Washika

Robert A. Poirier

Washika

A Novel

Baraka Books
Montreal

Cover illustration by Dean Ottawa
Cover by Folio infographie
Book design by Folio infographie
Editing by Mary Bialek
Map on p. 12 by Robert A. Poirier
Photos by Douglas Gagnon: p. 13, The ***Basko*** operated by the late Arthur Gagnon, and p. 227
Illustration p. 305, other photos and back cover, by Julia Philpot

Legal Deposit, 4th quarter, 2012
Bibliothèque et Archives nationales du Québec
Library and Archives Canada

ISBN 978-1-926824-53-6 (Paper)
ISBN 978-1-926824-72-7 (PDF)
ISBN 978-1-926824-71-0 (Epub)
ISBN 978-1-926824-73-4 (Mobi/Kindle)

Published by Baraka Books of Montreal
6977, rue Lacroix
Montréal, Québec H4E 2V4
Telephone: 514 808-8504
info@barakabooks.com
www.barakabooks.com

Printed and bound in Quebec

Société de développement des entreprises culturelles Québec

Baraka Books acknowledges the generous support of its publishing program from the Société de développement des entreprises culturelles du Québec (SODEC) and the Quebec Government's Programme de crédit d'impôt for book publishing.

Canada Council for the Arts

We acknowledge the support of the Canada Council for the Arts for our publishing program.

Trade Distribution & Returns

Canada
LitDistCo
1-800-591-6250
ordering@litdistco.ca

United States
Independent Publishers Group
1-800-888-4741
orders@ipgbook.com

To Louise and Pete

Table of Contents

Foreword

This is a story about twenty-one students who recently completed their final year at the Collège de Ste-Émilie, a high school in the small Quebec town of Ste-Émilie. The students signed up to work for a major forestry company, a summer job on the beautiful Cabonga Reservoir located in the heart of the La Vérendrye game reserve some 270 kilometres north of Montreal. The students were hired to work on the sweep, an integral part of the log drives that took place for years on the Cabonga.

This story, although told in English, actually takes place almost entirely in French. All of the characters are French speaking, with the exception of Emmett Cronier who speaks French but always swears in English. A glossary at the end provides definitions for the French terms and expressions and for some English words specifically related to logging.

Washika is a story about young students working with older men, about discovery of attitudes and selfishness, and about situations never dreamed of. It is a story of change, experienced either willingly or unwillingly, but change that leaves its mark for as long as water flows from the Cabonga into the mighty Gens-de-Terre River.

Map of the Cabonga Reservoir

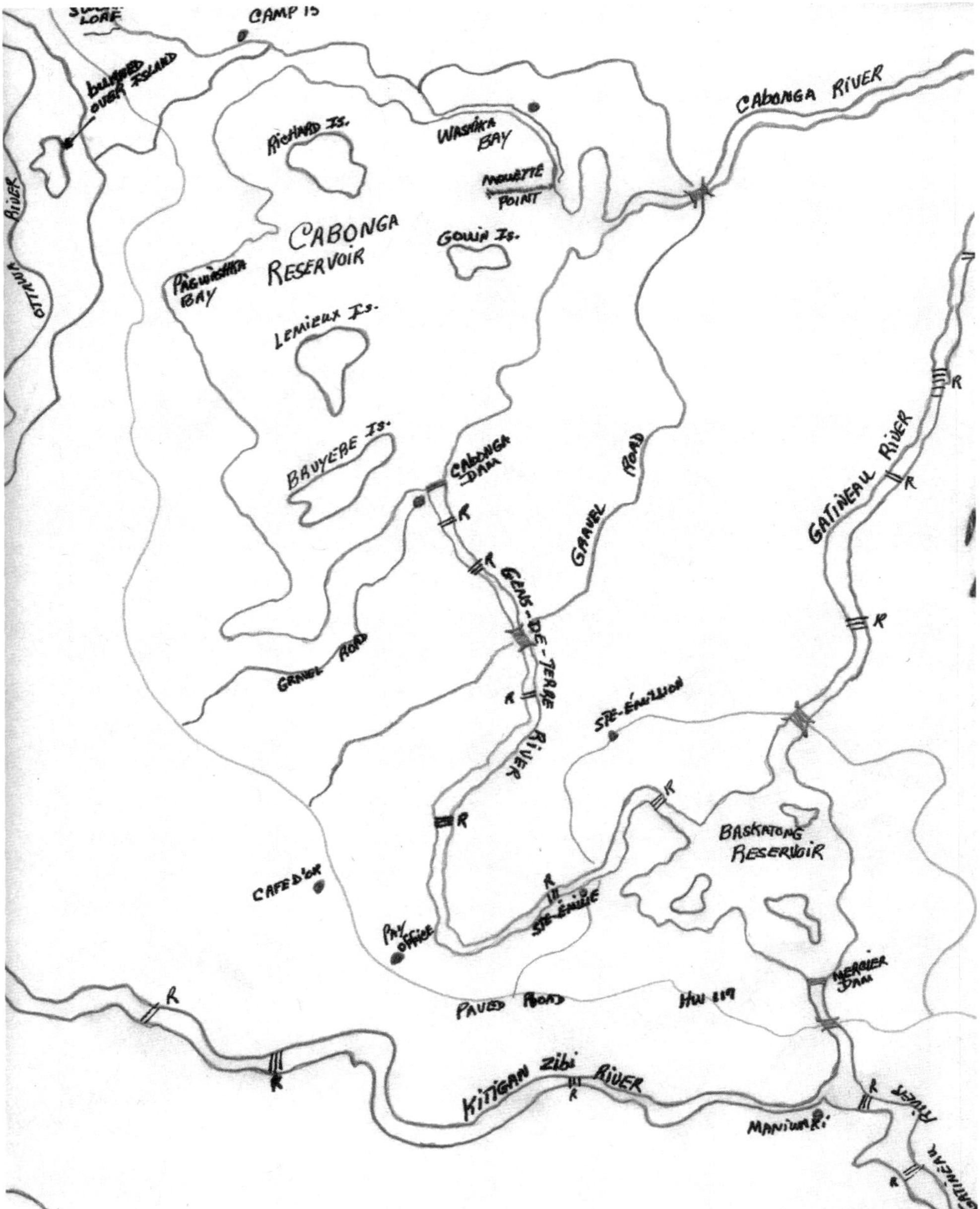

PART I

Chapter 1

Cabonga Lake was quite a large lake, famous for its long sandy beaches that stretched great distances along the shore and deep into the jack-pine forests. With the arrival of the white man and the forest industry, the lake and its surroundings were slowly but irreversibly changed. More and deeper water was needed for transporting the trees felled by the lumberjacks and so a dam was built at the south end of the lake, just where the mighty Gens-de-Terre River begins its flow southward. After the construction of the Cabonga Dam the water flowed steadily from the Cabonga River in the northeast and Cabonga Lake was gradually transformed into a larger body of water, the Cabonga Reservoir. Some of the former beaches remained, though smaller in size, while others disappeared completely. New shorelines were created, flooded areas of jack pine suddenly appeared, and new islands, that had once been lesser mountains in the forest, sat above the water.

Washika Bay was one of the larger areas to survive. Before the flood, the bay, with its extensive volume of beach sand, had been almost desert-like, a natural clearing stretching more than a mile in length and almost as deep. Even after the water level rose the clearing remained, as long though not as deep as it had once been.

Washika Bay was a camp site, a Company depot of sorts, for those men who worked the waters of the Cabonga in tugboats, rounding up logs that came from the logging camps and towing them downstream to Cabonga Dam.

All of the buildings at Washika Bay were painted green, a deep forest green. However, the camp itself was well organized and anyone visiting the site could see immediately, that much thought had gone into planning the layout of the buildings. The infirmary, for example, had been built on a section of beach that sloped upward from the water to the main plateau where the rest of the camp was situated. This provided for a quiet, peaceful environment should any patient have to spend an extended time there. The camp was built along the north-south axis of the bay, the infirmary being at its northern extremity. Just above the infirmary, a gravel road arrived from the lumber camps to the north, went straight by the camp, and ended at a log dump, at the extreme south end of the bay. The next most northerly building was the generator shed where a diesel engine-generator combination created electricity for the camp during certain fixed hours. The shed had been situated far enough away from the other buildings that the noise from its diesel engine did not disturb the residents of the camp or the infirmary. Next to and south of the generator shed was the garage-cum-machine shop. There, two men maintained and repaired the tugboats and the two tractors that were used for manipulating logs at the log dump.

The camp itself faced west, looking out onto the Cabonga. To the east was the jack-pine and white-birch forest. The main sleep camp was a long, narrow building, placed lengthwise and close to the forest and just south of the garage. There was a den at its north end with a hallway leading to the common washbasin and the two washrooms. On both sides of this hallway were individual bedrooms, each housing two beds. In front of the main sleep camp was the cookhouse, which consisted of a kitchen and a separate dining area where all the men at the camp took their meals. Just south of the cookhouse was what the men commonly referred to as the bunkhouse-and-office. This building was unlike the others in that half of it served as a sleeping area while the other half was an office for the camp clerk and two scalers, a radio room, and the van, a simple store with numerous articles for sale to the workers. Directly west and in front of the cookhouse was a small hut containing the truck scales. The west side of the hut had a large window facing the gravel road. Less than three feet from the hut were long wood planks laid down, level with the road. What could not be seen were the mechanical parts of the scales beneath this wood planking. When the trucks stopped there with their loads of logs to be weighed, the total weights appeared as a numerical reading on a scale inside the hut.

Settled in next to the forest and several hundred feet from the camp were three other small cabins. Like all of the buildings at Washika, these three cabins were painted green and had black, tarpaper roofs. The first of these cabins was a small one-room structure where P'tit-Gus, the chore boy slept and rested when he could. Next to this cabin was a three-room building where the cook, Dumas Hébert, resided. There was a small den and a spare room for an assistant, if and when he had an assistant. The last of these cabins was somewhat more elaborate: not only did it have a separate bedroom and living room but also running water, a kitchen sink and a washroom. This was where Simard-Comtois, the superintendent of the camp, spent a major portion of his time.

Not a single superfluous person lived at Washika Bay. Nor were individual tasks vague or lacking in apparent usefulness. The staff members were middlemen of sorts, intermediaries between the lumberjacks and the pulp mills hundreds of miles to the south, and without them the connection between the former and the latter would simply not exist. The whole scheme of things was simple enough to be effective. The tractor-trailers arrived from the logging camps with their loads of logs. The wood was weighed at the truck scales and measured by the scalers. This same wood, once measured and stamped by the scalers using a hammer-like tool with a Company insignia on one end, was pushed off the log dump into the Cabonga by one of two huge tractors driven by Percy Dumont. The logs floating by the log dump were gathered up by the tugboat captains and their crews. Large pockets of this wood were towed downstream to Cabonga Dam. When enough wood had accumulated, the dam was opened, allowing the wood to pass through the opening and into the Gens-de-Terre River. The logs followed the current and the rapids of this and other rivers until they reached their final destination. There the sawmills and the pulp and paper mills transformed the logs into profitable commodities.

One Monday morning, at the end of June, a Company bus drove up to the sleep camp at Washika Bay. Twenty-one high school students stepped down from the bus and, with loaded packs on their backs, stood in a circle around the superintendent of the camp as he delivered his welcoming speech. No one paid much attention to André Simard-Comtois' words of welcome. The students were intrigued by the buildings at Washika, the generator noise, and the tractor-trailers arriving at the scales but, mostly, they marvelled at the great expanse of beach sand before them and what seemed to be an unending body of water to the west.

The students were finally introduced to one of the tugboat captains, Alphonse Ouimet, and they took an immediate liking to him. They were especially amused when he called them his "little ducks" not knowing, of course, what the man was referring to. Alphonse issued instructions: they were to enter the sleep camp, select a room and a bed, store their packs, and then head to the office where they would be supplied with hard hats and gloves. Their hard-toe safety boots, it was assumed, had been purchased in town. After lunch they were to follow him down to the wharf.

"And don't forget the meal tickets," Alphonse concluded. "Be sure you get tickets at the van or you won't eat!"

These instructions were delivered in a friendly manner and the students, although feeling a bit jarred after their bus ride from Ste-Émilie, felt immediately at home. They entered the sleep camp and, before long, all available beds were spoken for.

Alphonse had followed them into the sleep camp. He counted seven students standing by the washbasin, heavy packs on the floor by their feet.

"There's another sleep camp," he said. "But first, is there anyone who'd like to work in the kitchen? You'd be like an assistant to the cook."

None of the students responded to the man's request. They looked at each other and then back at Alphonse.

"You," Alphonse pointed to one of the students. "What's your name?"

"Morin," the student replied. "Henri Morin."

"Okay," Alphonse said. "Listen, Henri. Go to each of the rooms and tell the guys what I've just said. The one who accepts the job will have his own room in the cook's cabin."

Henri left then and, stopping by the door of each room occupied by the students, he relayed the message about becoming the cook's assistant. It wasn't long before he returned to the washing up area, followed by a tall, slim boy whose head was a mass of tight black curls.

"Good," Alphonse nodded towards the boy. "And what's your name?"

"Richard Gagnier, *monsieur*," the boy replied.

"Okay, Richard. Take your pack and go to the cookhouse. The cook there is Dumas Hébert. Tell Dumas that I sent you and that you'd like to work with him this summer. He'll fix you up."

"So," Alphonse turned to the others, "that leaves one more bed here. One of you guys can take that one and the rest of you come with me."

One of the students lifted his pack and followed the young man who was soon to be the cook's assistant. The six remaining students followed Alphonse across the yard and into the bunkhouse-and-office.

"This is the bunkhouse-and-office," Alphonse smiled. "The other half is the office. The van is there too. When you hear a bell ring, go to the cookhouse for lunch. And don't be late. The cook's pretty strict about that. You'll see."

The students went to the van as he had instructed. Afterwards, they sat on their bunks adjusting the straps inside their hard hats for a better fit. They flexed their new work gloves and folded the long string of meal tickets. Suddenly, an irregular bell sound could be heard coming from nearby and, shortly after, they saw the older men leaving the sleep camp. The students followed the older men and joined them at the cookhouse landing. There, they saw Dumas Hébert for the first time. The students smiled as they handed him their meal ticket. Dumas did not return the smile. When the last of the students had gone inside, Dumas entered, closing the screen door behind him. He walked to the centre of the dining area and addressed the students.

"My name is Dumas Hébert. I am the cook here at Washika. Your table will be that one there to my right. You will be ten on each side. As you can see, it is crowded so no elbows on the table. Be sure that your hands are clean and that your hair is properly combed when you come in here. There are two bells for the meals. One bell is to warn you, and the second is for the meal. So, do not be late. Also, after breakfast, there is one bell, for making lunches. That is all."

It was all very clear and simple. There would be no foolishness in the cookhouse. There was plenty to eat and the food was delicious. All agreed that Dumas was an excellent cook even if he was a *führer* of sorts.

After lunch the boys followed Alphonse to the wharf where they were introduced to the *Madeleine*, a six-cylinder tugboat and its two drive boats. They were issued life jackets and, when all were aboard, Alphonse backed the *Madeleine* away from the wharf and swung her bow around in a southerly direction.

After what seemed like less than an hour, Alphonse veered to port towards a stretch of beach sand spotted with logs of various lengths. He shut down the engine, allowing the *Madeleine* to drift up onto shore. Alphonse stood on deck and spoke to the students.

"Well, my little ducks," he began. "You see the shore there and all the logs on the sand. Use those hooks I showed you and pick out the logs and toss them into the water. Over there, where those dead *chicots* are, there are logs in the water behind them. Some of you go in there and pick those logs out and toss them over here. I want two or three of you in each drive boat, with pike poles. Now, here's the thing. We want to pick out all of the logs along here and toss them into deeper water. You see those square timbers here. They're called boom timbers. I'm going to make a kind of corral with them. When we've picked out enough logs I'll close the corral around them and snub the corral to shore. One of the tugboats will pick it up on its way to Cabonga. There are logs like this all along the shoreline. These are logs that got away from us during the drive to Cabonga. It gets pretty windy here. Sometimes the logs are on shore, sometimes not. That's when you boys have to go into the water. And so, this is the sweep. We always have to come back like this after a drive. Okay? Now, my little ducks, to work!"

So began the summer job at Washika Bay. All of the students working there were from the Collège de Ste-Émilie. Over six thousand people lived in the town Ste-Émilie, which was built up on both sides of the Gens-de-Terre River about eighty-five miles south of Washika Bay. The town had two beautiful stone churches, a bank and post office, and two large brick-covered schools which served both elementary and high school students. One of the schools was run by the brothers of the Sacred Heart. It was the brothers who had named the school Le Collège de Ste-Émilie. Also covered in brick and run by the "Grey Nuns," or the Sisters of Charity, was the hospital, L'Hôpital de Ste-Jeanne d'Arc, and the convent known as Ste-Véronique's where the young girls of Ste-Émilie received both their primary and secondary education. After graduation the choices open to the students were limited. The girls could follow nursing courses at the hospital and the boys could attend a trade school or find work in the local sawmills. Failing this, the boys could always sign up with the Company for work in the bush. The more advanced students could apply for acceptance at the university or the various colleges in the Capital. For these students, this usually meant an end to living in their hometown of Ste-Émilie.

The students adjusted well to life in the camp. There were occasions when their behaviour came into conflict with the habits of the older workers but these obstacles were soon smoothed over, mostly in favour of the older residents. Their behaviour in the cookhouse was impeccable, much to the satisfaction of Dumas Hébert. As far as work was concerned, Alphonse was very happy with his crew. They whined and complained some, that was true, but after bouts of encouragement on his part and the odd extended break, they worked with great enthusiasm and got plenty of work done. And besides, Alphonse reasoned, they were young. They had formed worlds of their own, some of them, based on their studies and all of the events that had occurred in their short lives.

Alphonse was correct in this assumption. The students had indeed created worlds of their own. Most were harmless, idealistic summaries of what life was all about, of what was expected of them as members of the future generation. Their most profound thoughts, it seemed, centred around the pleasures that life could offer them and, these, with a minimum of effort on their part. Despite these commonly shared opinions of life, their personalities were as varied as there were students in the camp. On the whole, however, they were a rambunctious, fun-loving crew. Two students stood apart from the group. André Guy was a short, skinny boy of seventeen whose most pronounced attribute might be described as his ability to attract attention. André believed firmly that the emptiness in his life could instantly be relieved by the numerous pranks that he played on his classmates. He did not perform these pranks to be boisterous and wild like his fellow classmates; his pranks were meant solely to attract attention. This was the only path to self-esteem that he understood. This was what he believed, what kept him going in his social life, the only life he knew. There was another student, Henri Morin, who seemed not to fit the same mold as the other students.

Alphonse had noticed Henri's enthusiasm and his keen interest in all that surrounded him. Henri accepted the teasing and the jokes played on him by the others with an attitude almost approaching the philosophical. In their discussions, Alphonse admired the young man's maturity while, at the same time, he was astounded by his innocence. At the risk of sounding mysterious, or even mystical, one might say that Henri possessed a personality that attracted people who seemed to have a deeper understanding than most, whose compassion for their fellow human beings was surpassed only by their desire to illustrate the importance of living life to the full. Alphonse belonged to this group and he had singled out Henri Morin as a young man that might be in need of his support however limited that might be.

Before Henri arrived at Washika, another such person had entered his life. Brother André, a member of the Brothers of the Sacred Heart of Jesus, was a mathematics and science teacher at the high school. He had noticed Henri's diligence in his studies and his precocious attitude to life, but he had also detected an inner struggle, a certain innocence that the young man camouflaged with his outwardly open personality. After a time, especially during the last semester at high school, Henri and Brother André spent a great deal of time together. Henri would remain after the mathematics or biology classes and, there, he and Brother André would discuss all manner of subjects. Brother André always expressed a great interest in Henri's opinions and this, coming from such a highly educated person, had a profound effect on Henri.

Throughout these discussions it soon became apparent that, deep inside this young man, there were ongoing perturbations that needed to be addressed. The discussions became somewhat more personal. Henri disclosed more of his inner self. The good brother offered more opinions. Henri was unable to live the carefree life of the other students, he explained to Brother André. To partake in boisterous behaviour at the games, or at the dances, was something so foreign to his nature that it almost prevented him from attending these events. To be carefree and wild was not something that came naturally to him. He had had a girlfriend, a year earlier, he told Brother André, and he believed that he had loved her very much. He had loved her and she had loved him. He was convinced that he had done everything right. But she had left him for no reason that he understood. He had been respectful and honest, and he had openly expressed his love for her. But, she was gone and Henri had died some with her leaving.

One afternoon, immediately following the algebra class, Brother André sat on top of the desk next to Henri's.

"Henri," he said, calmly. "I think that we should talk about you today."

"If you like," Henri replied. He closed his notebook and the algebra text. "I seem to be catching on to the equations now."

"Oh yes, I'm not worried about that. You know, Henri, there are things in our lives that we do not always understand. We give them names and sometimes that helps us to deal with them."

"And that helps?"

"Sometimes, but there are occasions when we give a problem a name that implies permanency, with no hope for solutions. You know how you are, Henri. You're unable to fall into place. Just being with your friends is often difficult. You're a misfit in this universe of ours."

"But why is it like that?" Henri felt the stinging in his eyes. "I have friends, you know. They seem to like me. I work hard and I've got good grades and everything. My parents seem to be happy with my work."

"I know all that, Henri. But I also know that there's not much happiness in your life. There must be a change in how you see life."

"I can do that?"

"Yes, I believe so. But it must be you who sees the possibility of change. Do you understand that, Henri?"

"Not really."

"Think about what I've just said. Think about those people you know who seem to float through life without a care, how everything just seems to fall naturally into place for them. These are people we might describe as having it all—*ils l'ont l'affaire.* Then there are those, much like you, Henri, who struggle through life—*ils ne l'ont pas l'affaire*—they just haven't got it. Let me show you something."

Brother André slid off the desk and went up to the chalkboard. He picked up a piece of chalk from the ledge and wrote in large capital letters: HAVES / HAVE-NOTS.

"There you go, Henri," he said. "Two labels for life. The line I've drawn between them is to denote 'time and experience.' Together, the words and their dividing line imply that the latter can be transformed into the former, and vice versa, of course. If you believe this, then there can be hope."

The man stood facing Henri, his hands clasped in front of him. He looked kindly upon his student, this young man who would be leaving high school soon.

"This is all I can offer you, Henri. I know that you'll be leaving soon for the lumber camp and then for the Capital most probably. I want you to think of these two words, every day if you can. At this moment you belong to the 'have-nots,' you just haven't got it. But that's okay. Let the dividing line between the words remind you that things can change, there's hope that your life can be transformed and then when they speak of you they'll say, *il l'a l'affaire*, now he's got it, now he's a have."

"You think that can happen?"

"I believe so, Henri. Just think of that dividing line and the strength it carries. And I'll pray for you, that life will allow you the option of change."

From that day onward, Henri adopted the two words given to him by brother André. He thought of all his classmates, all of his close friends, and he saw only 'haves.' Not a single one of them resembled him. None seemed to suffer the isolation that he experienced in his life. Brother André had not offered him a solution but he had presented him with the possibility of hope.

Chapter 2

More than a month had gone by. After the first three weeks the students were sent down to Ste-Émilie for the weekend. The trip down was almost as eventful as their time at Washika. There was the stop at the Cafe D'Or, a restaurant on the main highway, where they flirted with the American tourists' daughters and caused no small degree of disturbance in the restaurant itself. Later they were introduced to the clerk at the Company's Pay Office where they were treated like men for the first time in their lives. Saturday night in Ste-Émilie was the big night: drinking and storytelling and swinging the girls around the dance floor at La Tanière, seeing the girls shaking their bodies and waving their arms above their heads, the music so loud that you could feel its notes in your beer glass. And now they were back. They had returned to Washika on a Monday, their heads still filled with the pleasures of town life. Two weeks had gone by and their weekend in town was little but a memory as the students were once again absorbed by the Cabonga and the logs on and around its shoreline. This was, in fact, their thirty-second day on the sweep.

That morning no one wanted to work in the water. Everybody was tired of the water and the rotten smell it left on their clothes, and the leeches that swam around them trying to find an opening in their clothes.

So they worked on shore. There, the logs had settled on the sand and some, in the wet places, were half buried in mud. But mostly, the shore was fine beach sand and, just above where they worked, the sand was transformed to a brown humus covered in grasses and other low foliage and short blueberry plants. Above the shrubs tall white birch stretched outwards towards the water.

Twenty young men, armed with steel hooks and peaveys, jabbed at the logs and tossed them into the water. That was the job. During the previous log drives there were logs that had managed to escape the confines of the boom timbers. With the opening and closing of the dam at Cabonga, the water level of the lake had changed leaving these logs stranded on the beaches, or in the mud of the low, swampy shores. Now they, the sweep crew, had arrived to clean the shores of these strays so that they could be once again corralled within boom timbers and towed down the lake to Cabonga where, once the dam was open, they could be sent on their way down the mighty Gens-de-Terre River. All along the bay where they had worked that morning a line of logs hugged the shore, floating to and fro with the waves, and held there by a west wind blowing in towards the shore.

By eleven o'clock sandflies were everywhere. At that time of day they were especially bad on shore. Everyone knew that they were not as bad when you were working in the water but then there were the leeches, those blood-sucking aquatic worms so common to the shallow waters. Ten of the students put on life jackets and boarded the two drive boats snubbed alongside the *Madeleine*. They untied the boats and poled their way in among the floating logs. Standing in the drive boats they were able to spear the logs with their long pike poles and drag them out away from shore into deeper water and, eventually, past the tugboat. There, at least, they managed to avoid the wrath of the *brûlot* attack since these little sandflies were more commonly found close to warm beach sand and rarely over water, especially if there was a breeze.

Alphonse had driven the *Madeleine*'s bow up onto shore where the water was deep enough. The old grey tugboat's engine idled softly there, creating a backwater at her stern. The students pushed the logs into the current of the backwater, sending them even further from shore.

He stood on deck at the stern and watched how they walked slowly from one log to the next, picking at a log with their hooks until it caught well and then tossing it out on the water. Those with the peaveys worked the larger logs. At opposite ends and on the same side of a very large log, two fellows would jam in the swivel spear-point of their peaveys and, heaving together, roll the log down towards the water. The boys in the drive boats would take over from there, spearing the log with the point of their pike poles and, flexing their arms, guiding it into the backwater current of the *Madeleine*. Alphonse slid his watch out from the side pocket of his trousers. He looked at it briefly and entered the cabin. Suddenly it was quiet. He had shut down the engine. Sticking his head out through the cabin doorway he hollered, "Lunch!"

There was no longer the chug-chugging of the *Madeleine*'s six cylinders, no banging of pike poles on the drive boat gunwales, no logs splashing water. Now there were only the voices of the students, their lunch pails striking the metal of the *Madeleine*'s cabin as they climbed aboard and fought for a good place to lie on deck in the sun.

The waves ran softly onto the beach; this was almost the only sound to be heard. But then as the crew settled down in their places with their open lunch pails beside them, the birds appeared, high in the sky and silent. Before the last lunch pail had been opened, the barking of the gulls was upon them like a storm. Some of the birds were content to sit on a boom timber and wait for the bread crust or cheese to hit the water while others attacked the morsels in mid-air.

The students ate their sandwiches, and cheese, and biscuits, and washed all of these down with gulps of hot tea. There was the rolling of cigarettes and a second cup of tea; and then came the real quiet. After they had closed their lunch pails and the last barking gull had left, the boys lay stretched out in the sun, with their heads resting on life jackets or rolled-up wool jackets. Then there was only the rhythm of the waves as they slapped against the hulls of the boats or gently washed up and away from the shore. Sometimes the leaves of the birch trees hissed when a breeze came. The sun was warm on their faces and chests and they could feel it through their thick denim jeans. Even their feet felt the sun's rays through their heavy wool socks.

Alphonse was older. He had spent most of the summers of his life on this very lake, eating his lunch like this and afterwards hearing the quiet. He sat on a high stool in the cabin, out of the sun. He knew how the sun could make him sleepy and how difficult it would be to return to work. He poured a second cup of tea and smoked a cigarette. It was enough just to listen to the quiet. Sleep would come later.

Chapter 3

The *Madeleine*'s engine roared. That was the first sound they heard. Next came the yawning and the stretching and the exchange of curses. Alphonse came out of the cabin. It always amused him to see these poor fellows staggering around on deck, searching for their boots or a last cup of tea.

"Work!" he yelled above the roar of the *Madeleine*. "*Allez mes petits canards!*"

It was difficult not to smile. He could imagine all of those uncomplimentary thoughts going through their young minds at that moment. Still, they were polite, a good bunch of boys. They were young students, from town but not so bad after all.

It had been paradise sleeping on deck in the sun, or sprawled out on the floor of a drive boat where, now and then, a breeze came to cool your face and maybe sway the boat a little. On shore there was only the heat and the sand or mud and, worst of all, the *brûlot*, that horrible little creature no larger than a spec of black dust.

Not one of them wanted to go ashore. No one wanted to work on shore where your very presence was an invitation to every sandfly that lived there to come forward and taste a bit of your blood. But, it was the shore or the water. And the logs, of course, were on shore. Those who had worked from the drive boats earlier that morning had eaten their lunches there to be sure of their places. As they began to pole the boats out among the remaining logs, the rest of the boys sat on deck at the stern. Every one of them knew that it was the water or the shore. It was the deciding that did not come easy.

"Come on, *mes petits canards*," Alphonse encouraged them. "Let's go now."

Slowly and without looking back at Alphonse, the ten students slid off of the deck and into the brown water. André Guy was the last to go over the side. For a moment all they could see of him was his hard hat sticking out of the water. Two of the taller fellows reached down and, with their arms beneath his armpits, dragged him to where he could stand with his head above water. André came up coughing, swearing at the two boys who were helping him and yelling at them to leave him alone.

At last everyone had returned to work. They worked with their shirts off in the afternoon. Those who worked in the water remembered to tie their bootlaces around their jeans at the ankles. This was enough to keep the leeches away from their legs at least.

They stood in a straight line in the water, at right angles to the shore. André Guy was at the head of the line, closest to shore. The boys picked at the logs with their hooks and passed them down the line towards open water. The logs that strayed from the line were speared by the boys in the drive boats.

Alphonse stood on deck rolling a cigarette and watched his boys move the logs out. He scanned the shore where they had worked in the morning and the depressions left in the sand where the logs had been. Now the logs were in the water and being moved out. Soon all of the shore of Lost Cabin Bay would be swept clean and that job would be done.

He looked along the row of young, tanned backs and yellow hard hats. At the end of the line André Guy stood hooking the logs and firing them back with one motion of his arm. He never looked behind to see where they went. He didn't care; that was what the others were there for. They were there for that. He stood knee deep in the water with logs floating to his left and in front of him up to the shore. These were the logs they had tossed off the shore that morning. To his right were the brown water and the shoreline with its sand and mud and old, grey driftwood and entangled pulpwood.

"Listen to me," Alphonse called out to the boys. "Those logs will not jump off by themselves. Come on now. A few of you guys on shore there."

"*Sacrament*!" André swore softly.

"Look at you," Alphonse continued. "Five in a drive boat, that's nonsense. I want at least three over there. You, St-Jean. And you Lavigne. Who else?"

The boys in the drive boats leaned on their poles. Everyone had stopped working. There was only the *Madeleine* chugging her backwater.

"Me, I'll go," said a voice at the rear of one of the drive boats.

It was François Gauthier. He was a tall, thin fellow with thick blond hair and very pale blue eyes. As he made his way forward in the drive boat, he carried his lunch pail and had his shirt and jacket draped over one arm.

André Guy had also stopped working. He stood in the water, watching François as he made his way to the *Madeleine*. He knew about François. So did Alphonse and everyone else. Everyone knew how much François disliked sandflies and mud and, most of all, how he disliked getting wet. In the thirty-one days that they had worked out of Washika Bay, François was known to have returned to camp wet only once, and that was because of a storm. It was such a certainty that François would not go into the water any deeper than the soles of his boots that, early in the morning on their way out to work, the smokers among them would give him their tobacco and papers to hold until it was time for a break.

François, along with St-Jean and Lavigne, went aboard the *Madeleine*. The two who remained in the drive boat poled back to where the logs were next to the second drive boat. Everyone had started working again. Only André Guy was not working. He stood in the water watching François.

"Well, well," he said. "Hey Gauthier, what's the matter? Find a leak in the boat?"

François did not answer. He, St-Jean, and Lavigne went about the business of preparing to go ashore. They placed their poles in the rack on the cabin roof and removed their life jackets. They entered the cabin then to pick out the best crochets they could find in the box. The crochets, the hooks used to work the four-foot logs, were not always the same. Sometimes the points were dulled or the wooden handles were cracked and could pinch your hand if you were not wearing gloves. The three boys then jumped off the bow onto shore. They had put on their shirts; their faces and exposed arms were shiny from the fly oil Alphonse had given them.

As the three boys worked their way along the shore, André Guy kept a close watch on their every move. He knew what could happen next. In fact, he knew what would happen next. He knew it as well as if he were there on shore himself. But he was ready. He held a good-sized four-foot log cradled in his left arm with the L-shaped point of his crochet well embedded at one end. He bent his back slightly so that the water just covered the log from view. He watched them and waited for them to come closer, to walk past where he was. It was an old trick and André was soaked anyway. He knew they would get to him eventually since he was closest to shore. Now, he waited for what he knew would be his only chance.

At last it was time. The boys approached the spot he had picked out in his mind. They walked in single file along the beach with François at the rear. As they moved directly in front of him, André let fly with the log, sending it high and parallel to the water. The old spruce hit the water flat, sending up a wall of dirty brown water.

Everybody cheered. André tipped his hat and bowed to the applauding crowd. He had achieved his revenge for what would surely happen to him some time during the day. The others were pleased to see justice done. It was too bad about St-Jean and Lavigne but they were happy to see François get a soaking for a change.

Alphonse also was pleased. It was too bad for the boys on shore but that was the way. It was always that way. He knew that André's little trick had cheered everybody up and now they would work well.

The three boys on shore went on to where the logs were. They tried pretending that nothing of any consequence had happened. But, it was difficult not to feel ridiculous standing there and seeing the water dripping off of their hard hats.

Chapter 4

At a quarter to four in the afternoon Alphonse called to the boys that they had done enough work for one day and that it was time to head back. Beyond the *Madeleine* were the logs they had taken and the boom timbers stretched across the mouth of the bay and the open water with its blackness and its silver waves. On the opposite shore, the sun was just above the tall grey trees that stuck out of the water.

Alphonse eased the *Madeleine* out, away from shore, towing the boom timber snubbed to her stern and rounding up the day's work. He took her back to the south side of the bay, to where the opposite end of the chain of boom timbers was held fast to an enormous old pine. The tree was now grey and lifeless with small holes and long narrow tracks left by beetles. The shore there was steep and rocky and the water black from its deepness. Alphonse snubbed one end of the boom to the other and then returned to where the students were waiting in the drive boats.

The two drive boats were tied, one behind the other, and then snubbed to the tugboat by a thick yellow rope knotted around one of the short metal posts sticking up through the deck at the stern. The drive boats were long narrow double-bowed vessels with wooden hulls painted an orange shade of red. When Alphonse returned the students boarded the tugboat, except for two who remained in the drive boats for the ride back to camp.

With the drive boats in tow Alphonse steered the *Madeleine* out of the bay and, at full throttle, headed north across open water for Washika Bay.

The students, one in each drive boat, were sleeping on the floor at the stern. They had their orange life jackets pulled up under their necks and their hard hats covering their eyes. One had taken off his boots and socks and, with his legs raised on the plank seat, cooled his feet in the breeze. There were black metal lunch pails on the floors of the boats and bundles of jackets and heavy checkered shirts. Hanging from the gunwales were several crochets with the curved steel of the hooks painted red and the wooden handles smooth and shiny from use.

André Guy had crawled up into the lifeboat on the cabin roof. The lifeboat was normally fastened with its bottom facing upward to keep the little dinghy from filling up with water during a rainstorm. André had rearranged things; flipping the tiny boat over and fastening it to the roof, he could sleep in the tiny boat and not have to worry about falling off the roof. He slept with his mouth open and his arms wrapped around his head. The rest of the students were scattered about the deck. Some were lying flat on the deck with their shirts open and their hard hats covering their faces. Others sat astern with their backs against the cabin wall. Several of the boys were up front, sitting in the shade of the cabin and enjoying the cool breeze the *Madeleine* made as she cut through the waves.

Henri Morin had been sitting at the stern when they left the bay. Later, he had traded places with François and sat at the bow, against the cabin wall, with his knees tucked up, his chin resting on his knees and his mackinaw draped over his shoulders. He tried to sleep but the noise of the engine travelled through the bones of his knees and his chin, and inside his head. It was no use. Three miles out from Lost Cabin Bay, he edged his way towards the door of the cabin, holding on to the rack on the roof. He went inside then and sat down on an overturned wooden box that had contained the dozens of crochets used by the students.

It was cool in the cabin. Alphonse stood at the wheel, staring ahead through the tall narrow windows.

"Want to take her?" he asked.

"No, not now," Henri replied.

"Be a couple more days in there."

"And after?"

"Pàgwàshka Bay, most likely. Maybe the islands."

"Yeah?"

"There's tea if you like."

Henri was shivering. He sat on the low wooden box with his heavy wool jacket buttoned up to the collar, his shoulders rounded up near his ears and his hands together between his knees.

"Go on, Henri. I've had enough."

Henri unscrewed the plastic cup and placed it on the floor. He poured tea from the thermos. There was steam rising from the cup. He took a drink and then began to roll a cigarette.

"How long at Pàgwàshka?" he asked.

"Depends. Could be three, four days. Maybe a week."

"That long, eh?"

"We'll have to finish up here first."

"I'm sick of them, you know. Those damned *brûlots*, they're everywhere."

"There's always a good breeze at Pàgwàshka."

"Always?"

"Oh yes. You can be sure of that. Here Henri, take her for a while. Just keep her straight for the point there."

Alphonse went astern to see how things were and to check the knot of yellow rope at the tow post and the towrope between the *Madeleine* and the two drive boats. He went there to stare at the westerly shore, to see how the sun made the trees look like silver slivers growing out from the water, to smoke a cigarette, and to feel the sun and the wind on his face.

There was only a strong breeze and the whitecaps seemed to disappear almost as quickly as they came. Henri corrected now and then, sighting over the anchor to keep her straight.

The shivering came in waves. The cotton shirt scraped at his chest. He had been so stupid. Alphonse had warned him about it. He had been working in the water with his shirt off since lunchtime. When they had stopped for a break and sat in the drive boats smoking cigarettes, Alphonse had spoken to him about it. He told him that he had better put on his shirt and that, if he wanted to, he might work from one of the drive boats or from the stern of the *Madeleine*. After the break he had gone aboard the *Madeleine* and put his shirt on. It was only then that he could see the pink colour of his chest and how, whenever he touched it, his fingers left white marks that just as quickly turned to pink again.

Henri looked out through the window, along the thick cable to the anchor and, above it, to the point up ahead. He unbuttoned his jacket and then his shirt. In the shade of the cabin, the colour seemed to be even worse—a deep scarlet covered with goose bumps. Perhaps that was because of the shivering, he did not know. All he did know for sure was that the pain was much worse, like the colour, and that he was chilled throughout and he could not stop shivering. He had been so stupid. He had put his shirt on all right. He had put his shirt on as soon as Alphonse had spoken to him about it. He put on his shirt but he did not fasten the buttons. Instead, he had tied the ends like he had seen the girls in town do. Three times that day he had had to re-tie the shirt ends. Even with the ends tied, his shirt opened whenever the wind blew or he pushed the logs with his pike pole.

As Alphonse entered the cabin, Henri looked over the anchor and corrected to starboard.

"And, how's she going?"

"Pretty good."

"And the burn?"

"Not so bad. A little worse maybe."

"I'll take her now. Stay inside, Henri. Here, have some more tea."

"Maybe I'll see the nurse."

"Oh yes, as soon as we get in. That's a bad one you have. She'll fix you up, don't worry."

Henri hung his life jacket from the railing behind him. He sat on the box with his back against the life jacket. He poured tea from the thermos and rolled a cigarette. He tried to keep his shirt from scraping against his chest. He tried not looking at it. Finally he decided not to even think about it until he could see the nurse at Washika. He listened to the roar of the *Madeleine*'s diesel engine and the rhythm of her six pistons. He looked at the dark, almost black tea in the cup on the floor and tried matching the ripples in the teacup with the beat of the engine. He looked down at his scarlet chest and then he tried blowing smoke across it hoping that maybe it might do something.

Chapter 5

Alphonse eased up on the throttle and veered to port making a wide circle away from the point. Mouette or Sea Gull Point, which seemed to Henri to be nothing more than a long, narrow finger stretching out across the water, was an outcrop of grey weather-beaten rock, three feet above the surface of the water, that stretched out a hundred yards from the shoreline. There was not a tree to be seen, or flowers or grasses of any kind. There was nothing but a bed of solid rock, pockmarked with cavities and jagged edges and the whitish droppings of the gulls. There were sea gulls everywhere. As the *Madeleine* circled around the point, the gulls grew more excited. Some of the gulls sat on their nests barking loudly while others stood up on their nests and waddled awkwardly on their large webbed feet, stretching their wings and crying out to the sky above them. Seven gulls leaped from the rocks, flying low over the water to starboard and then astern, making a graceful sweep upwards and circling the *Madeleine*. They hovered above her with their beaks open and pointed downwards. All of them were screaming as if to chase the tugboat away.

For twenty years Alphonse had navigated the *Madeleine* around this point in exactly the same manner. His reason for doing so was simple and personal and had nothing to do with the safety of the tugboat or the solitude of the gulls. When the *Madeleine* and her two drive boats had reached midway between the point and the furthest northerly shore, Alphonse veered hard to starboard and headed east for Washika Bay.

Washika Bay was a mile wide at its mouth and the tugboat was well inside the bay and a half-mile from camp. Alphonse checked his watch. It was a quarter to five. He eased back on the throttle and sat up on the tall wooden stool behind him. He would maintain that speed until the last quarter mile and then, at full throttle, pull in to the dock at exactly five o'clock.

Alphonse enjoyed this time of day. He sat on the stool with one foot resting on its highest rung and his back against the wall. He rolled a cigarette, working the paper over and over again until it was perfectly round, licking the glue side with one sweep across his tongue, and then rolling it a quarter turn to finish the job.

He looked out through the tall narrow windows, beyond the anchor and the open water, to Washika Bay. To starboard, he could see the steep bank of the log dump where Percy Dumont worked. Seen through the windows of the tugboat, it was the southern extremity of the long, natural clearing that was Washika Bay. There the expanse of beach sand ended and the forest continued with a narrow beach between it and the Cabonga. At the site of the log dump, the bank had been built up with large timbers and filled in with gravel so that there was deep water just in front of the bank. People even went there to fish for bass in the evenings since the water was so deep. Above the oil-blackened timbers of the bank, Alphonse could see Percy wheeling his tractor around. At first he saw only the pencil-yellow cab behind a great pile of logs. Then, as the logs came off the bank making a great splash in the water, he saw the tractor as Percy slammed her into reverse with her blade up high over the engine and her enormous black tires digging into the sand.

Alphonse was alone with his thoughts and his great joy. Only the beat of the *Madeleine*'s six-cylinder engine penetrated his being. All of that moment lay before him through the narrow windows of the tugboat. It was all there in a perfect half-circle: from the log dump to the thick green forest with its tall, white birch and the sloping beach sand; to the green buildings of the camp and the wharf where they would dock; and far to port, the long, narrow, flat-roofed infirmary where Henri would visit *Mademoiselle* Archambault.

This was the one thing he had. As long as there was water and logs and he had this job with the Company, he would have it. There was really no necessity to approach Washika from the centre of the bay as he did. The other tugboats kept close to the southern shore after circling the point. It was the shorter route to camp. But, to have it as he did meant seeing it all at the same time, from one point and without tricks of vision or the imagination. Alphonse had it, he knew, and he never wanted to lose it. He reasoned, also, that few men of his lowly education and intellect could have such a thing. For this, he considered himself especially fortunate and thus never talked about it to anyone lest he should lose it; having this, in addition to his normal life, made him a very happy, contented man.

Alphonse opened one of the windows and felt the cool breeze on his face. He stared across the water, from port to starboard, from the infirmary to the log dump and back again. It was good to know something so well. He knew the camp better than he knew any of the twenty young students; better even than Francine, his wife, or their seven children. One glance at the Westclox they had given him four years ago and he would know almost precisely what was going on in each of the buildings at Washika Bay. Just as he had seen Percy working his tractor at the dump, he could easily imagine the expression on his face when the *Madeleine* first came into view. As he headed the tugboat east into the bay, Alphonse saw the trailer with its load of logs stopped at the truck scales in front of the cookhouse. In his mind, he could hear Emmett Cronier speaking to the driver from the window of his little hut: "Yes, it's a hot one all right. Christ Almighty!" Then Emmett would tilt back the tiny straw hat with the blue feather in its brim, a hat he had won at the fair in Ste-Émilie many years ago, and say, "Yes sir, too god damn hot for any man to be working on a day like this."

To know each individual and each building at Washika, to get to know each one of his twenty young log drivers, to know Francine and their seven children, to know everything well in its separate parts was, to Alphonse, a most wonderful gift. Any man with eyes and ears and a willingness to learn could have it. The ultimate goal and supreme pleasure, however, was to see it all at one moment in time. This was very difficult. Although the difficulty lessened as he grew older, he had found it useful to devise little tricks to be able to do it well. There were times when he would imagine himself standing at the summit of a very high mountain where, looking down, he might see each individual part, each minute detail magnified a thousand times, where he might hear every expression uttered, and see every piece of action taking place. From this elevated position, Alphonse could see all of it, the whole, all at a particular moment in time.

Alphonse stood at the wheel. They were less than a quarter-mile from shore. Gently, he moved the lever and the *Madeleine*'s engine began to roar, faster and faster, until the chugging of her six pistons became one and the same. At full throttle she rode the water high with her rounded stern only inches above water.

Everybody knew the signal. The two boys in the drive boats were awake and trying to find their shirts in the bundles at the bows. The students who had been sleeping on deck were doing up their shirts while others who had removed their boots and laid out their socks to dry in the sun were busily lacing up. Of the twenty-one people aboard, only one person remained unaware that they would all be ashore in a matter of minutes. Curled up like a dog in the lifeboat on the cabin roof, André Guy slept as soundly as if he were at home in his bed.

François stood to port, on the narrow section between the gunwale and the cabin wall. He was ready. He looked at the bundle in the lifeboat: the faded blue jeans, the green and black checkered shirt with the sleeves rolled past his elbows and the long, skinny sunburned arms wrapped around the yellow hard hat covering his face. François looked to stern for a place to stand when the time came. The timing would be important.

As the *Madeleine* approached the dock, her engine seemed to stop and then, as suddenly, speed up again as Alphonse shifted her into reverse to keep from ramming the wharf.

François looked around. Everyone was leaving the tugboat. It was time. He lifted his hard hat high above his head and, swiftly, whacked André's hat with his own. There was a dull sounding crack as the two hard hats met.

André rolled over onto his back. His face was pink and wrinkled from sleep. He looked down at the guys filing past him. They were laughing and shoving each other and, one by one, they jumped off the *Madeleine* and onto the wharf.

Henri Morin left the cabin holding his shirt out, away from his chest. Shortly afterwards Alphonse appeared in the doorway. He carried his lunch pail and extra-large thermos in one hand and his jacket draped over one arm.

Everyone passing the cabin door looked up at André. Everybody looked the same to him. No one wore that look of guilt André was searching for. Alphonse looked up at him as he came out of the cabin.

"Have a good snooze?" he said.

"Just wait, *sacrament*!" André stood up in the lifeboat.

"Another bad dream?" Alphonse laughed. "That's what you get, sleeping in the sun like that."

André looked away. He could hear Alphonse laughing as he stepped off the tugboat. He could hear them all laughing.

He sat down on the wood seat of the lifeboat. Although his socks had dried—he had hung them from the gunwales of the tiny lifeboat—his boots were still wet inside. He put them on but did not lace them up. He looked for his jacket and gloves. They were not in the lifeboat. He looked to stern, to the drive boats where he had left his lunch pail. There, at the stern stood a solitary figure. André looked at the blond hair sticking out from the ridge of the hard hat and, immediately, he knew. He knew exactly what had taken place and, as quickly, reacted in the only way he knew.

Alphonse and the others heard the screaming as they reached the crest of the hill on the path to the camp. Beyond the knoll of fine sand and sparse tufts of short grass, they could just see the roof of the *Madeleine*'s cabin and her tiny lifeboat. There, in the lifeboat on the cabin roof stood short, skinny André Guy waving his fist at the open water of the bay and screaming, "Gauthier! Gauthier, *mon tabarnacle*!"

Chapter 6

Henri removed his wet wool socks. He slid out of the damp jeans and underwear and replaced these with dry ones from his duffle bag by the bunk. He hung the wet clothes from a wire stretched across the room. After he had stored his hat and work gloves, he got a towel and comb from the orange crate shelves between the two bunks and left the bunkhouse-and-office.

At the main sleep camp Henri stood at the galvanized washbasin with the others. They were eight at a time at the basin. Henri was at the end and he could see everyone's grey, soapy water as it floated by him, circled and finally disappeared down the screened hole. He washed his hands and face and wet his hair to comb out the stiffness that came from wearing a hard hat all day.

He did not waste any time. Stopping only long enough at the bunkhouse-and-office to drop off his towel, Henri ran to the van. There he stood in line with the others and, when his turn came, he bought tobacco and papers, two chocolate bars, two soft drinks and a pair of bootlaces. He signed his name in the book and returned to the bunkhouse-and-office. He stored his things under the bunk, checked his hair in the broken piece of mirror on the wall and then left the bunkhouse-and-office. He was off for a visit with *Mademoiselle* Archambault.

Henri walked on the fine sand between the cookhouse and the bunkhouse-and-office. The windows of the cookhouse were open and he could smell the freshly baked bread and hear Dumas, the cook, barking orders at the cookee. Just beyond the cookhouse, he stopped at the truck scales to say hello to Emmett Cronier. The door to the small hut was open.

Emmett sat on a low stool, sharpening his pencil with a penknife. He was wearing an athletic undershirt, the kind with no arms. Tilted back on his head was the straw hat with a blue feather stuck in the headband, the kind of hat that Henri had seen people win by swinging a heavy mallet and ringing a bell at the top of a high column. He had seen it at the annual farmers' fair in St-Émillion, a village northeast of Ste-Émilie.

"Hot one, eh?" Henri greeted the man.

"Yes, by Christ, you can say that again."

"Wonder if the nurse's open?"

"Always open. Christ though, you can never tell with all them curtains."

Henri opened his shirt and looked down at his chest.

"Not bad, eh?"

"Christ Almighty!"

Henri buttoned the lower half of the shirt but left all of it loose, outside his trousers. He walked across the heavy wood planks of the truck scales and on to the gravel road towards the infirmary. He kicked at the larger stones as he walked along the road.

Reaching the infirmary, he left the road and followed the sandy path to the verandah. The floor of the verandah had been painted grey, like the *Madeleine*. The screen door banged against the jamb when he knocked.

"Yes?" a voice called from inside.

"Hello," Henri answered.

"Yes? What is it?" the same voice replied.

Henri cupped his hands around his eyes and his nose pressed against the screen trying to see inside. There, a short, stout woman stood before him. She was wiping her hands with a towel.

"Come in," she said.

Henri opened the door and went inside. It was dark and cool in the room. There was a strong breeze coming in off the lake, whistling through the screens and making the long white curtains stand out away from the open windows beside each bed. He looked at the woman standing before him, at her spotless uniform, white like the curtains. She was staring at his boots.

"Just stand right there," she said.

There was a smell of strong soap as she came closer. There was another smell but Henri was not certain what it was.

"Now, what can I do for you?"

Henri unbuttoned the lower portion of his shirt and as he held the shirt open he looked down at his boots. The sand that had collected around the soles of his boots had begun to dry and there was a scattering of it on the small square of orange carpet where he stood.

"Hold it open so I can have a look."

Mademoiselle Archambault scanned his chest with her little green eyes while Henri studied her face and the way her hair was combed back from her forehead, dark brown and shiny and twisted into a ball at the back of her head. She had slender ankles and her legs were not very big up to her knees but, from the hem of her uniform, they seemed to grow larger. He liked the sound her uniform made when she moved, and how smooth it was and how the plaits were long and straight and running parallel to each other.

"Painful, isn't it?"

"A little, yes."

He looked at her eyes as she spoke to him. He had not noticed before. Perhaps it was because she was looking at his chest. Or, perhaps, it was because he was trying to imagine the shape of her breasts. But now, he could see it plainly as she looked into his eyes. He had seen it at a funeral once, in the faces of the people standing in the pews and watching the coffin being wheeled out, followed by the grief-stricken relatives who had sat at the front of the church. He had seen it one hot afternoon by a roadside when a crowd of grown-ups stood around looking at a little girl crying and hugging and caressing a long-haired collie that had just been run over by a truck.

"There is not much I can do."

"It seems to be getting worse."

"That is a very bad burn. I can apply a salve. That will ease the stinging a little."

She left him and went into the back room. Henri looked around the clean white room, at the six empty beds with their white sheets stretched tightly across the mattresses, the white metal bed stands with their little wooden wheels and the thin black trim around the white bedpans placed under each bed. The floor had been covered with tightly fitted sheets of varnished Masonite and so highly polished that he could see the reflections of the beds on it.

Mademoiselle Archambault came in carrying a purple glass jar with a wooden tongue depressor sticking out from the top.

"What is your name?"

"Henri. Henri Morin."

"Hold your shirt out, Henri."

With the wooden instrument she brought out globs of pale yellow salve and applied it to his chest, starting at the top just below his neck and sliding it all the way down to his navel. She used long gentle strokes and Henri could feel the coolness of the salve each time she applied a new glob of it. He was beginning to feel better and he wanted to tell her that, and that he even liked the smell of the salve. He wanted to say that, although he liked the smell of the salve, there was another smell that he liked even better, and that he liked the soft way she touched him and that he didn't care if she was older than him.

"There, that should do it."

"It feels better already."

"Try to sleep on your back. And, of course, stay out of the sun."

"Should I come back?"

"See how it is in the morning. Probably it will blister. So do not pick at them."

"That's it then?"

"Yes."

Henri had not felt this way before. It was simple enough. All he had to do was to thank her and leave. He carefully buttoned his shirt, leaving the ends loose outside his trousers. He looked at the nurse, at the way her eyes were a light green and how quickly they darted from side to side when she looked at him.

"Was there anything else?"

"No, that's all. Thank you."

"You are welcome, Henri."

There, it was done. Now all he had to do was to leave.

"*Mademoiselle* Archambault?"

"Yes, Henri?"

"I'd like to know. What is your first name?"

"Lise."

"Mine is Henri."

"Yes, I know."

"Well, thank you again."

"You are welcome."

"You want me to shake the mat outside? My boots, you know."

"No, do not bother. I will do it later."

"All right. Well then, good-bye."

"Good-bye, Henri."

"Hey! You like raspberries?"

"Yes Henri, I like raspberries. Now go, you hear!"

Lise Archambault, twenty-eight years of age, an excellent nurse, systematic and tidy about everything in her life, a lonely woman who had not made many friends since the dispersal of her graduating class, laughed for the first time in the three long years she had been at Washika.

Henri opened the door to leave.

"I'll be back," he said. "You'll see. As soon as they're out, I'll bring you a pailful."

As Henri walked down the gravel road away from the infirmary, Lise Archambault watched him for a long time through the screen door and, after, through the curtained window of her bedroom.

Chapter 7

At four o'clock in the morning it was raining and cold. It had been raining softly but steadily since midnight.

P'tit-Gus walked quickly across the yard. He wore a heavy wool mackinaw with the collar turned up so that, at times, it touched the rim of his hard hat. He was a short, stocky little man and there was a no-nonsense look about him as he made his way from the main camp to the bunkhouse-and-office. With his hand in his pocket, he carried a bundle of newsprint wedged under his arm. Walking along the wet sand and lighting his way with a hunting lamp, he could see his breath in the cold air and the fine drops of rain falling in front of the lens.

Arriving at the bunkhouse-and-office where six of the students slept, P'tit-Gus scraped his boots on the short length of square timber at the door. He cupped his hand over the latch of the screen door as he opened it and went inside.

The air in the room was damp. It smelled of tobacco smoke, and fly oil and wet woolen socks. One of the students was snoring.

P'tit-Gus moved swiftly to the north side of the room where the oil space heater was. It was an older model, a brown, rectangular, upright metal box with a grilled front and a small fuel tank at the back. From the top of the heater, a grey galvanized pipe rose to within two feet of the ceiling, turned sharply, and ran the full length of the room before entering the south wall. Grey metal chairs were scattered around the space heater with wet jeans draped over the backs and, directly over the heater and suspended from a wire hung several pairs of woolen socks of all colours, but most were the grey ones sold at the van, with red and white bars at the tops.

P'tit-Gus reached around to the back of the heater and turned the flow valve to "half." He opened the grilled door and then, very quickly, he opened the small round door of the firebox. The hinges were rusted and P'tit-Gus knew the noise they would make if he opened the door slowly. In the twenty odd years he had worked as chore boy in dozens of lumber camps, he had learned about such things.

P'tit-Gus aimed the light down inside the firebox. He could see the velvety coat of blackness along its wall. At the bottom, the ashes were a dull grey except at the back where the oil had begun to flow and reflect the light of his lamp. He was very careful about things like that. He remembered well that cold February night in another camp when he had come so close to burning his shack to the ground. It was a good old heater, very much like this one but, for some reason that he never understood, the fire had gone out while he had been off attending to his chores. It was twenty below that night and, even though he had a good down-filled bag to sleep in, he knew what it would be like in the morning if he did not light a fire, and how miserable it would be shivering into his clothes. He crumpled up some paper, set a flame to it and dropped it into the firebox. Instantly, the flames went shooting past the door of the firebox and up into the pipe. For three hours that night P'tit-Gus sat by the stove, listening to the roar of the flames and the cracking of the stove and its pipes as the metal expanded, and he held the damper open with a hunting knife to try to keep the flames down. He sat in the dark in his shack as the light generator had long been shut down. He could smell the heat of the old stove and see the cherry-red circle of heat growing on the wall of the firebox.

P'tit-Gus learned his lessons well. He remembered, yet there were always the reminders. There was the memory of the grey-white circle on the belly of the old stove to warn him about the lighting of fireboxes half-filled with fuel. There was the stump of an index finger on his right hand. That was from when he was a young boy and had not yet learned to sharpen a scythe without slicing off part of his hand. There was his short, stocky body to remind him of his poor old mother and her constant nagging when he began to use tobacco at the age of fourteen. Then, there were reminders that no one could see. There was one reminder that not even P'tit-Gus could see, but he knew about it and he never talked about it and, always, he tried not to think about it.

Her name was Claudine and it was a long, long time ago. He was a young man then, full of joy and hope. He was working the lumber camps but he was still able to return to Ste-Émilie every other weekend. During one of these weekends, he met Claudine at a dance at the church hall. He walked her home after the dance that night and it was decided then and there that they were meant for each other. P'tit-Gus was in love and his days could not pass swiftly enough. He worked extra hours to help pass the time, to bring the time closer to when he could be with his Claudine.

With the extra hours he worked, P'tit-Gus was able to place a down payment on a small but clean two-bedroom house, just below the rapids on the Gens-de-Terre River, where it entered the town of Ste-Émilie. On the weekends when he was in town, P'tit-Gus and Claudine worked in their new house: linoleum on the kitchen floor, curtains for the windows, and boiled linseed oil on the small area of hardwood flooring in the living room. They were to be married in June. Claudine worked as a secretary for an automobile dealer in town. Two car salesmen worked there. One of the salesmen was happily married while the other was known to have ruined more than half a dozen lives. He was a handsome man, and charming, so much so that his very own mother referred to him as a snake in the grass.

One weekend when P'tit-Gus was in the camp, Claudine worked alone in their little house. She was preparing bed sheets for the new mattress they had purchased. She heard the door open and before she could rise from over the bed the handsome young man from the automobile centre was standing in the bedroom doorway. Claudine had never been with a man before. She and P'tit-Gus had decided to wait until Father Landry had blessed their marriage. The man entered the room. He held Claudine in his arms and before she knew it, this snake in the grass was lying on the bed beside her. He was gentle for such a big man. He caressed her softly and kissed her and, slowly, removed her clothes. Then, he was inside her. Her heart screamed, no! Yet her body squirmed and convulsed to his every touch and finally exploded in waves of pleasure that never seemed to end. And then he left, without a word, not even a kiss. Claudine removed the blood-stained sheet from the mattress and threw it into the wood stove. Later that afternoon, she sat in the hotel lobby waiting for the bus. There was a sweater draped over her tiny suitcase and in her hand she held a one-way ticket for the Capital.

One week later, P'tit-Gus was surprised to see that Claudine was not at her work place when he dropped by, as he did every time he returned from the camp. He rushed down the street to their little house by the river. There he found her letter on the kitchen table. He opened the envelope and, trembling, read how she had been unable to wait for him, how her craving had led her to take on another man, in their house and on their bed. What she had not written was that she had been attracted to the handsome salesman for quite some time. The weeks without seeing each other, while P'tit-Gus was working in the bush, only served to increase her desire for this handsome young man. She was ashamed, she wrote. She would never forgive herself. There was nothing to be done. She was leaving Ste-Émilie and he would never see her again.

P'tit-Gus threw her letter into the cold, iron stove. As he did so, he saw the crumpled bed sheet and the blood stains, a rusty shade of brown. He returned to work on Monday morning and never mentioned the woman's name again, not once in the thirty years since those events had taken place.

P'tit-Gus flipped open his Zippo, lit the paper ball and, when he could no longer hold it without burning his fingers, dropped it into the firebox. The ball moved slightly, folding and unfolding. As it became a mass of black weightless petals, the last of its flame began to creep towards the back of the firebox and then around, until the remains of the ball were surrounded, first yellow, then yellow-red. He watched until the flames came like long, red tongues from the whole circumference of the firebox, darting higher and higher until they touched just above where the paper had been. He watched for the quick bursts of the shorter tongues, deep purple and darting out between the longer ones.

P'tit-Gus shut the small round door and closed the grilled door after it. He stood facing the heater, listening to the puffing of the flames and the cracking of the cold metal as it began to warm. He stood before the grilled door, feeling the heat coming through his trousers. With his lamp, he scanned the room to make sure that the windows were shut. He walked around to the back of the heater and turned the flow valve to 'one quarter'. Then he moved a chair with its damp jeans up closer to the stove and started to leave.

"What time is it?" a voice asked.

"Early," P'tit-Gus replied. "Go back to sleep."

"Is it raining?"

"Yes."

"How bad?"

"Not enough."

"*Sacrament*!"

In the dark behind the glare of his lamp, P'tit-Gus smiled. He did not smile often. There were times when he smiled though, even chuckled, when there was no one around. As the years passed him by, he had become somewhat disconnected from everything modern. He was considered by some to be an aging hermit of a man, completely out of touch with the world around him. But, P'tit-Gus had his life, whatever it was, and there were moments of joy. He would sit on the verandah in the early evenings, smoking a cigarette and chuckling to himself at the best of all jokes, a page in God's great comic book, he would say, as the sky grew black and the clouds grumbled and the lightning came in long zigzag chains. The boys could not play volleyball in the yard behind the cookhouse, the radio-telephone might cease to function and the wires from the generator shed might spark and sizzle. There would be a puff of smoke and all the lights would go out. It was a time for God's little joke—*la farce de Dieu*—and, whether they liked it or not, and P'tit-Gus certainly did, there was not a damn thing they could do about it. That, above everything else, was what gave P'tit-Gus the most pleasure.

Standing in the room, behind the glare of his hunting lamp, the joke was almost as good. This young man, he mused, this student from Ste-Émilie who has come to Washika to work and earn money during the summer months, has only one prayer in the evening and that's for it to rain hard enough in the morning so that he won't have to go out to work.

The rain pattered softly on the tarpapered roof. P'tit-Gus smiled. He could hear the stretching of the flat springs of the bunk as the student who had spoken to him rolled over onto his side and pulled the blankets up over his head.

During the summer months the inner door was held open by a wire twisted around the latch and wrapped around a nail on the wall. P'tit-Gus removed the wire and closed the door behind him. As he shut the screen door, another student awoke and P'tit-Gus could hear him and the one he had spoken to swearing, and then a third one yelling at them to shut up.

Chapter 8

When Henri opened his eyes that morning, he was not sure that he was really awake. He tried looking about the room. It was dark. He could not see where the windows were. The first bell had not sounded. He was sure of that. He was a sound sleeper and, except for the first night at Washika, always slept until the very last moment when Dumas Hébert, standing outside on the cookhouse landing, would lift the steel rod from its hook, place it inside the triangle, beat all three sides with a circular motion of his arm and fill the camp with a sound that no one could ignore.

It was warm under the grey blankets and his throat was dry. He lay on his side with his head resting on one arm. He could smell the ointment. He closed his eyes and he saw Lise Archambault lying in her bed, with her hair untied and floating across the pillow. Because it was so warm, she had rolled the covers back and unlaced her nightdress. Henri could see one of her breasts pointing upwards from her chest. He ran his hand along his chest. It was greasy, and he could feel the scales, like when he had once ran his hand over the back of a dead fish.

He listened to the quiet. Someone was snoring. There was another sound. At last, he was sure. It was not a dream. He listened to the puffing of the oil stove and remembered P'tit-Gus saying that it was raining. But he also remembered P'tit-Gus saying that it was not raining hard enough. He raised himself on his elbows and listened through the quiet, and the snoring, and the puffing of the oil stove. It was raining. He could hear the soft but steady patter of rain on the tar-papered roof. It was raining! Henri smiled in the darkness. Please God, he prayed, let it keep on. Let it be thunder and lightning if You want, I don't care. But just keep it coming. Harder and harder. Alphonse is a good man. He's a good and kind man but it'll take more than this to convince him. Just a little harder, Lord. Please. And lots of black clouds. If it keeps on like this, he'll want us out there by seven. And besides, dear God, if it doesn't rain, even a little, I won't be able to go out to work. I can't work in the sun, remember. That's what she said.

He rolled over onto his side and closed his eyes. He no longer heard the stove, or the snoring, not even the rain. It was soft and warm in his bed and he could see the little green eyes looking into his and smell her good smell and feel the touch of her hair on his arm.

Chapter 9

At a quarter to six Dumas Hébert stepped out onto the landing of the cookhouse and rang the bell. Almost immediately lights could be seen through the windows of the camp buildings and there were sounds of low murmuring voices, boots shuffling, doors closing and, throughout the camp, the older men could be heard enduring their morning cough. Some of the men were worse than others. Télesphore Aumont was forty-one years old and captain of the tugboat, *Hirondelle*. Every morning, he would walk to the washroom with his back bent. Before he would reach the washroom, his face would be very red from coughing and his eyes so large and wet that the students would watch him attentively to see if this was the day his eyes would come popping out of his head. Télesphore smoked cigars and he had, most certainly, the worse cough of the whole camp.

In the bunkhouse-and-office, the students stumbled around the space heater trying to find their jeans and socks and bumping into one another. They no longer noticed that, from the waist up, their bodies were a light brown while their legs and feet were the colour of white chalk. Henri was a special case. In addition to his light tan, his chest was covered with a thin rust-coloured scab. Lavigne came closer to look at it as Henri buttoned his shirt.

"*Et calis*!" he said.

Henri said nothing. It was bad enough without talking about it. It made him feel sick just looking at it. Maybe he would see Lise about it after breakfast. He could not work with a chest like that. That made him feel better, that, and the rain, and maybe seeing Lise later.

As Henri prepared to leave with the others it struck him suddenly that André Guy was not with them. He had not noticed earlier. Perhaps it was because of the scabs, or the rain, or the excitement of seeing Lise Archambault again.

"Hey, you guys! Look at that," Henri called to the others.

The guys came over to where Henri was standing. There, on the bed closest to the stove, was a mound beneath the grey wool blankets with several strands of brown hair sticking out at one end.

"I'll get some water," Lavigne offered.

"No, leave him alone," Henri said. Already he regretted having spoken about it.

"You've forgotten the French bed, Henri?" one of the guys added.

No, Henri had not forgotten. It was another of André's many pranks. He would simply remove all of the blankets from the bed, take the sheet from the foot of the bed and fold it up to the head. The blankets were then returned to the bed as they had been previously. That night, when Henri drove his feet in under the blankets there was some resistance at first, and then he heard the sound of cotton tearing as his feet went through the sheet. There was another sound in the darkened room, insane laughter, coming from the bed closest to the oil space heater.

"Come on, Henri," Lavigne pleaded. "Don't miss your chance. I'll do it for you if you want."

"No," Henri said flatly.

"Wait! I've got an idea," said St-Jean.

Maurice St-Jean stood by the door with a towel draped over his shoulder, his sandy brown hair rumpled from sleep, and with that grin that always gave him the appearance of not having any teeth.

"Hurry up, Gaston," he said, nodding towards the bed. "Grab one end. Henri, you hold the door."

St-Jean looked around the room. The other two roommates, Pierre Morrow and Gaston Cyr, stood by the oil furnace waiting to see what would happen.

"Go on!" St-Jean turned on them. "Get going before he wakes up."

Morrow and Cyr left, running across the yard in the rain. Henri tied the inner door open with a length of wire. He held the screen door open with one hand while he remained standing inside.

St-Jean signalled to Lavigne and, together, they lifted the bed off the floor. They walked slowly, shuffling their feet and carrying the bed at arm's length.

As they carried the bed past Henri and out through the doorway, St-Jean stumbled on the square timber landing. He was a strong young man and the muscles stood out on his neck as he squatted on the sand with the foot of the bed against his chest. Stepping backwards on the sand, St-Jean pulled himself upright. He and Lavigne carried the bed out to the centre of the yard and lowered it to the ground. Henri covered André's feet with a section of blanket. The three boys ran then, crossing the yard in the pouring rain.

That morning, the older men were surprised to find the washroom so quiet. They found the students gathered around the windows and looking out through the rain. Some of the men went to the windows and looked over the students' shoulders of. There, in the centre of the yard in the pouring rain, was a bed and a mound of wet, grey blankets.

St-Jean was beginning to have regrets. The joke was not going well. How could anyone go on sleeping in the rain like that? Several of the students began to leave. They didn't want to miss anything but it was late. The bell would ring in a few minutes and they had not even washed yet. St-Jean was about to give up. Then he heard the screen door slam shut and he saw Gauthier walking across the yard. He was headed towards the cookhouse.

As Gauthier walked by the bed, the mound of blankets began to move. He paid no attention to the bed. He continued walking towards the cookhouse and then as the rain started to come down in large, heavy droplets he began to run. Suddenly, a violent scream erupted from behind him. Gauthier glanced over his left shoulder; André was coming after him, running barefoot on the sand and wearing only his white cotton underwear.

In the main sleep camp, laughter filled the washroom as André chased Gauthier around and around the camp yard in the pouring rain.

Chapter 10

At exactly six o'clock, Dumas Hébert came out of the cookhouse and, without looking at the men gathered before him, took the rod down from its hook and rang the second bell.

André Simard-Comtois, superintendent of the camp, was often late for breakfast. So was P'tit-Gus, but that was not his fault since there were often last minute chores to attend to. Jean-Luc Desrosiers was often late as well but that was also understandable since his position as Inspector of Sweeps kept him on the move most of the time. Often, he would arrive at Washika just in time for the breakfast bell. There were times when he would arrive much later, in which case he would be at the cook's mercy. If Dumas was in a good mood that morning, there would be leftover toast, and tea, and perhaps some buns and warmed-over potatoes and ham. Otherwise, Jean-Luc would have to settle for strong black tea and cakes. Or he might be informed that the cookhouse was not a restaurant and that if he wanted to eat there he should arrive on time like everybody else.

That morning, as Dumas rang the bell, all of the older workers at the camp were present with the exception of P'tit-Gus. Dumas placed the rod on its hook and stood by the open doorway. As each man filed past him, Dumas collected the green meal ticket. He did not smile or speak to the men. He stood straight in his white, short-sleeved shirt and trousers and examined carefully each hand that held out a ticket. He would not tolerate a lack of cleanliness in his cookhouse. Dumas was forty-two years old and he had not been a cook all of his life. He had worn many different hats in his life. Before becoming a cook in the lumber camps,

Dumas had tried his hand at several different trades in the cities he lived in. It was said that, although he was not more than five foot eight and weighed scarcely more than one hundred and thirty pounds, whenever he grew tired of the cookhouse he would trade in his white uniform for work boots and wool shirts and there was hardly a lumberjack around that could keep up to him.

Gauthier was at the end of the line. As he handed Dumas the ticket, the cook glanced past him. He could see how Dumas's eyes changed and how his cheeks moved showing the outline of his jaw. The students came, running across the yard. Some came from the main sleep camp while others appeared from around a corner of the bunkhouse-and-office. Dumas counted eighteen of them. The students lined up, single file, and marched past Dumas. Each one of them handed him a ticket and went in to the cookhouse without once looking at him.

When the last student had passed, Dumas put the tickets in his shirt pocket and, as he reached back for the handle of the screen door, he saw P'tit-Gus coming across the yard. He was half-walking, half-running on his short, stocky legs, his heavy work boots slipping in the sand. As he walked, his head moved up and down and just looking at him moving that way, Dumas could tell he was angry. Without stopping, P'tit-Gus pulled out his watch, looked at it, and then returned it to its pocket, muttering something that Dumas could not make out. When P'tit-Gus finally arrived at the landing, Dumas held out his hand for the ticket. P'tit-Gus trembled slightly and his face and neck were covered in sweat.

"*Gang de p'tits chrisses*!" he said.

"*C'est rien, mon Gus*," Dumas said softly. "It's nothing."

There was a faint smile on Dumas's face as he closed the screen door behind them.

Chapter 11

In the cookhouse the men sat at long wooden tables with plank benches. The twenty students sat facing each other, ten on each side of the table next to the front wall of the cookhouse and nearest the door. The table opposite them was where Simard-Comtois took his meals, along with Jean-Luc Desrosiers and the two scalers. Along the same wall, beyond the kitchen entrance, was where the older men ate. They were only ten at this table, five a side, but they had been in logging camps a long time and they treasured their lifelong habits: they enjoyed eating in silence and resting their elbows on the table as they ate.

The table opposite the older men, along the front wall and just beyond where the students were, was not used for meals. Running down its centre in a straight line were five large metal wash pans: one pan for scrapings from the plates, two for spoons, knives and forks, and two for cups. The scraped plates were piled next to the first pan.

Dumas stood at the centre of the room with his arms locked across his chest. He stood at the centre point of the four tables and his small black eyes scanned the three tables where the men ate. There were pancakes and thick slices of toasted homemade bread piled onto platters. There were greasy, twisted slices of bacon, and beside them, pork-chops, chunks of fried potatoes and large plates of fried eggs laying one on top of another. Running down the centre of the tables were small jars with spoons sticking out of them: bottles of jam, ketchup, molasses, and brown sugar, salt and pepper, margarine, jugs of powdered milk and pots of steaming, hot tea. Dumas kept a close watch on everything. He saw and heard everything, and never did a bowl, or jug, or plate come close to being half full when Dumas would arrive with a fresh supply, leaving just as quickly with his swift way of walking. Never could it be said that there had been some item missing or in short supply in Dumas Hébert's cookhouse.

At a quarter past six the cookhouse door opened and André walked in. His hair was wet and there were several strands standing straight up on his head. André walked between the two long tables. He did not look at the students as he walked past them. He walked softly but quickly, like in Ste-Émilie when he would arrive late for Sunday mass at St. Exupéry's. Dumas held his arms across his chest. André held out a meal ticket but Dumas did not look at him. He scanned each table diligently as he spoke.

"You have been in this camp how long?" he said.

"Thirty-three days today."

"And, you are enjoying yourself? Everything is to your liking?"

"Yes *monsieur*. Everything is fine," André replied.

Dumas turned to examine the table behind him, where the older men were seated.

"And you are well?" he continued. "You are not sick or anything?"

"No, no. Everything is fine."

"Perhaps it is the hours then. It is early, is it not? You could speak to Simard-Comtois about it, you know. He would agree with you, I am sure. After all, breakfast at six o'clock in the morning, that is crazy."

"No sir. That's fine sir."

"What do you say, eh? Simard-Comtois is the big boss here. He could fix it for you."

"No sir. That's fine. Everything's fine."

Dumas had been looking towards the table where Simard-Comtois sat as he spoke. He turned then and looked at André with his deep, black eyes.

"I will tell you something then," he said. "The next time you feel like having your breakfast a little later than usual you can join your friend Simard-Comtois in his cabin. What do you say, eh?"

"Yes sir."

Dumas took the meal ticket from André and put it in his shirt pocket. He stared at the table opposite the students, where Simard-Comtois sat, and a faint smile appeared on his lips. At the end of the table, nearest the door, Simard-Comtois had stopped eating. He was breathing silently through his nose and staring hard at the cook. Desrosiers and the two scalers looked at each other and at their plates. They did not look at the superintendent.

Chapter 12

Sometime during breakfast it had stopped raining and the dark clouds had disappeared leaving only scattered puffs of white ones in a blue sky.

Henri was disappointed. He sat on his bunk in the bunkhouse-and-office rolling a cigarette. There was not much time. In less than ten minutes the bell calling all to make their lunches would ring. He could not decide on his own not to go out to work. If he made up his lunch pail, there was no longer any decision to be made. He lit his cigarette and left the bunkhouse-and-office.

When he arrived at Alphonse's room in the main sleep camp, the air was thick with tobacco smoke. Alphonse was sitting on his bunk talking to two men sitting on the opposite bunk.

"Well, well," Alphonse said. "And how's my little copilot this morning?"

"Oh, fine," Henri replied.

"A lot drier than the one in the yard this morning," one of the men said.

"Dumas fixed him all right," the other man said.

"And so, Henri," Alphonse said. "What can I do for you this morning?"

"It's the burn," Henri said. "I went to see the nurse, you see, and she put on a salve and said to stay out of the sun and it's not raining anymore and look how it blistered."

Henri opened his shirt. Alphonse looked at the scabs covering Henri's chest.

"All right, Henri," he said. "You stay in camp today. I'll speak to P'tit-Gus. He'll find you something."

"Okay. I'll see the nurse later. And I'll tell Dumas that I'll be here for lunch."

"Yes, that's right. Remember now, you'll be working for P'tit-Gus today. It's him that will be your foreman today."

"Yes sir."

Henri went out of the room. As he walked down the hall he could hear one of the men in Alphonse's room saying something about P'tit-Gus and then all of them laughing.

Henri went back to the bunkhouse-and-office. Most of the fellows were stretched out on their bunks, smoking cigarettes and waiting for the lunch bell to ring. André Guy sat alone at a small table shuffling a deck of cards. His hair was still wet and he did not look up when Henri entered the room.

"And? Did you see Alphonse?" Lavigne inquired.

"Yes," Henri replied.

"And? What did he say?"

"It's all fixed. I'm not going out today."

"Really?"

"Yes."

Maurice St-Jean came over to where Henri and Lavigne were standing by the bed.

"Seeing as you have nothing to do all day," he said. "You might hang out André's sheets and blankets. It seems that they got kind of wet during the night."

"Don't laugh," Henri said. "I'll be working for P'tit-Gus today."

"Good!" St-Jean went on. "That's good, Henri. At least you'll get paid for doing André's laundry."

St-Jean walked over to the table. He put his hand on André's shoulder.

"What do you think, André? Henri here will be doing your laundry. Like having your own personal maid." He turned to Henri. "Go on, Henri. Show him those good legs of yours."

André's gaze never left the cards. He shuffled them over and over again, like a cat's tail swaying from side to side before a strike.

"Leave me alone, *sacrament*!" André warned.

"Now, now André," St-Jean continued. "You don't want to hurt his feelings. This is Henri's first time. Look how nervous he is."

André stood up quickly, his fists clenched. Henri and Lavigne and the two others moved in closer. There had not been a good one in camp since their arrival and, with St-Jean, it promised to be a good one. André rushed St-Jean but he did not move. His feet stayed in one spot as his left shoulder dropped and then he popped André a left to the eye. Just like that, and André was sitting on the floor rubbing his eye.

St-Jean turned to leave when André attacked him from behind. They went down together. St-Jean got a right arm around André's head and, with his left, hit him three times in the face.

"Enough?" said St-Jean, still holding André by the head.

"*Mon tabarnacle*!"

Three more punches to the face.

"Enough now?"

"*Mon sacrament*!"

Another shot to the face. The lunch bell rang, clangity, clangity, clang. St-Jean let go his hold on André. He walked over to the bunk, picked up his lunch pail and went out with the others.

André sat on the floor in the corner. He sat on the floor facing the wall and he was crying softly.

Chapter 13

Dumas stood in the centre of the cookhouse collecting the green tickets. The men carrying their lunch pails handed Dumas a ticket and then went on to the table where the older men had eaten earlier. Now there were large platters on the table: ham and pork slices, bread, cheese, pickles, and round, hard biscuits and doughnuts. There were bottles of ketchup and mustard, salt and pepper. At the opposite table, where the pans for dirty dishes had been, were several pots of steaming tea and coffee. There were cans of evaporated milk as well as jugs of powdered milk, ice water and bowls of white sugar for the coffee.

The students stood on both sides of the table with the platters of food. There they made sandwiches with the thick slices of white bread. They wrapped the sandwiches in small squares of waxed paper and stuffed them into their lunch pails. On top of the sandwiches and in vacant corners of their lunch pails, they jammed in cookies and cheese and pickles, also in waxed paper. After they had filled their thermos bottles and placed them inside the covers, some had to lean on their lunch pails to be able to snap the fasteners shut.

Henri stood at the end of the line, the only one not carrying a lunch pail. He felt a fool being there like that and already he was regretting not going out with others. When his turn came, he stood with empty hands before Dumas. He felt naked.

"*Monsieur* Hébert," he began. "I won't be going out today. I got a very bad burn yesterday."

"I am not the nurse. Do I look like the nurse, eh?"

"No sir."

"So, why should I want to know that you got a very bad burn?"

"Yes, well you see, I'll be here for lunch today. I'm not making a lunch. So, I'll be eating here today."

"And why should that concern me? Eh? Why should I have to know that?"

"If I don't make a lunch that makes one extra person here for dinner"

"And?"

"I just thought you should know."

"Now I know."

"Yes. I'm working for P'tit-Gus today. *Monsieur* Hébert, I was wondering?"

"Yes?"

"Well, does it ever happen? I mean, is it possible someday to have chocolate pudding?"

Dumas looked at Henri. He smiled without moving his lips, more a look of disgust than a smile, and one that made Henri wish he was standing somewhere else at that moment.

"You think that this is a summer camp?" he said. "Maybe I should visit in the evenings with cookies and milk? Eh?"

"No sir."

Dumas turned and walked quickly into the kitchen, leaving Henri standing alone in the centre of the cookhouse. Henri felt more a fool than ever. He wished that he had not spoken of the pudding. Then he thought about P'tit-Gus and he wished that he had not gone to see Alphonse, and he wished that he had not become so excited about seeing Lise Archambault later and, finally, he wished that he had buttoned his shirt properly when Alphonse had spoken to him about it.

Henri left the cookhouse and walked across the yard to the bunkhouse-and-office. Through the screened windows, he could hear Richard Gagnier, the cookee, singing, and pots banging on the stove. As he reached the bunkhouse, he met André Guy. André was carrying his lunch pail and he walked past Henri without looking at him. He was very red around the eyes and there was a swelling above his right cheek.

Henri entered the bunkhouse-and-office. The students had already left and gone down to the wharf. It reminded Henri of once when he had visited his school during the summer vacation, how empty the classroom had seemed and how he could see each of the faces of his classmates at their desks. He had looked at the dull, black chalkboard and imagined that he could see the words and the numbers that had once been written there.

"You're ready?"

Henri turned quickly. He had felt alone in the room. Now the voice had frightened him. He had not noticed the man sitting by the stove.

"There's lots of work to do," P'tit-Gus declared.

"Yes sir," Henri said, looking down at the man. "But first, I must go see the nurse."

"Did Alphonse say that?"

"No sir."

"All right, you can go. But remember, you're working for me today."

"Yes sir."

"Go and see the nurse then. And after, come back and sweep up this place."

"Yes sir."

P'tit-Gus pulled at the string that was tied to his pocket watch. He looked at the watch and put it back in its pocket. He walked over to the door and, turning, looked once around the room and went out.

Henri looked out the window. He looked at P'tit-Gus making his way to the main sleep camp. It had clouded over once again and he could hear a light rain falling.

Chapter 14

Henri opened the screen door and then knocked on the thick, hardwood door of the infirmary. It was cold and damp standing on the verandah and his hair was wet from walking across the yard in the rain.

The door opened and Lise Archambault stood in the open doorway. She was wearing a pink nightgown with lace at the wrists and all down the centre. Her brown hair was untied and it slid over her shoulders and down to the small of her back.

"Yes?" she said.

"Hello," Henri said. "It's about the burn."

It was warm in the room and the windows were closed and the curtains hung straight down past the sills. It was almost dark in the infirmary but there was a light coming from the back room.

"They are waiting for you?" the nurse asked.

"No, I'm not going out today."

"Yes, well, have a seat then. You have had your breakfast?"

"Yes."

"I am just finishing mine. Would you have a coffee while you wait, Henri?"

"Yes, that would be good."

"Come with me, then."

He followed her and, as they walked into the light of the back room, she turned to guide him into the small kitchen and as she did so he could see the shape of her breasts and her legs through the pink of the nightgown.

"You take sugar and cream?" she said.

"Yes, that's fine."

Henri sat at the varnished wood table. The nurse set a place mat in front of him. She brought a cup and saucer with a spoon and placed two small porcelain bowls near them. Henri looked at her hands as she poured coffee from the glass coffeepot. She sat across the table from Henri. There were orange peelings on the place mat and she ate cereal from a white porcelain bowl. Henri added sugar and cream and stirred his coffee with the spoon. He had never felt this way before.

"*Mademoiselle* Archambault?"

"Yes?"

"I was wondering. Maybe I could. Well, what if I were to call you Lise?"

She looked up at Henri.

"Yes. If you like," she said.

The nurse smiled and Henri looked at her green eyes and how her hair was parted in the middle and flowed down both sides of her head, curving around her cheeks to her neck and shoulders and down her back. Her hands were tanned, like her face. Henri wondered about that. Where would she go to get a tan like that?

Henri drank the coffee. He looked around the room, at the varnished walls and the white refrigerator and stove and the pine cabinets on the wall. At one end of the kitchen there was a couch with lace-covered cushions and, in front of the couch, was a low table with a small bowl of yellow flowers on it. Beyond the couch was a closed door.

"Lise?"

"Yes, Henri?"

"You like it here? Working at Washika?"

"It is not so bad."

"You must be well paid, being a nurse."

"Yes, the salary is quite good."

"Someday, when I finish school, I'll have a job. I'll have a job that pays well and a car. A sports car, you know, like a racing car with spokes on the wheels, and no top."

They both laughed. Lise got up from the table and gathered the dishes and utensils and placed them in the sink. She ran water over a cloth and passed it several times over the place mat.

"You would like another coffee, Henri?"

"No, thank you."

"Well, if you will excuse me, I will go and change."

"Lise?" How he loved to say her name like that.

"Yes?" she said, as she entered the bedroom.

"Would you like me to wait on the other side?"

"No, Henri. Finish your coffee. I will be only a minute."

Henri drank the coffee. The door to the bedroom was open, he could see the light was on and he could hear the nightgown being slid off her shoulders. Perhaps she would be angry. She might even see *Monsieur* Simard-Comtois about it. But, what if it was not like that? He would hate himself after. There was not much time. In fact, there was only now.

"Lise?" he said.

"Yes, Henri?" she called from the bedroom.

"Lise, would you mind if I came in?"

There, he had said it. It was quiet in the kitchen. Only the clock was ticking on top of the refrigerator. The ticking seemed to grow louder with each passing second.

"If you like, Henri," she said, at last.

Henri went into the bedroom. The room smelled of her hair and it was dark except for a lamp by the bed. Lise stood by the bed, in front of the lamp. She was naked and she stood with her head bowed so that her hair covered the side of her face. She was beautiful. Henri had never seen anyone so beautiful. He had seen naked women before, in the magazines, with their slim legs and flat bellies but, here, standing in front of him, was the most beautiful woman he had ever seen.

Henri began to unbutton his shirt. He could not take his eyes off of her. Then she looked at him with her green eyes and he prayed, dear God make it good and let me hang on and not be a fool.

"Henri," she said.

"Yes Lise."

"Close the door, will you."

Chapter 15

It was ten o'clock. It had stopped raining and the sun was out. Henri smelled the good smell that follows a rainfall as he walked across the yard. He went to the bunkhouse-and-office. P'tit-Gus was sitting at the table leafing through one of the picture magazines.

"At last," he said. "Where have you been all this time?"

"With the nurse."

"Yes, well don't stand around. I've got lots of work for you."

Henri did not wish to argue. He stayed away from the man. Her smell was still on him. He could still smell her sweetness and taste her in his mouth. There was still that good flushed feeling and he did not want to lose that arguing with P'tit-Gus.

"What's there to do?" he asked.

"What's there to do," P'tit-Gus repeated. "I'll show you what's there to do. Come with me."

Henri followed P'tit-Gus out of the bunkhouse-and-office and across the yard to the main sleep camp. Walking behind the man, he thought about Lise and the last time he had looked at her and how she had stood, naked, behind the screen door.

"Now, first you start at this end," P'tit-Gus began, "and work your way down to the other end. Clean everything, wastebaskets, ashtrays, anything dragging on the floor. And check under the beds. Here, take these." P'tit-Gus handed him several black, plastic garbage bags.

"When that's done," he continued, pointing towards the corner of the room, "there's the broom there. Start from this end again. And don't forget to spread the dust bane."

In one corner of the common room, next to the broom, was a large green barrel containing the soft, sand-like, green dust bane that was used for keeping the dust down when you swept. Henri liked the smell it made on the floor.

"And when you've finished, do the same over at your bunkhouse."

"Is that it?"

"Oh no. After, there are the sheets and pillowcases. Come on, get a move on. I've got work to do."

Henri could not imagine what work there was left to do but he said nothing. He did not want to argue or even speak with P'tit-Gus. It had been wonderful being with Lise. He was feeling so happy and he did not want anything to spoil that.

Henri spent the rest of the morning doing the jobs assigned to him by P'tit-Gus. He picked up, swept and changed the bed clothes in both sleep camps. But, she was always there. He could not stop thinking about her. What was supposed to have been a simple visit to the infirmary had, in fact, produced a profound change in his life. Prior to his visit with Lise Archambault, Henri had made love only in his dreams. Lise had been most patient with him and guided him and held him until it was time, and after, she made love to him in her way and the experience was one that Henri would remember for the rest of his life.

At noon, Henri went to the cookhouse for dinner. He avoided the eyes of the older workers who were there. Maybe just thinking about her would show on his face. Perhaps someone had noticed how long he had been at the infirmary. And there was her smell, that sweet smell of her that was still on him. He sat apart from the others at the table. After dinner, Henri stretched out on his bunk to read and wait for further orders from P'tit-Gus. He could not read. He listened to a bumblebee and watched it banging against the screen, trying to get inside. Later, he thought, he would visit Emmett Cronier at the scales. Perhaps Lise might sit on the verandah in the afternoon. He would be able to see her there from the scales. There would be nothing wrong, just walking down to the infirmary and speaking with her on the verandah. No one would think anything wrong about that. But, he had promised. That very morning, as they sat together with their backs propped up against the pillows, she had made him promise. They would not be seen together, ever. On Sundays, she would pack her fishing gear and sandwiches and head south and out of the bay as she did every Sunday morning if it was not raining. No one would suspect a thing. If he wanted to be with her, she would be by the log dump. There, she would wait for him in her little skiff, fishing for bass in the deep water by the square timber wall and out of view of the camp. There was a beach two miles south of Washika with a dense growth of evergreens above its sloping sand. Behind this thick wall of trees, a circular patch of beach sand lay hidden from view. From this patch of sand one could easily see out towards the lake while no one could see in past the trees. It was there that she went swimming every Sunday and, afterwards, lay on the sand in the sun behind the row of trees. That, she explained to Henri, was how she came to be tanned all over. She would take him there and they would swim together and, after, they would make love on the sand. And maybe, sometime during the day, they would fish a little. Also, she had made him promise; he must bring along his life jacket, the one he used on the *Madeleine*. She insisted strongly on this point. Henri was curious about that but he did not wish to say or do anything to ruin the moment they were living. And, she insisted, they must never be seen together and he must not speak about it to anyone.

That was the difficult part. When the others arrived at five o'clock, he would have liked to stand aside with St-Jean, and maybe Lavigne, and tell them what an extraordinary day it had been. He wanted to say how beautiful she was and how she made soft sounds in her throat when he touched her and, later, how she made love to him. But, he had promised.

"And how were the flies?" he said to Lavigne.

"*Sacrament*! Always the same. And you?"

"Not bad. The burn's not so bad now."

"No, no. P'tit-Gus, I mean. Didn't work you too hard? He was pretty pissed about us this morning."

"No. Not so bad."

"Tell me. Maybe I'll get a burn tomorrow."

Henri had not thought about that. Suppose Lavigne was to get a burn and be forced to stay in camp, and see the nurse. Would it be the same with Lavigne?

"No, my poor Lavigne," Henri said. "It's not worth the trouble. P'tit-Gus is so hard to please and, besides, it's so boring here all day with no one to talk to. Believe me, you're much better off out on the lake."

"I suppose you're right. A guy alone like that, he starts to think. It's bad enough on Sundays. Hey! Can you imagine, Henri, some poor young girl wandering in here on a Sunday?"

"Like those tourists near the log dump," Henri laughed. "Remember them?"

"Yeah. And that wasn't even on a Sunday."

They both laughed. Henri remembered that day and he often wondered how the two girls must have felt. It was close to five o'clock and Alphonse had suddenly veered to starboard, steering the *Madeleine* towards the log dump and the two two-hundred-gallon fuel tanks strapped to the square timbers of the wall. Between the log dump and the dock at Washika, a car was parked on the road just above the beach. An aluminum boat was tied to a rack on the roof of the car and, as the *Madeleine* went by at a slow speed, they saw a short, fat man wearing sun glasses and a baseball cap, fishing from the shore, casting out onto the water, spinning the reel and casting again. Just beyond the fat man, two teenage girls ran along the beach. Both girls were deeply tanned and their long blond hair flew freely as they ran along the beach together. They wore shorts and light T-shirts, and the older girl was not wearing a bra. It had been a long time for the students from the Collège de Ste-Émilie. It had been almost two weeks since their last trip down to Ste-Émilie. It happened suddenly, and spontaneously, and without warning of any kind. As the *Madeleine* went by the tourists, nineteen young men jumped overboard, each one yelling madly as he did so. The water was shallow there and soon they were running in the water towards the shore. The girls looked frightened. They turned and ran back towards the fat man. He reeled in quickly and all three of them got into the car and sped off towards the log dump.

The students dropped onto the sand, laughing and catching their breath. Only one of them was missing. François Gauthier had been the last to go over the side. He was not interested in the girls on the beach. He was dry and warm and he wanted to stay that way. Still, he had learned not to like being different. At the very last, he had jumped from the stern. He had felt stupid as he did not believe that the young girls would have anything to do with them. It was stupid, and senseless, but so was putting up with their needling. So, he jumped. He sighed and looked up at the sky and stepped off the *Madeleine*'s rounded stern. The water had been shallow when the others left the tugboat. Gauthier was not so lucky. He managed to tread water, held afloat by his orange life jacket and wearing his hard hat. He felt a fool in his wool mackinaw that would take days to dry.

"They sure were good-looking," Lavigne said.

"That's for sure. And remember Gauthier?"

"Poor Gauthier. And him not even interested in girls. I can hardly wait. Only three more days."

"Three days?"

"Today is Wednesday?"

"Yes."

"Well? This is our weekend to go down."

Henri had not thought about that. On Saturday, it would be three weeks since their last weekend off in Ste-Émilie. That was it, then. He would not have to tell her. Lise would see the bus arriving. She would know that he could not stay behind. They would think he was crazy not to go down.

"Of course!" he said. "I forgot it was this weekend."

The bell rang. It was time for supper. Henri was not thinking about food. It would be a long weekend without her. He reached into his wallet for a ticket and left the bunkhouse-and-office.

PART II

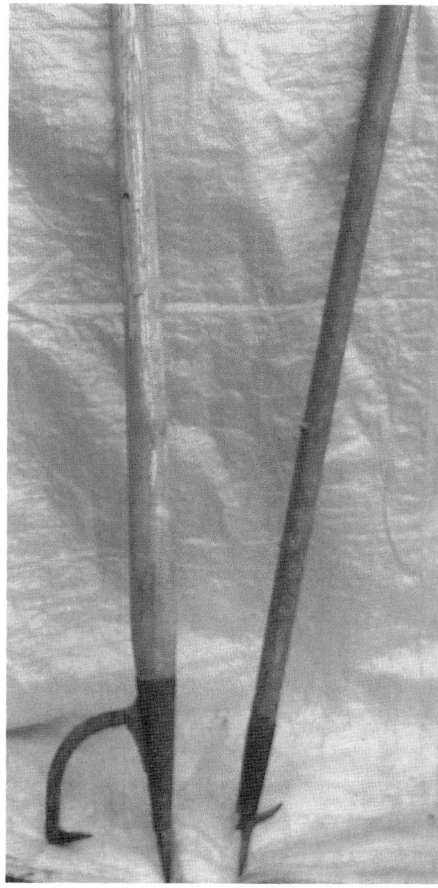

Chapter 16

That morning it was not raining. It had rained during the night so that the sand did not give easily under their feet, and the air was cool and the sky a dark shade of blue. The students walked in single file, over the knoll and down towards the dock and the grey tugboat. By the dock the water slapped against the *Madeleine*'s hull. It was quiet, and damp, and only the sound of the waves slapping against the *Madeleine* made it real.

"Come back!" a voice called from the crest of the knoll. "Come back, you guys!" It was Alphonse. He waved to them to return to camp.

"Good old Alphonse," someone yelled.

Henri looked up at the sky. It was not so dark. To the east was a clearing. It would probably not rain at all.

They were happy. Alphonse was a good man. He would not make them work in the rain. Maybe they should buy him a little something in Ste-Émilie during the weekend. That was it. They would buy him something together.

"Well, my little ducks," Alphonse began as the last of the students reached the circle around him. "I have some good news this morning."

Alphonse turned to look at the man standing behind him. "*Monsieur* Simard-Comtois here has something to say to you."

The superintendent cleared his throat and stepped into the circle.

"*Messieurs*," he began. "*Monsieur* Ouimet here informs me that you have been doing excellent work out on the lake. In fact, he is quite proud of you all."

The students looked at the sand. Then they looked at Alphonse. Alphonse lit a cigarette and smiled at them.

"You know," Simard-Comtois continued, "the Company takes great pride in being able to assist any young man in getting a start in life. It is hoped that by the end of the summer you will have not only achieved financial gains but it is also our belief that you will have accumulated a certain degree of experience that will remain with you..."

No one was listening. They looked at Alphonse for a sign but Alphonse just smiled and smoked his cigarette. What did he want? They had heard this kind of talk before, that first day at Washika as they got down from the bus. He was there that day, speaking in the same way. After lunch that day, they had had to go out on the *Madeleine*, pick logs off the shore and stand in brown stinking water with leeches sneaking in under their jeans, all that after the long, sweaty bus ride from Ste-Émilie to Washika.

"And in conclusion," the man went on, "I'm sure that you will not disappoint us in this next endeavour."

They looked up from the sand. They stared at Alphonse as if staring at him like that would somehow change things

"Well, my little ducks," Alphonse smiled at his crew. "We have a new job for you today. You see, there's a fire started up on the Ottawa. It's been going strong for twelve days now. Men are tired and it's time for fresh meat up there. Leave your life jackets behind. The bus should be here any minute."

The students left the circle without saying a word. There was nothing to say. They were not going out on the Cabonga today. That at least was clear. In the bunkhouse-and-office the guys were worried.

"I wonder if we should bring fly oil?" Pierre Morrow asked no one in particular. He was the youngest and the smallest person in the camp.

"Fly oil?" Lavigne turned on him. "You worry about fly oil at a time like this? Don't you realize what could happen to us?"

"You mean it's dangerous?"

"Dangerous? What's the matter with you anyway?"

"Leave him alone," Henri interrupted.

Lavigne moved in closer. "Listen, my friend," he said. "You know what day this is?"

"Thursday?" Morrow was not sure. He looked at the others sitting on their bunks.

"That's right. And do you know what week this is?"

"Sure, I know."

"Well?"

"It's our week to go down; on Saturday, right after breakfast."

Lavigne had made his point. He smiled at Morrow but Morrow did not return the smile. No one was smiling. They were looking at the grey plywood floor and taking long drags on their cigarettes.

"You think so, eh?" Lavigne continued.

"All right, Gaston," St-Jean got up off the bunk. "That's enough." St-Jean looked out the window to the yard where the bus would arrive. "For me, we've had it," he said. "There'll be no going down this weekend. I've heard about these fires. We could get stuck a couple of weeks up there if it's a big one."

"But they're expecting me at home," said Morrow. "We have visitors coming. It's *maman*'s birthday on Sunday."

"Poor little one," André Guy began. "He's lonesome for his *maman*."

"Your mouth, *calis*!" St-Jean looked over at André.

"It's here!" Lavigne shouted.

They could hear the engine running. They looked out the window and saw the pencil-yellow bus with a black bar running along its length. The students picked up their lunch pails and their gloves and hard hats and went outside.

Outside, Alphonse stood talking to the driver. They stood by the open door of the bus. The driver reached into his shirt pocket and offered Alphonse a cigarette from a light blue package. Alphonse lit the driver's cigarette and then his own. He turned to the students gathered around him.

"All right now," he said. "Everybody in the bus and if you're smoking be sure to butt them out on the floor. We have enough with one fire."

The students lined up alongside the bus and, one by one, they stepped inside. The inside of the bus was pale green with a black rubber mat running down the aisle between the rows of seats. They were bench seats with leatherette covering and chrome bars above the backs. Everyone raced for a window seat. The boys placed their gloves and lunch pails in the racks above the seats and, as quickly, fought for a place next to a window. They fumbled with the latches and pulled at the glass until all of the windows of the bus were open.

Alphonse entered the bus and sat down beside François Gauthier in the front seat, to the right of the driver's seat. At last the driver appeared at the front of the bus. The students could see the back of his head in the mirror as he counted the passengers in his bus. The driver pointed an index finger towards each one of the students as he counted. Then, it was time. The driver reached over to the handle and swung the door shut. He shifted into gear and they were off.

They went around the bunkhouse-and-office. All of the students waved to Emmett Cronier as they crossed the truck scales. From there, they drove down the gravel road, past the infirmary and north to the Ottawa River. Henri had been careful to choose a seat by a window on the driver's side of the bus. He had raised the window up to its highest and he looked out onto the water of the bay as they went by the infirmary. Lise Archambault was not there. She was not on the verandah or even at the door. He remembered being able to see out through the curtains when he had been there with her. As they sped by the building, he gave a little wave towards the windows, just in case.

The engine groaned going up some of the hills and there was often a grinding sound as the driver downshifted at the start of a new hill. Some of the boys tried to sleep but the road was very rough. Mostly hey smoked and looked out the windows at the thick green forest, the swamps and beaver ponds in the lowlands. Once, going down a steep hill, they saw a moose standing in the water. The moose lifted its head to look at them. Water dripped off the large dewlap hanging from its throat.

At exactly ten o'clock they drove into a widening of the road. The bulldozer had cleared away a strip thirty yards wide on both sides of the road. At the end of the clearing on both sides were broken trunks and roots and a mixture of light sand and stones piled up where the tractor had pushed them. A narrow house trailer stood alongside the road with several Company trucks parked beside it. The trucks all had long steel antennas on their roofs and at one end of the trailer stood a thirty-foot pole with a radio antenna at the top. On the opposite side and further back from the road were two tractor-trailers with their low-beds empty and long lengths of chain lying on the sand beside them. They could hear the heavy machinery that the trucks had transported there on the low-beds and smell the burning forests through the open windows. To the northwest the sky was a grey-black and it had begun to rain softly. The bus stopped in front of the house trailer. Alphonse stepped down from the bus and walked towards the set of steps leading to the door. As he approached, the door opened and a tall, thin man with grey, curly hair waved to him to come inside.

The driver shut down the engine and sat at the wheel smoking a cigarette. The air was damp and heavy and drops of rain began to cover the windshield. Most of the windows were still open and the boys sat quietly, listening to the rain and the mosquitoes entering the bus.

Alphonse came out of the house trailer office followed by the tall, thin fellow they had seen earlier.

"That's it, then," Alphonse said. "We should be there sometime around noon."

"Oh yes," the tall man answered. "No problem at all. We opened a new road in just yesterday."

"How long do you think?"

"Well, that's hard to say. With the wind and the rain, who can tell, eh?"

Alphonse turned his back to the bus. No one could see him as he quickly winked at the tall man in front of him.

"At least three weeks, what?" Alphonse asked, loudly. He wanted all of his little ducks to hear.

"Oh yes, at the very least." The tall man smiled and looked towards the bus and its open windows.

No one was speaking in the bus. It was quiet, except for the mosquitoes. The boys looked out at the man who had said, "Oh yes, at the very least," and they hated him then, even if they didn't know him. They looked at his clean white shirt, freshly pressed trousers and clean work boots and they hated him again. When he lifted his hard hat to scratch his head through the thick grey curls, they hated him some more.

Alphonse waved good-bye to the man as he entered the bus. He spoke to the driver and they both laughed.

"Sometime tonight," he said to the driver. "I have no idea what time. They'll reach you somehow, with their radios, probably."

"You bet," the driver said.

Alphonse turned to the students. They sat in the seats, some with their heads resting against the windows, others smoking, and all being very quiet.

"All right, you guys," Alphonse began. "Here's how it is. The fire is sixteen square miles now. We'll be staying pretty much together but, if we do get split up, don't worry. At the end of each day, all the men are assembled at Camp 15. That's where we'll take our bus back to Washika at night."

This was different. The students felt it as soon as Alphonse had begun to speak. Out on the Cabonga, on the sweep, Alphonse was in charge. If they had put in a good morning and it was especially hot in the afternoon, he would go easy on them. They might move to another shore, running the *Madeleine* at slow speed, or they might stop at a nice windy beach and roll out a log or two. There, it was Alphonse who decided, and he had always been good to them.

"What about you, Alphonse?" Lavigne spoke up.

"Yes? What about me?"

"Will we still be working for you?"

"Yes, in a way," Alphonse smiled. "As long as you're with me. But there are a lot of foremen here. You may not be working with me."

"How's that, *sacrament*!" Lavigne whined. "I didn't come here to fight forest fires. I came here to work on the sweep, same as everybody else. *Calis*!"

Alphonse did not answer him. He took a notebook and pencil out of his shirt pocket.

"There's a truck over there by the trailer," he said. "The one with the caboose. Get ready to get on. It'll take us out to the fire."

The students gathered their gloves and lunch pails from the racks above the seats. They came out of the bus, one by one, walked past Alphonse who was standing by the door, and headed towards the caboose. As Henri stepped down from the bus, Alphonse made a sign with his hand to come closer.

"Henri," he said. "I have a little job for you if you want."

Henri looked at him. Alphonse had changed. He was not like he had been on the Cabonga. This was not the *Madeleine* and they were not at Washika Bay. He could not say exactly what was different about the man, but he could feel it. And he was sure that Alphonse felt it also.

"Yes, of course," Henri said.

"You see, Henri," Alphonse held out the small, black notebook and pencil, "they have asked me to keep track of the hours. I'm not very good with numbers, you know. Just write down the names there and mark down the hours we work every day."

"You want me to keep the book with me, Alphonse?"

"Well, I'd better keep it. They might not like that. At the end of each day, come and see me and enter the hours beside each name."

Henri took the notebook from Alphonse. He pressed it against the hood of the bus and with the lead pencil wrote down the names of the students. At the top of the page he wrote the date and, just below the date, he underlined the word "HOURS" in capital letters. He folded the notebook and handed it and the pencil to Alphonse. Alphonse and Henri walked across the fresh sand, past the trailer office, to the caboose. As they reached the truck, Alphonse waved to the bus driver.

"Sometime tonight," he shouted.

"You bet!" the driver called back as he started the engine.

They did not find it funny being told to board a caboose. There wasn't a railway line within at least a hundred miles, maybe more. Being loaded into a wooden box attached to the frame of a one-ton truck did not amuse them, nor did the fact that the box was called a caboose. They climbed the two steps at the rear of the truck and entered the caboose through the open doorway. When the last student had entered, the driver closed the door behind them. They could hear him securing it with an iron bar across the back. There were small openings about six inches by six inches covered by wire mesh on both walls of the caboose. The only other opening was a rectangle cut out of the wood panelling adjacent to the rear window of the truck. Sitting on the plank benches along the walls of the caboose, they could lean over and look through the rear window of the truck and the windshield and see the bulldozer road ahead of them. They could see Alphonse sitting in the truck, smoking and talking to the driver, but they could not hear what he said.

The road was very rough. The benches were not bolted down and the boys had quite a time trying to keep from sliding around inside the caboose. It was raining. They could not hear them but they could see the drops forming on the windshield between the sweeps of the wiper blades.

It seemed endless. They swayed back and forth with the changes in the road, holding on to the plank benches as best they could. Suddenly they felt a change in the truck's speed as the driver geared down and finally came to a stop.

Up ahead, Company pick-up trucks were parked at different angles along the side of the road. Among the pick-up trucks there was a larger truck, dark green with a wooden rack and a light brown tarpaulin stretched over the top of the rack. Further up the road, past the truck with the tarpaulin, a bulldozer was parked with its blade resting on the sand, and roots and pieces of branches caught in the cogwheels of its tracks. Beyond the bulldozer the students could see the trail it had made through the bush. All along the trail they saw through the windshield lay long lines of grey, canvas hose. They could see where the hose crossed the road, entered the trail, and then disappeared behind the clumps of charred blueberry bushes and fallen jack pine.

They heard the bar being lifted and then the door opened. The air entered the caboose, damp and cold, along with the smell of diesel fuel and smoke from the burning forest.

"Okay you guys!" the driver said. "End of the line." The driver was a short, stout man. His skin was deeply tanned and his curly brown hair slipped out below the rim of his hard hat. Although they knew little about the man, his accent told them that he was not from anywhere that they knew of. And besides, his clothes were neatly pressed and clean and he wore new steel-toe safety boots.

Alphonse stood by the truck as the students came out. He had his lunch pail and his extra-large thermos.

"We'll eat now," he said. "There's a good fire over there to warm us while we eat. If you want, you can eat in the caboose."

Alphonse turned to the driver.

"You are not leaving right away?"

"No. I'll hang around for a while."

None of the students wanted to eat in the caboose. They stood around the fire, eating their sandwiches and drinking tea. All of the thermos bottles were the same: black with red plastic tops that served as cups. Only Alphonse's thermos was different and that was because he had brought it with him from his home in Ste-Émilie. It was not one of those small black thermos bottles sold at the van. His thermos was brown with a white cup and at least three times larger than those used by the students.

A very thin old man was feeding wood to the fire. The way he placed each chunk of wood just so, walking around the fire with an armful of wood, had attracted the attention of all who stood there. No one knew why but they had the feeling that they were in the presence of a very special event. The man trimmed a spruce sapling with his axe and when he had notched the top end he placed the butt end into the sand. After piling three large chunks of wood together, he leaned the pole on them so that the notched end stuck out over the fire. Then he reached behind him for a blackened pail full of water. The pail had a wire handle. He placed the handle in the notch and lowered the pail over the fire. The flames, one after another, licked the bottom of the pail.

The old man stood leaning on one leg, watching the fire and the steam rising from the pail. He held a paper bag in one hand and at his feet was a cup of cold water that he had taken from the pail before putting it over the fire. His gaze never left the pail or the water inside. At last the water began to bubble. The old man reached into the bag and brought out a handful of black leaves that he immediately tossed into the pail. He stood back from the heat of the flames. The water bubbled and tossed and suddenly took on a golden brown colour. The old man reached down for the cup of water and quickly emptied it into the pail.

Next to the cup the students had noticed a straight branch with a short stub of a side branch at one end. As he set the cup on the ground, the old man picked up the forked branch and, with its stub of a side branch, removed the pail from the end of the sapling and placed it close to the fire. He stood there for a while, staring at the fire as he probably had done hundreds of times before, giving thanks for his life, the fire, the water, and anything else that happened to come his way.

When the students had finished eating their sandwiches and drank the last of the tea in their thermos bottles, they dipped their cups into the pail by the fire and drank the golden brown tea. Along with the tea, they ate doughnuts and biscuits that Dumas had baked that morning. Mostly, it was warm and pleasant by the fire. They felt the heat on their faces and through the denim of their jeans but when the wind shifted the smoke blew into their eyes. The rain came down in a fine spray but it did not touch the fire and only the backs of their mackinaws and their hard hats were wet. Standing by the fire, with its warmth and soft crackling sounds, their thoughts shifted elsewhere, to some other world. Each person's thoughts were within him, safe and warm.

"Work!" Alphonse said. He threw the last bit of his cigarette into the fire. "Leave your lunch pails in the caboose."

Alphonse picked up his lunch pail and extra-large thermos. He pointed towards the green truck with the tarpaulin-covered rack.

"Over there, you'll find shovels and grub hoes. Come on, now."

The brown canvas that stretched across the rack had begun to sag with the weight of the rain, but it was dry inside. The students picked out shovels and hoes that had been placed in neat rows between bundles of canvas hose, portable water pumps and canvas water bags with hand pumps.

The students waved good-bye to the old man feeding the fire. Only he and the caboose driver remained behind. Alphonse and the twenty students left the road and entered the trail cut by the bulldozer. They walked along the road in the rain, single file, not speaking. They followed the canvas hose and, like it, they disappeared behind the clumps of charred blueberry bushes and overturned jack pine. The most amazing thing about it all was the mosquitoes. As Alphonse and the students followed the canvas hose through the burned-out section, it seemed impossible to them that anything could still be alive in such a black, devastated mess. They walked in ashes that were still warm and, everywhere they looked, black, dead trees lay in a tangled maze or stood apart without leaves or needles, just black skeletons of what they once were, all very dead. The mosquitoes came in droves and the guys joked about the female attack. After the first wave, they did not joke about them anymore. They put on fly oil and tried keeping their mouths shut just to keep from swallowing them.

As they reached the crest of a hill, they saw the smoke down below and could hear wood cracking and chain saws working. When a breeze came, they could see the flames. There was smoke everywhere and men with chain saws cutting down trees that were burning at the tops. Others worked around smoldering roots and stumps with grub hoes. Several men were walking over the burned-out places with shovels. They dug around smoldering pieces and covered them with earth. Two men at the bottom of the slope held canvas hoses and were watering down trees that were still green. Their faces were dirty and the fronts of their trousers were wet from the leaking hoses.

Alphonse turned to the boys walking behind him.

"All right," he said. "We can start here. Just do like the others. We can't leave anything smoking. We have to put it all out."

Alphonse left them then. He walked down the side of the hill to where the portable pump was. A short length of canvas hose attached to the pump disappeared into the water of a small creek nearby. On the opposite side of the pump, the hose fanned out into two sections, each section leading to one of the men hosing down the green jack pine.

The pump operator and a foreman sat together on a log by the pump. As Alphonse approached, he could hear the steady whine of the gasoline engine.

"Yes sir," the foreman said. He stood up as Alphonse arrived.

"Ouimet, from the drive," Alphonse introduced himself. "Nice little mess."

"Could be worse," the man replied. "That rain yesterday, it helped some."

"I brought in my gang. All students from Ste-Émilie, but they work well. Anything special you want done?"

"No, no. Just keep them going like that, maybe one or two down here. Those guys would like to eat soon." The foreman pointed towards the two men working the hoses.

Alphonse looked at the two men. He could see how they shot water up into the thick evergreens and how, when the stream of water hit the trunk of a tree, the bark would fly off from the pressure. Beyond the tall, skinny trunks Alphonse could see clouds of smoke and occasional sheets of flame.

He returned to where the students were scattered around the burned-out section on the side of the hill. They walked slowly, carrying their shovels and grub hoes. The shovels were the long-handled, round kind that were good for digging the soil while the grub hoes had flattened blades that could slice through roots and burned humus. The grub hoes had wooden handles, painted red. The boys dug around stumps and exposed roots and buried them until smoke could no longer be seen. Occasionally, a smoldering trunk would suddenly come to life with flames flickering in the breeze. It was not long-lived as the students rushed it together and beat it with their shovels and their boots. Everyone looked pleased when they had finally put it out.

Alphonse joined some of the students standing around a large stump that had been cut by one of the men with a chain saw. The wood was still white where he had cut it but the rest was black and the branches looked naked without their needles. The boys stood around the stump, leaning on their shovels and looking at the smoke coming out of the ground where the roots entered.

"They need a couple of guys down there," Alphonse said.

Henri looked around him. There was no way to tell. All the trees were burned. There were no needles or leaves to be seen anywhere.

"Which way is the wind blowing, Alphonse?" he said.

"Hard to tell, there seems to be none right now."

"There's nothing left to burn here." Henri had read about forest fires somewhere and how they made firebreaks with the bulldozers and felled all the trees in front of the fire. Then they set fire to them so that, when the fire finally arrived, there was nothing left to fuel it and the fire would simply burn itself out. "What about there, Alphonse?" Henri went on. "Where those men are with hoses?"

"There's a break on the other side. It should burn itself out soon."

Alphonse put out his cigarette on the stump. He looked at his watch, wound the spring and put the watch back into the slit pocket of his trousers.

"Henri, would you go down there on the hose. They'll show you what to do."

Alphonse looked behind him. The boys were scattered over the hillside. He turned to Henri and the boy he had been speaking to.

"You, St-Jean," he said. "What's your first name?'

"Maurice," St-Jean replied.

"Ah yes. Maurice, would you go with Henri? I'll be down there in a little while."

Henri and Maurice left then, going down the side of the hill, using their shovels to keep from sliding in the steep parts and to keep from falling when they had to climb over felled tree trunks. They went straight to where the pump, the pump operator and the foreman were.

"We've come down to help out on the hoses," Henri said to the foreman. It was always easy to tell who was a foreman by the colour of his hard hat.

"Good! Good!" the man said. He turned to the pump operator and made a sign to shut down the engine. As the engine sputtered to a stop, Henri and St-Jean watched the men with the hoses and the look on their faces as the stream of water curved towards the ground.

"Fresh meat!" the foreman yelled to the two men.

The two men dropped the canvas hoses and returned to where the pump operator and the foreman were speaking to Henri and St-Jean. It was quiet then except for the spitting and crackling sounds that a forest makes when it's burning.

After instructing Henri and St-Jean on the use of the canvas hoses, the foreman and the two men who had been working the hoses left, working their way slowly across the hill. Henri reached the end of the hose before the operator had started up the engine. The operator's name was Jean-Louis Venet and he lived in Ste-Émilie like Henri and the rest of the students. Although he did not look old enough, he had a daughter, Marie-Josée Venet. All of the students at the Collège de Ste-Émilie knew about Marie-Josée. Some knew her better than others and some even claimed to have relieved her of her virginity. Henri was not sure about all of this. Of one thing he was sure, however: he would never speak about Marie-Josée in that way. Was it because he was now working with her father? Did it have anything to do with his time spent with Lise Archambault in the back room of the infirmary? He wasn't sure. At that moment, standing in burned jack pine branches waiting for the pump engine to start, there were beginning to be many things that he was not sure of.

Henri held the cold, metal nozzle and with one hand, the wet canvas hose, now limp and empty with the other. He heard Jean-Louis pulling the starter rope, then the sputtering and, finally, the engine whining at full throttle. Henri braced himself and waited for the pressure to build up inside the hose. It seemed a long time coming. At last the hose stiffened and jerked him sideways and the water came, suddenly, in powerful spurts at first and then in one long, steady stream. Henri glanced over at St-Jean. He had straddled the hose and was aiming high, towards the tree tops and then down along the trunks. It was easy after they learned to balance the hose and its nozzle. They could almost handle it with one hand. He and St-Jean amused themselves, cross-firing, or both attacking the same tree and watching its bark and needles fly.

St-Jean stood to the left, towards the slope of the hill. On occasion he tested the strength of his hose by aiming high and up towards the side of the hill where the students were working. With more pressure he could really send them running for cover. He thought of asking Jean-Louis if he could open the engine up a little more. But St-Jean was one of the students who claimed to have slept with Marie-Josée in the back of his father's station wagon after a Saturday night dance at the high school. He thought perhaps that Jean-Louis might have heard mention of it and, besides, the guys on the hillside were yelling and waving their fists at him so the pressure was probably good enough as it was.

Gradually the students moved across the hillside, digging at roots and shovelling fresh, brown earth on the smoldering, charred wood. They moved across the slope like grazing cattle until around mid-afternoon, and then, they were gone. They had reached the easterly crest and, just as slowly, disappeared below it.

Henri and St-Jean poured water onto the thick wall of jack pine but they saw fewer and fewer flames and the clouds of smoke rising from behind the evergreens seemed smaller than before. Henri heard the engine sputter and finally come to a stop. Almost immediately he saw the stream of water drop from where he was aiming to the ashes on the ground before him.

"Hey, you guys!" Jean-Louis waved at them. "Take a break, eh!"

The two boys dropped their hoses and walked over to where the pump was. Jean-Louis offered them filtered cigarettes from a pack. The man had made himself comfortable. Resting against a large round log, he had placed several pieces of split log to form a backrest. On the ground just in front of the backrest, was a thick layer of jack pine branches. These he had covered with a length of brown canvas. By the log was a cardboard box partly covered with branches and next to the box was a thermos bottle. The pump operator stood up when they arrived. He unfolded the brown canvas he had been sitting on and spread it out along the log.

"Here," he said. "Sit down here while it's still dry."

He opened the thermos and filled the plastic cup. He took a drink and, without swallowing, spit it out on the ashes.

"*Sacrament*!" he swore. "Want some?"

"No thanks," Henri answered. "You've been here a long time?"

"Forever!" Jean-Louis chuckled at his own little joke. "Sometimes, it seems that way."

"Not much action here, eh?" Henri continued. St-Jean, it seemed to Henri, was being especially quiet.

"Mosquitoes are pretty bad."

"How about when there's wind? Fire must get pretty bad then."

"Oh, you bet. When the wind shifts, the flames roar and you see it jump from the tops of the trees and you run like hell."

"Did that ever happen? You had to run?"

"No. I've been sitting here a long time. So far, nothing like that."

"Where's Alphonse?" St-Jean spoke up for the first time. He had been thinking about Marie-Josée lying in the back of his father's station wagon. He remembered the trouble he had undoing the clasp of her bra and how she had ripped away three buttons trying to get his shirt off. He was not sure if she was a virgin that night. He only knew that he was and that when he dropped her off two streets before her house, he no longer was.

The pump operator smiled. The man was about thirty-five years old and seemed to be intelligent enough. But, sometimes, he would laugh suddenly as if he had been thinking of something that was very funny. He would stop, just as suddenly, look at Henri and St-Jean, and then grin and poke at the ashes with a stick.

"Where is your foreman?" St-Jean asked.

"He's gone for a walk," the man answered. "And your boss too. They went up over there to check."

The man pointed towards the eastern slope of the hill, where the burned out section ended and the almost blue sky began.

"What about the two guys we replaced?" Henri said.

"Them too."

"I thought they were going to eat."

"So did they," the man said. "So did they! Ha! Ha! Ha! Ha! Ha!"

Henri got up off the log. He walked away from the pump and standing with his back to St-Jean and the pump operator he pissed on the ashes. It had stopped raining and he saw the sun beginning to show between two, thick white clouds.

Later in the afternoon, the sky was clear and it was very warm. The students who had gone over the easterly crest were spread out in groups of three and four among the charred tree trunks on the burned-out section of the hill. They worked steadily. They broke through the charred humus of the forest floor and then they shoveled out the yellow sand. They went at it two at a time, until they were tired and then two other students took over. They dug and shovelled until there was a mound of yellow sand all around them and only their hard hats and shoulders could be seen above ground.

It had started with an idea. The students were tired and bored with the whole business. All they wanted to do was lie in the sun and get as far away as they could from the black, dead world of ashes and burned trees. But, there was not a single green, unburned piece of ground anywhere. Every inch of ground, every felled tree, even the rocks that could be found, were covered in black soot. François Gauthier had an idea. With his shovel, he marked out a circle in the ashes about three feet in diameter. He dug inside the mark, removing the burned needles and humus until he had a perfect circle of yellow sand. He sat in the circle on the sand, with his knees raised and his chest resting against them. He rested in the sun and was very happy with himself. He said nothing to the others. He was content to sit there, warm and dry and happy in the sun, until someone or something forced him to do otherwise.

The others were quick to recognize the worth of François' idea. But they could not let it alone. They seemed compelled to modify his plan somewhat. Together, in groups of three or four, they dug holes in the ground large enough to sit in with their knees tucked up and their backs resting against the walls. When they finished digging and sat down in the holes, they were disappointed. Sitting in the holes, with only their hats showing above ground, was uncomfortable. The sand slid down the mounds onto their necks and inside their shirts when they leaned their backs against the walls. The earth was damp on the bottom of the holes and they had to place their gloves beneath them just so as to keep their buttocks dry. It was cool and damp where they sat hidden from the rays of the sun. They came out often to take the stiffness from their legs and to warm themselves in the sun. At such times, they could see François sitting on his circle of warm, yellow sand, with his knees pulled up and his chest resting against them. His hard hat was pulled down low over his eyes and they guessed that he was sleeping. Some swore they could hear him snoring.

It was boring. After the digging it was boring and dull and the only diversion was when they came out of a hole to stretch and warm themselves in the sun. Suddenly, they heard a sound coming from the west. It was the steady drone of an engine that grew louder and louder. Then, it was above them. All of the students stood up in their holes. They waved at the yellow aircraft with their hard hats and yelled, "Over here! Over here!" The large, twin-engine water bomber circled in low and dipped its wings. The students cheered, realizing that the pilot had seen them. They were excited about seeing the CL-215 and how the pilot had recognized them as part of the firefighting crew. They watched the plane as it flew eastward and disappeared behind a ridge of tall jack pine. The boys returned to their holes then and waited for the day to pass.

It was close to sunset when Alphonse arrived. The boys in the trenches could not see the sun from where they were and they were cold and bored again. Alphonse stood by one of the holes and looked down at the boys inside. Henri and St-Jean stood behind him.

"Hey, hey," Alphonse said, nodding his head in disapproval, "a nice bunch you are."

Alphonse did not approve of them hiding like that and not working. They were not getting any work done but they were not unhappy. There was that, at least. Later, they would get some work done.

"All right," Alphonse said," Fill up the holes. As soon as you're finished, we'll head back to the road. The caboose should be there by now. We'll be eating at Camp 15."

"We're not staying there, are we?" Morrow wanted to know. "We're going back to Washika, aren't we?"

"Yes, later," Alphonse replied.

Chapter 17

After the boys had filled in the holes, Alphonse and the crew went back along the trail, following the canvas hose in the almost dark. It was dark when they reached the road. They saw the fire, and the old man and the driver standing by it, almost exactly as they had left them. They both had cups of tea and the old man had a pipe dangling from a corner of his mouth. The students noticed the pipe and they wondered how he did that. They had noticed earlier that day that the old man did not have any teeth. As they came closer to the fire they could hear him speaking. They had never heard him speak before.

"*Oui sacrament*!" he said. "You can be sure of that."

The caboose driver laughed and tossed the rest of the tea in his cup towards the fire. He turned and looked back as Alphonse arrived.

"Yes sir," he said.

"Yes sir," Alphonse greeted the man. He nodded towards the old man who acknowledged the gesture with a short wave of his pipe. The old man added water to the pail suspended over the fire. Beyond the fire, it was dark. From where he stood, Alphonse could just make out the reflections of the fire on the door of the truck.

"Ready to head back?" Alphonse said to the driver.

"Sure thing. No problem at all."

"What about the shovels? The truck's gone."

"Leave them here for tonight," the old man spoke up. "Just pile them right up here." The old man pointed to the cord of firewood behind him. Folded over the wood was a thick tarpaulin similar to the one the students had seen on the truck rack. "Just cover it all with the tarp," the old man added.

The students rushed to the woodpile and deposited the shovels and grub hoes, leaning them against the wood. When they had finished, they covered the tools and the wood with the tarpaulin.

"Anyway," Alphonse said to no one in particular, "there's no guarantee we'll be back here tomorrow."

"Ha!" the old man laughed, showing his bare, toothless gums. "There's no guarantee of anything around here. With that gang in charge here, we could all be dead in the morning."

The driver laughed, and as the old man smiled at Alphonse saliva dripped down from the corner of his mouth where the pipe was.

"I'm an old man," he continued. "I'm an old dried up thing and I've been around a long time and I've seen lots of them guys, them guys from the head office. *Calis*! Do I ever know about them."

Alphonse laughed along with the others, but not too much. In his heart he knew that the old man was right. The man had the knowledge of years and his age allowed him to speak out without fear. Alphonse, however, was a foreman. He wore the hard hat of his rank. He had his job to think of, and his wife and his children. And then, there were the students. They respected him, he knew that. And he always wanted to be good to them. On the drive, that was easy. He was in charge, miles away from the camp, out on the Cabonga where no one could see them, and they worked well. Some days they did not do very much, that was true. But there were other days when all of the students did excellent work. It would all balance out in the end. But here, it was different. Here, many were in charge and considered themselves beyond reproach. Not all of them believed as he did, that all things happen for a reason, that a balance is almost always reached one way or another.

The driver offered his cup to one of the students and each, in turn, dipped it into the pail and passed it on to the next student. Finally, Henri filled the cup and offered it to Alphonse.

"How long to Camp 15?" Alphonse spoke to the driver.

"An hour, hour and a half," the man answered.

"Guess we'd better get going then."

"Yes sir. No problem."

Alphonse turned to the old man.

"Are you staying?" he asked.

"All depends."

Alphonse looked at him, at his tired old eyes and the deep lines stretching over his brown skin.

"All depends," the old man repeated. "All depends on you."

"How's that?"

"How's that, you say? You're the last truck out of here tonight. Think they'd send someone out just for me? Ha!"

"No problem," Alphonse replied. "Get on with us."

"No favours, eh? I don't want no favours me."

"It's no problem at all. There's room for the three of us in the truck."

"Na, na, na!" the old man waved his pipe back and forth in front of his face. "I'll sit in the caboose like everybody else. Na, na, *sacrament.* I'm too old now to start that kind of stuff."

Alphonse looked at the man once again, and as their eyes met across the fire both men smiled. He was at least seventy-five years old. He was tall, probably as tall as François Gauthier if he would hold his back straight, which he never did. He was tall and very thin and his long-legged trousers were held up tight to his crotch with police suspenders that made his legs look longer than they were. The old man had spent many years of his life in the sun and it showed on his hands and his face. The skin, brown and lined, was taut on his face and around his cheekbones and his long nose curved like the beak of a falcon. His name was Frederick Garneau. Alphonse stared at the man and realized what a good time the old man was having there. It was not true that they had left him behind. He had probably refused several rides back to camp. And he probably did not dislike the bosses, at least not all of them, as much as he said he did. He was an old man who had come to spend his last days where he belonged and to poke fun at the younger men as they struggled to learn some of the things he had known for years. Alphonse wondered if the old man, in his wisdom, was aware that somewhere in the head office there was someone who understood and had given the okay for a man of Frederick's age to be there, in the bush, working on a forest fire.

Two of the students drew water from the stream and helped the old man put out the fire. The wood sizzled and a large cloud of smoke went up from the wet, black wood. As the students poured the last pail, they heard the truck's engine and saw a large section of green forest lit up by the headlights.

"Okay, let's go." Alphonse said.

The door to the caboose was open and the inside of the caboose was lit by a small dome light on the ceiling. The boys climbed the two steps and went inside. The last to go in was Frederick Garneau. The driver pushed him from behind after Frederick got a foot up on the first step. The old man laughed. But he forgot to duck going inside and he swore as his hard hat crashed against the upper portion of the open doorway.

The boys sat on the benches along the walls of the caboose. As the old man entered, Henri moved down along the bench and motioned to the old man to sit down beside him and next to the rear window opening.

"Sit here, *Monsieur* Garneau," Henri said. He had heard Alphonse asking the old man what his name was.

"Na, na!" the old man replied. "Fred. My name is Fred, you hear?"

"Yes sir."

As the truck moved along the gravel road, the students held on to the benches and looked at one another. Hardly anyone spoke. They were quiet going along the new rough road. The only thing attracting their attention was Fred, sitting there in the dim light with his eyes closed trying to sleep. He would grimace with pain when they hit a bad spot on the road, causing the skin, stretched over his skinny limbs, to pinch on the hard wooden bench.

About an hour down the road, Lavigne rapped on the window and signalled to the driver that he had to go outside. When the bar was removed and the door opened, several students went out to relieve themselves. After he had finished, Lavigne had gone to speak to Alphonse and the driver. When he returned to the caboose he was carrying a grey felt cushion. He handed the cushion to the old man and returned to his place along the opposite wall.

Neither Lavigne nor the old man had spoken. Lavigne had handed him the cushion without saying a word. All along the road the rest of the way to Camp 15, the boys sat without speaking and, in the dim light of the caboose, tired old eyes looked at them kindly.

Chapter 18

Camp 15 was very different from Washika. More than three hundred and fifty men lived at the camp and everyone seemed to be in a hurry and going about different tasks. Not everyone ate, or washed, or slept at the same time of day. The sleep camps were two-storey buildings with long wooden stairways on the outside at one end. In the cookhouse there were places for two hundred men at a time and the cook had five cookees helping him. Everyone passing with a tray could see them working the pots and pans in the open kitchen. This was so very different from the cookhouse at Washika where Dumas ruled over all including his small kitchen and one cookee. During the meals Dumas stood at the centre of four long tables surveying all who ate in his cookhouse, making sure that nothing was missing and that the fellows ate without chatting. His food was delicious, his discipline supreme. Here at Camp 15, the cookhouse was much like the cafeteria at the Collège de Ste-Émilie and the food just as mushy and tasteless; the students immediately took a great dislike to the camp and its inhabitants. None of them spoke during the meal and they ate very little and drank tea, and all appeared distraught.

Outside, it was raining. The bus was parked alongside the cookhouse landing with its engine running. As the students came out of the cookhouse they could see Alphonse inside the bus talking to the driver. They were both having a good laugh. The students stepped into the bus and sat down. No one fought for a window seat. It was quiet, and dark, and damp. Before the bus was a mile south of Camp 15 the students were curled up in their seats with arms wrapped around themselves, swaying freely with the bumps in the road and just barely hearing the engine groan and the wipers squeaking across the windshield.

"Work!" a voice called out.

It could not be. Surely it must be a nightmare. The students groaned and squirmed in their seats. They rubbed their eyes and stared at the dim light on the ceiling.

"Come on now, my little ducks," Alphonse called out in a loud voice. "We're home. Wake up now!"

Alphonse and the driver stood at the front of the bus looking at the students stumbling about and searching for their gloves and lunch pails. They swore and mumbled, and all were in a very bad mood.

"After you've dropped off your things," Alphonse shouted from the front of the bus, "come over to the kitchen. Dumas will have cakes and tea for you."

The camp was asleep. The generator had been shut down but there were dim lights coming from the main sleep camp and the bunkhouse-and-office as well as from the cookhouse kitchen. As the students stepped down from the bus they saw P'tit-Gus walking across the yard with his hunting lamp. It was still raining softly. In the bunkhouse-and-office, a naphtha lamp hissed loudly on the table. The guys dropped their gloves and lunch pails on the beds and left for the cookhouse. André Guy undressed quickly and before the last guy had left the bunkhouse he was in his bed with the blankets covering his head.

Dumas smiled at the students as they entered the rear door of his kitchen. He did not even seem to mind that they had not removed their hard hats. He stood in a corner of the kitchen talking to Alphonse, stopping only to smile at the arrival of yet another student. The students did not know what to make of this sudden change; they were never permitted to enter the cookhouse wearing their hard hats or without washing their hands thoroughly and combing their hair. They stood on both sides of the long wooden table and ate cookies and doughnuts and drank several cups of hot tea. They were happy to be home. Eating slowly, they looked at the array of pots and pans hanging from hooks on the walls, felt the heat of the large wood stove and smelled the fresh bread stacked in racks near the windows. They were happy and tired and each of them was feeling very special for the way Dumas was treating them.

Chapter 19

Henri could not remember having fallen asleep. Now, he listened in the dark and wondered who was walking around outside. A beam of light came through the door screen and into the bunkhouse. The door opened and P'tit-Gus stepped inside. He walked quietly over to the table by the old space heater.

"What time is it?" Henri whispered.

"Time to get up," P'tit-Gus replied. He had placed his hunting lamp on the table. Henri could see his arm moving and hear the wheezing as he pumped air into the naphtha lamp. P'tit-Gus lit a match and stuck it through the hole to the inside of the lamp. The gas hissed as it entered the mantle and ignited, filling the room with a soft yellow glow.

"Up!" P'tit-Gus said loudly. "Time to work. Let's go now. Up!"

P'tit-Gus chuckled behind the glow of the naphtha lamp. This was almost as good as a storm. He watched the roundness of the blankets begin to move. Suddenly a head popped out from beneath them. The student closest to the table squinted as he stared at the lamp. He turned his head slowly to look at the darkness through the windows and back to the lamp in disbelief. The young man groaned as the truth of the matter filtered through.

"Are you crazy, *calis*?" Lavigne yelled at P'tit-Gus. "It's four o'clock in the morning!"

"He's just trying to get even," someone said.

"Yeah, he's still pissed about the other day," another voice commented.

"Hey P'tit-Gus!" Lavigne said. "Do you know what time we got to bed last night? Eleven o'clock, *sacrament*! And you wake us up at four o'clock in the morning!"

P'tit-Gus said nothing. He was enjoying the whole thing immensely. He would have to wake the boys in the other bunkhouse individually so as not to disturb the older men. But here, he was able to stand back and see the whole effect of his efforts at one moment in time. A strange feeling of joy seemed to rush through his spine. On those rare occasions when he experienced a sudden moment of joy, like when he witnessed an electrical storm, his whole body would shudder and then, it was just a memory, a very pleasant memory. Now, the pleasure of it was past and P'tit-Gus picked up his hunting lamp and walked towards the door.

"Breakfast in fifteen minutes," he said, and went out of the bunkhouse.

It was difficult to believe. Henri dressed slowly. Could it be that P'tit-Gus would do such a thing? After all, it was the bunkhouse-and-office and its occupants that caused him the most trouble. Henri sat on the edge of the bunk rubbing his face, his bare feet resting on the cold floor. He put on his socks and boots. He went to the north window and looked out at the darkness.

"Oh no!" he swore softly. "Dear God, no! It can't be." But as he looked again, he saw Dumas rush past a window in the kitchen. There was a dim light in both the kitchen and the dining area where they took their meals. It was a dim light but it was still a light. The kitchen being lit was normal, as Dumas always began his day around four in the morning but he did not light up the dining area until much later, when the generator was running. Henri was not sure just what time Dumas turned on the lights but he was convinced that it was not at four in the morning. P'tit-Gus had awakened the students in the bunkhouse-and-office. That was one thing. Possibly revenge on his part. But P'tit-Gus would never dream of tricking Dumas into preparing an early breakfast, as a joke on the students. So it was true. They were, in fact, being awakened at four o'clock in the morning to go out to work on the fire.

The door opened and Alphonse stood in the doorway. "Breakfast in ten minutes," he said. "We'll leave right after breakfast. Leave your lunch pails behind. They'll be sending us out some. Come on now, you guys. Get a move on!"

"How come we have to leave so early, Alphonse?" Lavigne wanted to know. "We've only had five hours sleep and it's even dark out."

"That's the way," Alphonse replied. "That's the way it works on the fire."

"It's not right. I don't care what they say. It's not right," Lavigne mumbled to himself as he put on his boots.

Alphonse took a last look around the room. Most of the boys were dressed. Some already had towels on their shoulders and were preparing to leave for the washroom. On the bed nearest to the old space heater, André Guy sat wearing only his underwear. He sat facing the wall with his mouth open and staring at the grey plywood floor.

"Come on, André," Alphonse encouraged him. "Hurry now."

André nodded his head. "Yes, yes," he said. "I'm coming." And then his eyes closed and his head drooped, causing strands of hair to stand straight up on top of his head.

Chapter 20

It was quiet in the cookhouse. Dumas did not ring the bell. He collected the tickets inside as they went to their places at the table. It was strange not seeing Dumas beating the inside of the triangle with the bar. There was no bell, no Dumas on the little porch landing and not even a light above the door. There was of course no generator, only the hissing of the naphtha lamps and the darkness outside.

The students sat at the long wooden table and ate more from habit than any desire for food. No one spoke or coughed or even looked at each other. The twenty young students sat at the table with their hair still wet, forcing in bacon and eggs and potatoes and pancakes and sipping at cups of steaming hot tea.

Alphonse sat alone at the older men's table. Halfway through breakfast Dumas came out from the kitchen with a cup of coffee and joined Alphonse, sitting down just in front of him.

"Looks like more rain again today," Dumas began.

Alphonse washed down the toast with some tea. He poured more tea from the pot and sucked at his teeth with his tongue. Back home in Ste-Émilie, his wife would not hear of it. It was strictly forbidden to do that at the table. But, at this table at Washika, it was accepted behaviour, even in the presence of Dumas.

"It rained pretty well all night," Alphonse replied. "It wasn't raining when I came in just now. But you could feel it in the air. What do they say on the radio?"

"Sun and cloudy periods. But that is in Ste-Émilie. And who can believe them anyway? Probably it will rain all day. That should keep your gang happy, eh?"

Alphonse glanced around the room. They were not sad or angry. They sat there, silently putting food into their mouths looking very dejected. Some were eating with their eyes closed.

"They're not too happy now," Alphonse said, finally. He picked up his plate and cup along with knife and fork, took them over to the opposite table and dropped them into the wash pans. These would be picked up later by Richard Gagnier, the cookee. That was one his jobs, that and washing all of the soiled dishes and cutlery left in the pans. There was only one cookee at Washika and Dumas made sure that his life was a busy one.

The students left the cookhouse and walked across the yard towards the sleep camps. It started to rain. They heard it, first, on the tarpapered roofs, and then on the bus parked in the yard between the main sleep camp and the bunkhouse-and-office. The driver and Alphonse were talking by the door of the bus as they walked by.

"Get your stuff," Alphonse said to them. "And get on right away. You can have your smoke as we go."

No one said anything. The students went on to the main sleep camp and to the bunkhouse-and-office without saying a word. They returned shortly afterwards wearing their wool mackinaws and hard hats with their gloves sticking out of their back pockets. They boarded the bus and sat at the first empty seats that they came to. No one fought for a window seat and no one opened a window. The bus quickly filled with smoke.

The driver switched on the headlights, closed the door and shifted into gear. The wiper blades squeaked and the rain pattered on the thin metal roof. The springs of the bus stretched and groaned as they went around the bunkhouse-and-office and crossed the truck scales. From there they drove down the gravel road, past the infirmary, and north to the Ottawa River.

Henri did not look up from his place as they went by the infirmary. He did not think about Lise Archambault and he did not worry about the fire and not going to Ste-Émilie for the weekend. He was tired. He dragged on his cigarette and felt sick to his stomach. He tried not to think about that. He tried not to think about anything at all.

They were only five miles out of Washika when it happened. As they reached the crest of a very steep hill, the darkness suddenly changed to the semi-darkness of dawn. They could make out the shores of the lakes and swamps and see clearly the jack pine silhouetted along the roadside and the shores of the lakes.

The driver shifted gears and began a long descent towards a bridge at the bottom, with swamp on both sides. Floating shrubs like tiny islands lined the shore between the water and the trees. As the bus headed down, Henri could feel the heaviness of his stomach rising up to his throat. It was difficult to swallow. He heard the snap of the window fasteners at the front of the bus and felt the cool air on his face as it rushed towards the back of the bus. Suddenly, someone yelled, "Ah no, *sacrament*!"

Henri looked from his seat to the front of the bus. François Gauthier was kneeling on the seat with his head sticking out of the open window. All of the windows from François down were splashed with a pink, creamy substance. Looking out through the window beside him, he could see the vomit sliding down on the glass.

CC Coulomb sat next to Henri and beside the window. He sat with his eyes closed and his mouth shut very tight and Henri could hear noises coming from his throat. The bus had just crossed the bridge when CC quickly snapped his hard hat off his head and held it in front of him like a soup bowl. Without retching more than once, the hat was filled almost to the brim.

Chapter 21

It was after six when they arrived at Camp 15. There were men rushing down the long stairways of the sleep camps and heading towards the cookhouse. There were trucks arriving with men who had worked all night and other men on the verandahs of the sleep camps waiting to take their places. The bus stopped outside the camp office and the camp foreman they had seen the day before, with his grey curls and neatly pressed trousers and clean shirt, waved to them from the office verandah. They could not see his clean shirt and trousers under the black rubber raincoat but they knew they were there and they hated the man again.

Henri looked at the man and guessed that perhaps he had a son about their age and he wondered if his son hated him too.

"Yes sir!" Alphonse greeted the man as he stepped down from the bus. The foreman stayed on the verandah, out of the rain.

"Nice weather for ducks, eh," the man replied. "Your boys in good shape today? Ha! Ha! Ha!"

The boys stared at the foreman from the windows of the bus and they hated him and they hated his white hard hat and his grey curls and his black rubber raincoat.

"Where to this morning, Georges?" Alphonse inquired.

So, that was his name. Georges. Now they had a name. That goddamn Georges! That goddamn Georges and his lousy goddamn curls and his goddamn clean clothes and his lousy son-of-a-bitch of a forest fire. There, they felt better now. It was like a cyst they had been pressing from all sides and now, finally, it had burst and the creamy, yellow pus had come shooting out. Afterwards, the red scar would heal over and the skin would be as if the cyst had never been there at all.

"Well, you see," Georges said. There's been a little change in plans. The men finished up on one of the islands just this morning. There'll be some cleaning up to do in there. And patrolling, after. Maybe five, six days."

"Oh, at the very least!" twenty voices called out from inside the bus.

The man looked up at the windows of the bus. "Well," he said. "They're in good shape this morning, aren't they?"

"They'll be all right," Alphonse said.

"It's the hours. It's not the work so much. It's the hours that get you."

"They're a good bunch. Give them a few days."

As the two men stood talking, the caboose arrived alongside the bus. The old man, Fred Garneau, was sitting up front with the driver. The fellows waved to the old man and he smiled back at them, showing his bare gums. The driver got out and went to join Alphonse and the camp foreman.

"You know Jacques here," the foreman said.

"Yes, we met yesterday," Alphonse nodded to the man.

"Jacques will take you out to the island. There'll be boats there so you can get across, and spare ones for loading the equipment. You can start patrolling as soon as that's done."

"What about the old man?" Alphonse inquired. "Does he stay with us?"

"Do you mind?"

"No, not at all."

"He can make tea and take care of the lunches and everything."

"No, we don't mind," Alphonse repeated. "In fact, the boys seem to like him. It might cheer them up."

"He's a funny one," the driver said. "And *sacrament*, you should hear him swear."

The foreman stretched his arm forward and looked at his watch. Alphonse stared at the gold watch with its flexible metal wristband and, for a brief moment, he compared it to his own ordinary Westclox ticking loudly at the end of a leather thong in the slit pocket of his trousers. He felt a cut below Georges and his gold watch and his neatly groomed hair and expensive clothes, but only for a passing moment. He thought of that night, after midnight mass, how Francine and the children had sat around the tree. Not one of them would open their gifts until he, Alphonse Ouimet, father of the family, had opened the little square box wrapped in fine, soft paper with a red silk bow and held up the Westclox pocket watch for everyone to see. The look of pride in the eyes of his seven children was worth more than all the gold watches in the world. But there was another gift as well. Alphonse looked at his wife Francine. The children were far too busy tearing open their presents to have noticed. The look they shared that Christmas Eve, brief as it was, would remain with them for the rest of their lives.

"Good," the foreman said. "That's settled then. I'll let you go now. If you need anything. Any problem. Don't hesitate. You can always get in touch with me through Jacques here."

"Sure thing! No problem," the driver snapped.

"Well, we'd better get going," Alphonse said.

"Yes sir!" the driver snapped again. "No problem."

Alphonse turned to say good-bye to the foreman but the man had left and Alphonse could hear him laughing loudly as he stepped into the dry, warm office.

Chapter 22

The island was completely burned. All along the shore the charred stems of the bushes stuck out over the sand. Inland, there were black, standing tree trunks and the tangled remains of the ones that had fallen or had been cut down by the men with saws. Grey canvas hoses sat in the ashes on the forest floor and were spread out all over the island.

As the students stepped out of the boats they could hear the mosquitoes. It had stopped raining but it was hot and humid. There was no breeze and the only moving thing was the flat brown water of the river beside them.

"All right," Alphonse said. "Now here's what we do."

Alphonse picked up one end of a canvas hose from the ashes. He bent two feet of the hose along itself, turned it edgewise, and rolled it two more feet, on the ground this time.

"Now, you have to get the water out," he said. "Squeeze it out as you go. It's not hard. Just roll one way and then the other. Keep it up until you reach the end. You disconnect the brass connector and then you make a little knot with what's left. That's the handle. Here, I'll show you."

Alphonse followed the canvas hose through the ashes, over stumps, around trees and through charred bushes, rolling two feet at a time until he reached the place where the hose was joined to another by a brass connector. Alphonse disconnected the two hoses. He passed the loose end through the bundle he had formed. He gave the remaining piece of hose a sharp tug and swung the bundle over his shoulder.

"You see?" he said. "That's all. It's called a *banane* and you carry it like this. Okay? Here, Henri, you try one."

Henri picked up the hose end that Alphonse had disconnected. The hose was stiff in his hands and left them covered in soot. It was flat in places, but where water remained inside it was round and difficult to bend.

"Go on, Henri," Alphonse encouraged him. "Press hard. You have to get all the water out. That's the way. Press hard and get it out as you go. That makes nice tight *bananes*, and not so heavy to carry."

The students stood in the burned-out section fighting off the mosquitoes and watching Henri roll his way along the length of hose in the ashes.

"All right," Alphonse called to them. "You see how it works now. I want you to make *bananes* with all the hoses you can find. Bring them back here and put them in the boats."

The group spread out across the island. They searched out the grey hoses and held the ends up to force the water down. Then they rolled them into *bananes* and carried them off to the boats as Alphonse had told them.

Alphonse and Fred Garneau had gone for a walk. As soon as Alphonse had finished telling the crew about rolling the canvas hoses into *bananes*, he and Fred each took a shovel from one of the boats and left, following the shoreline and examining the damage that had been done by the fire.

"A real goddamn shame," Fred said.

"What's that?" Alphonse said. His eyes followed the slow current the Ottawa made around the island.

"All this mess, what good does it do, eh?"

"Good? I don't know. They say it grows blueberries. And jack pine."

"*Calis!*"

"Yes, yes, I know," Alphonse laughed. "I don't know Fred. They say that God has put everything on this earth for a reason. But, the fires? I don't know. Makes jobs for fellows like us, I guess."

"Maybe a cleanup, eh? Maybe that's His way of starting over again."

Alphonse jabbed the shovel into the sand. He reached into his shirt pocket for his tobacco. He slid the thin package of papers out from the cellophane wrapper and began to roll a cigarette.

"Yes," Alphonse answered. "I heard that once. I heard a man speaking about Hitler that way and how that was God's way of cutting back the population, of starting over. I couldn't believe it."

"*Calis*!" the old man swore. His cheeks sucked inwards over his toothless gums and he spat on a grey log lying on the sand. Alphonse watched the yellow liquid sliding down off the log and onto the sand.

When Alphonse and the old man returned, the students were sitting in the boats that were tied to driftwood jutting out from the shore. A breeze had sprung up and tiny waves slapped against the boats. Two boats had their bows pulled up onto shore and were loaded to the gunwales with the grey-black *bananes*. A brown canvas bag in one of the boats contained the portable pump that Alphonse had asked Henri and Lavigne to pick up. In the end, it was much too cumbersome to carry the pump in its canvas bag so Maurice St-Jean, the strongest of the group, ran his arms through the straps and carried the pump out on his back the way it should be done. The job was done. At least, that part of it. Both Alphonse and the old man were surprised to see that they had done so much work in so short a time.

"It was the mosquitoes," Lavigne explained. "It was hurry up or be eaten alive."

Alphonse was pleased. They had done a good job. Now, they sat in the boats and rolled cigarettes and waited for the morning to pass.

At eleven o'clock a man arrived and, without stopping the motor of his boat or even coming ashore, he threw off a cardboard box and a tin pail. "Lunch!" he said. He smiled at the students and then, swiftly, turned the boat around, heading away from the island and leaving only small waves slapping against the shore.

The old man placed the box in the shade of the boats snubbed on shore.

"Here," he said to François Gauthier. "Fill this up to about three quarters."

Gauthier took the pail and, stepping on the seats, made his way to the stern of the boat furthest from shore. Closer to shore the water had been stirred up when the boys stepped in it.

Now the old man was in charge. It was Fred Garneau's time. Like Gauthier, each of the students carried out his orders and returned as soon as they had completed them.

"No, no, *sacrament*!" he swore. "That won't burn, not even in hell. Dead wood, you hear? But, not lying on the ground. *Calis*!"

They laughed as Fred pretended to be angry with them. Alphonse was pleased with his boys. He watched as they gathered piles of driftwood and held them up for the old man's approval before laying them by where the fire was to be.

"Atta boy! Now you're talking!" the old man yelled. "You'll learn. When you get to be my age, you'll see. You'll know then how to make fire. Ha, ha, ha!"

Fred lit the ball of dry grass covered with thin, dead spruce branches from the tree he had found along shore. They could hear the dry twigs snap as they burned. The old man added larger twigs and smaller pieces of driftwood until the flames touched the pail suspended over the fire. The students were quiet as Fred worked at his fire. It was his fire and his time. They watched the dried old hands placing each piece of wood just so, and how the flames did not seem to bother him.

"There," he said at last, in a low satisfied voice. "Now you, Henri, get that box over there. We're not working for the devil. We can take time to eat, eh? Ha, ha, ha!"

There was bread and margarine and mustard along with slices of roast beef and bologna wrapped in wax paper. There were several cans of warm apple juice and a large bag of flat, thin biscuits. At the bottom of the box was a metal can full of black tea leaves.

"The water, Fred" Lavigne said. "It's ready"

The old man got up from where he was sitting. His face grimaced with the pain. "I'm getting old," he said.

The boys stood around the fire and watched closely as Fred threw in one handful of leaves, and then another. They saw the water boiling, turning the leaves over and over again, and then changing to a golden brown. The old man took the pail off the branch and set it down near the fire. He dipped his cup into the river and emptied it into the pail of steaming hot tea.

"What's that for?" Gauthier wanted to know. "Eh Fred? Why did you do that?"

"Aha!" the old man smiled, showing his wet, bare gums. "Now that's the secret. That comes from my old grandfather all the way from Charlevoix in Ireland. Yes sir! Passed on to me by the old fart himself. Ha! Ha! Ha!"

Chapter 23

The breeze had grown into a light wind, twisting the flames away from the fire and rocking the boats tied to shore. Alphonse looked at his watch and walked over to the boats loaded with the shovels and hand pumps. There were eight pumps and more than enough shovels.

"Work!" he yelled out.

The young men looked at him. This was not the *Madeleine*. They sat around the fire and there was a look of emptiness in their eyes when he called them to work. Out on the lake, on the sweep, they would groan at first, that was true, but once they were fully awake and they had begun to work, they were a good happy bunch. Here, it was quiet. Nobody said a word. The only sounds were the fire crackling and the waves slapping the shore and the boats snubbed to driftwood sticking up from the sand.

Fred took a long drag on his pipe. He looked into the bowl and then tapped it lightly on a stone showing itself above the sand.

"*Bon*," he said. "Time to earn a living again."

The old man's face twisted in pain as he got up from the log. He had been sitting too long and now he was paying the price. It was always like that. While he and Alphonse were walking around the island he had told him that, "when you're old, all the pleasures are more expensive."

The students got up slowly and left the fire. They joined Alphonse by the boat with the pumps and shovels. Fred had motioned to François Gauthier to stay behind. As the students gathered around Alphonse they heard a loud hiss coming from the fire and, turning, they saw a cloud of steam rising and Gauthier behind it with his empty pail.

"More!" the old man said. "More water. Don't be shy. It's not expensive here. Come on, *sacrament*! Get a move on it. Hee, hee, hee!"

Gauthier rushed back towards the water. He stepped on the seats of the two boats tied in tandem and loaded down with hoses. As he reached the end of the second boat, a place where he could get to deeper water, he slipped sideways. The students roared and slapped their thighs. Even Alphonse could not keep from laughing. Gauthier had slipped and now was sitting on the bottom of the river with water up to his armpits as he held the empty pail above his head.

"*Et bien calis*!" the old man muttered.

The boys were feeling better now. Even André Guy seemed to be coming back to his normal self. Waking up in his bed in the pouring rain, and the beating he had suffered from St-Jean's solid fists, had quietened him down some.

"Hey Gauthier!" he yelled. "Find a leak in the boat?"

Everybody laughed, and cheered. They were happy now. Even Gauthier, wading out of the river, did not feel badly as he could see that Fred was having a good laugh over the whole affair. On shore, the old man was bent almost in two, laughing and showing his bare gums and slapping his thighs and saying, "*Et bien calis*! Hee, hee, hee!" He even had tears in his eyes. It was difficult not to smile; the smile grew and grew until Gauthier was laughing along with everyone else, no longer feeling a fool seeing the water dripping from the pockets of his mackinaw.

"Fred," Alphonse said, "make another fire, will you. We'll go ahead now and you can meet us later."

"Well, well," the old man looked Gauthier up and down. "Now I'm a nurse for one of Ouimet's little ducks. Come on, then! Let's get a move on. Get me some wood!"

Alphonse turned to the others. He picked up one of the pumps from the boat and held it up by its nylon webbing arm straps. A three-foot long rubber hose was attached to the tank with a straight section of metal pipe and a nozzle at one end. Alphonse lowered the tank into the water, holding it there until it was filled. He placed one arm through the nylon strap and pulled the tank up onto his back. He put his other arm through the second strap and adjusted the weight on his back. Holding the section of straight metal pipe in one hand, he slid a piston back and forth along the straight pipe with the other hand. Water shot out of the nozzle and, when

Alphonse aimed it at the shore, the stream of water from the pump cut a small groove in the sand.

"These are the hand pumps," Alphonse explained as he continued pumping water onto the shore. "The men here call them *crosseuses*." The students looked at each other and smiled. Just the name, and the sight of Alphonse pumping away and the water squirting out of the nozzle with added strength each time the piston moved...it was all too much.

"Hey Alphonse!" one student yelled. "Give one to André. He's good at that. Every Sunday at Washika he practices in the washroom."

"Now," Alphonse continued, "we have only eight pumps. The rest of you can use shovels."

There was a sudden rush for the boat. It was not long before eight students had the pumps filled and strapped to their backs. Even standing still, the boys with the pumps leaned forward because of the weight.

"We'll start by patrolling the shore," Alphonse said. "It's not very complicated. If you see smoke you put it out with the pumps, or bury it. Okay now, let's go."

Alphonse led the group along the shore of the island. Eight students with pumps and eleven others with shovels on their shoulders followed Alphonse as they walked single file, around the black burned-over island.

When the last one had disappeared around the bend, Gauthier took off his trousers and hung them up on a branch along with his mackinaw and shirt and wool socks. The branch bent over low with the weight. He stood with his back to the fire wearing only his wet underwear while the old man added more wood. It was a good fire. Fred hung the tea pail over it and sat on a log again, resting his bones and waiting for Gauthier and his clothes to dry. He would worry about the pain later.

The boys walked on the sand of the shore. Where the island dropped suddenly into the river and there was no beach, they walked on the ashes among the black stumps and fallen trees.

They walked. There was not much else to do. Now and then, smoke could be seen rising lazily from the base of a stump or from the end of a charred branch; immediately eight guys attacked the site with their pumps while the others leaned on their shovels and made jokes about the washroom at Washika on Sundays. But mostly, they were bored, again. They were tired of being there on the fire. The guys operating the hand pumps complained that their shoulders ached from the straps and that their backsides were wet from the tanks leaking. Those further down the line were not so gloomy. They walked along quietly at the end of the line, pumping water and emptying their tanks on cold, black ashes and the flat, brown water of the river.

Henri walked third in line behind Alphonse. He stared at the sand or ashes and brittle, black branches as they walked. His eyes were fixed on either the beach sand or the imaginary trail that consisted of ashes and charred lichen, and only when he raised his head could he see the plaid shirt of the fellow in front of him and the blade of the shovel resting on his shoulder. The straps made Henri's shoulders ache but the tank did not leak. He had that at least. And there was Lise. This fire could not last forever. Things would eventually calm down and they would be at Washika again. The first Sunday he was back, he would go to see her. Walking that way in the black nothingness of the island, he remembered her clearly and nothing interrupted his thoughts of her, those green eyes. How they spoke to him. As he walked along the trail with the others, he recalled how he had stared into her eyes for as long as he could manage it while he caressed her with the flat of his hands. He had tried looking into her eyes as he bent down to kiss her lips, or the high bones of her cheeks, but they were always lost, those searching beautiful eyes were always lost in the blur. Henri saw her back stretch and curve like a cat as he ran the tips of his fingers over her breasts, along the side of her neck to the back curve of her ears. Her breasts were firm and moved with her breathing and they touched his chest when he leaned down to kiss her.

"Break!" Alphonse yelled from the front of the line.

Henri looked up from the ashes. A red, plaid shirt was suddenly in his face and, as suddenly, there was a sharp crack as the fellow's shovel sliced into his forehead.

"*Sacrament*!" the plaid shirt said. "You okay?"

"Yes. It's nothing," Henri said.

"Lucky for you, you had your hat."

"Yes, I guess."

There was a mark on the front of the hat. That was all. He had not been hurt and it had really been his fault after all. Worse still was the moment with LIse that he had suddenly lost. Just the remembering had made him feel empty and alone. The shovel hit to the head was nothing at all.

The group stood around Alphonse, rolling cigarettes and watching the slow current of the river. The boys with the pumps had removed the straps from their shoulders and let the tanks drop to the ground.

"Henri," Alphonse said. "Your head? It's all right?"

"Yes. I'm okay."

"We should be meeting up with Fred and François soon."

"You think they can catch up?"

"They'll come the other way around."

"But, they have no pumps."

"Yes, I know." Alphonse replied. "Anyway, there's not much to be done here."

Henri looked at him, at his thick, sad eyebrows and the heavy moustache of the same dark brown drooping over the grinning lips. But it was the eyes that said it, those hazel eyes that smiled out of the leathery tanned face.

"Then why, Alphonse? Why are we here?"

Alphonse gave a short laugh and pulled deeply on his cigarette. He leaned back with one eye shut to keep out the smoke.

"We're here," he said, "because they want us to be here. Today, perhaps, and maybe even for a couple of days, we might not find any smoke. But they'll want us here longer, and we'll be here longer even if we know that there is not a single spark left anywhere on this island."

Henri looked at the man. There was neither weakness nor bitterness in his eyes. He was a man like any other man standing by a river with a black, burned-over forest behind him.

"But why," Henri seemed almost to be whining. "If you know that it's useless us being here like this. How can you accept that? You're not bitter. You're not even angry. I don't understand."

"You're young, Henri, you and all the guys here."

"I know. So?"

"You see, Henri, it's your time, yours and the others here. It's time to ask why, and to question everything. It's your time, just like it's Fred's time to swear and tell lies and poke fun at the bosses. When you're older, you'll learn not to take things so seriously, only the important ones."

"You think so?"

"Sure. And besides, Henri, I can tell right now that you'll be all right. Or maybe you'll grow up and wear fancy clothes and give orders and have people like Fred making fun of you."

"Never!" Henri replied.

Alphonse took out his watch. He looked at it, turned it over in his hand and then put it back into the slit pocket of his trousers.

"Courage, my little ducks," he said. "The way I see it, we'll patrol this island for another four or five days and then they'll be sending us back to Washika. We'll be finished with the fire then and back on the lake. About another five days."

"Oh yes," the boys yelled out together. "At the very least!"

Alphonse smiled. At least the group had not been split up. Soon, they would be together on the lake. But, for now, they were content and happy standing on the shore of that burnt, black island on the Ottawa.

Chapter 24

There was a thick fog in the morning. The students could barely see each other in the boats. As they moved forward, the fog seemed to split open and expose another stretch of river.

It was their third day patrolling the island. They had not seen any smoke on the second day and, with the storm the night before, they did not expect to see smoke on this or any other day. They pulled the boats up onto shore when they reached the island. After tying the boats, they sat on the gunwales waiting for orders from Alphonse.

Alphonse turned to the old man.

"Fred," he said. "You know how to run the boat, eh?"

"Yes, sure." the old man replied.

"All right then," He looked at the boys sitting in the boats and the others standing around him. "Henri," he continued. "You go with Fred, here. Take the boat and patrol around the island."

"Should we take a pump, you think?"

"Be better, yes. You never know with these things. And bring a couple of shovels."

The boys were slow getting started. They stood on shore, smoking and talking quietly. They were cold and wet from the fog and not one of them had removed his life jacket.

"All right, you guys," Alphonse shouted. "Get your stuff now."

The students groaned, some swore softly. They removed their life jackets and tossed them into the boats. From one boat they hauled out the shovels and pumps.

"We're going straight through today," Alphonse began.

"Through all that?" Lavigne pointed to the thick mass of black, fallen trees and burned shrubs.

"Yes sir!" Alphonse smiled at the crew. "What's the matter my little ducks? Afraid to get your boots dirty, eh?"

"*Sacrament*, he's serious," a voice said.

"I never would have believed it," another voice added.

"No, it's not that," Lavigne explained. "It just doesn't seem worth while going in there. I mean, we haven't seen any smoke for almost two days now."

"Well Gaston, maybe we'll see some today."

Alphonse went over to where Fred and Henri were preparing to leave. They had a hand pump in the boat, two shovels and an axe. There was a metal gas tank on the floor of the boat, with a black rubber hose going along the floor and over a seat to the outboard. The old man sat forward, at the bow. He had just finished filling his pipe and was puffing loudly. He held a match over the bowl and pushed the tobacco down with his finger as he puffed. At the stern, where he sat by the outboard, Henri could smell the sweet aroma of pipe tobacco as the smoke drifted his way.

"We'll meet back here around noon." Alphonse said. "Watch out for sand bars. No need to go too close."

"Don't worry," Fred said. "With me up here and my little engineer at the controls, there's no danger. No danger at all. *Calis*, you worry for nothing."

Alphonse laughed. Perhaps he was being a bit of a mother hen at that. It was not as he had planned. He had counted on Fred handling the boat. Still, it was perhaps better that way. The old man had much better eyes for spotting sand bars.

"It's all right, Alphonse?" Henri said.

"Yes, yes," Alphonse replied. "I forgot how good you are on the *Madeleine*. Just follow Fred's directions. Everything should be fine."

Alphonse smiled at the old man. "No problem, Fred. Henri's all right."

"That's what I said," Fred snapped. The old man twisted his face sideways, jutting his chin over his left shoulder. "Engineer!" he barked. "Come on, *sacrament*. Let's go!"

Henri started the engine and, as they backed away from shore, the old man waved to Alphonse with his pipe.

Alphonse watched them as they headed east and disappeared around a point on the island; the old man at the bow puffed on his pipe and barked orders at Henri, his little engineer. Never once did he take his eyes off the water in front of him.

Alphonse returned to where the students were waiting.

"And now," he said. "Let's go in there and see if we can't stir up a little smoke, eh?"

Chapter 25

On the east side of the island, the sun was burning through the fog and the fog itself had lifted so that Henri could see the flat, brown water and the sand and boulders on the shore of the island.

Fred Garneau knew about boats. In just a few sentences he had explained the general mechanics of the outboard, the right speed to be using, what to do if the prop should hit a log or some rocks, and where the sheer pins were kept in a little box taped to the motor. He showed Henri the rubber bulb and how to get the gas flowing from the tank on the floor up to the outboard. "Now, all you have to do is keep us going straight, and slow down when I tell you."

"What happens if we hit one?" Henri said.

"Nothing. That's because we won't. The sand bars are as big as trees. Bigger. And even if we did, nothing. We might get stuck. And then you'd have to get out and push. What do you think of that, eh? Ha! Ha! Ha!"

By ten o'clock the fog had lifted completely. They could see the island now and the burned trees, and the black, forest floor. Seen from the river, it looked different. Henri guided the boat along the contours of the island. Gripping the helm, he could feel the vibrations of the engine and the numbness in his hand.

"Not too close," Fred yelled over the whine of the outboard.

Henri veered to port and then straightened out.

"How's that?"

"Good. Now slow down a little."

The old man stood up and motioned to Henri with downward motions of his open hand. "Easy now," he said. Holding on to the gunwales, Fred looked over the starboard side.

"Slow down!" he yelled back. "Left Henri. Left!"

Henri pushed hard to the left. It had only taken a second. In that second his hand had pivoted clockwise and the boat had run aground at full throttle.

Henri looked forward. The old man was on his hands and knees in the bottom of the boat. Henri shut down the engine.

"*Monsieur* Garneau?" Henri called. "*Monsieur* Garneau, are you all right?"

"*Saint sacrament*," the old man mumbled to himself. He held on to the gunwales and lifted himself up and sat down on the seat. He leaned over and picked up his pipe at the bow. He aligned bowl with stem and put the pipe in his shirt pocket. He brought his hand up to his forehead. Henri could see that his hand was trembling.

"*Calis*!" the old man swore.

"You all right, *Monsieur* Garneau?"

"Fred! Fred! ..." the old man spun around on the seat. "How many times I have to tell you. Yes, yes I'm all right."

There was blood flowing from a cut above the man's left eye. He dipped his hand into the water and scooped some up to his eye. The blood smeared over his forehead and dripped down the side of his nose. He took a wrinkled handkerchief from out of his back pocket and held it over the wound.

"I say left Henri, and you go right. I say, slow down, you go full speed ahead." The old man looked up at Henri. "How come, Henri? Eh?"

Henri realized by this time what had happened but he did not want to try to explain it. Explaining would only make it worse. He had acted badly. It was his fault and that was that.

"I don't know, Fred," Henri said. "I guess I got a little excited. Maybe I'd better sit up front."

"Na, Na!" the old man shook his head. "If we're going to crack up I'd like to know, at least, what I'm hitting. Anyway, it's nothing. See? The bleeding's stopped already."

"Then you want me to keep on here?"

"Yes, yes. But first, let's see how we're fixed here." The old man looked over the side. Holding on to both gunwales, he rocked the boat from side to side. "See if you can back her off."

Henri started the engine. He slid the engine into reverse and rotated the throttle for more speed. As the engine whined and made white water at the stern, Fred continued his rocking maneuvers. Slowly, inches at a time, the boat seemed to be moving backwards, off the sand bar. It was difficult to tell with Fred rocking it from side to side like that.

"There," he said. "We've got it. Give her hell, Henri."

Henri opened up, full throttle, and the boat backed off of the sand bar in a lurch. The old man was seated and he held on tightly to the gunwales.

"Good, good," he said. "Now, take her slow. When you get past the bend there, we'll shut her down for a minute."

There was no mistaking the bend. There was only the one up ahead. Henri fondled the helm nervously. He was nervous and felt badly about the sand bar and the cut above *Monsieur* Garneau's left eye. He thought about how Alphonse had praised him and how *Monsieur* Garneau had called him his "little engineer." Some engineer. He watched the old man vigilantly; at any moment a hand might rise, telling him to slow down, or turn. Now, the old man sat staring forward, one hand gripping a gunwale and the other on his forehead holding the handkerchief against the wound.

The river was not very wide where they were. It was less than fifty feet across from the island to the opposite shore. Henri could easily make out the raccoon tracks alongside the small mound of clamshells on the muddy shore. There, the shoreline was different from that of the island. All along the shoreline across from the island, the shore was a muddy grey soil descending at a steep angle, with alders sloping out over the water. Beyond the alders the land rose suddenly and was covered in jack pine, white birch, and occasionally, spruce and balsam fir.

"Looks different from here, eh?"

"Yes. All right, Henri, shut her down here."

Henri shut off the engine. The boat coasted along at their original speed and then, slowly and silently, drifted with the current.

"There," the man said. "We'll rest our ears a little."

He stood up and, holding on to the gunwales with both hands, he lifted first one leg and then the other over the seat. Being as tall as he was did not make it easy and he grimaced as he forced his back forward and down in order to turn himself around on the seat. At last, he sat down, facing Henri. He took out his pipe and tobacco pouch from his shirt pocket. The bleeding had stopped and now there was only a smear of dried blood over his left eye.

"Want a fill?" he said.

Henri held up his tobacco and papers.

"Yes sir," the man said. He puffed at his pipe and looked at the forest beyond the alders.

"Nice and quiet here," Henri said.

"Yes, and in my day it was always like that. We wouldn't be patrolling around with a loud stinking motor like that." Fred nodded towards the outboard motor. "No sir. Men knew how to paddle in those days."

Henri watched as they drifted towards the island. There were places there where even the driftwood on the sand had burned. All of that part of the island that they could see from the boat was a solid mass of black, naked trees leaning against each other or lying on the ashes with their branches sticking up.

"*Et bien, calis*!" the old man swore. "Will you look at that?"

Henri looked towards the shore of the island, to where the old man's gaze was directed.

"Quite a mess, eh?"

"No, no. Look there. There, beside the big rock."

Henri had not noticed the rock and the clump of bushes on the lee side that had escaped the fire and still had leaves that were green.

"Paddle over closer," Fred whispered. "And don't make any noise."

Henri grabbed the paddle at his feet. It was stuck under the pump and the shovels. He pulled hard and it came, suddenly, striking a gunwale. The noise echoed over the flat water of the river.

"*Sacrament*! Look at her go," the old man pointed with his finger.

Henri turned and saw the large brown animal rushing inland through the blackness of the forest.

"A nice big one," he said, looking at where the moose had lain on the sand. "I wonder what he was doing here?"

"She," the old man snapped. "That was a cow. Probably tired, poor thing. Could be, she's been running since the fire started here."

"But moose can swim," Henri was not absolutely sure about that but it seemed he had read about it somewhere. And he had seen them standing in water before. "And besides, it's not far to cross."

"Sure they can swim. And they can have little ones this time of year. Probably, the calf burned."

Henri stared across the flat water and the island of burned trees but he could not see her. Given the direction she had fled in, Alphonse and the others might meet up with her. It was something, seeing one close like that. He would remember what he saw of her for a long, long time.

"Why does she stay, Fred? There's nothing left here."

"Hope maybe. I don't know."

Chapter 26

Some time around noon, Henri and the old man came around the southwest side of the island. They could see the boats tied to shore, the smoke of the fire and the boys standing around it with cups in their hands. Alphonse grabbed the point of the bow and pulled the boat up onto shore as Henri cut the engine and let the boat drift in.

"Well?" Alphonse said.

"Nothing," Fred replied. "There's nothing left here."

"Your eye? What happened?"

"It's nothing. I drink too much tea. I'm all the time pissing."

"Yes, but your eye, Fred?"

"Yes, yes. That's what happened. I went ashore and I was in such a rush, and my goddamn zipper stuck and me walking and trying to get it down. And that's how it happened. A branch sticking out about that long," Fred held his hands out about three feet apart. "Caught me, paff, right in the face. You should have seen the blood. *Calis*! Anyway, it's nothing."

Henri did not look at the man as he spoke. He had tilted the outboard motor forward. He knelt on the floor of the boat and turned off the fuel supply.

"We saw a moose, Alphonse," he said. "A cow. Fred says she probably has a calf."

"Yes," Alphonse said. "We saw her."

"You saw her, eh. I kind of thought you would, the direction she was going."

"No, Henri. We didn't see the cow. It was the calf we found." Alphonse turned to the old man. "The boys took it pretty bad."

"It's dead, then?" Henri said.

"Yes."

The old man stepped ashore and tied the boat to a tree trunk. When he had finished, he and Alphonse and Henri went over to where the fire was. The guys were standing around the fire, drinking tea.

Fred and Henri made sandwiches and took small chunks of cheese from the box, and biscuits. The old man dipped his cup into the tea pail and then set it aside to cool. Henri sipped at his tea. It was hot and burned his lips even when he slurped it like he had seen Fred do so often. He looked around at the guys. They were being very quiet. St-Jean stood next to him, staring fixedly at the fire.

"Maurice," Henri said. "We saw a big cow moose this morning. I heard you found a young one."

"Yeah." St-Jean replied.

"Probably the smoke got it." Henri continued. "It couldn't have burned alive."

"Ah no," Morrow interrupted, "you should have seen its face, Henri. Just like it was screaming. For sure, it burned alive."

The guys looked away from the fire. No one wanted to be the first to talk about it but, now, that was done. They were feeling badly about the thing and they had a need to say something about it.

"You should have seen it, Henri," Lavigne began. "It was terrible. And CC found a rabbit."

"Yeah," CC said, nodding. "Only the head wasn't burned."

Henri's face twisted in disgust. How was it that they had not seen these things earlier? At the first place they had gone to, they had seen no signs of wildlife, except mosquitoes. Even around the island. They had walked around it for two days and seen nothing.

"But, how come?" Henri said to no one in particular. "We walked all around here before and saw nothing."

"Me and François, we found eggs," André announced.

"Probably partridge," François added. "They were close together on the ground."

Alphonse listened to his log drivers speaking as he had never heard them speak before. He tried to recall a time in his life when he might have spoken as they did now. It was a long time ago and he could not remember it well but he knew it had happened and he knew how he had felt about it. As the students spoke, Alphonse glanced at Fred sitting on a fat, grey log. He was eating his sandwich and pretending not to hear what was going on across the fire in front of him. The old man looked up at Alphonse through the flames of the fire. He washed down the rest of his sandwich with two quick gulps of tea and dipped his cup into the pail.

"Who's responsible for this stuff?" he asked, nodding towards the tea pail.

"Me," François Gauthier spoke up. All heads had turned towards the old man. Was Gauthier going to get a talking to? Things were not going well. Might just as well be Gauthier's turn. "What's the matter, Fred? It's not okay? I made it too strong, maybe?"

"Too strong? Ha!" the old man glared at the students.

"I find it not bad," Henri said.

"Not bad?" Fred turned to look at Henri. "Not bad you say?"

"Hey Fred," André Guy stood next to François. "Maybe it's the sandwich left a bad taste in your mouth. Even if it's Gauthier who made it, I think it's pretty good."

Now, the fellows looked at André, signs of surprised disbelief on their faces.

"*Sacrament*!" Lavigne just could not avoid a comment. "What's happening to you?"

"Well it is," André argued. "Eh Alphonse? It's not bad, eh?"

"If you say so," Alphonse smiled.

"Listen here, *calis*!" Fred stood up and jabbed a thin brown finger at his chest. "I'm the expert around here. Not bad...pretty good. *Sacrament*! This here is the best tea I've ever had in all my life. Yes sir. Better than the old fart in Charlevoix ever made. Ha! Ha! Ha!"

Standing by the fire and kicking at the sand with the toe of his boot, François Gauthier felt both pride and embarrassment. Although the boys felt badly about the animals and all that had happened, they could not ignore the opportunity just presented to them.

"Hey Gauthier," Lavigne snuggled up close to him. "You'd make somebody a good little cook, eh? A bit ugly but still pretty good in the kitchen."

Lavigne tried to fondle François' hair beneath the rim of his hard hat but François pushed him away.

"I wonder if they make skirts that long?" St-Jean wanted to know. "Hey Françoise, my dear. Pour me another tea, will you."

André moved in closer. He tapped François' hard hat lightly with his hand. "Well Gauthier," he said. "Guess you won't be using this where you're going."

François was quiet during the whole ordeal. He had learned earlier that summer how to handle himself with them. He did not say a word. He just smiled and endured and, when he was convinced that they had had enough fun with him, he dipped his cup into the pail and then, closing his eyes, he savoured what Fred Garneau claimed was the best tea he had ever tasted, better even than his grandfather's who had lived in Charlevoix in Ireland.

The old man reached behind him to the pile of driftwood the boys had collected. He pulled out two of the twisted, grey pieces and added them to the fire. It was quiet again. They sipped their tea from the brown melamine cups that came with the lunch boxes and watched the flames curling around the pointed ends of the wood. Around one o'clock Alphonse would call out, "Work!" and they would douse the fire and Henri and Fred would leave in the boat while the others would follow Alphonse back into the bush. That was what they had to do and it was not much different from the day before, and the day before that. But, they were not the same. They felt differently now, about the forest and the fire and what they were supposed to be doing there. They had behaved badly. They knew that now. And they wished that they had been otherwise but what was done was done and there was nothing they could do about it. They could only hope that, someday, they would have the opportunity to go about things in a proper way. But perhaps time would have softened their memories of how they had behaved. They might have forgotten how they felt now, standing by their little fire on the island. Maybe, all those years later, they would behave badly again.

Chapter 27

The students never returned to the island. On Sunday, their fourth day on the fire, they were sent further north on the Ottawa to a place the men called Sugar Loaf. They were there for thirteen days and worked very hard. On the last day it had rained all morning and the boys hid under the largest spruce trees they could find, rolled cigarettes and waited for the rain to stop.

Henri Morin was alone under his tree. It took him a long time to try to roll a cigarette without the paper getting wet from the water dripping down from the branches. Later that morning, he leaned against the trunk of a large spruce with its branches almost sixteen feet long at the bottom, and fell sound asleep, half listening to the rain.

When Henri awoke, it was still raining. He was damp and hungry. He walked out along the firebreak to the road. The caboose was gone. There was not a truck to be seen. No trucks, no people, nothing but the rain and the sand and the quiet. Henri climbed into the yellow tractor that had been left by the side of the road. He tried to understand why he could not hear the whine of the pump motors or the chainsaws working the trees. The only sound disturbing the quiet was the rain tapping on the roof of the tractor. At that very moment, some thirty miles south, the rest of the guys were finishing up their lemon meringue pie and sipping hot tea in the cookhouse at Camp 15.

After lunch Alphonse was in a hurry to settle up with the camp foreman. They would be going back to Washika. They were finished with the fire and he wanted to make sure that his and the students' time was properly recorded and that it was clear that the cheques should be sent to

Washika. He did not like Camp 15 and he hoped that he would never see it again. All he needed now was the little black notebook with the hours. For the past week or so Henri had been in the habit of keeping the little notebook with him. Once he had the book in hand, Alphonse could report the students' and his own hours to the clerk and say good-bye to Georges and never have to look at the place again.

"Gaston," he said. "Have you seen Henri?"

"No," Lavigne answered. "I haven't seen him all morning."

"He wasn't in the caboose when we came in," François added.

"But there was a second," Alphonse said. "He must have come back in that one."

"No, I don't think so," Lavigne said. "I was in the second. I didn't see him."

Alphonse looked around the camp yard. Nothing had changed since the morning: trucks arriving, some leaving and men rushing everywhere. He returned to the cookhouse and scanned the rows of tables. Finally he went to the camp office and reported that Henri Morin was missing.

"Can't be," Georges said. "We always take a count of the fellows for the hours. You know that, Alphonse."

"Yes, I know that. I also know that in our gang, it's Henri Morin who takes the count."

"Christ! That's all we needed. I can just hear them at the head office."

"There'll be a bigger fuss if we don't find him." Alphonse was suddenly angry. Before, he had been worried. Now, he was worried, and angry with this man with the clean clothes and grey curls and everything so neat in his office and everything arranged just so. "Never mind about the people in town, the head office and all that gang. Get a truck out there right away."

"Yes, yes. You're right. I'll send someone right away. Where was he anyway?"

"On a pump. The first one on the creek that crosses the break."

"That was on number nineteen?"

"Yes."

The man snatched his immaculate white hard hat from the rack and rushed out of the office. Alphonse stood in front of the large oak desk. He stared at the map covering one wall, at the red, and blue, and yellow pins sticking out of the contours. He tried to imagine which pin showed where Henri might be. He walked around the glass-topped desk and sat down in the chair. He heard the spring stretching as he leaned back and placed his feet up on the desk.

Out at number nineteen, it was still raining. Henri sat high up on the seat of the tractor with his mackinaw buttoned up to his neck, his collar up and his arms folded, trying to keep warm. He was cold and hungry and there was a strong, stale taste of tobacco in his mouth. He was tired and could easily have fallen asleep again but the shivering kept him awake. He was not worried. Eventually someone would notice that he was not there. They would send someone. It was just that it had to happen to him. And on the last day! Finally, he got bored thinking about it and fell asleep.

It was two o'clock in the afternoon when Jacques, the caboose driver, pulled up beside the tractor. He got out of the truck but did not close the door. He took soft, careful steps going towards the tractor. Once close enough, he grabbed Henri's foot and shook it violently.

"Hey, hey!" he screamed.

Henri opened his eyes. He turned his head slowly to glance down at the man. He felt good seeing that the driver looked disappointed.

"What time is it?" he said.

"After two."

"Well, it sure took them long enough."

"Shouldn't have been hiding in the first place."

"Hiding? Who was hiding? If they had honked the horn when it was time, I wouldn't be here now."

"We did," the driver smiled. "Three sets of short ones. I know. It was me on the last run."

"Anyway, I wasn't hiding."

"Well, let's go," the driver said. He looked around him. To Henri, he seemed to be checking for any other stragglers. "Everybody's waiting for you."

Henri had only been cold and damp and hungry before. Now, the driver was making him think that all this was his fault, and that he should feel guilty. He knew that he was being stupid but he was beginning to feel guilty anyway. He looked across at the driver with his brown curly hair and clean boots and gold-capped teeth and, slowly, he began to hate the man and the smug look on his clean, shaven face.

When they arrived at Camp 15, Henri could see Alphonse and the driver standing by the open door of the bus. The caboose pulled up alongside the bus. Henri opened the door and stepped out of the truck. He did not speak to the driver.

"You okay?" Alphonse said.

"Yes."

"Go on in to the cookhouse, Henri. Maybe there's something left."

"No, that's okay. I'll eat at Washika."

"You have the book, Henri?"

Henri handed over the notebook and pencil. He had filled in the entry for the last day on his way in to Camp 15. The driver had made a joke about it, about not forgetting to put in two extra hours alongside his own name. Henri had not even looked up from the notebook and the driver did not speak to him after that.

Finally, Henri decided to see what he might find to eat at the cookhouse. He returned shortly afterwards with a paper sack and a jam jar full of tea. He sat up front, to the right of the driver, ate the sandwiches and biscuits and drank tea from the jar with his glove on. He had missed the old man. He was sorry about that. After their last day on the island, Fred Garneau had been assigned tasks at the camp. He must not have liked that. That afternoon, while Henri sat in the tractor waiting for a ride back to Camp 15, the old man had taken the Company bus back to Ste-Émilie. The fellows had lined up single file to say good-bye and to shake his firm brown hand. As he boarded the bus, Fred waved to them with his pipe and smiled his famous toothless smile.

Henri had just finished eating when he saw Alphonse and Georges coming across the yard from the camp office. The two men stood a short while in the rain alongside the bus. The zipper on Georges' jacket was done up tight to his neck and he kept his hands in his trouser pockets. Finally he jerked one hand out of his pocket, shook hands with Alphonse and turned to leave. As he did so, he looked back towards the windows of the bus and gave a short wave. He waved a second time and smiled up at the raindrop-covered windows. The man turned then and walked back to the camp office. He did not look back again.

As the bus turned in the yard, Alphonse was feeling sorry about Georges. It must not be easy to do his job well and not be hated by some of the men. It must not be easy being hated. He must not forget to tell Georges that the next time they met in Ste-Émilie, which was not very likely. But anyway, if ever they should meet, he would invite him to join him at the tavern for a beer. No man that Alphonse was aware of, regardless of his position, could let a short stay over a tavern table with a tall cold beer pass him by. While they shared this neutral territory, Alphonse would tell him how all of the students had waved back to him that last day, and how they had said very nice things about him. The last part was not true of course but Alphonse believed that the man would feel good about that. A man like Georges must not feel good often. And anyway, it was not a very big lie.

PART III

Chapter 28

As the bus came to a stop between the main sleep camp and the bunkhouse-and-office, the students could hear the clangity, clang of the supper bell. The older men had already gathered around the cookhouse landing. They were waiting for Dumas to finish beating the triangle, calling all to the evening meal.

"Hurry and wash up," Alphonse called from the front of the bus. "We don't want to keep Dumas waiting, eh?"

They were happy to be back. They pushed and shoved each other stepping out of the bus and, standing at the basin later, there were elbows swung back at ribs and short shoulder jabs and the best name calling they had heard in over two weeks.

The students were late arriving at the cookhouse, not very late, but still late by Dumas' standards. They came in together, single file, with their hands well scrubbed and their hair wetted down, each holding out a ticket. Dumas stood between the four tables with his arms locked across his chest. He smiled at the boys.

"Glad to be back, I'll bet," he said, loudly. "Well, sit down. There's plenty to eat."

The older men looked up from their plates. They looked over their shoulders at the cook and they looked at each other across the table.

"He's started drinking," Percy Dumont whispered to the man beside him.

"You think so?" the man replied.

"For me, yes. You've been here as long as me. Ever see him like that?"

"No. Still, I don't know. A person can change."

"Dumas Hébert change? Ha! Listen to me. I saw him in the hotel in Ste-Émilie once. He was laughing and talking with everybody. Liquor. That's what did it. For me, he's started again."

"I don't know," the man argued. "I saw him go to the infirmary twice this week. Maybe he's very sick. The pills, you know. Sometimes they make you act a little crazy."

"That could be. Still, he looks drunk to me."

The students sat down at their usual places at the table and Dumas went back to the kitchen. They could hear him yelling something to the cookee and then both of them laughing loudly. They had never heard Dumas laugh before. No one in the cookhouse except Percy Dumont had ever heard him laugh. The effect was immediate. Within seconds of hearing him, everyone in the cookhouse was smiling and waiting for Dumas to come out of the kitchen. They were curious to see if his face looked the same. Still, a few of the older men were convinced that the cook was drunk and they waited anxiously to see him drop a plate or trip and fall flat on his face.

After supper the students showered and those who had begun to grow hair beneath their noses or on the points of their chins, shaved. They dropped their blackened clothes into plastic garbage bags to be washed in Ste-Émilie but, most probably, never to be worn again. Clean and fresh in white T-shirts and jeans, they played cards in the common room or lay on their bunks, talking and smoking cigarettes. In the bunkhouse-and-office, it was the same except that, there, the guys were worried.

"And today's only Friday," Lavigne argued. "You know what that means."

"Tomorrow's Saturday," Morrow volunteered.

"Of course, it's Saturday. We know that. But it's also a workday around here. We work six days a week here. Remember?"

"You think they'll send us out tomorrow?" Henri said.

"Could be. Why wouldn't they?" Lavigne replied.

"Well, I don't know." Henri tried to reason the thing out. "I mean, we've worked sixteen days straight and two Sundays on top of that. Seems to me they owe us a couple of days."

"Yeah," Morrow interrupted. "And besides, we missed our weekend because of the fire."

"You don't understand," Lavigne began. "The fire's the fire and the sweep's the sweep. The way I see it, we'll have to work two more days before we can get two days off. Look, it's simple. We finished on the sweep on a Wednesday of the week we were supposed to go down. There were still two days left to work. So, if we work two days, we can go."

"You'd like your time off on a Monday and Tuesday?" Maurice St-Jean joined the conversation.

"*Sacrament*! I forgot about that," Lavigne said.

"You're all wasting your time," St-Jean continued. "We'll get a week-end off when they decide and not before."

"He's right, I think," Henri said.

"Maybe we should speak to Alphonse," Lavigne tried again.

"No, I don't think so," Henri said.

"We can make them an offer," André spoke up suddenly. He had been shuffling cards at the table where he sat alone. He tossed the cards onto the table and joined the others by Henri's bunk.

"What do you mean, a bargain?" Lavigne inquired.

"Sure," André answered. "It's too late tonight but, tomorrow, when were ready to go out, we can talk about it with Alphonse and Simard-Comtois. We can say to them that if they let us go down this weekend we'll make up the time by working a couple of extra hours a day next week, or maybe go out next Sunday."

"Whoa!" Lavigne stood up. "Not Sundays. We're not going to start that. Still, I think you have a good idea there."

"Sure," Morrow added. "And what's a couple of hours more a day anyway."

"What do you think, Maurice?" Lavigne said.

"It sounds pretty good to me. But we'll have to speak to the others."

"Hey, I can't think of anyone who would be against it," Lavigne said, looking across the room. "You Gaston, you're with us on this?"

Gaston Cyr was sitting reading a picture magazine with the back of his chair leaning against the wall.

"What's that?" he said.

"You'd like to go down this weekend?"

"Don't ask?"

"Be willing to work extra hours next week?"

"No problem."

"There, you see," Lavigne turned to the others. "Everybody will be like that."

That night, lying in his bed, Henri was both happy and unhappy, so much so that he was unable to sleep. He was very happy to be finished with the fire and to be back at Washika. Maybe tomorrow they would be sent down to Ste-Émilie for the weekend. He could hardly wait. There were his parents, and all of his friends, and the stories he had to tell them about his experiences on the fire. With his best friend, David Greer, he would share his experience with Lise Archambault. Lise, that was the sad part. He had not seen her for a very long time it seemed. With the crazy hours they worked on the fire, even dreaming of her did not come easy. Once, hiding beneath a spruce tree out of the rain, he had thought about her and he remembered being aroused instantly. Sitting there under the wet, dripping branches, he had never felt lonelier in his life. And now, if they were to go down to Ste-Émilie for the weekend, he would not see her on Sunday. He would have to wait until the next Sunday before seeing her again, and then, it could rain.

Henri tossed around under his blankets. He lifted himself up on his elbows and tried to look outside. It was dark everywhere. He could not even make out where the windows were. He would think about something else. He was warm and dry in his bed, he was back at Washika, finished with the fire, and maybe in the morning he would be on the bus, going home. He tightened the blankets around him and closed his eyes. He thought about Alphonse and Simard-Comtois and what he would say to them after breakfast. It had been decided by the others that he should be the one to speak to Alphonse and the superintendent. It would be simple enough. They would like to have their weekend off, he would tell them, but since they owed the Company two days before being entitled to a weekend off they would work two extra hours each day the following week to make up the time. And...Henri lifted his head off the pillow. Then, he sat straight up in his bed. It could not be! How could they have been so stupid? And yet, it was simple. They owed two days. That made eighteen hours. At two extra hours per day, they would have to work nine days, almost two weeks putting in extra hours each day.

Henri drew back the blankets and slid his feet across and onto the floor. He sat on the edge of the bed and looked into the darkness. Perhaps Maurice would be angry. Henri felt the need to talk this over with someone but Maurice did not like being awakened before the bell, whatever the reason. What could they do? Two weeks working extra hours and coming home late for supper every night. Dumas would be furious. Dumas! They had not thought of Dumas. That was it then, the end of their plan. Dumas would certainly not change the hours of his cookhouse just for them and, of course, he would not serve them two hours late for supper either.

Henri laid his head on the pillow, still happy and unhappy. He was disappointed now that they would not be going down to Ste-Émilie for the weekend. He wrapped the blankets around himself. He closed his eyes and was warm and happy again, lying on the hot sand, looking up into her green eyes and feeling the roundness of her breasts against his chest. Later, they would do a little fishing or, maybe, just lie there in the sun and wait for the day to pass.

Chapter 29

After the first bell, when all of the students were up and searching for their clothes, Henri broke the news to them.

"How's that, *calis*?" André was not happy.

"Mathematics," Lavigne snarled. "Two into eighteen gives nine. Nine days. *Sacrament*!"

"And then there's Dumas," Henri continued. "You know how he is about us being late."'

"I've got it!" Morrow was excited. "I've got it!"

"Well?" Lavigne stood with his palms up. "Come on, out with it."

Morrow walked around to where Henri and Lavigne stood by the table. "It's so simple," he said. "I don't see why you didn't think of it, Henri."

Lavigne grabbed Morrow by the shirt and started to lift him.

"Listen you," Lavigne hissed. "You're the one who'll be simple if you don't stop screwing around."

"Leave him alone," Henri said. "It's no use. Forget it."

"Wait," Morrow said. "Listen Henri. What if we were to talk Dumas into making two lunches in the morning? What do you think, eh?"

Henri stared at Morrow. Then both he and Lavigne walked out of the bunkhouse-and-office without saying a word. As they crossed the yard to the main sleep camp, they could hear Morrow explaining his plan to the others.

"What an asshole," Lavigne mumbled.

"He's all right," Henri said. "He just wants to be part of it. That's all."

In the main sleep camp, the students went to the washroom and washed up at the basin. They looked at each other and smiled as Télesphore Aumont coughed his way to the washroom. They were happy to be back.

Walking across the yard to the main sleep camp, Henri had seen the bus parked behind the cookhouse. Lavigne also noticed it as they made their way to the cookhouse.

"What do you think, Henri?" he said. "Not another fire, *sacrament*?"

"No, I don't think so. Probably just the driver was tired."

"Did you ever notice his eyes?"

"From driving at night," Henri replied. He did not know this for certain but he had read it somewhere.

"Yes, I suppose. You know, every trade has its eyes. Ever notice an undertaker? Their eyes are always sunk back in their head, especially the old ones. It's the chemicals, a guy told me once."

"Yes, I suppose," Henri said. He believed Lavigne's theory about undertakers' eyes as much as he was certain about truck drivers' eyes. It was all beer talk, and the wrong time of day. In Ste-Émilie, after two or three beer they would talk like that. But now it was six o'clock in the morning and Dumas was waiting for them on the cookhouse landing.

Henri and Lavigne joined the others in line. No one was speaking and Henri could hear the breeze whistling through the screened windows of the kitchen. Out in the bay small whitecaps were forming.

It wasn't long before everyone had noticed the change. It seemed impossible. A few of the older men sniffed quietly going by the cook. As each person handed him his ticket, Dumas would smile and say the person's name.

"Ah, Morin," he said, as Henri held out his ticket. "Henri Morin, the chocolate pudding man. Come in! Come in!"

Henri did not know what to say. He handed Dumas the ticket and tripped on the doorsill going in. It was like that all during breakfast. Dumas rushed in and out of the kitchen, carrying fresh platters full of eggs and fried bacon and mountains of toast, humming as he worked, and smiling at each individual who caught his eye.

After breakfast everyone was talking about it. He had started to drink was the theory held by most of the older men. There were some, more charitable, who suggested that maybe he was, in fact, very ill and that the medication was affecting his brain. Of all the older workers at Washika, only Alphonse claimed that it was all very normal and that the poor man was probably in love. In the bunkhouse-and-office the boys were much too concerned with their own problems to be worried about the erratic behaviour of the cook. They had only one thing on their minds and that was the possibility of returning to Ste-Émilie for the weekend. Someone suggested a petition. Gaston Cyr stood up on a chair and with one fist in the air called for a strike. The others looked at him in silence. Gaston felt a fool then and stepped down off the chair.

Just minutes before Dumas signalled that it was time for them to make their lunches, Alphonse stepped into the bunkhouse-and-office.

"Well, my little ducks," he said. "I have some good news for you this morning."

"Ah non! *Sacrament*!" Lavigne swore. "Not another fire."

"Now, now," Alphonse smiled. "Don't take it so hard. The bus is waiting. Be ready in fifteen minutes."

"Where is it this time, Alphonse?" Henri asked.

"What do you mean, Henri?"

"The fire. Where's the fire this time?"

"What fire? Who said anything about a fire?" Alphonse looked at the boys standing around him.

"But the bus?" Henri continued.

"Pack your rags, my little ducks," Alphonse grinned. "There's only one bus leaving for Ste-Émilie today."

Lavigne rolled off his bed. He danced around the room screaming and holding his clenched fists high above his head. Some sat silently on their bunks with their eyes closed, wearing wide, happy grins. Morrow was already busy throwing clothes into a long, narrow duffle bag. Alphonse left the bunkhouse-and-office. As he walked across the yard to the main sleep camp, Gaston Cyr ran past him and into the main sleep camp yelling, "We're going down! We're going down!"

In the kitchen, Dumas and the cookee and the bus driver were sitting at a small table drinking tea. Dumas had a towel draped over his shoulders and Lise Archambault was cutting his hair.

Chapter 30

When the driver came out of the cookhouse, all of the students were seated in the bus. They had combed their hair and put on their cleanest jeans and shirts with the sleeves rolled up to show their tanned arms. Above them in the racks were duffle bags and packsacks stuffed with dirty clothes. The windows were open and the boys smoked and drank soft drinks saved up from before the fire. Everyone was bored waiting for the driver to arrive.

Alphonse stepped into the bus after the driver had started the engine. He stood at the front, holding onto the chromed post by the door.

"Well my little ducks," he said. "This is it. Don't spend it all in one place now. Be good and have fun and get well rested up for next week, eh."

The students cheered. Some of the students invited Alphonse to join them for a beer in Ste-Émilie. Alphonse smiled. Someday his sons would be speaking like that. They would be wild like this bunch thinking only of drinking, running after the girls and having a good time. Would he smile then, and also find them amusing? His father had not been amused when he, Alphonse Ouimet, had been young and crazy. Ah yes, he had been wild in his younger days. Not in the same way as these guys from Ste-Émilie. Worse perhaps. But it had been so much fun. Now, he was older and mature, as Father Landry would say, older and wiser perhaps, but what a price to pay. No longer could he do and say all the foolish things of his youth and still be considered a normal, adult human being. But what was normal? These wild, screaming students from Ste-Émilie, that was normal. They were young and their behaviour was acceptable... up to a point. After that, they would have to get serious and make something of their lives. That was it, serious. After a point in time, when a young man has reached a certain age, he has to get serious about his work, his ideas and his life. And then what happens? Alphonse thought of the young men he had known in his youth and how some of them had been very serious and had achieved success in certain disciplines. One day they discovered that they had spent most of their lives being serious about life. Many of the young men and women around them, those less-serious, light-hearted fools, had been busy enjoying their lives to the fullest and would continue to do so with or without the consent of their serious, intellectual counterparts.

Alphonse waved to the students as he stepped down from the bus. "Have a good time, my little ducks!" he shouted.

The driver pulled the arm back, closing the door. All of the students waved to Alphonse through the open windows. They were off, and happy. As the bus drove by the truck scales, Alphonse could hear them singing a familiar drinking song.

Chapter 31

It was different. It was the same type of gravel road with long uphill climbs and grinding gears and sharp turns and travelling less than five feet from the swampy water in places and plank bridges with the planks rattling as they drove over them and, always, the winding, curving gravel road lined on both sides with jack pine and white birch sticking out through the green pine needles. Nothing had changed for the snowshoe hare that hopped across the road in zigzag fashion, or the raven, wonk-wonking its presence high up on a tall grey *chicot*. But, for the students from the Collège de Ste-Émilie, it was not the same. They were going home, after almost five weeks. Now the jack pine and the birch trees were no longer boring, and the swamps no longer the foul-smelling, sucker-infested cesspools they once were. Now, through the open windows of the bus, going home, they were all of nature's beauty and life.

After they had tired of singing and every story had been told, the boys grew silent. They gazed out through the open windows, thought private thoughts and praised the beauty of nature in their own ways. After an hour, staring at the green jack pine and the white bark of the birch and the waters along the way, they dropped their heads back, some forward, some leaning against the open window frames, and slept as they would have on the deck of the *Madeleine*, or wrapped up in blankets on their bunks at Washika.

It was the sound that woke Henri. He could not remember having dreamed. His neck was sore from leaning his head sideways. He had slept well and now he was awake but the sound persisted, a humming, whining sound that was louder than the engine.

"We're on pavement," Lavigne said. He had noticed the puzzled look on Henri's face.

"Long?"

"Ten minutes. *Sacrament*, you snore loud, Henri."

Henri smiled. Lavigne had sat beside him when they left Washika. Shortly after turning right at the forks and along the gravel road that led to the main highway, Lavigne's head had dropped back and he began to snore. Henri looked around him. The students were awakening, stretching, reaching into their shirt pockets for tobacco, and rolling cigarettes.

"How much further?" Henri said.

"Another half hour we should be there."

"I hope Sylvie's working today."

"Ah, Sylvie," Lavigne moaned.

"She goes to Ste-Véronique's."

"I would take her for a ride in my father's car any day." Lavigne stretched his legs out and closed his eyes. "Such legs, and those eyes, and..."

"Ask her. Maybe she's going down this weekend. She might go out with you," Henri laughed.

"Are you crazy? My girlfriend would kill me. Five weeks I haven't seen her. I didn't even answer her letter two weeks ago. I'm in trouble now, for sure."

Henri thought often about Sylvie after the first time they had stopped at the roadside café. It was the only restaurant along the sixty miles of paved highway and its door was open twenty-four hours a day. Sylvie was a student from Ste-Émilie and her uncle, who was the cook at the restaurant, had gotten her the summer job there. She was a very pretty girl. All of the students had noticed her and voiced their desires. Henri had even thought of asking her out to a movie in Ste-Émilie, but he was never able to be alone with her long enough to speak to her about it. Once, on their way back to Washika, he sat at the counter. He had hoped to speak to her between customers but she was always very busy, filling coffee cups, punching keys on the cash register, carrying orders off to the tables. At one point, there was a lull in business and she stood behind the counter where Henri sat and she wiped it with a damp cloth, then lifted the ashtray and his cup of coffee and wiped it there again. She had smiled at Henri. It was his chance. No one else was sitting at the counter. It was the chance he had been waiting for but he said nothing. It was the button on her uniform that was to blame, the one she had left undone and which let the fold of her blouse fall forward when she rubbed circles on the counter with the cloth. Henri wanted to speak but he could not. He could not utter a sound nor think of anything but the two chalk-white lobes and the thin space between them and, for a fraction of a second when she leaned further over the counter, there was an opening still greater than before, and Henri stared. And then she blushed and Henri felt a hot flash grow across his face. She had seen him looking at her breasts. What did she think of him? Was he just like all the others? How could he ever think of asking her to go out with him? And besides, now there was Lise. Why should he complicate his life like Lavigne and a lot of the others? With Lise he was free to do as he pleased and every Sunday, if it did not rain, he would share pleasures with her that the others experienced only in their wildest dreams. What more could a fellow want? Henri did not dwell on the question. He had thought about it before, about love and relationships that last a long time. He was not ready for that. Probably, he never would be.

The bus slowed down and turned in to the right by the sign saying "Café d'Or" in large letters made of bent ash wood. Alphonse had told them about the letters being made of ash wood but he didn't know where they got the wood as there were no signs of ash trees anywhere nearby. Alphonse had also mentioned that the native people who lived in the area used this same ash wood for making their snowshoes. Several cars were parked in front of the restaurant and most had trailers with canvas-covered boats with only the outboard motors showing. All of the cars had orange and blue license plates. These were the American tourists from New York State, the only Americans the students had ever seen.

The students stepped out of the bus and walked in a group towards the Café D'or. They looked in through the windows past the curtains, smiled at the customers inside, and scanned the tables, looking for the *petites Américaines*. Henri was a bit shy with girls, and so were Lavigne and André Guy. Most of the guys were that way. But, as a group, and with the jukebox jammed with quarters, they were beyond shyness; there was no girl too beautiful or parents too reserved or protective to prevent them from openly expressing admiration for their female progeny.

Henri sat at the counter, near the cash register. The swinging doors opened and *Madame* Laviolette, the proprietress, backed into view carrying four plates of steaming hot stew. She nodded towards Henri and went over to the tables by the window. Henri was able to look past the doorway into the kitchen when *Madame* Laviolette had come out. Sylvie was not there.

When the elderly woman had finished with the customers by the window, she returned behind the counter and, after turning several pages back in the receipt pad, stood in front of Henri.

"Yes *Monsieur*?" she said.

"Just a coffee," Henri replied.

"One coffee," she repeated.

"Sylvie's working nights?"

The woman placed the coffee before Henri and added a small plastic container of cream onto the saucer.

"One coffee. There you are."

"Thank you," Henri said. Perhaps she had not heard him. Henri cleared his throat. "The girl who works here, Sylvie, she is working nights this week?"

"Yes, yes, I know her," the woman replied. She wrote numbers on the receipt pad. "Your name is Henri Morin?"

"Yes."

"Sylvie has gone down for the weekend. She asked me to tell you that if you happened to stop in here."

Henri was certain that he had blushed. He could feel the heat on his face. The woman looked at him without smiling. She tore the receipt from the pad and placed it on the counter by his cup.

"*Merci Monsieur*," she said. She placed the pad in the pocket of her skirt and returned to the kitchen.

Henri put two spoonfuls of sugar in his coffee and emptied the plastic container of cream into the cup. So, now it was Sylvie. And what about Lise? That was how it was, all or none at all. Still, Sylvie was more his age. They could go out together, to the movies or to the restaurant. With Lise, it could only be on the sand behind the row of trees. How long would it be before it could be like that with Sylvie? And with Lise, how long would that last? Until the end of summer? What did they do at Washika in the winter? He did not know the answer to that one, or the others. And Sylvie was really more than pretty. She was very beautiful. All of the fellows spoke about her at the *collège*. She was beautiful and she was waiting for him in Ste-Émilie. Henri was excited, wondering what he should do. Should he call her? No, it would be better to play it by ear, to meet her on one of the main streets in town or at the hotel perhaps. She might be there if there was a good band. By nine or ten, if she was not there he would call her from a pay phone. And Lise? Well, he would see. Lavigne had it all right: the fire's the fire and the sweep's the sweep. He would see later about Lise. And besides, it was different with Lise and him. It was not one of those affairs, like Lavigne and the others who had steady girlfriends. With Lise, it was different. They were not tied to each other, only on Sundays on the sand behind the trees.

Henri finished his coffee and stood up from the counter. He handed the receipt and a dollar bill to the woman behind the counter and turned to leave.

"Your change, *Monsieur,*" the woman called to him.

Henri waved his hand without looking back and left the restaurant. The woman shrugged her shoulders and dropped the change into a glass under the counter. The students began to line up at the counter. Each student handed the woman his receipt and, each time, she held it at arm's length and stared down at it through the lower half of her glasses. She punched the keys and looked up at the numbers in the display window of the cash register to see if she had punched the right ones. Each time she handed out change the student would raise his hands and she would say, "*Merci Monsieur*," and, more often than not, the student would say, "We just come off the drive, us."

When the last student had left and the bus was easing its way back onto the highway, the woman began to clear away the dishes from the tables where they had been. A man and a woman and a teenage girl were sitting at a table by the window.

"Quite a gang, eh?" the man said.

"Oh, they're not so bad. It's only when they come out of the bush they get like that."

Chapter 32

Almost everyone in the bus was smoking a cigar, raising their lips and showing their white teeth as they bit into the plastic tip. They spoke with the cigars still in their mouths.

"Well," Lavigne began. "One more stop and then...a good bath, couple of beers at the tavern, pick up my old lady and..."

Lavigne did not finish. He sat back in the seat with his legs outstretched, passed one hand between his legs and massaged his groin.

Henri was silent. He took long drags on the cigar Lavigne had given him and inhaled the smoke. After smoking only half of it, he was beginning to feel dizzy.

"Wish I had a beer," he said to Lavigne.

"Yeah, me too."

"Do you ever drink at home, Gaston?"

"Me? Sure. But mostly just at Christmas and Easter. Anyway, there's hardly ever any around. You?"

"No. Once, at a wedding party held at our house."

"Ah yeah! *Calis*, do I ever get into the beer then! And it's free and everybody's in such a good mood and they don't get on your back if you're pissed."

The tires hummed and the boys smoked their cigars and looked out at the green forest and the rock cliffs that had been sliced to run the highway through. They read the words, "*Joe aime Marie*", "*Elmo était ici*", and "*Sarah suce*" written in red and orange on the rock face walls. One hour exactly after leaving the Café D'or, the bus slowed and left the highway, turning onto a semicircular driveway covered with white crushed stone. Within the boundary of the crushed stone driveway was a well-kept lawn with a small rose bush at one end and a flagpole in the centre with a Union Jack flapping in the wind.

The bus stopped in front of the two-storey frame house. The house had been freshly painted, white with green trim around the windows and the railing of the verandah on the second floor. There was a verandah on the main floor as well, with a very wide oak door and a varnished pine board inscribed with the words "Pay Office" in solid black letters. The students had been given strict instructions regarding their behaviour in the pay office. *Monsieur* Lafrance, who was the chief and only clerk there, was a very serious man who had a reputation for near genius when it came to figures. But he would not tolerate noise, shouting, laughing, swearing or any other shenanigans from the students of the Collège de Ste-Émilie.

The twenty students stepped quietly into the office and, those who could, sat down on the chairs by the wall. The others stood along the opposite wall, waiting for their names to be called, or for a chair to be liberated. It was quiet in the office, like a bank or a post office. It was clean and smelled of pencils and paper. The students could see their reflections on the varnished floor. Most of the students spent much of their time staring at the floor. It was the only way they knew how to avoid the usual chain of events that led to nothing but trouble in the end. And here, they did not want any of that.

"Henri Morin," *Monsieur* Lafrance said loudly and clearly.

Henri moved up to the counter. The clerk punched the keys on the machine and pulled on the handle several times. He ripped off the slip of white paper that had a column of figures in black ink. Some of the numbers were in red ink. He stapled the slip to a long form that was green, like the jack pine, with a black trim around its edge.

"Sign here," he said, making an X with his pencil at the beginning of a dotted line. He pointed to a row of figures. That is for unemployment and this one is tax deductions. And that one, under 'other,' is for the van."

The whole transaction had taken no more than thirty seconds. In less than one minute, *Monsieur* Lafrance handed Henri a cheque with the Company's name in large green letters at the top. "That's for three weeks less two days," the clerk said as he handed him the cheque. "The fire cheques will arrive at Washika in four days."

Henri looked at the man's well manicured fingers, large like his hands, and the glistening grey hairs combed just so over the tanned, balding head. *Monsieur* Lafrance did not smile but, when he spoke, Henri noticed that he was as serious with them as he would have been with the older, permanent employees. Money was serious business with the clerk and he treated the students as he would the other men. It was the only place where they felt as if they were being treated as adults and they treasured this fact so greatly that all of students were constantly vigilant of each other's behaviour.

Above the large desk where *Monsieur* Lafrance worked the adding machine, there was a shelf with many books, mostly thick books with leather bindings. Beside the books, on the same shelf, was a radio the likes of which Henri had never seen. The radio itself was enclosed in a polished wooden cabinet and a loudspeaker in a similar wooden cabinet sat on top of it. The knobs were of polished wood, like the cabinet, and the dial was a vertical red line that moved horizontally across a rectangle of yellow parallel lines. Along these parallel lines were numbers, written in kilocycles and megacycles, and, in gold letters, the names of countries, Sweden, France, England, Germany, and so on. Henri had never seen such a beautiful radio. He promised himself that when he had finished school and was working he would get himself a radio like that. He would sit in the dark in his room at night and listen to the peoples of the world.

When all the students had received their cheques and folded them four times and placed them neatly within the folds of their wallets, they went outside and boarded the bus. In the yard behind the house, they saw *Madame* Lafrance. She was wearing a large straw hat and tending to the vegetables in her garden. She was a plump, elderly person like her husband, and she displayed the same degree of efficiency in her garden as he did in his office. They waved to *Madame* Lafrance as the bus followed the driveway out onto the highway. The woman nodded slightly and returned to her work.

The students were quiet, speeding along the highway with only the tires humming and the wind rushing in through the open windows. They had crossed the line, the one that divided the wild and crazy *étudiants* working in the bush for the summer from the wild and crazy beer drinking, girl-chasing *étudiants* just come down from working in the bush.

The line, *Monsieur* Lafrance's pay office, was neutral territory and it always had a sobering effect on them. They were, after all, not such a bad bunch. It was only when they came out of the bush that they got like that, as *Madame* Laviolette at the Café D'or had mentioned earlier.

Chapter 33

Ste-Émilie was not a very large town. The sign at the entrance to the city said "Population 6921," but the sign was not new. The paint on its frame had already blistered and was peeling off in long, orange fingers.

"Well, now it's six thousand nine hundred and twenty one again," Lavigne smiled as they went by the sign, down the hill and onto Boulevard Carrion.

"You think there are that many?" Henri said.

"You saw the sign."

"Yes, but it's old. Older than both of us maybe."

"Some come, some go," Lavigne held up an index finger meaning to imitate Brother André at the high school. "But the numbers remain the same."

"I don't think so," Henri argued. "We are after the war. There are many old people dying."

"So?"

"Don't you see? Most of the population here is young people, like us. When we finish at the *collège*, and the girls finish at Ste-Véronique's, we leave for university, or to work in the Capital."

"There'll be more young ones, Henri. What's the matter with you?"

"Yes. And where will they come from, these young ones? From us, Gaston, and where will we be, eh?"

Lavigne twisted his face as he was in the habit of doing when he saw or heard anything strange. He lit up a cigar and handed one to Henri.

What you doing tonight?" he said.

"Oh, I don't know." Henri slipped the cigar into his shirt pocket. "You?"

"I'll call my girlfriend, of course. But after, probably La Tanière. Maybe we'll go there. Supposed to be a good band. Helène wrote me about it last time."

"They'll still be there?"

"Three weeks, she said in her letter."

"Oh, for sure then," Henri said. "I don't know what time. Late, maybe."

"Aha!" Lavigne smiled. "You have someone special in mind?"

"No, no."

"How come, Henri, we never see you with a girl?"

Henri shrugged his shoulders. It was too complicated to explain to Lavigne, or anyone else. It was all he could do just trying to understand it himself. It had taken some time before he was convinced that, for the moment, it was the only choice he had.

"It's not good for a guy, you know," Lavigne went on. "Me, I have to have a girlfriend. To me it's only natural. You better be careful, Henri. You'll finish like André in the washroom on Sundays."

Lavigne laughed and he looked down the row of seats to see if André Guy had heard him.

"Don't worry," Henri said. He wished, then, that he could describe how it had been in the room that smelled like her hair. How, after he had closed the door that day, Lise had come towards him in the dim light, and how the nipples of her breasts had rubbed against his chest when she moved in closer to slide his shirt down off his back; and when she kissed him, how her tongue worked, and he thought she would swallow his, and all the time her fingers moving like waves below where his hair fell on his neck and, after, how surprised he had been to find her hand there. He had not felt the button loosen and his blue jeans falling to the floor and then they were together on the bed. It had all been too much for him, and Lise had laughed and caressed him and told him not to worry about it. They were lying side by side on the bed when it happened: Henri kissing her breasts, and her sliding her legs between his and running her fingers along the spine of his back. He tried hard to think of something else but he could not, and then his forehead, covered in sweat, rested on her breasts and he looked down at her abdomen, round and deeply tanned, and he saw his wetness all over it. But she had been so wonderful about it that he had not felt badly for long. Soon, she was touching him again and they made love the only way Henri knew how and, after, Lise showed him more ways and they made love again, each time finishing like after a long, hard run, and Lise making soft crying sounds in her throat.

He wanted to say all of these things to Lavigne, to show him that he was just like everybody else and that he had no need, at least not more than anyone else, to stay a long time in the washroom at Washika on Sundays. He wanted to tell Lavigne how wonderful Lise was, and how he was free, and how his life had not become complicated by a "steady." But, he had promised and, although neither he nor Lise had made any sort of commitment, Henri felt that he owed her that at least. He would not share what they had with anyone. Not with Lavigne, anyway.

The bus slowed at the sign with the Company name and drove into the paved parking lot next to the sprawling white building with three floors of Company administration. The students pulled their packs from the racks and left the bus. They said, "*Salut,*" to the driver who nodded to each of them.

The students left then, shouldering their packs and walking down the streets in as many directions. Some left in groups of four or more while others walked alone. Henri walked alone, down Rue Leblanc, and when he reached the Hotel Chamberlain he opened the door to the main lobby and went inside.

Chapter 34

After walking through ashes and burned, fallen trees for sixteen days, Henri strode across the sky blue carpet in the lobby of the hotel as if he were wearing no boots at all. He was light of foot, and tanned, and he had never felt better in his life.

"Sign the back," the woman said. The woman behind the counter scanned the cheque quickly, turning it over once. "And put your address and telephone number too."

Henri scribbled his signature above the line and below it he wrote his address and telephone number. He liked the sound the pen made on the counter top.

"Could I have it all in ones?" he asked.

"Let me see," the woman examined the cheque again. "You want all ones?"

"Yes."

"Hold on then."

The woman opened a set of cupboard doors at knee level and opposite the counter. Inside was a black metal door and Henri watched her turn the bright metal dial: clockwise twice, counter clockwise once, and clockwise again. She pulled up on the handle and opened the thick, black door. When she stooped down to reach into the safe, Henri could not see inside. All he saw was the tightening of the skirt around her large hips and her white skin showing above the skirt where her blouse had slipped out.

The woman removed the elastic band and counted out the bills.

"There," she said, tapping the bills on the counter top and squaring out the edges. "Count it."

"No, that's okay," Henri trusted the woman.

"No, no," she said. "Count it. I could make a mistake. Sometimes they stick."

Henri counted out each bill and placed it on top of the previous bill, making a neat stack as he had seen the woman do. When he had finished, he placed the bills in the fold of his wallet and stuffed the rounded wallet into the back pocket of his jeans.

"*Merci Madame*," he said to the woman

"You're welcome. Good day," she answered without looking up from the typewriter. Henri had often gone to the restaurant attached to the hotel. He knew that she was typing up menus for the Sunday dinners.

Henri walked along the lobby that opened onto a cocktail bar. The customers were mere shadows seated at small tables with their backs to the walls. The girl behind the bar looked at him and the bulky sack on his back. Henri smiled at her but she did not return his smile. He looked back at the girl, at the mirror behind her and at the glass shelves upon which stood tall, slender bottles containing assorted liquors and aperitifs. He could see the back of the girl's head in the mirror and the leather band with its wooden pin that held her long hair tucked up in a bun.

At the opposite end of the bar an archway opened onto the restaurant. Henri had hoped to see some of his friends there, the ones who had found summer jobs in town or those who were just loafing away the summer in Ste-Émilie. Perhaps some of the girls he knew might be there drinking cokes on such a warm afternoon, Sylvie, maybe. The blades of a large fan suspended from the ceiling of the restaurant turned silently and slowly. Beside each booth and tacked onto the wall was a picture of an animal drawn in pen-and-ink by an artist who lived on the reservation just south of Ste-Émilie. Henri walked along the rows of tables with their ashtrays and sugar bowls and salt and pepper shakers. He looked at each of the paintings and how the signature at the bottom of each one was the same. There was no one in the restaurant. He felt disappointed, let down. There could have been at least someone to talk to. He had been away for some time. He had things to say, stories to tell. But no one was around. Going out the restaurant door, he looked back towards the counter. The woman who had cashed his cheque for him was there, still typing up the menus. She had tucked in the loose end of her blouse. She was sitting with her back straight and Henri saw her stop typing just long enough to take a drag on her cigarette.

Henri walked slowly, going along Rue Leblanc, looking at the people rushing by and the traffic moving along impatiently. Everyone was hurrying to prepare for the weekend. He stopped to look at the displays in the shop windows and noticed that, as usual, the price tags were placed in such a way that you had to go inside to inquire. At the intersection of Leblanc and Chemin de Notre-Dame, he turned to the right and descended the long, steep hill, leaning back because of the weight of his packsack. At the bottom of the hill the street followed the curve of the river, La Rivière Gens-de-Terre, the pride and joy of the people who lived in Ste-Émilie. Here, along the curve of the river, a wooden walkway had been built. Along the walkway the grass was kept well trimmed and there were trees, maple, birch, and spruce, all well spaced above the riverbank. At one point along the river, within a deep curve of its bank, the town had set aside a piece of land with picnic tables and garbage tins and a paved parking space. As Henri walked by where the metal barrels were, the sea gulls barked at him and flew out over the water. Henri wondered if any of these birds had ever been to Washika. Had they sat on boom timbers on the Cabonga waiting for the students to toss bread and cheese to them?

Along Chemin de Notre-Dame, Henri walked past the Église de St-Germain, a beautiful stone structure almost a hundred years old, and then stepped off the sidewalk onto the gravel driveway of his parents' house. He was home. Why he felt nervous, he had no idea. But he did anyway. This was his home, after all. He knew that his father was not home. The car was gone. Albert Morin was probably at the tavern. After doing all of the *commissions* madame Morin had listed for him as she did every Saturday, he needed a beer or two. Henri walked around to the rear of the house. He opened the screen door and went inside.

"Henri!" his mother cried. "Henri, I'm so glad! Come Henri, so I can give you a nice big kiss." She wiped her hands on her apron, held him with both of her hands on his cheeks and kissed him gently on the mouth. "Oh Henri, Henri," she hugged him and spun him around like a child. Looking over her shoulder, Henri saw his sister, Céline, and his brother, Gilbert, standing in the open doorway.

"Hello Monkey," he said.

"I'm not a monkey," the little girl protested.

"Ah, don't start, Henri," the woman ran her fingers through his hair. "And you, Gilbert? What's new with you, eh?"

"He's been good lately," the woman said. "Your father had to speak to him the other day. You know what that means."

"Aha! What was it this time? Snakes? Bugs? Surely not spiders again."

Gilbert was small for his eight years. He adjusted the glasses on his nose and kicked at the doorsill.

"Gilbert!" the woman raised her voice. "The flies! Close the door, will you." The boy stepped across the sill, pushing his sister ahead of him, and closed the screen door.

"No," the woman continued. "This time papa had reached the end of his patience. Imagine, during the night, we were all in bed and suddenly we hear a great noise and then a lamp falling and then my curtains in the living room, and banging against the window."

Gilbert lowered his head but, when he saw that Henri was looking at him, he smiled, showing where he had lost a second front tooth.

"Oh, I'm telling you," his mother continued. "I was terrified. Finally, I wake *papa*. He was not in a good mood, you can imagine."

"So, what was making all the noise?" Henri laughed.

"You'll never guess. I was so afraid I hid under the blankets and all I could hear was the scratching against the window glass, and your father swearing. Oh, I was so scared."

"Me too," Céline added.

"Go on," Gilbert spoke up suddenly. "You weren't even awake. Monkey."

"*Maman*!"

"Now Gilbert, don't start!"

"Anyway *maman*," Henri said. "What was it, finally?

"An owl! Can you believe it? Mother of God, an owl in the house… in the middle of the night!"

"Wonder how it got in here?"

"Don't ask, eh? You know how he is with animals. Anyway, *papa* got the bird out somehow. Oh, he was mad. Lucky for you young man, *papa* waited until later to speak to you. The air in the room was blue. Oh, he was mad."

Henri laughed. He sat down at the table opposite his mother. He pulled the plastic-tipped cigar out of his shirt pocket.

"Here, Gilbert," he said. "A cigar."

"Henri!" the woman's voice rose again.

"A joke, *maman*."

"Okay, I'll take it. Can I have the cigar, Henri? Please."

"You're too young, you know. And besides, you're liable to feed it to your fish, or your turtle or whatever else you've got up there in that zoo of yours."

"Yes, you can well call it a zoo," his mother laughed. "I'm almost afraid to make the beds in the morning. You never know what will crawl out on you. Oh, it makes me shiver, just thinking about it."

"Ah, *maman*." Gilbert looked at Henri and then at his mother. "It's not that bad. And they're all in their little boxes and everything."

"And the lizard! Eh?"

"Is it my fault? Eh? *Papa* won't buy me a real cage."

While they spoke, Céline had moved in closer and she pulled at the straps on Henri's packsack.

"What's that, Henri?" she said.

"That's your brother's packsack," the woman replied. "Now, go and play outside, my sweet. You too, Gilbert. *Papa* should be home soon."

"There's something in there, Henri?" the little girl tugged at the straps.

"My clothes. And a baby raccoon."

"Henri!"

"Where? Let me see!" Gilbert begged.

"A joke, Gilbert. There's nothing in there."

"Aw, how come?" the boy was let down.

"Ah, that stinks!" the girl cried. She had loosened the straps and slid the top cover back.

"You brought your washing, Henri." Henri recognized, by the tone of her voice, that it was not a question.

"Yes, *maman*. And that reminds me. Some of the clothes I put in a garbage bag. I don't think they can be washed. We were on a forest fire."

"Yes, I know. So, was it very bad?"

"You knew about the fire? How come?"

"A man from the Company phoned to say that you wouldn't be down. He said that the fire was very bad."

Henri smiled. He was thinking of Lavigne who had been worried because he had not answered his girlfriend's letter. It was probably she who had worried more about her precious Gaston fighting those "very bad fires."

"It was not so bad, *maman*. At least not for us."

His mother passed her hand over the tablecloth, smoothing out the long narrow plaits. For a brief moment, Henri was reminded of some other long, narrow plaits that now seemed so very far away.

"I was worried," she said. "You never know. It could be dangerous. We hear stories. *Papa* just laughs at me when I worry like that but I can't help it."

"No, no, *maman*," Henri laughed. "There's no danger. Come on!"

Henri had planned on telling her all the stories: the hours they worked, CC vomiting into his hard hat, patrolling around the island, the animals that had burned alive and him being left in the bush on that last day.

"*Maman*," he said. "Got anything to eat?"

"Poor Henri. Don't they feed you up there in the bush?"

"Sure. But, we ate at six this morning."

"Look in the fridge, there." she got up from the table and went into the dining room. "Wrapped in foil. There's a ham."

"Yes, I've found it."

Henri was hungry. He had not eaten like the others at the Café D'or. Should he call her from the upstairs phone? It was only three thirty. She might not be home. On Saturdays the girls sometimes took a walk downtown. No. Better to call her later, from a pay phone at the hotel. Maybe he would not have to call. Sylvie might be there to hear the new band. They could spend some time together.

"Henri," his mother called. She came in from the dining room. She was carrying a large brown envelope. "Henri, I've got some news for you."

Henri looked at her face, at the envelope in her hand and, suddenly, he was not hungry any more. That's it then. I'm paying for it now. It was all wrong with Lise. It was good and wonderful but it was wrong and a sin and now I'm paying. Henri's throat was dry and his stomach felt the way it had early one morning on the bus going out to the fire.

"Yes *maman*?"

"It's from the provincial exams," she said. His mother was not smiling. She removed the letter and the attached form from the envelope.

"It says here," she held the letter up to the light. She lowered the letter and looked into Henri's eyes. Henri could not look at her. More than anything at that moment, he wanted to be somewhere else. He looked at the flower patterns on his mother's apron.

"It says here, Henri," his mother repeated, "that you passed with seventy-nine percent and that you will be accepted into university!"

"*Ah oui*," Henri said, neither believing nor disbelieving. "Not bad, eh? Seventy-nine, you said?"

"Yes, Henri. Oh, we're so proud of you. *Papa* was mad at first. He said that being so close they could have made it eighty. Eighty percent sounds better than seventy-nine percent. But he's proud too, Henri. You can be sure of it. Naturally, he might not mention it. But he's very proud of you, Henri. I know that for sure. Believe me."

"Anyway, I'm glad that's over," Henri said.

There was the sudden sound of tires rolling on the gravel driveway and a car's horn honked twice.

"There's *papa*," the woman said. "I told him not to toot the horn like that."

The screen door opened and Albert Morin, father and provider, entered the kitchen carrying two large paper bags, followed by Gilbert and Céline carrying smaller bags.

"Here on the table," the woman said.

"Well," the man said, looking at Henri. "Back from the bush, eh. How was it on the fire?" The man put a large hand around Henri's neck and slid it across his shoulders. There was a smell of beer on his breath.

"Pretty good, *papa*," Henri replied.

"Pretty good? Christ, when I was on the fire..."

"Albert!" the woman looked up from the paper bags she was emptying. "The children!"

The man wiped the perspiration off his upper lip with the palm of his hand. "As I was saying," he continued. "When I was on the fire it was pretty rough. Molasses and salt pork, and not too often at that. And the flames chasing after us. And I seen men on their knees, praying, and me, I was running like hell. Christ, I was never so scared in all my life."

"Albert!" the woman stared hard at the man.

"Yes, yes. I forgot."

The man looked at Henri and brought one of his great big hands down gently on his shoulders. He winked at Henri.

"The bush's been good for you, my boy. I can see that, just looking at you."

"Yes *papa*," Henri said. He bent down to the sandwich he had been preparing. He could feel the stinging coming to his eyes and he did not want his father to see that.

Albert Morin burped loudly as he opened the refrigerator door. "Hey *maman*," he yelled back from the open door. "My beer, *maman*. I knew it. Just leave the house for a couple of hours and all the hens come around to your house and drink your beer."

"Albert! That's not true and it's not nice either. Anyway, look in the cellar. Next to the potato bin. I needed room in the fridge."

"Ah, saved. I thought that old gobbler, *Madame* Brisebois had paid herself a few."

"Albert!"

"All right, *maman*. Can't we laugh a little, eh? Henri?"

"Yes *papa*?"

"A cold one?"

Yes sure. Wait *papa*, I'll go and get them."

"*Ah sacrament*! They learn things on the fire."

"Albert!"

"Yes, yes, *maman*. I forgot. I know, I know. The children."

The man approached the table, covered in small parcels taken from the large paper bags. "Come here, *ma belle maman*," he said. "A nice big kiss for your poor tired old man."

"Get away from me," the woman laughed, stepping around to the other side of the table. "You maniac. You smell beer."

"Come here," he teased. Suddenly, he lunged across a corner of the table and locked his large hands around her waist. The woman did not pull away. Her arms went up to his shoulders and her hands caressed the sides of his face, and she kissed him with her mouth open and her fingers playing with his hair that curled at the back of his neck.

"*Maman*!" the man whispered. "The children."

The woman laughed and pushed him away. She looked at Céline and Gilbert who had been opening the parcels. The two were standing close together with their heads just barely above the table. They looked at the man and the woman with inquisitive eyes and their mouths open and waiting for whatever was supposed to happen next.

"Come on, now," the woman said to them. "What're we waiting for, eh? Help me put these in the fridge, my sweet. Gilbert, you take the cans."

Henri arrived with the beer.

"You want a glass, *papa*?"

"Oh yes."

"*Maman*, I brought an extra one for you."

"What's got into you, Henri? You know I never drink that. But, don't worry. It won't go to waste. *Papa* will see to that."

"Your mother," the man said. "Always on my case. I don't know how I manage. Tell me, Henri, you made good money on the fire?"

"I don't know."

"*Bon*. You don't know?"

"No. We haven't been paid yet."

Henri felt the lump against his right hip. "I almost forgot," he said. He opened his wallet and dropped the one hundred and seventy-eight one-dollar bills on the table.

"And that's just for the last three weeks on the sweep," he explained. "There'll be more when we get our fire pay."

"Be careful, Henri." His mother looked at the bills spread on the table. "You shouldn't leave money lying around like that."

"No, *maman*."

"How much?" his father asked.

"One seventy-eight." Henri gathered up the bills. "That's three weeks less two days. The rest is fire pay and we should be getting that in a few days."

"Not bad," the man said. "Should pay your room and board for the weekend."

"*Papa*!" the woman scolded.

"A joke, *maman*. Everybody knows you're worth more than that, eh?"

"Don't try to flatter me, old man. I see it coming."

"Now I'm an old man. Imagine!"

Henri's parents loved each other very much. It was obvious every hour of every day and it always made him feel wonderful and secure. Many times he had wanted to ask them what it was like before, when they had been younger and just starting to love each other. There was so much about loving that he did not know. His father never talked about such things. Perhaps he was just good at it naturally, without knowing anything about it. His mother rarely spoke of it and when she did it was always about someone else. None of it had been of any help to him.

Henri finished the sandwich and drank the cold beer. He gathered the one-dollar bills into a neat stack and went up to his room.

Once again there was the feeling of visiting a former classroom. It had been only five weeks but he felt a stranger in a familiar place. Everything was the same: the pictures on the wall, the map of the world, his writing desk and his bed with the thick down-filled comforter his mother had made for him and that he used both winter and summer. Still, there was a presence in the room, as if he had been there, thinking, being, only hours before. Henri pulled open one of the bureau drawers. He looked back to reassure himself that the bedroom door was closed. He slid back two heavy, wool shirts and, from beneath these, he withdrew a plain wooden box held secure with a tiny brass padlock. He sat down on the bed, with the money beside him in a pile, and held the wooden box on his thighs. Just touching the wood made him think of her. He had promised himself at Christmas that he would go on with his life, a life without her. He was young, after all, and there would be others. But there had not been others. Not like her.

Henri opened the box. He took out the magnifying glass, the Lone Ranger ring and the plum-sized chunk of Pyrite that he had, for many years, considered as precious as real gold. He removed the square of white canvas and took out the flat cigar box that had been hidden underneath. He opened the cigar box and saw the bundle tied with green fishing line just as he had left it. The letters had been tied like that for more than six months but he knew every word of every line of every page and remembered the pictures of them together, at the lake, huddled together in the tiny rowboat. He saw every smile and every hair in and out of place. There were seven pictures in all, but he had a favourite and it still hurt him, just thinking about the day he had taken the picture of her with the wind blowing her hair across her face. The two of them had chased each other through the park and he had finally caught her and thrown her to the ground covering her in the dry leaves and she, suddenly, not smiling and looking very serious, said, "I love you." And what could he say? He knew nothing of such things. "Yeah?" was all he could manage and she had pretended to be angry with him but she stood close to him and kissed him on the mouth and then she left him and ran down the street to her home. Henri had turned sixteen a few days before. The next day he was in love. Nothing else was important; nothing existed in his life but Shannon and what they had together. Imagine! Shannon Morin. They used to laugh about that. They were very happy and walked hand in hand everywhere and sat close together at the movies, with their heads touching. And Henri's mother had warned him not to get too attached and his father had made jokes about checking out the rest of the pond. And then, one day, it happened. The kiss was not as warm, they did not hold hands anymore and, at the cinema, Shannon sat with her arms folded beneath her breasts.

"I want to meet people, Henri," she said. "I want to live." And so Shannon went back to living and Henri crawled into his shell. The only time he left his home was to attend classes at the high school. He no longer went to the dances and changed his route home from school to avoid walking by the restaurant at the Hotel Chamberlain where many of the students gathered after school and on the weekends. Finally he got word that she was gone. Her parents had moved to Montréal. He found it easier then. To Henri, Montréal was far removed from his life in Ste-Émilie. As far as he was concerned, Shannon might have gone to live in Dublin or Chicago or Red Deer, Alberta. She was gone and now, perhaps, he could start again. And so, on Christmas Day, when everyone was sleeping in the afternoon, Henri re-read each letter she had written, looked at the pictures and then tied them in a bundle with a bit of green fishing line, never to be looked at again.

Henri moved the bundle to one corner of the cigar box. He placed the stack of one-dollar bills beside the other bills he had earned during his first three weeks on the sweep. He closed the cigar box, replaced the canvas, returned the lens, the ring and the chunk of rock and closed the box. Seeing the bundle of letters in the cigar box had awakened familiar feelings. One day, he thought, I'll burn them all. Someday, when I've got things straight, I'll do it.

Chapter 35

Henri sat at the table opposite his brother and sister. His father ate loudly at one end of the table while his mother rushed back and forth from the table to the stove, to the sink and back to the table.

"*Maman*!" the man said. "Sit down, will you. They can get their own."

"It's nothing," she replied.

"Ah."

"Céline, eat my sweet," she said. Then, turning to her youngest son sitting beside her, "And you too, Gilbert. No dessert, I'm warning. No one can live only on cake and ice-cream, you know."

"Why?" the boy said, pushing the glasses up on his nose.

"Albert, we're going to have to take him in for an adjustment. They're still not right."

"Sure," the man said. "Henri, pass the beets."

"*Eh, maman*? Why not?" the boy wanted to know.

"Why not what?" his mother replied. "Eat Gilbert."

"Why is it that we can't live only on cake or ice cream?"

"You can't. Ask your father, he'll tell you."

"*Papa*," the boy turned to the opposite end of the table. "Why can't nobody live only on cake or ice cream?"

"Eat," his father replied. That was the final word on the subject. Gilbert had learned to recognize the signal early in his life, as had Céline and Henri.

Henri looked up from his plate. His mother smiled. Both she and Henri knew from experience what Gilbert was not old enough to have learned. Someday, probably in the near future, Albert Morin would take him for a walk, to the park maybe, or along the shore of the Baskatong and, while they were watching the gulls flying overhead or the boats tacking along the widest part of the lake, he would casually start talking to his son about nature and animals and food chains and nutrition and finally, if the wind was right, he might answer Gilbert's question about cake and ice cream.

"*Maman*?" Henri said.

"Yes, Henri."

"Do you think I could have some money for tonight?"

The woman smiled at Henri and then she looked across the table where her husband was struggling with a chicken leg, pulling at the tendons with his teeth.

"What's that?" he said. "With all that money you threw on the table today, you want to bum money from your poor old *maman*?"

"Albert!" the woman's face grew stern

"Yes, *papa*," Henri said. "That money is for school, for the university. I can't touch that."

"That's right," his mother argued. "He'll have to buy clothes and books and who knows what."

"The tuition alone will cost several hundred. Maybe a thousand, Henri added. "Maybe, I won't go."

"Henri!" the woman scolded.

"Now, now, Bernadette." The man wiped his mouth with the back of his hand. It was not often that he called her Bernadette in front of the children. Henri remembered well the shock it had given him, when he was about Gilbert's age, to discover that his mother's real name was not "*maman*."

"It's all right, Henri," his mother said. "You save your money. It's not every young man your age that plans ahead like that. And don't worry. *Papa* will let you have some for tonight."

Albert Morin leaned over his cup and slurped the hot, steaming tea.

"That's it then," he said. "A man works hard at his trade and what does he get: a rich son who bums money off of him to go whoring around town until all hours while his poor old parents lie in their beds shortening their lives with worry."

"Albert Morin!" the woman snapped. Her face was red. Henri was afraid that she would cry. He wished that he had not spoken about the money.

"Now take your mother here," Henri's father continued, probing at his teeth with a toothpick. "She won't sleep at all. And she'll wake me several times during the night to tell me how she cannot sleep, worrying about you."

"*Maman*," Henri looked at his mother. "There's no danger. You worry too much, *maman*."

"Her mother was the same," Henri's father said.

"Yes, she did worry a lot," the woman said. "But then, she had reason to. Imagine, her innocent young daughter going out in the evenings with a wild man like you."

"Innocent!" the man chuckled.

"Albert!" the woman looked at him sternly. Henri noticed the change in his mother's eyes.

"Yes, yes, my little pigeon. Anyway, your mother was probably no worse than mine. My poor old *maman*, always worrying that I'd never amount to anything. Well, she was right about that at least."

The man laughed and poured himself a cup of tea. The dark, steaming tea fell loudly into the cup. The man looked up and saw his entire family staring at him. He felt, immediately, that now was not the time to be thinking about himself and his opinions of life. He had created a situation with his idle babble and, now, he was confronted with it and, because he loved his family more than anything in his life, even more than his life, he must make things right without hurting anyone.

"Yes," he went on, speaking over the rim of his cup. "*Maman* was right. She was always on my back about how a person alone thinks alone, and only about himself and, being that way in the world, can never amount to anything good. It's in the thinking and caring of others, she used to say, that you make something of yourself in this world."

Albert Morin lowered his cup and looked at each one of the children and, finally, his eyes found those of Bernadette, his wife.

"So, you see," he said, sucking at his teeth with his tongue. "My poor old *maman* was right. I'd be absolutely nothing at all if there were not a Henri Morin, and a Gilbert Morin, and a Céline Morin. And none of you would be anything at all if there was not a Bernadette Morin."

There, he had done it. He had saved them from the truth. Oh, it was true he loved Bernadette and the children. He loved them very much, more than life. But, he did not love life. How could he tell them? It would sound childish to speak of it, selfish even. When he was a young man, about Henri's age, he had one and only one love in his life, more a passion than anything, and that was the game of hockey. He had proven to be the best all-round hockey player on his high school team. In his final year a scout from one of the American teams had attended a game at the Ste-Émilie arena. After the game the man approached Albert, shaking his hand vigorously and spouting his disbelief that a young man with such great talent could be playing hockey in a small town league. There was glory to be had, and good money, if he would follow him to New York, to be signed up with a major farm team and then, eventually, with a major league team. Albert Morin was overcome. He could not believe his good fortune. Not only could he spend his life enjoying his great passion but he could earn a living doing it as well. He ran all the way home from the arena that night, clutching the scout's business card in his hand. It was with great pride that he informed his parents of his plans. He would be leaving for New York in one week. He would call them as soon as he was settled and he would write to them every week. And weren't they proud, Albert beamed, that their son was soon to become a major league hockey player? The answer was no, definitely and unequivocally no! Hockey is a game, his father said, flatly, not a job. New York is a big city, his mother said, where all manner of dangers lurk. Albert Morin was seventeen years old. His father had spoken. Albert tore up the business card and never played again. He did not listen to hockey games on the radio or attend games at the arena. Even later in his life, if someone turned on the television at La Cabane and there happened to be a hockey game being played, Albert would leave the tavern immediately. As he saw it, life had cheated him. But it had given him a family to love. He had that at least.

"What do you say, *papa*?" Henri said. "Would you pass me a few dollars for tonight?"

"We'll see, eh"

"Yes, *papa*," Henri was satisfied. His father had not said, no. After he had taken his short nap, Henri knew what his father's answer would be.

"And Henri," his father turned as he walked towards the living room.

"Yes *papa*?"

"Use your own razor, eh."

"Yes *papa*."

It was only seven o'clock but Henri moved quickly, picking out clean jeans and underwear, and a new sweater, a Christmas gift from an aunt in Vermont.

There were only two rules as such in the Morin household: *papa* had his nap after supper and was not to be disturbed between seven and seven-thirty, and *papa* took a shower at eight. *Papa* Morin was "available" at all other times. Bernadette was always there.

Henri shaved, feeling the thinness of the blade against his skin. After each stroke of the razor, he sloshed it around in the steaming water and tapped its handle on the edge of the sink to dislodge hair and soap. Once, as he slid the razor over his Adam's apple, he went too fast. After he had rinsed and toweled, small dabs of blood appeared on his neck.

Henri wiped the steam from the mirror. He looked at his face and the strip of sparse hair he had left beneath his nose. No, he was not ready yet. He dipped the brush into the hot water and stirred up fresh lather in the cup. He went slowly, and very carefully. Holding his upper lip rigid over his teeth, he shaved off the near mustache. Henri removed his T-shirt and trousers and slid the underwear over his chalk-white feet. He stood before the mirror on the door and looked at his tanned arms and chest and the brownish V extending upwards from his sternum to both sides of his chest. His legs were white, like his feet. He held himself sideways and sucked in his stomach and noticed that his arms were perhaps more muscular than before, but nothing else had changed. Everything looked the same.

Henri slid back the curtain and stepped into the shower.

Chapter 36

When Henri went into the kitchen his hair was still wet from the shower but he was fully dressed and ready to go out.

"You smell good, Henri," his mother said. The woman sat at the table leafing through one of the many catalogues she ordered from the Capital. She rarely purchased anything from the stores there but she found several good ideas for clothes for Gilbert and Céline, which she quickly put together on her old pedal sewing machine. "You smell just like *papa*," she laughed.

"Yes, *maman*," Henri blushed. "You think he's awake?"

"It's past seven-thirty. Anyway, he has to shower."

"I always hate to wake him."

"I know. I know. When your father and I were first married, it always frightened me. Sometimes, he would be late for work."

"He must have been really angry then."

"Oh no. He would reach for the phone without getting out of bed and he would tell them down at the office of some great catastrophe at the house and then we would lie in bed until noon and...anyway, Henri, go on. He won't say anything. Wake him if he's sleeping. If he yells at you, tell him I sent you to wake him."

Henri walked through the dining room and into the living room where his father was half hidden on the large leather-covered sofa. Walking across the carpet with his shoes on, Henri felt almost guilty, like at St-Exupèry's once when he had slipped on his cap as Father Landry and the altar boys disappeared around the altar and went into the sacristy. Henri liked to look at the books on the shelves that spanned one whole wall in the living room. Many of the books were old and had leather bindings and just looking at them brought back their unique smell. On the opposite wall was a single painting. It belonged to his father. They all liked to look at it and hear their father tell stories about it, but it was *papa*'s painting, set just above the chair where he read in the evenings after his shower. His good friend, Doctor Henri Major, from whom Henri got his name, had painted it one summer while the rest of the group was out on the lake with their lines. Doctor Major was not a very good painter but this one, as far as Albert Morin was concerned, was a masterpiece.

Anytime Albert Morin looked at the painting, he could smell the odour of hardwood smoke coming out of the tin stovepipe and he could hear the breeze whistling through the screen on the porch of the cabin and through the long, green needles high up in the white pine overlooking the lake. Along the ground and on the tarpapered roof were the orange pine needles from the previous year. He could feel them under his bare feet as he looked at the painting. Then, he was no longer in his chair or in the country of the book he had been reading. He was sitting in the sun on the dock, looking out over the water and watching the bamboo pole dip each time a trout took a bite off his worm. Behind him he could hear a garter snake sliding across the dry, sun-baked leaves on the rocky ledge. It was looking for the fish it could smell but which hung, safely out of reach, from the stub of a branch stuck into its gills and out through its mouth.

"*Papa*," Henri said softly, almost a whisper.

"Yes, yes," the man replied. "What is it?"

"I thought maybe you were sleeping."

"No. I'm awake. And now, to the shower. I have to smell nice or *maman* will kick me out of bed, eh?"

"Yes *papa*. *Papa*, about the money?"

The man sat upright on the sofa. He rubbed his face with both hands, massaging his eyebrows and the sockets of his eyes.

"Money?" he said. "Oh yes, the money you have but won't spend. Is that it?"

"Well yes, I suppose. I've got to save for school in the fall."

"Yes, yes. Your *maman*'s right. It's wise to plan ahead. Think of your future, Henri but not too much. Knock around a little. You'll be locked in your harness soon enough, my boy."

"You think so, *papa*?"

"I know it."

The man bent over his thick waist and put on his slippers.

"So," he said. "What's on for tonight?"

"I don't know. Probably, I'll go down to La Taniére. Supposed to be a good band."

"And the girls. Don't forget the girls. Anyway, after five weeks in the bush, I shouldn't have to tell you that, eh?"

"No, *Papa*. That's for sure."

"Taking anyone?"

"No. I'll just go down and see who's there."

"Ah yes. And you'll hang around the bar checking out the stock pretending not to be all that interested. And before you know it, the evening has passed and you have had too many beers and you end up staring at yourself in the mirror behind the bar, and sometimes you twist your head, or lift your glass, just to make sure that it's you."

"Was it like that, *papa*? When you were my age, did it happen like that?"

"Yes, something like that. That was before *maman*, of course. After I met *maman*, things were very different."

"Will you tell me someday? About you and *maman*?"

"Yes Henri. Some Saturday morning we'll go down to the tavern for a few. Just you and me. We'll play a little shuffleboard. It's always quiet in the morning and hardly anyone's waiting for the board. And then, maybe we'll talk about your *maman* and me, eh? But for now, Henri, be serious but not too serious. Have fun and live life while you can and be sad when it's time but don't let it eat you inside after the sad part has passed."

Henri had never heard his father speak this way. It was the longest conversation he could remember ever having with his father. What was it? He had been away. But, he had been away before. Or was it because he would be leaving home in the fall?

Albert Morin reached into his trouser pocket and pulled out a flattened bundle of paper money. He slipped off two of the bills and handed them to Henri.

"Here," he said. "Just remember, Henri, that your reputation is the most important thing in all of your social life. Apart from that, be crazy and have a good time and enjoy your life."

"Yes *papa*," Henri held up the two bills. "Thank you *papa*."

"Tomorrow!" his father waved without turning to look at him as he shuffled towards the stairs. "If you're very late, take off your shoes so as not to wake *maman*."

"Don't worry."

The man turned to look at Henri. "If you're up to all hours, bring her home for breakfast. That should give *maman* a shock, eh?"

Both Henri and his father laughed about that. Then, Henri stood alone on the thick carpet in the centre of the living room and he could hear his father going up the stairs to the bathroom. He felt the warmness of the bills that had been in the pocket of his father's trousers, and he looked at the books and the painting on the wall and the crease on the leather of the sofa where his father had lain and, for the first time in his life, he realized, truly, that someday his father would die.

Chapter 37

Norbert Lanthier: that was Sylvie's father's name. Henri had looked the phone number up before leaving the house. He had written it down on a piece of paper and placed it inside the folds of his wallet.

Outside, the air was fresh and smelled the way it always did after a storm. Henri walked quickly along the sidewalk, avoiding the puddles in the depressions of the concrete, and the reflections of the streetlights on the wet pavement. Walking like that, in the clean night air, always reminded him of a fresh start, of starting something new without attachments or ties. He thought of the Lanthier's house on Rue Deslauriers, and the slip of paper stored in his wallet. This was it then, a new beginning. And there were no ties. Sylvie and Shannon had never known each other. He was sure of that. And this would be different. Different? How would it be different? Henri stepped off the sidewalk and walked across the wet grass to the riverbank. He felt the damp coolness of the water and he could hear the swirling little eddies as they came and went going down river with the current. Different? That's how it would be different. One day at a time, like an eddy, and not looking ahead to the next one. Whatever it was that they would have would be like the river, alive and flowing, always flowing, but every day a little different with new eddies growing and disappearing, and always the river flowing.

Henri was very happy. He left the riverbank, happy, his shoes wet from the grass. He stepped onto the sidewalk and walked quickly along Chemin de Notre-Dame. Now that it was settled in his mind he was looking forward to the evening. He wanted to be with people while he was feeling this way, to drink and laugh and not be too serious. He wanted to be with Sylvie and talk to her. They would say things to each other that had only one meaning and maybe then they could love each other.

Henri ran up the climb to Rue Leblanc. The lights were numerous there, on both sides of the street, and all of the shop windows were lit up. He watched the light display on the roof of the Hotel Chamberlain. The man and the woman dancing on the roof seemed old and tired now that several of the bulbs had burned out.

When he reached Rue Pierre-Lemoine, Henri could see the club from where he stood, and "La Tanière" written in white letters across the blue canvas canopy that jutted out over the sidewalk.

There were cars parked on both sides of Rue Pierre-Lemoine, up to and past the club. The cars were still wet from the rain, and bright and shiny. Those cars directly in front of the club reflected the lights that were suspended along the verandah roof. As he approached the club, Henri could hear base notes and crashing cymbals and the screaming high notes of an electric guitar. He took one of the bills his father had given him out of his wallet and put it in his pocket. He walked quickly but, as he stepped in under the canopy, a drop of water rolled off the canvas onto his head and he felt it in his hair and then, finally, cold on his scalp.

The band had just finished a song and, as he opened the door and headed down the spiral staircase, he could hear them all, laughing and talking, some shouting across the room, and that special sound that glass makes that can only be heard in a crowded bar. There was a sudden, crisp chord slapped across a guitar and a voice saying, "one, two" and the band starting on the count of "three," loud and wild. People were on the dance floor with their arms raised, some dancing next to the bar, and the waiters held their trays above their heads going through the crowds.

There were red, blue and bright orange lights and a haze of cigarette smoke floating upwards to the low ceiling. Henri squeezed into a space at the bar, the barmaid leaned towards him and he shouted into her ear. When the young woman brought the beer, he poured it, slanting the glass like his father did. After he had drunk half the glass and sucked away the froth from his upper lip, he looked at himself in the mirror, and held up his glass; he could feel the vibrations between the glass and his fingers and thought, yes, Lavigne was right, it was an excellent band.

The beer was very cold. After the first glass, it went down smoothly and Henri was finding it difficult not to drink too fast. He smoked ready-made cigarettes from a fresh pack and peeled at the bottle label as he watched them dancing and shaking their bodies and having a good time. The girls were tanned and showing their legs each time they whirled in their light skirts, most of them barefoot on the dance floor. They wore brightly coloured cotton skirts and many of the girls had on strapless tops and often, while they were dancing, they had to pull up on the material to keep their breasts covered.

"Okay Morin, don't move!" a voice came from behind.

Henri felt a strong arm around his throat and a clenched fist pressing against the small of his back. He looked up towards the mirror, just above the rows of bottles.

"David!" Henri yelled. The fellow removed his arm and Henri turned to face him, holding out his hand. The two young men shook hands.

"Come on, slide in here," Henri said. "There's room."

Tall and muscular, David Greer was Henri's best friend. They had been friends all through high school and they had even tried to arrange it so that they would be attending the same university. But David had decided to study veterinary medicine. There was only one university with a college of veterinary medicine in the province that David could attend and Henri, thus far, had decided to attend the first university that would accept him, as he had no idea what he would study. They had also tried to arrange things so that they would be working together during the summer. David's father, Archibald Ulysses Greer, had taken care of that idea. David's father was district superintendent of Surveys and Estimates for the Company. Instead of being sent up to Washika with all of the other guys from the college, David was sent on the timber cruise along with a small group of university students, all two or three years older than he was. David was unhappy working on the cruise, as unhappy as he had been at home for most of his teenage life.

"So?" Henri said. "How did you make out? Mine came in the mail this week."

"Ah yeah. And, did you do all right?"

"Seventy-nine. You?"

"Don't know. Guess I'll have to give my old lady a call one of these days."

He had not been home. Henri had heard the others talking about it once on their way back to Washika. It was said that David Greer had not been home since his first day working on the cruise. When he came down for a weekend, he would rent a room at the hotel and wash his clothes at the laundromat on Rue St-Charles. He had not even phoned home since the beginning of the summer.

David leaned over the bar. He looked down towards the end where the girl was getting change from the cash register. She glanced his way briefly, closed the till and walked quickly to the opposite end of the bar.

"*Sacrament* I'm thirsty," David said. "What's her name?"

"Diane," Henri replied.

Before David had time to call out her name, the girl stood before him.

"Yes?" she said.

"Two beers," he said.

The girl looked along the length of the bar, towards the dance floor, and finally she looked at David.

"Look," she said. The girl was not smiling. "There are more than a dozen kinds of beer here. If you don't mind. eh?"

"Tell you what," David smiled at the girl. She had blue-green eyes, beautiful eyes, and David leaned closer and looked directly into them. "How about if I let you decide what I should drink tonight, okay?"

"*Sacrament*!" the girl swore, softly. She nodded to a guy standing behind David, waiting to be served.

"Yes?" she said.

"Okay, okay," David said. "Don't get pissed. Bring us two of those." He pointed to the half-peeled label on Henri's empty bottle.

The girl left and Henri watched her as she leaned down to open the heavy refrigerator door and bring out two beers and close the door with only a slight motion of her hand.

"Short fuse on that one, eh?" David laughed.

"She's pretty busy," Henri said.

"Yeah, I suppose. Not bad though. Give her a try?"

"No."

The girl brought the two beers and placed fresh glasses on the bar. David paid her with a twenty and, when she returned with the change, she placed the bills in front of him, flattened with the change piled on top, without looking at him. David slid the quarters and dimes off the bills.

"Here, that's for you, *ma belle*," he said.

"*Merci*," she said without looking at him.

"Hey, what's the matter?" David said.

"Nothing," she said. The girl jerked her head and the strands of coffee-brown hair bounced off her cheek. "I'm just tired. Okay?" She tossed the change into an empty beer glass on the shelf where the liquor bottles were, and left.

"They're all like that," David said. "Ask them anything and if they don't want to talk to you, or if they don't like your face, or whatever, they're just tired. They're tired, or they have a headache, or they have to go to the can. Pisses me right off."

Henri laughed. He punched David a short one to the shoulder.

"Good to see you, David," he said.

"Yeah, me too." He tilted the bottle back and drank a long time before setting it down on the bar. "That's what I needed," he said.

"You bet." Henri chuckled. "You're a regular rubby."

"Nope. You know, I can take it or leave it. Like women. I enjoy them while I can but if they're not around, well, it doesn't matter one way or the other."

"Sure Greer."

"Yeah, well, anyway, here we are and just look at them all out there. Tonight's tonight. See what happens and worry about it in the morning."

David was tall and, standing straight at the bar, his blond, wavy hair almost touched the plastic canopy that ran the full length of the bar. He drained the bottle and brought it down hard on the bar.

"Hey smiley!" he yelled towards the barmaid who was punching keys on the cash register. "Two more here."

When the girl had brought the beer, Henri brushed David's money aside and paid her. When she returned with the change, Henri tipped her generously and she smiled at him and said thank you.

"Now I understand," David said. "It's the silent types that she's after. I might have known you weren't hanging around here for nothing."

Henri laughed and tilted his glass, glancing sideways at the girl. She was talking to one of the waiters and the way they looked at each other as they spoke, him mopping his tray over and over again and looking straight into her eyes, Henri knew better. Silent or not, he was no match for the waiter and David had certainly been joking, or he had not seen how the girl's face changed when she was with her waiter. When there was a lull in business, she would lean against the bar and talk to him, looking into his eyes with their hands touching and only the bar between them.

"Well, old buddy," David said. "Think I'll mosey on down there and check out the pickings. Who knows? Maybe I'll get lucky and find some sweet young thing to play with. Won't get much from smiley here. Not with you hanging around, that's for sure."

Henri smiled. David was joking, of course. There were very few girls who could resist his charm. It was said that, at the dances, he had only to choose and the young lady was his. Even among the "steadies" his good looks did not go unnoticed, and it was only his height and firm muscles that saved him from many an unpleasant scene. David had been Henri's best friend for several years. Despite his constant teasing, which Henri knew was never malicious, David was the most likable person he had ever met. There was just one thing about him that Henri could not come to grips with. David Greer was the only person he knew who hated his father with such a passion that just to mention the man's name would transform him, the most handsome, the most popular student at the Collège de Ste-Émilie, into a silent portrait of bitterness and gloom. Henri had met his father several times while visiting David at his home. It was not long before he learned to keep his opinions to himself in the presence of Mr. Archibald Ulysses Greer. He recalled with horror one evening at the Greer home when David was explaining to him how the trade union movement had organized workers and how these unions could prevent the exploitation of the working class by the Company owners. David's father had been reading his paper in an adjoining room. He heard his son's discourse. He came directly into the room and, without uttering a single word, slapped David hard across the face with the back of his hand.

"That's for talking bullshit," he said. "And you can tell your friend to leave."

David turned towards Henri holding both palms upward as a form of apology and from the look on his face Henri could tell how badly his friend felt. It was then that his father came up from behind and whacked David a sharp slap across the back of his head.

"Insolent little bastard!" the man screamed. "Up to your room. And you, Morin, out!"

Henri watched David as he strolled in among the dancers. He was not bitter or gloomy now. Not while he was on the prowl. Henri looked over the tops of the liquor bottles and smiled at his face in the mirror. He hoisted his glass and smiled again as he thought of his father and how happy he was not to hate him.

Chapter 38

Time passes in a bar. Henri had gone over all of the days he had spent with Shannon, every word and every kiss. Then, he went over the details, the beginning of the end. He peeled enough of the label off of the bottle that the barmaid had to ask him what kind of beer he wanted. He drank them, one after another, and watched the girls, their twirling skirts and heaving breasts. Each time he went to the washroom it was a new challenge, just trying to walk straight.

Suddenly he remembered Sylvie and how things were going to be different and how wonderful it would be. But when he tried to explain to the young woman behind the bar that he would leave his beer there and would be gone only long enough to make a phone call, he realized that, in his mind, he was saying the right words but they were coming out all wrong.

"Another beer?" the young woman asked. She looked at Henri with kind eyes, and she laughed softly. "Maybe you'd better take it easy, eh?"

"Easy?" Henri replied. "You bet."

He looked across the bar, past the young woman. The bottles on the shelf swirled before his eyes. He stood up straight and stared above the tops of the bottles. The face looking back at him wore a strange, clown-like grin. Henri smiled at the face and it grinned even more, until both faces were smiling broadly. Henri held up his glass and nodded in a gesture of friendly camaraderie, which the fellow looking back at him returned in kind. Satisfied and happy in his mind, Henri returned to his slouched position at the bar while his new friend disappeared behind the bottle tops and the mirror behind them.

Henri decided not to call her. What if one of her parents answered the phone? They would guess that he had been drinking. No doubt. And if she answered, what would he say? "Oh, hello there, Sylvie. It's me, Henri Morin. I'm really drunk, you know, but if you'd still like to see me, I'm at La Tanière. The band is very good and there are lots of people here. Hurry though. I don't know how long I can stand here like this." How long would it take to say all that, answer her questions, and repeat word after word? No, better to stand here, and think; to drink, and think, and see everyone having a good time. Maybe she'll come along later. That's it. If she stops by to see me, fine. No reason to feel guilty. For sure, she will realize the shape I'm in. And I'll tell her I would have loved to see her tonight but I resisted calling her. I just didn't want to start a relationship on such a bad foot. Or was it footing? Anyway, she would understand. I know it. And then, probably, she would stay with me. And we'd lean on the bar together and talk, truly, shoulder to shoulder. Later, if I'm able to walk still, we might go down to Chemin de Notre-Dame, to the benches along the river, and watch the eddies swirling by.

"Hey Morin!" Henri felt the voice close to his ear, and he felt the moist, cold fingers squeezing his neck. "Come on, *sacrament*! Wake up."

"I'm not sleeping."

"*Sacrament*, you've been standing here with your eyes closed for ten minutes at least." Lavigne said. "Ask Diane."

The barmaid smiled. She held a folded towel in her hand. "Here," she said. "Wipe your face with this."

Henri wiped the cold, wet cloth across his face and around the back of his neck. He felt better.

"*Merci*," he said to the young woman behind the bar.

"*C'est rien*," she said. "It's nothing. You'll be okay in a while."

Henri looked at Lavigne. He looked at the way Lavigne stood leaning sideways, with one elbow on the bar. His hair was mussed and he drank from the bottle with his head tilted too far back.

"Well Gaston," Henri said. "You're looking good. How's the hunting?"

"*Sacrament*! All they want to do is dance."

"You see Sylvie Lanthier?"

"No. I've been out a while. Had to take Hélène home."

"So early?"

"You don't know her father. Thinks all that happens after midnight is between a sheet and blankets. He's so worried about her precious virginity it's a wonder he can sleep at all."

"Hélène's still a virgin?"

"Come on, Morin. We've been together almost two years."

"Were you together long before it happened?"

He was beginning to feel better. The words seemed to be coming out all right. The wet towel had helped.

"Five, six weeks," Lavigne said. "I don't know. Boy, I was glad when that night was over. *Calis*!"

Henri was feeling fine. He waved to Diane and motioned for beer for both himself and Lavigne. The young woman laughed and pulled at the handle of the refrigerator door behind the cash.

The barmaid brought the beer. She removed Henri's half-emptied bottle and glass and placed a fresh glass before him.

"*Ah bien sacrament*!" Lavigne swore. "Henri, take a look over there, in the corner."

Henri looked across the empty dance floor, to the corner behind the bandstand. There was a waiter there. He was wearing a white shirt and standing with his back to them.

"Who's there? I can't see anyone."

"Look there, where the waiter is."

Henri looked again. The waiter had left and there, sitting at a corner table along the wall, he saw her. She was beautiful with her hair down like that and sitting so straight. And sitting beside Lise, with his head almost touching hers, was Dumas Hébert.

"I knew it, *sacrament*!" Lavigne said. "I knew there was something happening with them."

"How's that?"

Henri could not think of anything else to say. What could he say? How could she do this to him? And after all she had said, about never being seen together and how they could be together only on Sundays, how she had held him close to her and whispered words in his ear. He made her feel so good, she said, and whole and normal once again.

"Come on, Henri!" Lavigne said. "Think about it: Dumas visiting the infirmary two or three times a day and, after, singing and dancing all over the cookhouse. You think it was the pills made him do that?"

Henri could not speak. He was afraid that there might be an accident. He could feel the beer rising in his throat.

"Hey Morin! What's the matter?" Lavigne said. "You okay?"

Henri leaned up against the bar. It felt so good to rest, to close his eyes. He could smell the detergent that Diane had used to wash the counter. Just five minutes, and he would be all right. Just five minutes with his head resting down like that. He felt warm and secure. Just five minutes more and he would be fine.

Chapter 39

There was nothing, not a sound or smell, not even a feeling of anything. He was not even conscious of thinking a single thought.

"Hey, come on Morin! Wake up"

Henri felt his neck, cold, his back, wet, and when he opened his eyes the bottles swirled in front of him and the coloured lights seemed suspended in a distant fog. Finally, he saw Diane standing in front of him. She was leaning back against the refrigerator door with her arms folded beneath her breasts smiling at him. He stared at the round bulges beneath her blouse, at her red smiling lips and wondered if she lived alone.

"Is it very far to walk?" he said.

"What are you talking about, Henri?" Lavigne's voice was beside him.

Henri smiled at the barmaid. He was sure she understood. He could see it in her eyes.

"Is it very far?" he repeated. He tried very hard to remain focused on her eyes.

"Where to?" the girl laughed.

"Your place."

"You mean, where I live?"

"Yes. You have an apartment?"

"Yes. About five minutes from here."

"Good. Could I take you home later? Maybe we could talk a little. You know."

The barmaid laughed. Henri grinned and almost fell backwards trying to stand up straight. He passed his hand over his mouth. His forehead felt wet and cold. He did not look at himself in the mirror.

"I'd better be going," he said. "What time is it?"

"Two-thirty," Lavigne said. "Listen Henri, you can't go home like that. Come with me."

"Oh yeah? Where to?"

"Your friend, Greer, he has a room upstairs. You can sleep there for a while."

"David?"

"Yeah. David Greer. There's a party on after closing. Come on, I'll take you up."

"Sure, okay. But wait, I want to say hello to Dumas and the nurse."

"They're gone. Almost an hour now. Besides, you already talked to the nurse."

Henri was suddenly almost sober. He looked straight into Lavigne's eyes.

"You don't remember?"

"No. Was I really bad?"

"No, not really."

"Oh yeah. So, what happened?"

"Nothing. She kept trying to speak to you but you kept turning your back on her. Funny. There she was, trying to speak to you. She even had her arms wrapped around your shoulders. And you, with your head down all the time and saying over and over, 'No, I'm never going fishing. I'm never, never going fishing.'"

"And then?"

"Then what?"

"What happened after that?"

"Dumas came around then. It was him squeezed cold water on your neck. He paid me a beer and asked me to take care of you. After that they left."

Henri stood up straight, holding on to the edge of the bar. He took several deep breaths. That always helped when he felt weak or if he thought there might be an accident with the beer rising in his throat.

"And Sylvie Lanthier? Was she here too?"

"No. I told you before," Lavigne replied.

What?"

"I haven't seen her all night."

"Oh."

There was that at least. Henri felt better. He drank a little from the bottle. He waved to the barmaid who was talking to her waiter. She did not return the wave. Henri summoned all of his strength and cleared his head of all other thoughts and started to walk away from the bar.

"Hey!" Lavigne said. "Where you going?"

"You said there's a party, didn't you?"

Chapter 40

They were all there. As Henri and Lavigne entered the room, André Guy let out a war whoop and was soon joined by Pierre Morrow and Gaston Cyr. Only St-Jean was missing.

"Where's Maurice?" Lavigne inquired.

"Busy," David Greer replied, nodding towards the bedroom door. "You next?"

"You bet. How's the beer?"

"Lots."

Lavigne went into the bathroom. The lower portion of the bathtub was covered in crushed ice with only the tops of the beer bottles showing. Lavigne brought out two bottles, sweating from the ice and the heat of the room. He opened them using the handle of the dresser drawer and handed one of the bottles to Henri.

"Want to go after me, Henri?" he said.

"Where's that?"

"Do you want to go after me? Or would you like to go first? It's okay with me."

"Go where?"

"I didn't tell you? I thought you knew. Remember Francine Villeneuve?"

"Sure."

"Well, she's in the next room."

"Francine Villeneuve. You mean Francine Villeneuve who used to live next door to your place?"

"That's her. Look, if you want, I'll let you go first."

"No, that's okay. You go ahead."

Lavigne grinned. He tilted back his bottle and swallowed several times. When he had finished he tossed the bottle into the empty case on the floor.

"Ready for another?" he said.

"No, I'm okay," Henri replied. He watched the door to the adjoining room. Who was Francine with now? Did she still look the same? Actually, he had never seen her naked. It had been dark in the car and, then, she had not really taken all her clothes off. The clothes had just been slid over and up here and there so he could touch her. He remembered how soft she was, that one hair near the nipple of her breast, and how she had begun to shudder and let out little puppy moans when he had moved his hand up in between her legs. But she had a steady boyfriend not long after that and, shortly afterwards, her family moved to the Capital and he never saw her again.

Lavigne opened a window. It was warm in the room and most of the boys sat on the bed with their shirts off, smoking and playing poker, and waiting their turn. David Greer sat in a bright orange lazy boy, drinking from a large pewter mug. He kept changing the station on the radio beside the chair and, whenever he found a good rock 'n' roll tune, he would turn the volume up full. Henri sat on the floor, next to the lazy boy.

"How is she?" he said. David winked and raised his mug in recognition.

"How is she?" Henri repeated.

David turned down the volume. "What's that?" he said.

"She pretty hot?"

"You bet."

"How long she been up here?"

"This afternoon." David laughed. He leaned back in the chair and put the mug to his lips. The beer leaked out over his chin and down inside his shirt.

"You mean, when I met you at the bar earlier, she was up here all that time?"

"Yup"

"Why didn't you tell me?"

"You were too busy hustling smiley then. And besides, she was out cold. We went on a bit of a bender together this afternoon. I just woke up when you saw me down at the bar."

"How is she anyway?"

"Go in and find out. Christ, you want me to take you in by the hand?"

"It's just that I used to know her and everything."

"So did I, old buddy. So did I."

The door to the adjoining room opened and Maurice St-Jean came out carrying his shirt in his hand. The fellows on the bed gave a cheer and all of them threw their cards onto the centre of the bed.

"Next," St-Jean grinned. He went into the bathroom and closed the door behind him.

The boys looked at each other. Lavigne got up off the bed.

"Everyone go yet?" he said.

The fellows nodded. All had been there and back.

"Maybe Morrow," André Guy said. "He was only three minutes. Maybe he wants to go a second round."

The boys laughed. Morrow blushed and tilted back his beer. He drank quickly and then began coughing violently.

"What about you, Henri?" Lavigne said.

"Go ahead," Henri said. He leaned against the wall and watched as Lavigne entered the dimly lit room and closed the door behind him. He had hoped to get a glimpse of her but he had not been able to see inside. He would ask St-Jean about her and, if she was all right by St-Jean, he would be next.

Henri lay sideways on the blue carpet. He was unable to stay sitting upright for long, even leaning against the wall. As he lay there, smelling the musty carpet, he could hear the rock 'n' roll music and the boys swearing, someone opening a bottle on the dresser drawer handle and cheering at the end of each hand and then the slapping sound of the cards being shuffled once again.

Chapter 41

The first thing was the smell of roast turkey. Henri raised his head off the pillow and the pain shot from his forehead across his skull to the back of his head. He tried to concentrate: to not smell the turkey and not move his head on the pillow. But the odour of turkey fat bubbling around the browning bird lingered and haunted him. He was afraid that there would be an accident. Just the thought of vomit soaked blankets on his bed was too much. His mother would not accept that. Slowly, Henri slid his feet from beneath the blankets and angled them downwards until they touched the floor. He stood up, letting the blankets fall back upon the bed, and for a brief moment, he held on to the bureau. He tried not to think about the turkey and how the sides of his head seemed to expand with each beat of his heart. If he did not think of these things, it was not so bad. Now, all he had to do was make it to the bathroom without moving a muscle or opening his mouth.

He made it in time. Just. He turned the faucet on full so that no one could hear. After he had cleaned up the carpet around the toilet bowl, Henri sprayed the room with lilac from a purple can. He lay on his back on the carpet and closed his eyes. It was cool on the floor. He listened to the water running into the sink. A chill came over his chest. The sound of running water had changed and he felt its coldness on his legs as the water flowed over the edge of the basin onto the floor. He turned the faucet off and watched as the water spiraled and disappeared into the blackness of the drainpipe. He reached behind him and turned the cold water on full. The loud rain shower noise of water striking the walls of the metal shower was what he needed. He went over to the toilet bowl once again. Kneeling down in front of the bowl, Henri tickled the back of his throat with an index finger. The liquid was a pale yellow and had a bitter taste but, afterwards, he felt much better.

He showered, combed his hair and brushed his teeth a second time. He looked in the mirror at the red veins on the whites of his eyes. By the time he had dressed and picked up his clothes from the night before, which he had found in a pile on the floor by his bed, Henri was not feeling too badly. If he did not have to enter the kitchen and face his parents and smell the turkey fat bubbling in the oven, he would not do badly at all.

"Hurry Henri," his mother called. "We'll be late. *Papa* is waiting in the car."

"Yes *maman*. Is there any coke left in the fridge?"

"Henri! Your teeth. There's some nice cold orange juice. But Hurry!"

"Yes, Yes. I'm coming."

Henri opened the refrigerator door and felt its coolness on his face, but seeing a half-eaten dish of rice pudding with raisins made him feel hot all over. He closed his eyes and held his head down as he brought out the pitcher of orange juice. He drank one glass and filled a second. There was an acrid taste in his mouth and, after the second glass, the tangy freshness of the toothpaste vanished. The sour taste of bile seemed to override any efforts he made to mask his early morning vomit.

Outside, they were waiting for him in the car. Céline and Gilbert were in the back and his mother sat close to her husband, leaving a place for Henri. The motor was running and the passenger door had been left open. Henri got in and closed the door. He lowered the window and tried not to breathe, or look at his mother, or the pavement moving past him as his father drove them away from their home.

"You were very late, Henri," his mother said.

"Yes, I suppose."

"And what does that mean?" she turned to look at him.

"*Maman*, leave him alone, won't you," Henri's father interrupted her. "Can't you see he's feeling badly?"

"Yes, well I still think that it wasn't an hour to be coming home. And the noise those boys made. And, Henri, tell me, who is Francine?"

"Oh, just a girl we met." So, that was it. The fellows had driven him home. And Francine. What happened with her? Had he gone into the room after Lavigne? Or was it before Lavigne? And how did they bring him home? None of them had a car.

"*Maman*!" Céline cried. "Make Henri close the window."

"What's the matter, my pet? Oh, look at your hair. Henri, close the window."

"It's warm, *maman*." Henri spoke without opening his mouth. He looked out at the pavement. He stared at the pavement up ahead but never just below the side of the car.

"Just a little, Henri." His mother leaned over the seat, combed the little girl's hair back and replaced the pink barrettes.

Henri rolled the glass halfway up and leaned his head against it. The pavement on Chemin de Notre-Dame was old like cobblestone and the vibrating window glass made his head ache even more. He wondered, as they drove on the hot, black pavement, why they bothered to drive to a church at the other end of town when their house was almost directly in front of the Église de St-Germain. But it was his mother's church, where she had attended mass as a young girl and where she was married and where, no doubt, her funeral mass would be said. Henri's father had no special church of his own. He drove them all to St-Exupéry's every Sunday. He led them up towards the front of the church, sat on the outside next to the aisle, furnished all of them with collection money, and hardly ever fell asleep during the service. There had been an understanding between Albert Morin and his wife, a pact made earlier in their married life. He would never complain or comment on his wife's devotion to the church if she would refrain from criticizing his Saturday morning visits to La Cabane where he shared a few quarts with his friends and played shuffleboard and told lies about his fishing trips. It was a wonderful arrangement and meant the end of all family troubles caused by *Monsieur* Morin's love of ale.

When they reached St-Exupéry's Henri saw his friends standing around the parked cars in front of the church. They were leaning against the hood of a grey Chevrolet and smoking. Both Lavigne and David Greer were wearing sunglasses.

"*Maman*," Henri said. "I'll be there in a minute. I want to talk to the guys. Okay?"

"You won't be sitting with us?"

"*Maman*!"

"Oh, all right. But don't be talking during mass. Remember how Father Landry stopped the mass on account of that young Lavigne boy."

"Yes *maman*. Don't worry."

Henri lit a cigarette as he walked over towards his friends. The cigarette tasted different. It smelled like La Tanière, and beer. He could still smell the odour of vomit on his fingers. Perhaps it was just lingering in his nose.

"Hey Morin!" Lavigne smiled. "How you feeling this morning?"

"Not bad. You?"

"Very best. You're looking better. Eh Maurice? What do you think?"

"At least he's walking," St-Jean grinned.

"Francine's really pissed about you, Henri," Lavigne said.

"Yeah?"

"You don't remember?"

"A bit vague," Henri lied.

"After I'd finished," Lavigne began. "You were sleeping on the floor. I woke you up and you went in with Francine. Not long after, we hear her yelling for you to get off and screaming for David."

"Ah yeah?" Henri said. It was all he dared to say. Already he had said too much. He knew Lavigne and how well he could handle his beer and still remember all the details the next day. He also knew how he loved to add new ones of his own.

"You remember going into the room, don't you?" Lavigne looked at the others.

"Sure. I remember that."

"And after?"

"Well, not too much. In fact, nothing at all."

"Okay Gaston, he's suffered enough," St-Jean said. He moved in between Henri and Lavigne. He put his hand on Henri's shoulder.

"You're not such a bad guy, Henri," he said. "So we'll tell you how it all happened."

"Don't forget about the pants," Lavigne interrupted.

"It's true," St-Jean continued. "You went in after Gaston. Not long after, two or three minutes maybe, we hear Francine screaming. David went in first and we could hear him laughing and Francine yelling at him and, finally, we all went in. And there you were, with your pants down to your knees and your shoes still on, and lying across Francine's naked body and snoring like you do at Washika."

"Did you at least have time to get it in, Henri?" Morrow laughed.

"I wouldn't talk if I was you," Lavigne said. "Just wait until the doctor gets at you."

"I'll be all right in a couple of days," Morrow said. "It's a little better already."

"What's the matter with him?" Henri asked.

"He got a good one off of Francine," Lavigne began. "Should see it, Henri. Blood coming off the end and everything."

The church doors were open and the boys, alone among the parked cars, could hear the organ music.

"We'd better get in," Gaston Cyr warned. "Come on, Pierre, let's go."

Gaston Cyr and Pierre Morrow left the group, followed by André Guy who had said nothing all morning.

"It's true then?" Henri said. "About Pierre, I mean."

"Sure, we all saw it," Lavigne said. "He showed everybody the bleeding, he was so scared."

"It was his first," St-Jean added. "And he was in such a hurry. Poor Francine, must have hurt her too. Probably he ripped something."

"Needn't worry about Francine," David Greer spoke up. "She may be a whore but she's clean at least."

Henri felt sorry for Francine. It made him feel bad to hear David call her a whore. She had shared an evening with them. So what if she was naked, and caressed and made love to them? Was that so wrong? What harm had she done to them?

"She's not a whore," Henri said.

"She's a hundred and fifty dollars richer this morning, lying in my bed, in my hotel room, eating breakfast on my bill and taking the bus back to the Capital tonight at my expense," David replied. "That doesn't make her Joan of Arc, does it?"

Henri had forgotten about the money. He had paid his share like the rest of them. He had paid only to drop his trousers and fall asleep across her naked body. He could not even remember seeing her naked. Henri felt cheated somehow. Still, somewhere in the back of his mind, he felt sorry for her. He didn't know why but he knew deep down that he had been raised that way. That there was some good in every person and, if only the bad showed, then there must be a damned good reason for that.

"Come on, let's go," Henri said. "We don't want Father Landry yelling at us again this morning."

Chapter 42

Henri lay on his back. He lay collapsed and stretched out on the swinging couch on the verandah. He could almost feel the heat rising from the pavement in front of the house. Two houses down, he could hear *Madame* Laviolette putting the metal cover in place on the garbage can and speaking sharply to Ponpon, *Monsieur* Lévesque's cat from across the street. The garbage was picked up on Monday mornings but *Madame* Laviolette always put her garbage can out right after the Sunday noon meal. Ponpon was orange with one ear tip missing and blind in one eye. He had been raiding *Madame* Laviolette's garbage can since he was a kitten.

Henri felt better. The taste of vomit was gone and his stomach was full: turkey and potatoes and beets with raisin buns, and hot rhubarb pie with ice cream for dessert. And his friends had cleared up things with him after mass. Yes, it was true that he had fallen asleep on top of Francine's naked body but he had not made love to her. She had not charged him and David said that she seemed put out about him not making love to her. She had always had a thing about Henri. And finally, the guys had thrown their change onto the bed and, with Henri's share that Francine had donated, they came up with enough to hire a taxi as far as Henri's house. They had all boarded the taxi, of course, and when they arrived, Lavigne and St-Jean each holding one arm, led him along the driveway to the back door. That was when they had awakened his mother. St-Jean and Lavigne struggled with Henri, trying to hold him up against the door while they searched for the key. Not far off, somewhere between the sidewalk and the back door to the house, David Greer and André Guy and Morrow and Gaston Cyr shouted moral support. During this time it was Morrow that Henri's mother heard yelling something about Francine.

Henri felt better now that it was cleared up. He thought about Lise Archambault and he tried to picture the nurse and Dumas naked together. He could not. Tomorrow, he would have to face Dumas in the cookhouse. How much would Lise have told him? His behaviour at the bar was an embarrassment in any case. If Dumas knew about his affair with the nurse he would simply consider Henri to be a poor loser, a very immature young man at best. If he knew nothing of the affair, he might simply conclude that Henri was lacking in experience when it came to drinking and that he might do some growing up before indulging in public places.

Perhaps the cook would be right about that. Henri thought about the blank spaces, the parts that were completely erased from his memory and, that, even after the boys described every detail. This frightened him as nothing had frightened him before. Was this to happen every time that he put back a few beers? Or was it, in fact more than just a few? Maybe he should quit. Never touch the stuff again. Ever. But then what? And his friends, would they still be there? Lavigne and the others would tap him on the shoulder and some would say, "Yes Morin, you're doing the right thing". And then they would leave him and head down to La Tanière, to the drinking and dancing and the girls with swirling skirts and heaving breasts. No. It was too much. He was too young, much too young to give up all that. He would learn to control it, maybe. There must be a way to do that. He would talk to his father about it some Saturday morning at the tavern. He was too young. There was too much life to be enjoyed before growing old and wise. He wanted to be wild and crazy while he was still young. Later, much later, he would be wise and think deep thoughts and be good to himself.

Henri soon fell asleep on the couch on the front verandah. A loud honking pestered him and he tried putting the noise out of his mind. The sun was hot on his face and he rolled over, facing the back of the couch. He smelled the warm canvas covering and he listened to the metal springs stretching as he shifted his position on the couch. But the other sound was still there. The honking would not go away.

"Hey Morin, you alive?" someone called from the street. This was followed by the honking sound once again.

The noise was unbearable. Henri sat upright on the couch. He looked out from the verandah, across the lawn and the sidewalk to the other side of the street. Everyone was staring at him. They were all there. Lavigne was at the wheel of his father's car. Beside him were André Guy and St-Jean. Gaston Cyr and Morrow were in the back seat and they all had a beer in their hand.

"Come on, Henri, let's go," Lavigne shouted.

"Be just a minute," Henri replied.

Henri rushed up to the bathroom where he splashed cold water on his face and combed his hair and brushed his teeth. He scraped vigorously across his tongue with the brush.

Downstairs, in the kitchen, his mother swayed in the rocking chair by the window.

"Is that that young Lavigne honking outside, Henri?" his mother looked up from her magazine. "He's going to wake papa."

"Yes *maman*," Henri checked his hair a last time in the mirror by the door. "I probably won't be in for supper, *maman*."

"Henri! You won't be back for another three weeks."

"Yes, I know."

"Well then, wouldn't you like to spend some time with us before you leave?"

The woman looked out the window at nothing in particular. Henri noticed a sudden moistness in her eyes.

"*Maman*," he said, "*Papa* is sleeping on the couch, Gilbert and Céline are who knows where and you always read your missionary magazine on Sunday afternoon. I'll be back early enough. I just want to be with the guys a little while."

"You're with them all the time."

"Yes *maman*, but we won't be in town for another three weeks. Okay?"

How could he explain it to her? It was like his father trying to explain his reasons for going to La Cabane every Saturday morning. His father did not wish to insult his woman or hurt her feelings by coming right out and saying that her company alone did not meet his needs completely. No, instead he went on about how he must speak to Albert Desforges about a new type of fishing reel he had read about in a magazine, or how he had promised Jean-Marie Lavigne, Gaston's father, that he would show him how to get to Ewen Lake where the trout were as large as walleye and more vicious than northern pike.

Now, it was Henri's turn. Poor *maman*. Both father and son loved the woman very much. They loved her so much that they could not tell her the truth, at least not the full truth.

"*Maman*," Henri began. "We're just driving over to St-Émillion to see the rides. The circus people arrived there on Friday and they say that there's a whole new bunch of rides. Okay?"

It was a lie. But it was a good one. And she would feel better if she knew where he was and what he was doing.

"Yes, yes. Go ahead," the woman said. "But watch out for that young Lavigne, if he's anything like his father."

"*Maman*!"

"All right, but don't be late."

Henri could hear the music from the car radio as he crossed the street. The rear door was open and there was a case of beer on the floor.

"What took you so long?" Lavigne snapped. He raced the engine as Henri got into the car.

"Take it easy," Henri said. "My old lady's probably watching at the window."

"Catch it for last night, Henri?" St-Jean inquired. He opened a bottle using the under part of the dashboard and held it up for Henri.

"No," Henri said. "Where we headed?" He took the bottle from St-Jean.

"St-Émillion," Lavigne said. "The circus is in town and they say that there are all new rides."

"*Ah bien, sacrament*!" Henri swore softly.

They stared at him. They had never heard him swear before, not even when he was drunk.

"What's happening to you?" Lavigne turned to look at him.

"It's nothing. Let's drive around town first, eh?"

It wasn't too late. Although the town would be deserted like every other Sunday afternoon, Henri remembered hearing that Sylvie's father had sold their cottage at Lac Sirois and so she might be out walking with some of the girls from her school.

"Oh no," Lavigne said. He turned north, and away from Ste-Émilie towards St-Émillion. "I told Hélène I wasn't going out today. If she sees me driving around town, I'm dead."

Henri shrugged. He lifted the bottle and swallowed several times before putting it down. So, this is what it's all about, he thought. There are those who have and those that do not. After his talk with Brother André at the high school, Henri knew that he belonged to the latter group. Perhaps he would spend his whole life that way, watching those who have and seeing them expend enormous amounts of energy avoiding what he, and others like him, strove for each and every day. Henri had better grades than Lavigne, he knew all the species of logs that they tossed into the water, just from the bark, and he could play the harmonica and dance. He was a fairly decent dancer and he even considered himself more intelligent than his friend Lavigne. But, Lavigne was a 'have,' just like David Greer was a 'have,' and all of those for whom life comes easy, just as naturally as breathing. They were all 'haves' but Henri knew, deep down inside, that he was not a 'have,' that he was a 'have-not' as Brother André defined it. There was perhaps hope that he might be like David or Lavigne and all of the others, that he might someday escape the confines of the 'have-nots' but Henri could not foresee that happening soon.

Chapter 43

The man at the gate was wearing a straw hat, just like the one Emmett Cronier wore at the truck scales at Washika. The fluffy blue feathers waved in the breeze of the passing cars.

"Yes sir! Yes sir!" the man said cheerfully. "And how many are we here, eh?"

Lavigne was wearing dark sunglasses. He looked directly at the man but did not answer him. The boys sat in the car with beers between their legs and stared straight ahead through the windshield.

"Let's see now," the man bent down to see inside the car. "One, two, three…all right. Six at fifty cents, that'll be three dollars even my young man."

Lavigne fished the bills out of his shirt pocket and paid the man without speaking to him. Before the man had time to back away from the car, Lavigne tapped the accelerator to the floor and Henri could feel the wheels spinning beneath him. When he looked back he could just make out the man waving his little straw hat in a cloud of dust.

"Hey Gaston," Henri asked. "You know that guy?"

"Yeah."

"So, who is he anyway?"

"He's the asshole who raped Francine Villeneuve behind the arena."

Henri remembered the incident well. They, all six of them, had been with Francine only a few hours earlier. Lavigne had parked by the river, where the town had set up picnic tables and a paved parking space. There were several other cars parked there and the tables were crowded with young students and their girlfriends. Lavigne and the boys sat in the car talking to Francine as she stood by the car window. She was wearing bright red shorts and her hair was let down so that it flowed past the small of her back. Every time she jerked her head to push the hair away from her face, her blouse opened wider, as did the eyes of Lavigne and the other boys in the car, even though they pretended not to notice. But, there was an understanding among them, tonight would not be the night. Tonight they would just talk and have fun. So, after some friendly banter, Francine left them to continue her walk. She wanted to get home before dark. That's when it happened. Instead of going up Rue Gendron and then on to Rue du Gap, Francine cut through the bushes along the east side of the arena. Arthur Lauzon had spotted her earlier as she walked towards the river. He waited for more than an hour. It was almost dark when Francine entered the bushes. With the high walls of the arena and the thick bushes no one could hear her screams, not even the gang at the river. Arthur Lauzon was a big man and the whole affair was over in a matter of minutes. The police were called and Francine was examined at the emergency ward. The last words she remembered hearing the examining physician saying to her parents was, "Well, *Madame* Villeneuve, I'm sorry to say this but there are no signs of sperm and no bruises of any kind on her body." That was the end of the investigation. But Francine knew, and so did all of her friends at school. Lavigne and the guys felt bad about the whole affair and, afterwards, became overtly protective of her. They were with her constantly and they continued to do so until the day she started dating a young man in town, and then she moved to the Capital with her parents.

Lavigne drove the car behind an enormous canvas tent and cut the engine. Each of the boys opened another beer. They drank the beer quickly and looked out from the car at the long wall of canvas. They tried to stay calm and drink their beer slowly but they were excited. None of them would admit to being excited, but they were. There was so much to do and so little time before they would be in the bus again, headed for Washika. Mingled with the sounds of engines revving and pipe music from the merry-go-round, they could hear the barkers calling and the girls screaming on the rides. There were bells ringing and rifle shots and the sounds of baseballs hitting canvas and the rapid tic-tic-ticking of the wheels of fortune.

"Well, what do you say?" Henri drained the bottle and slid it into the case. "Think we should have a look?"

"I don't know," Lavigne said. "Probably same old junk as last year."

"Yeah," Morrow added. "Remember that guy wrestling the bear. Poor bear must have been at least a hundred years old."

"Well, we're here anyway," St-Jean argued. "We might as well look around."

"Okay, okay!" Lavigne held his hands up. "We'll have a look around. You'd think you guys never seen a circus before."

The guys downed their beer and left the car. They walked along the canvas wall ducking under each anchor rope as they came to it. They passed through a narrow alleyway between two tents and out onto the main flow of traffic with people walking in both directions. Young men and women walking hand in hand, some with their arms around their woman's shoulders, carrying balloons and bamboo canes with miniature monkeys tied to them; young girls cuddled stuffed teddy bears and tall lanky fellows wore hats like the ticket man who raped Francine when she was barely sixteen years old. Children were everywhere, dodging adults and racing to and from the rides. There were fellows walking unsteadily and hanging onto counters and staring at the girls serving candy floss and popcorn, so beautiful under the lights that showed their breasts through their white cotton T-shirts.

Lavigne and the guys strolled between the rows of kiosks, continuing past the tent where the smell of frying hamburgers and onions made it difficult. They stopped by the booth with enormous orange juice coolers with droplets of sweat forming on the outside. They ordered drinks, served in tall paper cups, and left.

"Try your luck! Always a winner. Step right up. Three shots for a quarter!" The young woman held a dozen of the wooden rings on her arm. She held three separately in one hand and waved them above her head. "Step right up!" she called. "Three for a quarter. Pick your prize!"

Henri watched her walking around inside the booth, accepting bills and handing back change from a carpenter's apron before placing three wooden rings in the prospect's hand. Her legs were chocolate brown and, when she walked, her muscles showed just below the torn edge of her blue-jean cutoffs. Above, she wore a purple blouse with two of the four buttons undone. She wore no shoes and her feet were tanned, like her thighs. After everyone had tossed the rings and failed to place them around a prize on the floor, the girl walked around the blue satin sheet where the prizes lay, picking up the rings. Stepping lightly on the satin sheet, she would bend down over the prizes and retrieve all of the rings, calling loudly, "Step right up folks. Winner every time. Three for a quarter. Step right up!"

They walked along the main thoroughfare, between the rows of kiosks: Lavigne, St-Jean, and Henri, followed by André Guy, Cyr, and Morrow behind them. If Lavigne, St-Jean or Henri stopped to look at something, the other three were quick to mimic the gesture.

"Hey you guys," Morrow called from behind. "Look at that."

He pointed to several glass cases on a platform. All of the cases and platforms were covered by a canvas roof with light bulbs dangling from wires stretched above the cases. Inside the glass cases were miniature mechanical shovels. People stood in front of the cases, moving small rods that maneuvered the shovels. They moved the shovels back and forth, and opened and closed the shovels trying to pick up the quarters and silver dollars lining the bottom of each case.

"Morrow," Lavigne moaned. "That's as old as the earth."

The three up front continued on ahead, leaving Morrow and Gaston Cyr alone in the centre of the thoroughfare. André Guy stood between the two groups, undecided and looking back.

Chapter 44

Henri knew *Monsieur* Gaetan Lafond. He had spent hours watching *Monsieur* Lafond working a plane against a piece of pine, fitting it in place and returning it to the bench for a few more strokes of the long jack plane. Henri was with the man constantly: in the basement, up a ladder along the water troughs, standing on the scaffold as the man replaced window stops and trims. That was the summer his parents had hired *Monsieur* Lafond to refurbish the house. Henri watched his every move, and he loved how the man handled the wood and his tools and the soft way he spoke when Henri pestered him with questions.

After *Monsieur* Lafond had completed the renovations, Henri played with the short pieces of wood left over and piled neatly by the furnace in the basement. Henri felt the wood edge with his hands, and sighted along it with one eye closed; sliding his father's block plane along the grain and always doing his best to imitate *Monsieur* Lafond in the minutest detail. It was only at mealtime, or when he slept, that Henri could be seen without a wooden toothpick sticking out of the corner of his mouth.

Henri and the boys stood in the field, downhill from where the circus was. They stood with their arms folded, leaning back on one leg, and watching the tractors go by. The contestants drove by with raised plows gleaming in the sun, the black earth unfolding as they went forward with the blades lowered and turning furrow onto furrow. At the end of the square allotted each contestant, friends and neighbours stood with arms crossed, beer in their hand, and the visors of their caps low on their faces. And they all had a word to say.

"Atta boy, Gus!"

"Hold her steady, Ray!"

"Raise her some there, Pete. Jesus, them's pretty furrows!"

And while the tractors worked and the drivers strained their necks back and worked the lever and adjusted the height of their plows, a white-haired gentleman walked among the allotted squares, clipboard in hand. He sighted along the rows and jotted down notes, not once speaking to the drivers or the neighbours and friends at the ends of the furrows.

A short, stocky man wearing new overalls and a checkered shirt with the sleeves rolled just so was moving forward with the blades of his plow digging into the black earth. The tractor moved slowly but steadily and the man kept his left hand on the wheel and his right on the fender. His eyes scanned the furrows constantly and, as he worked, the small wooden toothpick wiggled steadily at the corner of his mouth.

"That's *Monsieur* Lafond," Henri pointed to the red tractor going by.

"Yeah?" Lavigne said.

"Yeah. You should see the tools he has. He fixed up our house a few summers ago."

The judge approached the square as *Monsieur* Lafond was finishing up. He walked back and forth, knelt on one knee. He jotted down more notes. He took out a measuring tape from his hip pocket and checked the width of the furrow.

Henri waved to *Monsieur* Lafond. "*Salut Monsieur Lafond*!" he yelled.

The man waved to Henri and smiled, and held the toothpick in the corner of his mouth.

"See?" Henri said.

"Yeah, okay," Lavigne said. "Hey, let's go see the bulls."

"I want to see who wins," Henri stated, flatly.

"Ah, come on. We can find out later."

"Yeah," Morrow added. "Anyway, the results will be in the paper."

Henri looked at the small gathering of people and the freshly plowed squares of black soil with the long, narrow furrows, damp and shiny. There were not many spectators for the County Fair Plowing Contest, about as many spectators as contestants. Henri felt bad about leaving. He had learned so much from *Monsieur* Lafond. And the man had been so kind to him.

The boys left then, heading back towards the circus tents, while the people strolled back and forth all along the thoroughfare. There the soundscape consisted of barkers, and merry-go-round music, screaming young voices, and the tic-tic-ticking of the wheels of fortune.

Chapter 45

The cattle barn was a long, whitewashed building at the north end of the circus thoroughfare. They could feel the warmth as they entered. Once their eyes adjusted to the dim light they could see the brighter light outside through the open doorway at the far end of the building. Lavigne strutted ahead of the others, shuffling his feet in the thick layer of wood shavings He liked the smell of the shavings and the sounds the cattle made, chewing constantly and eyeing them intently as they went by each stall. There were Hereford, Holstein, Simmental and Charolais bulls, some with horns and others with their horns burned short. Some of the bulls had stainless steel rings through their noses with short lengths of chain attached to discourage them from jumping fences when their neighbours' cows were feeling in a loving way.

Henri went closer to one of the stalls. He held his hand up between the rails and the enormous nose approached, its large round nostrils, pink and moist and vibrating with each curious sniff. Suddenly, the long, thick tongue slid along his hand. Henri pulled back. The animal stared at him, eye to eye, swaying its head sideways and shifting its weight from left to right. It looked at Henri, long and steadily, and Henri looked back into its large, dark eyes and, for the first time in his life, he did not feel the fear or anxiety that he had so often felt during similar encounters with members of his own species.

Outside, at the other end of the cattle barn, was a long row of wooden stalls with slanted, shingle-covered roofs. In each stall, the earth was covered with a thick layer of shavings. The guys walked along the row of stalls, sticking their heads in and, as they did so, each animal backed into a corner of its stall.

"Hey you guys!" Lavigne called.

The boys turned. For a second, they saw Lavigne leaning over the door of one of the stalls. And then, he was gone.

"*Sacrament*!" they heard him scream.

The guys ran towards the stall. As they ran past the stall fronts, the sheep and goats pranced nervously to and fro. Just as they reached the stall door where Lavigne was last seen, he stood up, leaning his body outward over the stall door. There were shavings in his hair, and on the right knee of his blue jeans was a dark brown stain. In a corner of the stall, a billy goat stood stiffly with his head down and his beautifully curved horns lowered.

"Come on, Gaston," St-Jean said. "Let's go have a beer before that fellow gets ideas. You never know, with that smell on you."

Lavigne turned and stared at the goat. It was standing in the corner ready for the attack. Lavigne moved quickly, forward and down, and he reached out with his left hand, making a grab for the goat's beard. But he wasn't quite swift enough. He missed the beard by inches. The goat charged. Lavigne turned and lunged towards the open upper-half of the stall door. With his hands on the edge of the lower door, he heaved upwards and let his head and trunk roll downwards to the ground below. There was a crash of horn against boards as Lavigne's legs came up and over the stall door. Lavigne was safe. Inside, the goat charged the walls angrily as the guys looked in at him.

"Okay," Lavigne said, shaking the shavings from his hair. "Now, let's go for a beer."

They walked together, into the cattle barn and down the alleyway between the stalls of prize bulls. Once outside the boys cut across the freshly mowed field to the dusty road and the parked cars behind the long canvas tent. There were men standing around the cars drinking beer. Some were standing with their backs to the grounds, their legs spread apart, and urinating upon the ground as they stared up at the blue cloudless sky.

Henri left the guys when they came out of the cattle barn. He walked on the stubble of freshly cut hay, past the corral where young boys and girls paraded the calves for coloured ribbon prizes.

Chapter 46

Henri entered the building where they showed the chickens and rabbits. There were shavings on the floor, like at the cattle barn, but the smells were different. The hens and the large white roosters cackled incessantly. And there were rabbits, white ones with pink eyes and long slender ears and pink noses wriggling and sniffing the air around them. Henri poked his finger through the mesh and stroked the back of a fat grey rabbit.

"Careful you don't lose a finger," a voice said.

Henri looked over his shoulder. The young girl was standing so close behind him their faces almost touched.

"*Allo* Sylvie," Henri said. "I didn't know you liked chickens. Or is it rabbits?"

"I like all of them," the girl said. She looked around the freshly painted building. "But I don't like to see them like that, in those little cages."

"Yeah, that's how I feel too."

Sylvie looked out through the tall rectangular windows that lined the south side of the building. Henri picked up a carrot top from beneath one of the cages and he tickled the rabbit's nose with the leaves. Sylvie looked back at Henri.

"Don't!" she said.

"I'm not hurting him."

"How do you know? How would you like to be teased like that?"

Seeing something in front of you, so close, and never having it; Henri looked at the girl. For a second, perhaps it was longer than that, they looked into each other's eyes, and Henri wanted to tell her all about the 'haves' and the 'have-nots' and what it was like always reaching, always searching, and never quite getting there. How, just as you thought that you had found it, and were taking the last step towards acquiring it, something would happen and all of it would disappear and the reaching and the searching would start all over again. But, just the telling of it was destructive, he knew that. Even the dreaming of it, seeing it only days ahead, could cause that thing you wanted so desperately to leave you disappointed, once again.

"No, I wouldn't like that," Henri squeezed the carrot top into the cage. The plump, grey rabbit hopped closer to Henri and began to nibble at the green leaves. They watched the rabbit taking small mouthfuls and chewing rapidly for what seemed to be a long time for such small morsels.

"Have you been here long, at the fairgrounds, I mean?"

"An hour maybe."

"How did you come?"

"Lavigne. He has his father's car. You?"

"My parents. Did you get my message at the restaurant?"

"Yes."

The girl stood before him with her eyes lowered. She stood close to him and Henri stared at her smooth-fitting jeans and the narrow plaits of her blouse rising upwards, and he remembered the white lobes. Suddenly, she was looking at him and he saw that her eyes were blue-green and that she did not lower her eyelids when he looked back into them. He did not know what to think. Before, he had wanted to speak to her about the 'haves' and the 'have-nots' but now he did not know what to think, what to say.

"I was drunk," he said finally. "I wanted to call you from La Tanière but I was so drunk."

"Why do you guys always do that?"

She liked Henri. She liked him the first time he stepped into the restaurant. She liked the shy way he sat alone at the counter, waiting for a chance to speak to her. She loved the way he blushed when she caught him looking down the front of her blouse. Even now, she loved him for not making excuses. He was drunk. That was plain enough. At least he did not go on about how he ran into his friends and was more or less obligated to get drunk with them. No reasons, no excuses, just drunk. He wanted to call her but he was too drunk. There was that, at least.

Drunk as he was, he had shown some form of respect for Sylvie by not calling her. She was beautiful, attractive anyway. She was not blind. She had looked at herself in the mirror. And besides, there were always guys wanting to take her out. But, it was always the same: first politeness, and then drunkenness, and her complaining and then, their leaving. She liked Henri. Perhaps, she might even grow to love him.

"Anyway," she said, turning to look out through the windows. "Now you're here."

Henri looked at the back of her head, and the wavy strands of blond hair and how they ended in an oval between her shoulder blades. He looked over her shoulder, past the windows. Even from inside the building, they could hear the circus sounds, and Henri listened to the shrill cries as the red tub whirled on its tiny metal wheels, around and around, sucking the air out of its passengers, and he watched the coloured seats of the Ferris wheel disappearing past the windows of the rabbit and chicken building.

"Yes," Henri said.

"Yes, what?" she turned to look at him.

"Yes, I'm here," Henri smiled. "Yes, I'm here and you're here and, now, we're both here."

The girl laughed. "You're crazy."

"Yes," Henri answered quickly. And, silently in his mind he repeated, yes, I'm crazy. Crazy for getting drunk and missing you last night, crazy for thinking of all those stupid schemes, and crazy for not having the courage to be honest and straight with you.

"Hey," Henri said. "Want to go on the big wheel?"

"Oh, I'm so afraid of that."

The girl looked out the window, at the wheel turning and carrying its red and green seats up and past the upper portions of the windows. The seats swayed as they went past the windows.

"Me too," Henri said. "Maybe together it wouldn't be so bad, eh?"

Sylvie shrugged her shoulders and tightened the muscles of her neck and face as if that would display her genuine fear of the wheel. Henri watched her lips part, revealing two rows of even, white teeth.

"Come on," Henri coaxed. Without thinking, he held out his hand and she, also not thinking about it, grasped his hand warmly. It was not until they were outside the chicken house, running towards the ticket booth, that they became aware of their sudden closeness.

"Hang on a minute," Henri said. He let go of her hand and reached into his pocket. He still had some money left from the night before, and he thanked his father for that. He took some cash out of his pocket and joined the line at the ticket booth.

He tried not looking at her but that, he was not able to do. Sylvie stood there with her arms folded beneath her breasts, staring up at the wheel and listening to the cries of the riders as they came over and down. Just standing there, she was so beautiful. But then, so was Lise, walking towards him in the dim light of the room with her eyes looking straight at him and her long flowing hair just covering her breasts and the brownness of them showing through. And when her fingers had played at the back of his neck he had grown more excited than he ever thought he could be. But all through the time he had been with Lise in the back room of the infirmary, he had never felt the warmness or the closeness he had just experienced when Sylvie had placed her hand in his back at the chicken and rabbit house. Was he making it all up? Henri looked at the mole on the neck of the woman in front of him. She was fat and her hair, the colour of iodine, fell in uneven strands on the back of her neck. And there were two folds of skin on her neck, and then, the mole. The woman glanced back and smiled at a tall, thin man standing behind Sylvie. The man smiled, weakly, and Henri, looking at the side of the woman's face, saw a space where a tooth was missing and the one beside the space was browning with decay. But he saw a look between them. There was something there. Or, was he making it all up? Was he? Sylvie was beautiful. She was beautiful and scared and she was going to ride the Ferris wheel with him. Just to be with him? Was she really that frightened? The thin man behind her looked frightened. Henri was frightened. He had been up once on the big wheel and he remembered the coming over and down and the chair swaying. Going over he had prayed like he had once prayed in the back room of the infirmary: oh please God, make it good and let there not be an accident and make me look a fool. He remembered going backwards, up and up, that had not been so bad but, when they had gone over the crest and started downwards, he had closed his eyes. He felt his legs rise as the chair tilted upwards, and the hamburger and candy floss and orange drink had risen in his stomach, threatening to come rushing out. That had been with Lavigne and St-Jean the year before.

The wheel was just as big now and the cries were the same and he repeated: God, please, let me pull through this without looking a fool. He placed the five-dollar bill through the opening and the woman behind the barred window of the ticket booth looked up at him.

"Two please," Henri smiled at the woman.

"One fifty," the woman said without smiling. "Your change sir."

Henri placed the change in his pocket and walked over to the fence. The fence covered a large area around the Ferris wheel with only two openings, one beyond and the other behind the ticket booth. Sylvie stood in line with others waiting their turn on the wheel. Henri joined the line and stood close to Sylvie.

"All set?" he said.

"Guess so," the girl nodded.

All eyes were on the wheel. Henri focused on two young girls in a green chair with the number eighteen written in white numbers on the back. He watched it rising backwards, and the girls laughing and waving to three other young girls standing by the fence. And then, as they approached the midpoint, the chair swayed upwards, feet first, and he could no longer see the girls from where he stood, only the number eighteen written in white paint on the bottom of the chair. As the chair descended there was a chorus of screams from number eighteen and, as they rode by the boarding platform, the girls opened their eyes and began to laugh and wave again.

Henri glanced at Sylvie. They both smiled. It was a brief smile and then, their attention returned to the wheel. Suddenly, there was a change in the sound. The engine driving the Ferris wheel did not sound the same. The man operating the engine was deeply tanned. He had thick, curly black hair and his arms were covered in blue-green tattoos: mermaid, Maltese cross, serpent and torch, and a heart with the word "mom" inscribed inside it. The man stared up at the numbers on the chairs and held onto a long metal lever. He slowed the engine and a chair stopped at the boarding platform. The man quickly stepped onto the platform, released the holding bar and held the chair to keep it from swaying as a man and a woman got out.

Near the ticket booth a tall, skinny man, deeply tanned with a small gold earring in his left ear lobe, collected the tickets from the people waiting their turn on the wheel.

"Okay!" he said sharply. He dropped the small length of chain barring the opening in the fence. Two people, a man and his young daughter, went by him and onto the platform. The man and his daughter sat down in the chair and, immediately, the operator brought down the holding bar and locked it in place. He hopped off the platform and stood by the engine. He pulled on the lever and, as the engine gained speed, the young man and his daughter began to move backwards and up with the little girl hanging on to her father's arm.

Henri and Sylvie waited their turn, watching people getting off and new ones getting on. And then, it was their turn. The operator smiled at Sylvie as she stepped onto the ramp and, when they were seated and the holding bar was in place, the man gave the chair a shove before returning to his engine. The chair swayed in midair and Sylvie held Henri's arm tightly and Henri prayed again for bravery and a strong stomach and whatever else it would take. They ascended slowly, one chair at a time, as previous passengers got down and new ones arrived. Henri held on to the bar with one hand. He could feel the smoothness of many coats of paint on the bar.

"See?" Henri smiled. "It's really nothing." They had reached the very top and there was only a slight breeze at that height. Henri could feel his knees begin to tremble but he fought it and pushed against the footrest with both feet.

"Look," he said. "We can see all of the grounds from here. Look, down there, Sylvie. There's Lavigne's father's car."

The girl peaked over the edge of the chair and quickly turned her head back towards Henri. The wheel began to move, downwards. It had moved slowly before, taking on new passengers. Now, they could feel it, the whole frame of the wheel vibrating with new speed and, down they came, their feet rising upwards in the footrest and their stomachs reaching out for air. Henri kept his mouth closed. He could feel Sylvie's grip tighten on his arm and, as they went by the loading ramp, he could hear the operator laughing, and then, backwards and up they went.

Henri could not think. He did not want to think. There was only one thing on his mind: dear God, dear, dear God, make it end soon and let me not be a fool and puke all over. And then, over they went again, and down, his stomach rising and the circus man's eyes smiling and him speeding up the engine and Sylvie's head buried on his arm. At last, the engine slowed. Sylvie lifted her head. Was it over? Not quite, but the worse was past. They were unloading. And Henri had made it without making a fool of himself. But he was not thinking about God now, or being a fool and vomiting all over everybody on the wheel. What next, he was thinking. What would they do now? Should they just walk around, stop and talk somewhere? Talk about what? Was he falling in love again? It was only a short ride on a Ferris wheel. She held onto his arm but only because she was frightened. Perhaps. Maybe she was in love with him. There, he was at it again. There he was, being a 'have-not' again.

They moved backwards and upwards, slowly now, as passengers got down and left, going through the opening in the fence on one side of the ticket booth while others replaced them going by the tall man taking tickets on the opposite side. Sylvie suddenly let go of his arm and waved to someone on the ground, *Monsieur* and *Madame* Lanthier; *Madame* waved a pink sweater at her daughter while her husband scowled and held up his wrist and pointed towards it with jerking movements of his index finger.

"Your father," Henri said, not looking at the man below. "What's wrong?"

"Oh nothing. He's just telling me it's time to go."

Henri felt sick again. So, that was it. A ride on a Ferris wheel and then, good-bye. He might have known. He was a 'have-not' and would always be a 'have-not' and there was nothing better that a 'have-not' could expect. When they reached the very top, Henri was feeling better. For a while there, I almost fell again, he thought, but no, I'm not ready for that yet. Sylvie is wonderful and beautiful and all I've ever dreamed of; someday, perhaps, but not now. No, I'm not ready yet.

Sylvie turned to look at Henri, who was peering over the edge of the chair.

"Henri," she said.

"Yes?"

"Henri, I'll be leaving with my parents as soon as we get off."

"Yes, I suppose."

"Henri, could I write to you at Washika?"

Henri's mind began to race: pencil, paper, not much time, wheel turning, parents waiting by the fence. 'Have-not?' Who was a 'have-not?' Henri? No, not him. He was with Sylvie and she wanted to write to him and they had less than a minute and Henri looked into her blue-green eyes and she touched his arm gently, and they kissed.

When they got up out of the chair and stepped down from the boarding ramp, Henri's legs felt rubbery. They walked past the fence to Sylvie's parents and she said, "*Maman, papa,* this is my friend, Henri Morin." After Sylvie had said good-bye, he watched her a long time going down the thoroughfare with her parents. He held onto the metal fence and watched the wheel turning and their green chair, number eighteen going by. He stood there a long time getting used to the new feeling for he had never truly been a 'have' before.

PART IV

Chapter 47

The sky was a bright blue, with not a cloud in it and, on the outskirts of the bay, the water had lost its early morning calm and whitecaps were beginning to appear. The students sat with their life jackets leaning against the moist grey steel of the *Madeleine*'s cabin. A few sat in the two drive boats in tow, with their collars up, smoking and facing back towards Washika.

Alphonse stood at the wheel. He touched the throttle lightly and reached back for the tall wooden stool.

"Well Henri," he said. "You passed a good weekend?"

"Yes," Henri replied. "And you?"

"Ha! At my age, you know, they're all the same."

Henri sat on the wooden box. He leaned back against the railing. Behind him the engine pounded out a steady rhythm with her six pistons. He slid a pack of cigarettes out of his shirt pocket. Henri opened the pack and offered it to Alphonse.

"Well sure," Alphonse laughed. "You know, you can always tell when a man gets to be my age. He rolls all the time, even weekends. So when he comes back after a weekend in town, he still has tobacco and papers in his shirt pocket."

"Yes, I suppose we spend too much. But, in town or out with a girl, rolling? I don't think I could do it."

"After a while, you stick to taverns. And the girls, well, they become women and they know what it is to save money."

Alphonse slid off the stool and stood at the wheel as they approached the point where the gulls nested. Henri looked out at the birds and how they became excited and lifted off the rocks and circled the *Madeleine*. They looked exactly the same, white with grey on their backs and long yellow bills with small, yellow bead eyes and feet like a duck: *Larus argentatus*, the herring gull. Henri had looked it up in his father's library. They were exactly the same as the gulls that gathered around the metal drums in the parking space on Chemin de Notre-Dame where people went to eat their noon lunches by the river. But here, at Washika Bay along the shores of the Cabonga, the birds were not the same. In town, most people looked upon the birds as just another form of nuisance to be endured. At Washika, however, the gulls were an important part of the Cabonga Reservoir, an element that contributed to its splendor. Many things were different at Washika. Even the air did not smell the same.

"Alphonse?" Henri said.'

"Yes, Henri," Alphonse replied before Henri had time to say anything further.

"Alphonse, would you like to live here at Washika?"

"I work here."

"Yes, I know. But, would you not like to live here someday? Maybe somewhere in off the beach?"

"Ha! You noticed it, eh?"

"What do you mean?"

"You've been here, what, a month and a half? And already you see the difference."

"From Ste-Émilie, you mean?"

"Ste-Émilie, Lac des Montagnes, Louville, any large town. You're lucky to see it so young. Me too, I learned it a long time ago. I didn't always work here. And I didn't always live in Ste-Émilie."

"But you like it here?"

"Oh yes. Still, there are some here who don't know anything. They hope all the time to find work in Ste-Émilie, or the Capital maybe. Somewhere, where they can drive to work in the morning, and visit the tavern on their way home at night. But, they don't know. They've always worked here."

"But you wouldn't live here," Henri continued. "You would rather live in Ste-Émilie."

"I didn't say that. My woman might say that."

Alphonse laughed and slapped Henri on the shoulder.

"Here, hold her steady," he said.

Henri got up from the wooden box to stand at the wheel.

"There, just like that," Alphonse said. "I won't be long."

Henri sighted over the tip of the anchor to a sandy cove shimmering in the early morning heat. The sun was at its highest and only slightly to the left and Henri guessed that they were headed almost due south.

"Where we headed, Alphonse?"

"Pàgwàshka Bay," Alphonse opened the door and went out on deck.

Pàgwàshka, at least there was always a wind. That's what the old ones said. No bugs and no water. Pàwashka, they said, was only a quarter the size of Washika Bay, with mostly dead trees, *chicots*, dotting its shallow waters and the shore. There was always a good wind, from the north, but it was not a good place for tugboats. For the drive boats it presented no problem. Even the Russel, with its two-cylinder engines and the steel cage around its screw propeller, could get around in there without too much difficulty. But for a six-cylinder tugboat like the *Madeleine*, the shallow water at Pàgwàshka Bay always meant trouble.

Henri held onto the wheel with one hand. He touched the throttle lightly with the other. The lever had been painted grey, like the *Madeleine*, but now it was ebony, mostly, from the paint being worn off, fondled by Alphonse and her captains before him. Henri felt near the lower portion of the lever, where it had cracked once and was now smooth and shiny from the bronze the welder had used to mend the break. Henri wanted to tell Alphonse about Sylvie. Later, he might speak to Lavigne and the others about her, but not yet. Things were just beginning. There was nothing solid yet. Telling them now, so soon, might spark their interest: if Sylvie Lanthier were willing to go out with Morin, she would probably like to go out with me…or some such nonsense. How many would think like that? Worse, how many would put it to the test? No. Later, when Sylvie was certain that it was he, Henri Morin, that she wanted and no other person would do, he might flaunt his love affair to the crowds, and never have to worry, or maybe he would come to speak like Lavigne and all the other 'haves' that he knew.

The door opened and the sound of the engine changed. Alphonse fastened the door open with a hook and eyelet.

"Okay Henri, I'll take her," he said.

Henri returned to the wooden box where he had been sitting, where he could feel the cool breeze rushing by the open doorway. He cupped his hands around the lighter and lit a cigarette.

"Alphonse," he said. "How old were you when you first met your wife"

"Too old. There were no women in the camps and we didn't go down often. When you reached a certain age, it was time."

"What do you mean, too old?"

"All my friends were married. I was an uncle to all of their little ones. When my woman came along, well, I was too old to say no. It was time to be serious and give up my wild ways."

Henri looked at him. It was difficult to imagine Alphonse Ouimet being wild. Henri could see him only as he was now, his deeply tanned face with the white hard hat tilted sideways and the thick, brown moustache and the piercing brown eyes squinting across the glaring water ahead.

"But you married her. You must have loved her?"

"Love? Well, yes. That came too, later on."

"Was she the first girl you ever went out with, Alphonse?"

Alphonse laughed. "She was the first I married," he said. Alphonse let go of the wheel and leaned out of the open doorway and glanced astern.

"There's Gérard," he said, stepping back into the cabin.

Henri stood and leaned out through the open doorway. Less than a quarter mile back, he could see the *Sophie,* riding the water with her bow high and her squat cabin appearing even smaller than it was. The *Sophie* was one of those two-cylinder tugboats, Russels, that were often used for rounding up logs within a corral of boom timbers.

"Is he coming to work with us?" Henri said.

"We might need him at Pàgwàshka. Besides, they had no work for him today."

Henri looked out through the windows, beyond the anchor, to the approaching shoreline.

"I met a girl on the weekend," Henri said quickly.

As the shoreline approached so it seemed that his time for such talk was quickly coming to an end. And he wanted so much to share this event, his becoming a 'have,' leaving the world of the 'have-nots' finally.

He wanted to share this with Alphonse. It felt strange to Henri but it was as if he needed Alphonse's approval.

"Good, good!" Alphonse said, smiling. "Now Henri, I want you to go stand at the bow. Watch carefully, and steer me through where there's deep water."

The *Madeleine*'s engine slowed and Henri went forward. Holding onto the anchor, he looked down into the clear water and the sandy bottom. From astern he could hear the guys talking and then, he heard the chug, chug, chugging of the *Sophie* as she came alongside. Henri lay down, flat on his stomach. The wood of the deck was warm on his chest and he stared straight down. The bottom seemed to move swiftly by even under the *Madeleine*'s slowest speed. Henri kept his eyes on the bottom and concentrated as best he could at his task because he knew that Alphonse and the *Madeleine* were depending on him.

Chapter 48

The bottom seemed so far away. With his hands cupped around his eyes, Henri stared down through the water, still very deep, and he watched it moving past, sand mostly, like on the beach, a huge boulder once and several waterlogged timbers sticking up out of the sand at an angle. But it was all far away, down deep enough not to be of any threat to the *Madeleine*. Henri watched a school of minnows swimming beneath the *Madeleine*. That should have been his warning clue. The little minnows were hardly ever seen in deep water. The grainy sand became more distinct. There was a sudden jolt that pushed him forward on the deck. They were aground.

Henri looked back at Alphonse. He could not see his face. The sun glared down on the cabin windows making everything black inside. He heard Alphonse shifting into reverse and the engine revving, and then shifting again and the engine revving once again. Then, it was quiet. The boys leaned over the sides and spoke softly among themselves. Alphonse came out of the cabin, a fresh cigarette dangling from beneath his thick moustache.

"It happened so fast," Henri called from the bow. "I'm telling you, Alphonse. It was deep and then, all of a sudden, it was only two feet."

"That's the way here," Alphonse replied. "It's nothing, Henri. We'll get her."

Astern, the *Sophie* bobbed listlessly while her captain, Gérard Laporte, leaned against the low cabin of the tugboat, rolling a cigarette and looking very pleased.

"Problem, Alphonse?" he called towards the *Madeleine*.

"I suppose you could say that," Alphonse said. "Shouldn't be too bad."

"Want me to snub?"

Gérard hooked onto the *Madeleine*'s port gunwale with a pike pole and pulled the *Sophie* alongside.

"If you want," Alphonse said. "With this gang though, we should be able to rock her enough."

"I'll snub just the same." Gérard looked up at the students leaning over the port side. "Looks like you guys are going to get a little wet for a change, eh."

"Oh, they're real little ducks, these guys," Alphonse said. He turned to Henri and the boys behind him. "Get all the peaveys we have, Henri."

Alphonse went astern. He untied the drive boats and set them adrift. From a hook on the cabin wall he took down a coil of thick, yellow rope and made it fast to stern. As the *Sophie* approached the *Madeleine*, stern first, Alphonse swung the remaining yellow rope onto the deck of the little tugboat. Gérard came out of the cabin and fastened the rope to the metal tow post to stern. He returned to the cabin and, with frothy sounds coming from its exhaust pipe, the tugboat began to move forward.

Everyone was astern except Alphonse. The fellows watched the rope curving like a snake in the water and then straightening and, finally, lifting out of the water, taut, as the small tugboat no longer moved forward. Gérard revved her two pistons and her stern sank leaving her gunwales only inches above water. Both engines screamed: the *Sophie* going forward and the *Madeleine* in reverse. Nothing. Gérard shifted into reverse and approached to within three yards of the *Madeleine. He* shifted again and shot forward as quickly as a two-cylinder tugboat could shoot. Nothing.

Alphonse came out of the cabin. "Just keep her tight Gérard," he shouted over the sounds of both engines idling. He turned to the fellows standing behind him.

"Okay, my little ducks. Time to show your stuff!"

Henri handed out the peaveys. The rest of the fellows grabbed pike poles from the rack on the cabin roof.

"Okay now," Alphonse spoke to the fellows. "The idea is not to lift her. You couldn't do it anyway. Just rock her. Get a good hold in the sand and rock her from side to side. Okay, let's go!"

The boys jumped overboard, ten to starboard and ten over the port side. Alphonse went back inside. The two engines rumbled softly, sending up a foamy froth between them and, above water, the yellow rope strained between the tow posts sticking up through the decks to stern. Alphonse stuck his head out of the cabin doorway.

"Ready?" he called to the guys below.

"Give her hell!" a voice yelled back from somewhere in the water.

The *Madeleine*'s engine revved, louder than the *Sophie*'s but they could see the froth the smaller tugboat made with its exhaust and they could tell that Gérard was pushing her for all she was worth. And sometimes, when she slacked off a bit, her stern would rise up and they could see the metal cage around her screw propeller. The water was three feet deep where they stood, and the boys drove the points of their peaveys and pike poles into the sandy bottom and, leaning them against her hull, pushed hard on the *Madeleine*. They groaned, leaning into their poles and, gradually, the tugboat began to rock from side to side and her momentum increased as the groans grew louder with each roll of her squat grey hull.

And then it was over. The *Madeleine* slipped backwards as easily as she had slid up onto the sand. The fellows cheered and the two men shut down the engines. Alphonse stuck his head out of the cabin.

"Break!" he hollered.

The young men laughed and staggered through the water to shore. Along the shore, the two drive boats bobbed up and down in the waves the tugboats had made. And then there was only the wind whistling through the evergreen branches and the soft murmuring of the students already on shore, sitting on the warm sand with their backs against the smooth grey *chicots*, their eyes closed against the bright noon sun.

Chapter 49

The *Madeleine* was anchored offshore and the sun warmed her dull grey paint, and the red-orange of the drive boats pulled up onto shore. It was midday and the students had settled into a normal after lunch routine: a short nap on the sand beneath jack pine branches, with the smell of the ever-present sweet fern, and the feeling of the sun and the wind on their faces. It had been paradise, almost.

Gérard had run the *Sophie* ashore purposely: with her engine running at a slow speed, it created the backwater they needed for moving the wood out towards open water. There were plenty of *chicots* lying flat on the water with their roots lodged in the sandy bottom. The boys waded in among the *chicots* in the shallow water and hooked out the four-foot logs that had been trapped there. The water was not deep where they worked, two and a half feet at the most, and with the constant breeze and the sun on their backs, the fellows worked steadily and well.

André Guy was the first to see it. At first, he said nothing. He stood crouched in the water with his hook raised, leaning one way and then the other with his arms outstretched. Suddenly, he slashed at the water with his hook. It came up, point first, behind him. He had missed.

"*Brochet*!" André shouted. He ran through the water, lifting his knees high. "*Brochet*! Come on!"

The boys left the bundles of pulpwood floating among the *chicots* and joined André near a rotting stump jutting out of the sand. On both sides of the stump were fallen *chicots* forming a grey matrix in the shallow water. André pointed to the base of the stump, where the sand dipped and the water changed to a brownish-black as it disappeared beneath the stump.

"There!" he said. "See it?"

They shaded their eyes with their hands and peered down into the water. At first, it did not move, but then they saw the gills waving, and the tail, and as they moved in closer the fish backed away. Suddenly, the fish made its move, and the boys attacked with pike poles and hooks and some tried to catch it with their bare hands.

"*Sacrament*!" André swore.

"What's the matter?" someone yelled.

"Look at that," André said. He looked away from the others, from where the big northern pike lay still in the water, keeping a watchful eye on his assailants. "Some people, they have everything."

A snow-white skiff approached the *Madeleine*. Her wake caused waves to slap up on shore. The boys stood in the water, staring up at the craft with her white hull and tan canvas convertible cabin roof, and the swivel chairs and racks for the rods, and buckets of ice for the bait and cold beer. No one was thinking about the pike lying somewhere in the brackish water.

"Hi ya," the man at the wheel said.

"Yes sir," Alphonse replied.

"Beautiful day ain't it?" the man said. He was wearing a baseball cap and a white T-shirt with an angry bass jumping across his chest. The other man sat astern, fat and comfortable in the swivel chair. He wore wide-legged shorts and a white T-shirt and his legs were burned red, like his arms.

"How long ya been out here?" the driver said to Alphonse. "We been fishing 'round here all mornin' and we ain't seen nobody 'till you fellas com 'long. How's the fishin' in these parts anyhow?"

Alphonse glanced sideways. Gérard smiled back. He did not speak English well but he understood enough.

"Not too bad here," Alphonse looked across to the driver. "Pike. About twenty, twenty-five pounds."

"Didn't I tell ya Charlie?" the driver spoke to the fat man. "Northern pike fer chris' sake! Twenty-five, thirty pounds!"

"Ask 'm, Al," the fat man stood up in the skiff. "Ask 'm 'bout lures. An' he must know the spots. Ask 'm 'bout the spots, Al."

The driver lit a cigarette. He held the pack out towards Alphonse.

"Smoke?"

Alphonse nodded, yes, and the man tossed the pack to him.

"Keep 'em," the man said. "We got plenty."

Alphonse tapped out a cigarette as he had seen the driver do and then he stuffed the rectangular shaped pack into his other shirt pocket, his left pocket already filled with his tobacco and papers. He lit the cigarette and inhaled deeply, feeling the smoke filling his lungs and smelling that strange, pungent smell of blended tobacco.

"So, ya got big ones up this ways, uh?" the driver said. "Mostly pike, right?"

"Yes, that's right," Alphonse replied.

"Any special place?" the man winked at Alphonse. "Must be pretty good right 'round here, uh?"

"Yes," Alphonse said. "That's right."

"Ya must know where all a them big ones are hidin', right? What ya doin' here anyways?"

"Working," Alphonse said. "You, vacation?"

"That's right. Three weeks a nothin' but fishin' an havin' us a good time. No job, no wife naggin', know what ah mean? Left all 'em troubles behind. This here's the life, I tell ya. Yes sir! Fresh air an' good fishin'."

The driver looked back at the fat man, and then at Alphonse.

"So where d'ya say them fish were?"

The students had never heard Alphonse speaking English before. They were seeing another side of the man, something unexpected, almost strange, like the first time seeing their fathers drunk and slobbering, or like when they heard Father Landry letting fly with a few good swear words that morning when he was putting up the double windows of the rectory.

Alphonse pointed up and down the bay with his hand. "Anywhere along here," he answered the man. "These fellows saw one just a few minutes ago. Chased him all along the shore here."

The driver looked down at the boys.

"Rather chase 'em than hook 'em, huh?"

The fat man laughed. "Look at their hooks, Al. Chris', they's big 'nough fer barracuda."

"We got pike here just as big," Alphonse said to the driver.

"As barracuda?" the driver smiled. "Ya know 'bout barracuda?"

"Yes, that's right."

"Hey Charlie, did ya hear that?" the driver turned to the fat man. "Fella here knows 'bout barracudas."

"Well I'll be a son-of-a-bitch," the fat man stared at Alphonse. "What 'bout the pike. Al?"

"Hang on, will ya. Lemme talk to da man," the driver snapped. He turned to Alphonse. "Yep, this here's real God's country, ain't it?"

"Yes, that's right," Alphonse replied.

'"What you guys doin' here anyway? Why ya pickin' up all a dis wood?"

"Pulpwood, and some logs."

"Ain't it kinda old?"

"No, not too old."

"But, how's it git anywhere?"

"River," Alphonse pointed away from the bay, towards the southeast. "Down the lake there to the dam and down the river to the Capital."

"Chris', ya must lose lots on the way," the driver chuckled.

"Yes, that's right."

"An' then you guys pick 'em up, right?"

"Yes, that's right."

"Com' on, Al." The fat man was sitting down again. "The bugs are eatin' the shit outta me. Find out 'bout the fishin' an' let's git ta hell outta here."

"Hang on, will ya," the driver said. He did not turn to look at the man. He looked down at the fellows standing in the water. "Nice an' cool, huh?"

The boys returned the man's smile. They did not know what he was saying but it sounded friendly enough.

"They speak any English?" he said to Alphonse.

"No," Alphonse replied.

"So, how 'bout it m'friend. Ya know where them big ones are? Must a seen plenty, right?"

"Yes, that's right."

The fat man reached into a canvas pack and took out several small, rectangular boxes. He stood up and handed them to the driver. "Here Al," he said. "See if they'd like some a these."

"Aw fer chris' sakes, Charlie. They's almost kids."

"Naw. Go on, hand 'em out. We got plenty more. Find out 'bout the fishin', Al."

The fat man sat on the swivel chair. He bit the end off a long, green cigar and then he lit it pulling long drags as he held the flame of the lighter to one end.

The driver opened the boxes and brought out the cigars, wrapped individually in cellophane with a red-yellow band near one end. He held the cigars up in both hands.

"Here ya go boys," he said. "Come git 'em."

They understood well enough. And there were plenty enough to go around. Henri took two of the cigars and tossed one of them to Gérard. The boys stood in a circle in the shallow water, holding their Zippos up to the ends of the long, green cigars and puffing heartily.

Alphonse looked at his watch.

"Break!" he shouted.

Gérard stepped into the cabin and shut down the *Sophie*'s engine. When he returned on deck, he held the cigar tightly in a corner of his mouth, showing his yellow teeth when he sucked in air.

"Down over there," Alphonse began, pointing towards the southwestern portion of the cove. "Where you see the *chicots* piled up, lots of minnows. The pike, they like the minnows."

"Maybe we'll jest try trollin' along shore there. Any special plug? Should be good fishin' right along there, right?"

"Yes, that's right," Alphonse replied. It was difficult not to smile.

"We thank ya, m'friend," the driver said. He started up the engine. He waved to the students as he backed away from the *Madeleine* and out towards open water. Astern, the fat man puffed on his cigar. His face was red from sitting in the sun and all the more from leaning over and jostling the trolls in his tackle box.

Chapter 50

Most of the students were sick heading back to Washika later that day. It was the worst kind of "sick" they had ever experienced. Their heads ached and they felt a continual need to vomit but nothing ever happened. Several times, Lavigne leaned over the side with the waves slapping cool spray on his face but nothing had happened. He had even tickled the back of his throat with an index finger but only green-yellow bile was forced out and that had made him feel worse.

They were quiet going back to Washika. None of the students slept in the drive boats because of the waves and most of them lay on deck, astern. They watched the sun slowly descending upon the treetops at Pàgwàshka Bay and they stared at the wake the *Madeleine* made as it petered out behind them.

In the cabin, Henri sat on the low wooden box. He had not smoked a single cigarette since they left Pàgwàshka nor had he said a word to Alphonse.

"Feeling better, Henri?" Alphonse asked.

"Not too bad."

"Those were big cigars," Alphonse smiled.

"And cheap. I heard once that you get very sick on cheap wine. It must be the same with cigars."

"I'm not so sure," Alphonse said. "I got sick one time on very expensive wine. My brother and me, we were altar boys at St-Exupéry's. That was a long time ago, before your time. Anyway, one morning after the mass was over, our parish priest, the *curé*, left the sacristy early and me and my brother, Oscar, we got into a big bottle of holy wine. We had to drink fast, you know. The *curé* could return at any time. Anyway, it wasn't long, we finished the bottle and, just as we were about to leave, we hear the *curé* coming. It was always easy to tell. The floor boards in the sacristy always made a noise and the *curé* always walked fast so that you could hear his cassock."

"So, what did he say?"

"I don't know. When I heard him coming, I ran for the altar. I jumped over the communion rail and ran out through the side door. It was then the wine started to hit."

"And your brother?"

"Oscar wasn't so lucky. The *curé* found him in the closet where we hung up our cassocks after mass. Poor Oscar, he was very drunk. When the *curé* found him, he was sitting in the corner of the closet trying to hide under a bundle of cassocks. He still had the bottle in his hand."

"What happened to him?"

"Not much. He was fired, kicked out of the altar boys forever. *The curé* made him get on his knees, right there in the closet, and poor Oscar made his confession and told everything."

"And so, were you really sick?"

"Sick? *Et misère*! I don't think I have ever been so sick in my life. My mother said it was punishment from God. The *curé* had called to tell her what we'd done, and that we were no longer altar boys in his church. My father never went to church but even he said that it was punishment from God, us being sick like that. It could not be the wine, he said, since it was the best to be had anywhere in the province."

"Was it good? The wine, I mean."

"Oh yes, very good," Alphonse replied with a weak smile. "But you know, I've never put my lips to a bottle of wine since."

"Nor me, cigars," Henri said. "Not green ones anyway."

Henri was feeling better. The breeze rushing through the open doorway brought in plenty of fresh air, almost completely removing the odour of diesel fuel from inside the cabin. He opened his lunch pail and shook the thermos bottle. It was empty.

"I've got lots," Alphonse nodded towards the thermos bottle by his feet.

Henri poured black tea from Alphonse's thermos. He watched the steam rise as he filled his cup.

"It's still pretty hot, Alphonse. Want some?"

Alphonse shook his head, no. He sat back on the stool and began to roll a cigarette. He stopped, suddenly. He slid the tobacco off the paper and back into the pack. He folded the paper carefully and placed it back inside its little cardboard folder.

"*Une dure?*" Alphonse said. He held out the slim paper package containing the strange-smelling cigarettes that the tourists had given him.

Henri made a face: a disgusted, about-to-vomit face.

Alphonse laughed. "Better not, I suppose. Sick once during the day is enough, eh?"

Henri held the plastic cup in both hands and he blew across the rising steam. He thought about the Café D'or and the red and white checkered curtains in the windows, tied back with bright red bows, like Christmas decorations, and the small square tables with table cloths made of the same material as the curtains. There was an ashtray, salt and pepper shakers, a sugar bowl and an upright, rectangular chromed metal box containing paper napkins, all of these in the centre of the table. And he could see Sylvie standing at the counter and smiling at the customers in her teasing way.

"What time is it, Alphonse?"

Alphonse reached for his watch and held it out from his waist.

"A quarter to four," he said.

A quarter to four. He must remember that. Maybe better to write it down once they reached Washika. He would ask her what she was doing at that exact time when they met again, in three weeks, maybe. She would never remember that far back. He would write to her. That was it. He would write to her tonight, and in the letter he would ask her what she was doing today, at exactly a quarter to four, while he was sitting in the cabin of the *Madeleine* and thinking about her. She would like that. He could see her so clearly, standing at the counter, with her hair tied back, and the folds of her blouse as she rubbed circles on the counter with a damp cloth. Or, if she was working the night shift, she would still be sleeping perhaps. Henri had never seen her sleeping. Did all girls sleep alike? Did they always curl up in fetal positions with their hair seeming to float on the pillow and breathing softly and looking more like little girls? Henri had lain beside Lise Archambault as she slept, seeing her and listening to her breathing and waiting for her to open her eyes so that he could make love to her again. He could not bring himself to touch her or caress her while she was sleeping. He could stroke her hair and keep her back warm with his chest; and when she awoke, warm and rested, she would be close to him and already in his arms and they would love each other and afterwards they would rest until the next time.

"Hey!" a voice snapped.

Henri looked up from his cup. Alphonse was looking down at him, a wide grin on his face.

"In the moon, Henri?" he said. "Could it be some pretty young girl in Ste-Émilie, eh?"

Henri laughed. He drank tea from the cup but it was only lukewarm now. He must tell Sylvie about that in the letter as well. Not the part about Lise, of course. He would tell her everything: how he felt now, and the first time he saw her, and that time on the Ferris wheel. But wait. There he was doing it all over again. It would be like before, like with Shannon. He had been open with her. She knew everything about him. He told her everything. And what happened? No, with Sylvie, it would be different. Of course, he would be honest with her. Honest? What did that mean? Certainly, he would respect her and he would always be truthful with her. And how would he respect Sylvie? Could he dream of her and want every part of her, and still claim between gasping breaths that he respected her? And what if she felt exactly the same way as he did? Was there lack of respect as they slid over each other, bathed in each other's warmth and convulsing wildly from sheer physical joy?

He looked up at Alphonse. The man stared across the water, only half-seeing for he had crossed here many times in his life. It was always a time of rest, a time to think.

"Alphonse?"

"Yes, Henri," Alphonse replied without turning.

"Alphonse, what do you think about women?"

Alphonse smiled. He placed one of the long cigarettes between his lips and lit it.

"You know, Henri," he began. "Women to me are like life. A man learns as he goes along. But, he never stops. As long as you live and you are not a hermit, or a person who does not like women, you'll be learning. Life can be pretty good."

"And it can be bad."

"Well yes," Alphonse laughed. "Anyway, you asked me what I think."

"You're married a long time now, Alphonse. Would you rather be single, you know, a *célibataire*?"

"To be free is something, you know. Free to come and go. But then, I don't think anyone is *vraiment libre*. You're never really free. There's always something. I wouldn't want to be only a little free and be alone. Without my woman and my children, being without them but not really free would be worse. That, to me, would not be being free. Right now, Henri, you are free, probably as free as you're ever going to be, I think. Remember that, and enjoy this time while you have it.

"But the girls," Henri persisted. "What about them?"

"They're free too, for a time. Just like you. And you can be free together, for a time,"

"Then what, Alphonse? Why does it have to end?"

"That's the woman in your life, and the man in hers. Anyway, that's how I see it, Henri."

Henri was confused. He remembered his father's words during his last visit home. His father loved his woman very much. There was no doubt in Henri's mind about that. But his father was not happy.

"Alphonse, is it the woman that makes you not free?"

"Sometimes, yes."

"But, what about the *célibataire*? A bachelor has no woman, yet sometimes he's not free."

"Yes, that's true," Alphonse smiled. "It's not the man or the woman. It's life that takes away the freedom. Sometimes a woman helps. Sometimes not."

"I'm not so sure I understand," Henri held the empty cup in both hands and he looked at the stain the tea had made on the inside. "For me, it's all very complicated, you know."

"Yes, I suppose."

"Take for example, on the weekend," Henri continued. "Guess who I saw at La Tanière?"

"Poor Henri. I never go there, you know that."

"Dumas. Dumas Hébert was there with *Mademoiselle* Archambault. I couldn't believe it."

Alphonse smiled. "You know, I'm glad to hear that. And I'm not surprised. That's good news, Henri, after all that has happened."

Suddenly, Henri was torn between his respect for Alphonse and his promise of secrecy to Lise Archambault.

"What do you mean, Alphonse? What has happened?"

"Well," Alphonse lit up another cigarette." I don't know if I should be telling you this, Henri. So, keep it between us, okay?"

"Yes, of course," Henri replied. Alphonse looked serious, more serious than he had ever seen him. Henri prayed that he would not be hearing the story of his visit with the nurse at the infirmary.

"You see, Henri," Alphonse began. "When Lise Archambault first arrived here at Washika about three years ago, we did not know anything about her. She was a pretty young woman, a young woman from the city, from Montréal. You probably noticed how she speaks different than us. She was a recent graduate from a nursing school. That was all we knew about her. And Dumas, that's another one from the city, from Québec City. Ever notice how he speaks? Anyway, it wasn't long before Dumas took an interest in her. He invented all manner of aches and pains to visit her at the infirmary. She never left the infirmary, ever. She never even went outside. This went on for about a month or two and, finally, Dumas gave up. He stopped getting sick, and he stopped visiting the nurse at the infirmary."

"Do you know why?" Henri interrupted. "Did Dumas ever say?"

"Well, not at first. You know how it is with us men. But then, one day we met in town, at the tavern in Ste-Émilie. It was not often that we saw Dumas in the tavern. Anyway, after a beer or two, we began to talk about Lise Archambault. That's when Dumas told me that it had been a real *coup de foudre* on his part, love at first sight, as they say. But it had been very difficult. She wasn't easy to approach, I think that was how he said it, and he had been so patient, more patient than he'd ever been in his whole life. We used to see him marching down to the infirmary in the evenings, carrying little boxes of chocolate, sometimes flowers or wine. He did his very best. But, like I said, he finally gave up. You know, I was certain that he still had feelings for Lise, even if she resisted his wanting her. Anyway, that day in the tavern, he told me about her. It seems that during her *stage*, her training at the hospital, Lise met up with this young doctor, a recent graduate from the university. An intern, I think. And so, before long, Lise and this intern are madly in love and seeing each other whenever they can, and making plans for when Lise would be finished her nursing course. Then, it was the graduation. The young doctor accompanied Lise to *le bal* and, after the formal ball, they went to a party at someone's cottage. That's where the trouble started. It seems that the cottage was packed. Everyone was having a good time and then someone announced that it was time for the *bain de minuit*, a kind of midnight dip where everyone swims with no clothes on. Naked. I think. Maybe you know about this, Henri?"

"Oh yes," Henri smiled.

"Well, according to Dumas' story, everyone left the cottage and went down the long wooden steps to the wharf. There were no lights along the stairs and so the people hung onto the railing and to each other going down. Remember now, these people had been drinking since being at *le bal* in town. Anyway, the young doctor, Lise Archambault's young man, tripped going down the stairs to the wharf. It was a couple of minutes before he came back to himself, before he seemed almost normal. Lise worried about him. She passed a cold wet cloth over his face and neck, and tried to convince him to go back to the cottage. But, no, he wanted to join the others. He took off his clothes right there in front of her. Then he kissed her and jumped off the wharf, joining dozens of men and women floating in the water below. After a time, the swimmers climbed back onto the wharf, put on their clothes, and headed back up the stairs to the cottage. One person was missing. The young doctor was not with them. The police were called in and big search lights were used, but no sign of the young doctor. Early the next morning, his body was found floating under the wharf."

Henri did not speak. He sat there with his empty cup, waiting for Alphonse to continue. He understood now. At least, it seemed clearer now, her insisting that he wear a life jacket, that they should not be seen together, and that he not speak of their relationship to anyone. Now he understood the sadness he had seen in those green eyes. Still, it was unclear why she had accepted him. Why had she not accepted Dumas? Only Lise Archambault would know that.

"So, Alphonse," Henri spoke up, finally. "You think that's why it never worked for Dumas and the nurse?"

"Could be, but then who really knows. It's true, something must have happened to light the fire again for Dumas. And for Lise? What that was we'll probably never know. But, I'm happy for Dumas. And for her too. Now they can get on with their lives."

Henri stared back at the man and, in the short interval of time when eyes looked into eyes, all of the goodness of life and all of the women past and all of the women to come flowed between them. Immediately, Henri knew what he must do. He would write to Sylvie. He would tell her about the shoreline and the water with its whitecaps and the sun flowing slowly downwards, making the *chicots* silver in the shallow water. His love for her would show through without explanations and, if she loved him also, she would see the country that he worked in, clean and warm. She would feel as he felt and, if he wrote clearly and honestly, she would feel his love as real as if he had held her in his arms and whispered the words into her ear.

Chapter 51

The students in the bunkhouse-and-office were surprised to see François Gauthier poking his head into their room. He stood in the doorway and looked at each of them in turn.

"Alphonse sent me," he said." He wants to meet with us."

"So, what's up?" Lavigne said. He stood by the table. He had his lunch pail in his hand. The time for packing their lunches was just in a matter of minutes and Lavigne was always the first fellow in line with his little green ticket. It didn't seem possible, just minutes before the bell rang, that Alphonse wanted to meet with them.

"Alphonse wants to see us?" Lavigne stared at François.

"After we make our lunches," François replied. "Alphonse says for us to meet at Simard-Comtois' cabin."

Lavigne let out a soft, drawn out whistle. "*Sacrament*!" he swore. "This doesn't sound good."

François said no more. He turned and left the bunkhouse-and-office without saying another word.

"Maybe another fire," André Guy said. "Bet you anything."

"*Non*!" Lavigne brought his lunch pail down hard on the table. "No sir! I'm not going on another fire. Not me, *sacrament*. I'll quit, I'm telling you."

As Lavigne spoke they could hear Dumas ringing the lunch bell. The boys picked up their lunch pails and headed out the door. Lavigne was the last to leave and he slammed the door hard as he left the bunkhouse-and-office.

Inside the cookhouse Dumas Hébert stood in the centre of the room, collecting tickets and keeping an eye on the platters of cold pork and ham and the baskets of thickly sliced bread as the students made up sandwiches and squeezed in biscuits and cheese in all of the remaining spaces in their lunch pails.

At supper, on Monday evening, Henri had avoided looking at the cook. Tuesday morning, he had stared directly into the man's face. Dumas had smiled at him, his cold steel, uncommitted smile. Henri's eyes met the blackness of the cook's eyes now and, once again, he failed to detect any reaction, any implied comment. After all, he had made a fool of himself at La Tanière during the weekend. His behaviour was less than acceptable. There was no doubt in his mind about that. He wondered how much Lise Archambault had told him. If Dumas knew anything at all about their little arrangement it certainly didn't show. He wore only the face of confidence, of a man who had won a woman's favour totally and unconditionally. If indeed he was ignorant of the details of Henri's little adventure with the nurse, he was demonstrating an understanding and a forgiveness of Henri's foolish behaviour at the bar, an understanding that could only stem from a clear remembrance of his own troubled youth and that, coupled with the happiness and generosity towards one's fellow man, that new love brings. Certainly, love had softened the lens through which Dumas now saw the world. Otherwise, Henri might not have come through it all so easily. His carrying on at La Tanière might have caused him more problems than he was able to handle.

But now, there were new problems at hand. All eyes were fixed on the short, stocky man with the thick moustache, the thinning side-combed hair and the brooding eyes. Alphonse was not disturbed. He stared right back at the students, and he smiled at them, showing his one gold filling.

"Alphonse," Lavigne said softly. "Is it true, you want to see us?"

"Yes. As soon as you're finished here."

"What's going on? Another fire?"

Alphonse smiled. He leaned on the cover of his lunch pail and closed the fasteners. "Hurry up, Gaston," he said. "We don't want to keep *Monsieur* Simard-Comtois waiting."

Alphonse left then, walking between the rows of tables. At the door, he turned and waved to Dumas

Lavigne hurried along the table, tossing chunks of cheese and biscuits into his lunch pail. When he had finished, there were biscuits and cheese and corners of thick bread sticking up above the edges of the pail. He cradled the lunch pail under his arm without closing the fasteners and turned to leave.

Dumas stood at the entrance to the kitchen. From there he could keep an eye on the goings on at the lunch table.

On his way out, Lavigne stopped in front of the cook. "*Monsieur* Hébert?" he said

"Yes?"

"*Monsieur* Hébert, are you aware of a fire?"

Dumas' face stiffened. The old Dumas look. He stared at Lavigne.

"Fire?" he said. "Of course I know about a fire. What do you think? I don't know what goes on here?"

"Ah *sacrament*!" Lavigne swore, raising both arms above his head. His open lunch pail flew to the floor.

The cook stared into Lavigne's eyes and then he gazed at his immaculate grey plank floor, at Lavigne's open lunch pail and the biscuits, cheese and bread spread all around it. Dumas turned abruptly, without looking at Lavigne, and went into the kitchen.

As the last of the students filed past Lavigne picking his lunch up off the floor, they could hear Dumas and Richard Gagnier, the cookee, laughing hysterically. The laughter would stop momentarily, the cook and cookee making a brief appearance only to disappear as quickly to the sounds of laughter the likes of which had never been heard in the cookhouse before, ever.

Outside, the sun was shining and the dew sparkled on the sparse tufts of green grass growing here and there in the yellow sand. Just beyond the knoll, where the superintendent's cabin was, Alphonse stood beside Simard-Comtois and both men were smoking filtered cigarettes

"Is this all of them?" the superintendent said.

Alphonse looked at them. His lips moved as he counted.

"Yes," he said. "That's all of them."

"Good." Simard-Comtois said. He looked at the students and he waited until the last of them had stopped talking. "Well boys," he began, "we have some good news for you this morning."

A low murmur, more like a groan, arose from the fellows gathered before him. They had heard this little speech once before, begun with exactly the same words. Good news. Really.

"Now, now boys," Simard-Comtois continued." You remember, not long ago, we sent you up on the fire. I'm sure all of you appreciated that experience. Well..."

"*Calis*!" The word cut through the morning air, as sudden and as brutal as a rusted razor blade. It was not obvious who had spoken. All of the students wore faces of defiance, of total mistrust.

The superintendent pretended not to hear. He tried not to show how this apparent hostility affected him. Still, his voice seemed to crack some when he continued his discourse. "We have another little job for you," he said. "I am confident that this additional task will round out your stay with us here at Washika, or rather, on the Cabonga."

The superintendent glanced back at Alphonse with a quick smile. Alphonse did not return the smile.

"This morning," Simard-Comtois continued. "You will be leaving for Cabonga Dam, for at least one week, maybe two. They will be opening the gap today or tomorrow and they will need all the help they can get. It's a nice place, Cabonga. I am sure that you will like it there."

The superintendent lit a cigarette and turned his back on the students. As he was returning the pack to his shirt pocket, he stopped suddenly and turned to face the group.

"And don't forget, boys," he said. "Take everything you own with you. The bunkhouses have to be emptied of everything that belongs to you. And, oh yes, bring your mattresses along. There are none at Cabonga."

Simard-Comtois offered Alphonse a cigarette and the two men walked back together, to where the superintendent's cabin stood on the knoll overlooking the bay. The man had his hand on Alphonse's shoulder and he spoke excitedly, waving his free arm in the air.

Chapter 52

It was a perfect, sun-shiny day as the *Madeleine* backed away from the wharf and out towards the open waters of Washika Bay. It had taken over an hour to get the students organized and packed, and another hour to carry all of their gear down to the dock and load it onto the *Madeleine.* The last to go were the long, narrow black and white striped mattresses. The students carried them balanced on their heads, as they walked unsteadily down the sandy slope to the water's edge.

At nine-thirty, the last of the mattresses was piled on top of other mattresses, and packsacks, and green army duffle bags. The deck, both forward and aft, was littered with the students' belongings. As the *Madeleine* moved away from Washika in a southeasterly direction, the students sorted out their gear and arranged things so as to be as comfortable as they could be. Astern, in the last of the two drive boats in tow, François Gauthier lay back on his mattress wedged between the gunwales. Propped up by a large canvas pack, he read attentively as the breeze from the bay rattled the pages of his book. Today, it was, *The Elements of Physics* by Shortley and Williams. Gauthier had many interests. In the green canvas bag at his feet were other books: *Biologie* by Claude Villee, a translated biography of *The Life of Jack London*, a very thick book entitled, *Les Poissons d'eau douce du Québec* and, finally, an old and extremely worn copy of Constance Garnett's translation of the short novels of Fyodor Dostoevsky. François Gauthier spent much of his time alone.

Henri lay against the front of the cabin, stretched out on his mattress. He watched the shoreline spreading outward as the *Madeleine* made her way due south to Cabonga Dam. He had not written to Sylvie. After supper, the previous evening, he had fallen asleep on his bunk and, when he awoke, there had been only time to prepare for bed before the lights went out. And now this. Henri felt a bit apprehensive about this migration to Cabonga Dam. Alphonse had often discussed future work plans with him, mostly during the trips back to Washika after the day's work. He would talk about how the sweep was going and about how much work was expected of them, what shores had to be picked clean more so than others. He had mentioned the dam and how the gap would be open soon, and how some of the men at Cabonga Dam had been working there since the construction of the dam in the late twenties. Alphonse told him that he and Télesphore Aumont of the *Hirondelle* and perhaps Gérard Lapointe of the *Sophie* might have to spend more time there once the gap was opened up. There were jams, Alphonse had told him, sometimes so bad that they had to use dynamite to untangle the logs. But Alphonse had never mentioned that the sweep crew might be going to Cabonga. They had all the men they needed there, Alphonse had said, good old boys who knew their job and did it well. They had been there so long it was difficult to send in replacements, fresh young men willing to learn the job. The old ones did not take kindly to the arrival of younger men, to being reminded that soon they would be replaced. What would they do then? Being sent help from Washika was never graciously accepted. They enjoyed a quiet, peaceful life at Cabonga and that was the way they intended to keep it. The arrival of the tugboats from Washika was tolerated as a necessary intrusion when the gap was opened, but only for that time. And besides, the tugboat captains and the men at Cabonga were old friends.

Henri smiled to himself as he looked at the stack of mattresses and packsacks and sleeping log drivers piled haphazardly about the deck. Just imagine, he thought, how the poor old boys at Cabonga will react when they get sight of this. It did not make sense to Henri. And he tried to understand, going over all that Alphonse had told him; Cabonga Dam on the Cabonga Reservoir where they had worked all that summer, the gap being opened in the dam, and the logs being driven through the gap and down the Gens-de-Terre river, and the men who had drowned there on previous log drives and where you could still find crosses erected along its banks. He closed his eyes, thinking, and he could feel the sun heating his eyelids and his face was warm and his head fell back heavily and, soon, Henri was snoring loudly like Lavigne who lay next to him, and St-Jean at his feet.

Chapter 53

When Henri opened his eyes, the first thing he noticed was that the *Madeleine*'s engine was not running. But, there was another engine running close by.

"Lunch!" Alphonse called from the cabin. Almost immediately, the other engine shut down. It was the *Hirondelle*, a tugboat almost identical to the *Madeleine*.

Henri squinted against the noonday sun and his mouth was dry from sleep. He stretched and then he did up his bootlaces. After, he began the search for his lunch pail like everyone else. He suddenly remembered that he had left his lunch pail in the cabin so that it would be out of the sun. Alphonse stood in the doorway with a sandwich in one hand and, in the other, a cup of steaming hot tea.

"Excuse me, Alphonse," Henri said as he slid by the man. "I just want to get my lunch."

"You can eat here, Henri. You might be better in the shade."

Henri remembered a similar warning, several weeks past, and the fish-scale V formation on his chest, and the purple jar, and Lise Archambault sliding the wooden tongue depressor with its yellow glob of salve slowly, and delicately, down his chest.

"Yes, all right," Henri said. He moved the wooden box away from the doorway and sat down. It was cool in the cabin and a light breeze whistled through a crack in the starboard window.

Alphonse leaned back into the cabin and picked out another sandwich from his lunch pail. From where he sat on the wooden box, Henri could see Télesphore Aumont standing in the doorway of the *Hirondelle*. The two tugboats had been made fast with their gunwales touching.

"Well, you know how they are," Alphonse spoke as he poured tea from his thermos bottle. "You've been here as long as me, Téles. You must know by now how they think."

"Ah yes, that's true." the man said. "You're certainly right about that."

Henri looked beyond the space between Alphonse and the cabin doorway. He could see Télesphore framed in the red trim of the *Hirondelle*'s cabin doorway. He was wearing his black sunglasses as he always did whenever he went outside, and a white hard hat. He had never achieved the rank of foreman and he had no one working under him, but no one ever mentioned the hat. There was nothing unusual about Télesphore, except his ears. They were large, elephantine ears. In the bunkhouse-and-office, the boys had made a joke about them. In the morning, when Télesphore coughed his way to the bathroom, the boys no longer waited to see his eyes come popping out of his head since, as the joke went, he was not really going to the bathroom at all. In fact, Télesphore Aumont was taxiing up the runway, testing the air and revving his engine and preparing to take off with his large flaps angled just perfect for a perfect takeoff.

"Now take this gang here," Alphonse continued, chewing as he spoke and washing the sandwich down with hot tea. "You think they need them at the gap? Armand has been doing the job, almost alone, for more than thirty years."

"Yes, you're right there," Télesphore burped loudly. He threw a corner of the thick sandwich into the water. "So you think it's the gang below?"

"No doubt at all," Alphonse said. "Besides, and keep this for yourself, Simard-Comtois told me so himself just this morning." Alphonse looked over his shoulder at Henri. "This is between us, okay Henri?"

"Yes, of course," Henri replied.

"According to him," Alphonse continued, "they made a bit of a gaffe in Ste-Émilie, at the head office. We don't know who, but that doesn't matter. It seems that there was supposed to be only six fellows on the sweep this year. But, you know how it is, the son of one, and the friend of the son of another. So now, there are twenty students on the sweep plus one working as a cookee. But, at the head office in Ste-Émilie, there are still only six."

"*Et bien*," Télesphore sighed, as he pulled at one of his large, flat ears. "That complicates things, eh? It's a wonder they haven't discovered this already down below."

"It's not as bad as all that. It seems that the clerk here can fix it so nothing shows in Ste-Émilie. Simard-Comtois told me. But, the worst is that some big shot is coming to Washika this week. Some kind of *directeur*, very high placed in the Company. Imagine, just for a minute, what he would think when he sees my gang here. And there's supposed to be only six of them."

"*Et bien*," Télesphore pulled at his ear again. "So that's why were going to Cabonga."

"Not you, Téles," Alphonse brought a toothpick out from his shirt pocket and placed it in a corner of his mouth. "They might need the *Hirondelle* for a while. Maybe even the *Madeleine*. We've got to keep the booms and all of those logs moving. It's my gang they're shipping down to Cabonga, to hide. No one knows for how long?"

"So what will your gang do at Cabonga?"

"They'll help Armand at the gap. Maybe they'll do a little sweep above the dam. Armand has an Acadia. Those are good little boats for that kind of work."

Télesphore rubbed the stubble on his cheek and on the end of his chin. "And there's a Russel there as well," he said. "Bernatchez is handling her. Poor Armand, he'll find it hard with your gang. He's so used to the quiet."

"Yes, I think so too." Alphonse began to roll a cigarette. He sat down on the doorsill and leaned his back against the frame.

"*Et bien*, what can we do, eh?" Télesphore stretched his bulging waistline, rubbing the palm of his hand affectionately across his rounded belly. He reached behind the cabin door and brought out a casting rod. "Well I guess I'll try to scare up a few," he said. Télesphore went forward then, to stand on deck next to the anchor, and cast out into deeper water.

Chapter 54

It was cool in the cabin, and very quiet. Henri sat on the low wooden box near the open doorway. He could hear the water slapping the hulls of the two tugboats. Behind and beyond the *Madeleine*, he could hear the barking of the gulls as the boys tossed cheese and bread crust out onto the water. Occasionally, someone moved about on deck, striking metal with lunch pail or hard hat, or dropping a pike pole across the seats of a drive boat. But, mostly, it was very quiet and Henri listened to the breeze as it entered the cabin. It was a special time of day for Henri. It was a moment of quiet contemplation, not unlike the time he had spent in church, at the Église de St-Germain, the year that he had gone to mass every morning during Lent. He had arrived thirty minutes early one morning and the experience of solitude, of silent meditation, had touched him deeply. Thereafter Henri had arrived early every morning, to sit alone, unmoving in the wooden pew, to stare at the statues and think about everything in his life and the things he understood and those he did not. He would drop to his knees and look up at the statues and concentrate very hard and will the carved heads to move and their lips to part in smile.

"Alphonse," Henri almost regretted breaking the silence. "Don't you find it kind of special, this time of day, so quiet and peaceful."

"*Et oui*, Henri." Alphonse replied. "A time to think of old sins. And maybe some new ones, eh Henri?"

"But I like this time of day, you know. Here on the water like this."

"Yes, probably. I've been here a long time, Henri."

A strong breeze blew in through the open doorway, scattering the smoke as it rose from Alphonse's cigarette. Henri listened to the quiet, the water slapping against the hulls, the barking of the gulls. Suddenly, there were voices, and hurried footsteps on deck.

"Alphonse," Lavigne stood in the doorway. "Could we take one of the drive boats? The guys spotted a bark canoe on shore."

"Yes, yes," Alphonse stood up from the high stool at the wheel. "Go ahead, Gaston. But, make sure they put on their life jackets. You never know who might show up here."

"Yes. Of course, I'll tell them," Lavigne said as he stepped back from the doorway.

Henri could still hear his footsteps on deck as he yelled to the others that it was okay to take the drive boats.

"Have you ever seen that canoe, Alphonse?"

"Oh yes. You've gone by there often. I'm surprised you haven't seen it.

"How's that?"

"Look outside, Henri. You don't know where we are? It's true, we worked a little further down. This is Lost Cabin Bay here, where we cleaned up just before going on the fire."

Henri stood up and looked out beyond the bow to the sloping shore with its yellow sand, and the jack pine, and the white birch trees leaning outward over the shoreline, and the low bushes just beneath, mostly sweet fern and blueberry. To Henri, the shore was not unlike the others they had worked on the Cabonga. He looked again, at the grey *chicots* sticking up out of the sand and, further in from shore, the isolated stands of black spruce. Looking past the stern of the *Hirondelle*, he saw the grey, dead remains of an enormous white pine standing taller than the forest around it.

"That's a white pine over there, Alphonse?" Henri wasn't absolutely sure. "The big one, taller than the rest?"

"Yes, that's right," Alphonse replied without turning to look at it.

"And so this is Lost Cabin Bay?"

"Yes sir. Maybe you should have gone there with the others, Henri."

"To see the canoe?"

"Yes. But there's not much left. It's very old. It was very well made though, and if it hadn't lain on shore so long, probably it would still be in good shape. And then, there's the cabin."

"There's a cabin in there?"

"Yes. Only the walls now. The roof fell in because of the snow, and now the floor has rotted. The walls are solid though."

"Was it the same person, you think, who built the cabin and the canoe?"

"Oh yes. I met him one time in Ste-Émilie. A big man. George Opikwanic, a very strong man."

"An Indian?"

"Yes. He used to trap around here in the winter. That was a long time ago. He would stay here all winter. Just him and Katherine, his wife, and a beaver dog."

Henri looked out again at the shore and the trees. He tried to imagine what it would look like in winter, with the sweet fern covered and the boughs of the pine heavy with snow. It was difficult to imagine the Cabonga frozen.

"Did he travel in and out by dog team, Alphonse?"

"No. They would spend the winter here. They came in from Washika by canoe in October or early November and they would come out only in spring, when the ice was off the lake."

Alphonse turned to look at Henri. He looked at Henri for what seemed to be a long time but he seemed to be elsewhere. Finally, he said, "you are not going to ask me about the canoe?"

"The canoe? You already told me, Alphonse. It belonged to the trapper."

Alphonse smiled. "Think Henri," he said. "The man's cabin is abandoned, ruined, and his canoe as well."

"Yes?"

"And the trapper's not here." Alphonse lowered his head, covering his eyes with the visor of his hard hat.

"An accident. There was an accident with the canoe? Did they both drown?"

"No, Henri. It wasn't like that at all."

Alphonse slipped the pack of tobacco out of his shirt pocket and began to roll a cigarette. Henri noticed the change. Alphonse had suddenly become very serious.

"You know what happened?"

"Yes Henri, I know but I'm not proud of what happened. I can tell you that it's been a great shame in my family ever since. Remember my brother, Oscar? I told you about him."

"The altar boy?"

"Yes, that's him. Well, he used to haul supplies for the Company. He had his own truck. He was doing very well. A good worker, Oscar, but he liked to take a drink and, when he was drunk, it was the women. Anyway, one day in October, George Opikwanic asked Oscar if he would take him as far as Washika. Oscar says sure, and they made arrangements to pick up George's supplies at the store. There was only one general store in Ste-Émilie then. The morning they were to leave, George and Katherine and the beaver dog were sitting on the verandah of the store at seven o'clock. The stores opened early in those days. They had their packsacks, and boxes full of provisions, rifles and ammunition, and kerosene for the lamps."

"It was almost nine o'clock before Oscar arrived, loaded down with supplies for the camps. After they got all of George's supplies in the truck, Oscar was sweating. It wasn't the work so much but he had drunk quite a bit the night before. And he wasn't too happy because it was Friday morning, which meant that he would be spending most of the weekend in the camps. So, after they finished loading, he says to George, "How about a little beer before we leave, eh?" Now, George was in a hurry to get out of Ste-Émilie, to be in the bush and trapping and away from the ways of the white man. And besides, it was the end of October and who could tell when the weather would change. But, Oscar was doing him and his wife a big favour. He was hauling supplies in to Washika that day and so he was not charging George for the trip. Anyway, George said okay, and they stopped in at Duhamel's. You know the place?"

"Yes, I know where you mean." Henri had driven by the place many times with his parents on their way to Sunday mass at St-Exupéry's. The verandah slanted downward towards the sidewalk and all of the second floor windows had the blinds down, yellow, faded blinds. There were always old men sitting on the verandah on Sunday mornings, warming their bodies in the sun. Henri remembered the barn-red paint of the building with its cream trim around the door and windows but, mostly, he remembered the sign hanging from the second floor balcony, a faded lime-green with red letters saying, "*Chambre à Louer*-$5.00" and the price crossed out with a single stroke and the new price to rent a room, $4.00, written in its place.

Alphonse ran his tongue along the paper and rolled the cigarette between his fingers. He lit the cigarette, closing one eye to keep the smoke out.

"Anyway," Alphonse continued. "At noon, they were still at the hotel. George had fallen asleep, drunk, at the table and Oscar had taken a room upstairs with Katherine. It was almost three o'clock by the time they woke George, and the three of them headed for Washika. No one knows for sure what happened after that. Oscar says that they did not make any stops along the way but there were quite a few places then, on the way to Washika, where a man could buy a drink. It was late when they arrived and there are many who claim that Oscar fell out of the truck when he stopped at the storehouse at Washika. George and Katherine had to be held up by their arms going down to the dock. The men loaded the canoe for them and helped them in along with their beaver dog. That was the last time the trapper and his wife were ever seen alive.

"It was near the end of May and they had not come out yet. We thought maybe they had gone to Cabonga Dam but Armand said that he had seen no one since the break-up. Finally, Jean-Luc Desrosiers went down that way for his inspection before the summer sweep. He stopped in at the cabin. The canoe was right where it is today, but in better shape. Inside the cabin, he found George hanging from a crossbeam, the rope so tight that the skin of his neck covered most of it. In the corner, with blankets up to her chin, his wife lay dead. They had both been dead for a long time, possibly since that last night they came down the Cabonga by canoe. There was a brief investigation. Two policemen arrived there in a Beaver airplane on floats. In the papers, later, we read that Katherine had been strangled to death."

"And after?" Henri inquired. "What happened after that? Was the dog ever found?"

"No. There was no sign of the dog. Nothing happened really. When the investigation was completed they sent my brother Oscar off to the Capital where he began driving a truck for the Company. He never returned to Ste-Émilie after that. I have never seen him since…"

Chapter 55

The sun was high in the southwest when they arrived at Cabonga Dam. The *Madeleine* made her way in among the logs, followed by the *Hirondelle*. When Henri looked back, to stern, there were logs behind him for almost a quarter mile and, beyond the bow, they were jammed right up to the dam. In the bay, opening onto the dam, the pulpwood was packed tightly together among the larger logs. On the east side of the bay, a large grey island of broken rock sat above the water. On its westward side, hundreds of logs stood up out of the water, stranded there in a mound of entangled logs. Henri pointed to the logjam.

"There'll be plenty of those," Alphonse smiled.

It was a perfect little bay. The land sloped high on both sides and the bay narrowed as it approached the dam. To the east, high up on the bank, was a two-storey frame house, white with green trim around the windows and the railing that ran all along the verandah at the front of the house. A well-kept lawn sloped down towards the water. In the centre of the lawn a tall, peeled jack pine held a Union Jack waving in the breeze. Henri was puzzled by the flag. At the pay office where *Monsieur* Lafrance had prepared their pay cheques, there was also a Union Jack in the yard. Henri did not understand. His father said that they had their own flag but it was only seen during the Saint-Jean-Baptiste Day parade. A government agent lived there with his family, Alphonse had told him, perhaps the man and his family came from overseas, from England maybe. The agent's work had something to do with the control of water levels but Alphonse was not sure about that. Nobody was sure of what the government agent was supposed to be doing there. The man rarely went outside although the children were often seen playing on the lawn.

Henri stood on deck by the cabin doorway. He could smell the pulpwood and, as they approached the west side of the bay, he recognized the sweet fern growing along the hillside. The shore was littered with huge grey-black boulders and, above these, the bank rose steeply. There were tall, skinny jack pine all along the slope with blueberry bushes and sweet fern growing beneath. As Henri scanned the shoreline, his brain seemed to register what he saw but was constantly being pushed and shoved into another awareness, constantly being reminded of one prominent factor, the invariable, ever-present roar of the *chute* as the water rushed through the gap, brown and froth-white, with its cargo of logs tumbling end over end.

The *Madeleine* and the *Hirondelle* were made fast to the boom timbers less than thirty feet offshore. The students stepped onto the boom and made their way ashore. As they moved closer to the gap, they were forced to raise their voices in order to be heard. When a breeze blew in from the south, they could feel the moist spray rushing in from the gap. They stared at the black, rushing water, and the white foam forming around the groups of logs that swirled in the current as they were herded towards the gap.

A boardwalk had been constructed along both sides of the bay and ended at the opening in the dam, at the gap. The boardwalks were simple wooden platforms, lumber nailed across two long, floating logs with a railing on both sides. Henri stepped over the chain holding the boardwalk to shore and boarded the platform. Holding onto the railing, he could feel the rushing water vibrating the planks of the boardwalk. It made him dizzy just looking at it. Closer to the dam, the wood moved more swiftly, some logs swirling round, others following straight courses or sticking straight up out of the water. The logs danced in all of these ways, faster and faster, in one and only one direction and then they were gone, disappearing through the gap, that great hole in the dam. Henri looked up at the black, squared timbers of the dam, and those that had been raised to open the gap, and the gear wheels and chains where Armand had cranked up the timbers early that morning. Now, the gap was open, the wood was being moved out, and somewhere along the banks of the Gens-de-Terre, a lone raccoon sat puzzled by the sudden rise of water as he added another empty mussel shell to the pile in front of him.

Alphonse walked past the students clinging to the railing and looking at the fast-moving water. He made his way to the mouth of the gap where a short, elderly man poked at the moving logs with a pike pole.

"Yes sir!" Alphonse shouted.

"Yes sir," the man replied.

"Did you get word from Ste-Émilie, Armand?"

"Yes just this morning, by radio."

"No fun, eh?"

"You know how they are." The man spat on a log as it went by. "Anyway."

"Yes, I know. Open early?"

"Eight o'clock. Might have opened yesterday but *Monsieur* fancy pants up there," Armand jerked his thumb towards the agent's house. "He was not ready. You know how they are."

"Ah yes, I suppose. Anyway, Armand, this is my gang."

"Yes, eh?" The old man leaned on his pole and looked at the boys standing at the far end of the boardwalk. A smile grew on his face. "Pretty rough looking crew."

"Oh, they're all right. You just have to get used to them."

"I'm getting old, Alphonse. I tell you. I'm getting too old for this sort of thing."

"You?" Alphonse laughed. "I'll be dead and buried and you'll still be here, pushing logs into the Gens-de-Terre."

"Ha!" The old man raised a thumb against his left nostril and blew hard, wiping the remaining mucus with the back of his hand.

Further back along the boardwalk, the boys watched Alphonse and the old man as they spoke. They could not hear the words over the roar of the gap. But they could tell by the look on their faces, the way the old man spat on the water, and how they both laughed as Alphonse slapped the old one's shoulder. They could tell, just seeing them, that Alphonse and Armand Lafond were one of a kind. To the twenty young log drivers standing at the gap on the Cabonga, this was a very good sign.

Chapter 56

So, this was Cabonga. The fellows let their packs fall at their feet as they reached the crest of the hill. They looked at one another and smiled. This was not Washika with its green flat buildings and electric wires and enormous tractor-trailers stopping at the scales. This was what they had expected, what they had sketched upon their imaginations when they first received word that they were going to Washika for the summer; before them, in a sandy clearing surrounded by spindly jack pine, stood the camp. The building was longer than it was wide, made of logs with the bark left on. A low-sloping roof, covered in tarpaper, extended several feet beyond the front of the building and there was a small landing made of boards before the door. At the far end of the cabin, a rusted stovepipe stuck out of the wall, held up by two lengths of wire anchored to rafter poles near the edge of the roof. In the same clearing and overlooking the bay were two other cabins.

"In there," Armand said, pointing towards one of the smaller cabins. He had followed the students as they climbed the slope. "You can put your stuff in there and wash up. Be supper soon."

They went inside, carrying packsacks, some of them hauling mattresses. It was cool in the cabin, and dark, and there was a strong smell of fly oil. When their eyes adjusted to the dim light, they could see that the wall logs had been peeled, and oiled, and the floorboards, although unpainted, were clean and well swept. There were bunk beds on both sides of the cabin. Only one of the beds had a mattress and blankets on it. There was a large trunk near the head of the bed, and the bed was neatly made with a clean, white pillowcase and a grey wool blanket stretched tightly and tucked in under the mattress. At the far end of the cabin was a thin wall of boards and an open doorway. Inside this little room they found a washstand with a full bucket of water, a washbasin and soap, and a small round mirror above them. There was a door leading out of the room, directly onto the slope of the hill. To the right of the mirror, a tall narrow window let in plenty of light. From outside, they had seen a stovepipe, like on the largest of the three log buildings, but there was no stove in the bunkhouse. Suspended from a set of rafters, a section of stovepipe descended, turned a sharp ninety degrees and stopped abruptly. Its opening was stuffed with burlap to keep the bugs out.

The students claimed their bunks by dropping their packsacks on the springs, and then they headed down to the *Madeleine* for their mattresses. François Gauthier, like several others, had carried his mattress up first, along with his bag of books. He chose the bunk bed adjacent to the washroom wall and dropped his mattress on the bottom bunk. Before returning to the *Madeleine* for his pack, François arranged his books in a neat row along the windowsill.

It was not long before every bunk had been claimed, packsacks dropped upon them, or mattresses. A continual stream of boys marched from the bunkhouse to the *Madeleine* and back again. Once they were settled in, the students untied the bundles of sheets and blankets and pillows and made their beds. At Washika, before leaving, some of the boys had tried rolling up their mattresses with the bedclothes in place; these were later untied aboard the *Madeleine* as they wanted a comfortable place to sleep during the trip to Cabonga Dam. Now, they hurried with the sheets and blankets, searched the walls for nails to hang their clothes on, or simply kicked their packs under the bed as André Guy had done without a moment's hesitation.

Suddenly, a large form appeared in the doorway. The man stood on the doorsill, looking at the new arrivals. He nodded politely and walked by the bunks to his own bunk where he dropped his hardhat and lunch pail on the trunk. The man looked up at Henri, stretched out on the bunk above his own. He pursed his lips tightly together and nodded a greeting to Henri.

"*Bonjour*," Henri said. "We just came in from Washika. You work here?"

The man nodded, yes, and picked up a towel from a nail on the wall.

"Better hurry," he said. "Be supper soon."

"There's a bell?" Henri said.

The man smiled. "We're only five here."

As the man spoke, a tall, thin man entered the bunkhouse. He walked quickly, with his head down, as if he had not noticed the students, or was shy and did not want to look at them. He went directly to the end bunk, opposite François Gauthier's, pulled a towel off the foot of the upper bunk and went into the washroom.

"He works here too?" Henri nodded towards the washroom.

"Yes," the man answered. He looked over at the others, stretched out comfortably on their bunks and waiting for the supper bell to ring. "Better hurry," he said to Henri.

As the man walked towards the washroom, Henri stared at the back of his large head, covered in a mass of sweaty curls. His shoulders, Henri noticed, touched both sides of the doorway as he entered the washroom. Henri looked at the lunch pail on the trunk, the black tin scratched and dented from use. The hard hat was yellow, like the ones they wore at Washika but it seemed smaller, rounder, an older model perhaps. A name strip had been glued to the front: C. Bernatchez.

So, there would be two other fellows with them in the bunkhouse. Henri had not noticed the other man's bunk at the far end of the room, or his towel hanging from the foot of the upper bunk. The two men came out of the washroom together, their hair wet and combed. They hung their towels from the top bar of their bunks and started to leave.

"Is it time now?" Henri said to Bernatchez.

The man nodded. He held up a wide, muscled forearm and stared a moment at his wristwatch. "In five minutes," he said. Bernatchez and the thin man who had waited for him went out through the front doorway of the bunkhouse.

Henri jumped down off the bunk. "Hey, you guys." He hurried towards the washroom. "Hurry up. Supper in five minutes."

"Go on." Lavigne rolled over on his side. "It's only five o'clock."

"That's it," Henri yelled back from the washroom. "That's when they eat here."

Slowly, the students dragged themselves from their bunks, stretching and scratching at their hair. François Gauthier was hurrying, trying to finish the last paragraph in a chapter.

"Hey!" A voice, loud but friendly enough. Alphonse stood in the open doorway. "Not hungry today? Last call for supper."

Alphonse then left as suddenly as he had appeared. It was almost unreal. Supper at five o'clock. And no supper bell. The fellows were beginning to have doubts. What kind of place was this?

"*Calis*!" Lavigne jumped down off his bunk. "Morin was right. What an hour. *Sacrament*!"

Lavigne noticed the body on the lower bunk. The boy was curled up in sleep with several strands of hair standing straight up on his head. Lavigne reached beneath the mattress, getting a good grip on the edge, and pulled up sharply. André Guy rolled off the bed and onto the floor and, just as swiftly, he was sitting upright with his raised fists clenched and looking around him with half-opened eyes and jerking movements of his head.

"Come on, André!" Lavigne shouted over his shoulder. "Time to eat!"

Chapter 57

It was the last thing in the world they expected to see. Inside the cookhouse, the log walls had been covered with Masonite and painted white. In addition to several lengths of sticky flypaper, there were naphtha lamps hanging from the two crossbeams spanning the width of the building. And there were two tables with long, narrow plank benches running the full length of the tables. But none of these things had interested the boys much. From the moment they had stepped onto the landing and smelled the odour of freshly baked bread through the screen door, from that very instant when they had stepped inside, there was one and only one thing on their minds. As the students marched past the opened screen door and into the cookhouse, their reaction was an openmouthed silence as they handed their meal tickets to the young girl.

The cook's daughter smiled and looked boldly into each of the students' eyes as he handed her his ticket. For the first time in their short lives, they were quiet, without comment, without the ability to utter a single phrase. François Gauthier blushed. No girl had ever looked at him that way.

When everyone was seated a short, pale man with thick, black hair combed straight back from his forehead stood in the centre of the room. He held his hands clasped together in front of him as he looked at the new arrivals.

"My name is Germain Laviolette," he began. "I'm the cook here." He looked down at his fresh, white apron. "Me and my daughter, that's my daughter Nicole," the cook said pointing to the girl, standing, half-leaning against the open doorway that framed the roundness of her hips in the light from the kitchen, "we'd like to welcome you to Washika...I mean, Cabonga."

Everybody laughed. The cook looked over at Armand Lafond. He chuckled then at his own unintended little joke. "If there's anything," he continued. "Don't be shy. Just come and see me and we'll fix it up."

The cook turned then and slipped by his daughter and went into the kitchen. The young girl stayed a moment in the doorway, fixing her eyes on the twenty students from the Collège de Ste-Émilie. It was not until she turned to leave that forty eyes scanned and remained focused on her beauty. Hungry as they were, most of the twenty students found it difficult to eat. The food was excellent. That was not a problem. And *Monsieur* Laviolette, the cook, seemed to be a good-natured person as he laughed and bantered easily with the older men.

Alphonse sat beside Armand Lafond and Bernatchez, the tugboat operator, and his deckhand. Télesphore Aumont sat alone, opposite Alphonse and the others. Behind him, the twenty students sat at one table, eating in silence as they had been taught at Washika, even though Alphonse and Armand and the other boatmen spoke freely throughout the meal.

Henri was hungry. There were boiled potatoes and yellow wax beans that he covered with margarine and pork chops to which he added great globs of ketchup. There was plenty of steaming, hot tea and piles of thickly sliced warm bread which *Monsieur* Laviolette refurbished as soon as the stack had noticeably declined. And there was raspberry pie, made from fresh raspberries Nicole had picked that morning. The cook had told them about the raspberries.

The girl, Nicole, was not seen after her father's welcoming speech. She worked in the kitchen while her father rushed back and forth, keeping the tables well supplied. Then, they saw her moving past the open doorway, with her golden hair tied back tightly on her head and the rest falling leisurely in a thick wavy tail upon her back. And she wore nothing beneath the white T-shirt; there was no doubt in any of the students' minds about that. Despite the full apron that she wore, the fellows were certain about it. Even Gauthier, when he had blushed earlier at the door, had felt himself becoming aroused upon his observation of each mamma pushing forcibly against the thin cotton material of her shirt. The girl moved swiftly by the doorway each time but the boys were on the alert. They watched and waited for one more glimpse: the long, slender brown thighs culminating in the fire-engine red shorts, the slightly rounded belly and those eyes, those they could not avoid, the teasing, taunting, grey-green eyes staring out at them.

Henri was hungry. He was hungry and he filled his plate until it almost overflowed. He covered everything with ketchup and moved it all with a fork to his mouth, and his mouth worked, and molars ground against molars, and great gulps of tea flowed in to wash it all down, past the pharynx and into the esophagus. And then he filled half of his plate with two quarter sections of pie and felt the seeds lodge between his teeth and, through it all, through the potato and wax beans, and the pork chops and the pie, there was nothing on his mind, nothing but the tall, slim-legged Nicole, and how she stood with her back straight and, seeing her from the side, how her breasts hung like large, ripened pears over the rise of her chest and when she walked how the muscles moved, long slender brown thighs and when she turned her back on them, her buttocks stared right back at them, as round and as firm as her breasts.

Chapter 58

Gauthier was in love. For the first time in his life, he had taken notice of a girl. And she had looked back at him. Now, he was miserable. After supper, he had lain down on his bunk to read, as he was accustomed to doing at Washika, but he was unable to concentrate. Three times he had read the chapter heading, "Interference Phenomena; the superposition principle," and each time the page blurred in front of his eyes and he found himself lowering the book and sliding down against the pillow and seeing her, standing before him with her soft hand outstretched and staring into his eyes. And the other part; he tried not to think about that, but he could not.

François placed the thick, black book on the windowsill and took down another, slim, aqua-blue, with black and purple circles on its cover. He opened the book and flipped rapidly through its pages. Finally, he leaned back and read, "Schematic sagittal section of the pelvic region of the female human being showing the organs of the reproductive tract..." He examined the illustration closely but it did nothing to arouse him as did the touch of her hand as he handed her his meal ticket, and her girl smell so close, and the firm roundness protruding from the interior of her shirt. It was all too much for him. That, and the way she had looked at him.

François was miserable and confused. Never before in his life had he been confronted with such feelings and no form of logic he had ever understood could explain it. He understood easily enough the concept of limits, the value of a particle approaching zero but never quite attaining it, and the logical evolution of the differential expressing a minute rate of change. At present, he was working on the idea of integration and even that part of the differential and integral calculus was clear to him. But this new sensation, this sudden lack of control of what and how he thought was most disturbing while, simultaneously, exposing him to a pleasure he had never known. François closed the biology text and placed it along the protruding windowsill with his other books and walked out of the bunkhouse.

"Hey Gauthier!" André Guy called out to François as he went by his bunk.

François did not look back. He stepped over the doorsill and disappeared from view.

"What's the matter with him?" André inquired. He looked up at Henri.

"I don't know," Henri said.

"Who can tell with Gauthier?" Lavigne commented. "You know how he is with his books."

"Maybe we should fix him up with Nicole for a night, eh?" André laughed. "*Sacrament*, he wouldn't read so much after that."

"Never mind!" Lavigne sat up on his bunk. "If I can get her, I'll keep her for myself. Hey, did you see her, eh?"

Henri looked across to the bunk on his left. Maurice St-Jean was lying flat on his back with his hands clasped behind his head and looking straight upwards to the tiny strips of flypaper hanging from the crossbeams, their stickiness shining in the dim light and dotted with dead, desiccated flies.

"What do you think, Maurice?" Henri said.

"What?" St-Jean stared at the flypaper.

"The cook's daughter."

"Not bad."

"Come on, Maurice. You saw her. You can't say she's not beautiful."

St-Jean rolled over onto his side, facing Henri. He reached back, beside his pillow, and slid a tin ashtray across the blanket. He brought out two cigarettes from his pack of tobacco, the ends twisted to keep the tobacco from running out. He offered one to Henri.

"Sure," Henri said.

St-Jean lit up. "Yes, she's beautiful," he said. "Everybody knows that. Her too. Just look at her. You can tell."

"But it's not her fault she's good-looking. Come on."

"That's true. You know Auguste St-Jacques in town. It's not his fault he's so strong. Just like it's not his fault Gauthier's such a brain. Just like it's not his fault your friend Greer looks good and picks up girls like it was nothing. It all depends how you wear it."

Henri nodded. He had never heard St-Jean string so many sentences together. "What you say is true, Maurice. And so?"

"So," St-Jean continued, "just take Auguste, he wouldn't hurt a fly, strong as he is. And Gauthier, have you ever heard him try to make fun of someone with big words or fancy talk from his books? Never."

St-Jean stopped there. Henri wondered if he had purposely refrained from commenting on how his friend David Greer handled his attractiveness to the girls. David was Henri's best friend, that was true, but he could not deny being jealous of him at times and even, on occasion, disapproving of his behaviour. David was a 'have,' like Lavigne. Did all 'haves' abuse their good fortune at the expense of the 'have-nots'? Did just being good exclude one from the world of the 'haves,' doomed to remain, forever, a 'have-not'? Were all good people 'have-nots'? Were his parents 'have-nots'? No, he didn't think so.

"Are you saying, Maurice, that Nicole is not a good person?"

"She's good-looking."

"But bad."

"It's like I said before. It depends on how you wear it."

"I think you're being hard on her. You don't even know her." Henri paused for a time. "Do you?"

St-Jean did not answer.

"Anyway," Henri continued," she must have a boyfriend."

"That's for sure, and more than one waiting his turn."

"Come on, Maurice. You sound almost jealous."

"You don't understand, Henri. You can't know what it's like. I know, *sacrament*, let me tell you."

St-Jean returned to his original position on the bed. The conversation had ended. Once again, he stared at the flypaper and the dead and not so dead flies.

"Maybe you're right," Henri said. He thought about Sylvie, at the Café D'or, and how beautiful she was. And Shannon, how beautiful she had seemed to him. But the two girls were not the same. Perhaps St-Jean was right. Perhaps they did not wear their beauty in the same way. And this was surely something, St-Jean speaking out like that. A bad experience? With a girl like Nicole perhaps. What was it? Bitterness or fear? Anger and bitterness and the feeling of loneliness at being let down? Henri remembered the taste of it. He felt sorry for Maurice.

"Hey! Here's Gauthier," André Guy said loudly, turning from the window.

Henri raised himself on his elbows. Looking out through the screen door he could see the flat light on the sand outside and he suddenly realized how dark it had become inside the bunkhouse.

"André," he called down from his bunk. "Get the lamp going."

"It's no use," a voice said from below. It was Bernatchez.

Henri leaned over his bunk to speak to the man. "How come?" he said "There's fuel. I checked it earlier."

"Yes," the man replied. "But it's broken. The O-ring and valve stem have to be replaced."

"Isn't there another lamp?"

"No."

"So what do we do in the dark?"

"Sleep," Bernatchez answered. The man sat up then and began undoing the buttons of his shirt.

Henri looked around the bunkhouse. In the dim light he could see that several of the boys had fallen asleep already, fully dressed and lying on top of their blankets.

Suddenly, the room grew darker. François Gauthier was standing in the doorway.

"Aha, Gauthier!" André began. "And where have you been off to, eh?"

François Gauthier walked slowly as he entered the bunkhouse, looking at no one as was his custom but, as he went by André's bunk, he turned his head sharply and screamed, "None of your goddamned business! Okay?"

The students who were still awake could not believe their ears. Those who had been sleeping stirred on their bunks and looked about them in a sleepy, half-interested manner. No one could see the scarlet tinge on François' cheeks and forehead nor, in the semi-darkness, could they see André sitting on his bunk, his own vision blurred by the tears in his eyes. He had always believed that, deep down, Gauthier was really his friend.

Chapter 59

The students were handed pike poles and stationed ten on each side of the gap. The job was easy enough: just keep the logs moving and watch out for the jams. Henri was second in line from the gap. He leaned into his pole and straightened out the logs as they came rushing by sideways, or leaning on others, and he twisted the point of his pike pole out of the bark as the log swept past Armand and out through the gap in the dam.

"That's it, Henri," the old man said. "Keep 'em coming."

Henri listened to the water and imagined melodies, rhythms, and he smelled the good smell of spruce gum and he was happy standing in the warmth of the sun. He looked across the bay, to the other boardwalk where he could see Lavigne nearest the dam, and St-Jean, and André Guy up to his old tricks, smashing his nearest neighbour a crack of his hard hat. Things were almost normal. Henri found it strange not seeing Alphonse around. He had left after supper without stopping in to see them at the bunkhouse. Télesphore Aumont had left as well.

Henri was tired. Not from the work, for he always felt good and alive and happy working like this in the sun, with the water and the pulp smells and the gulls barking overhead. But, he had not slept well. It was always like that the first night. He could not remember having slept. *Monsieur* Bernatchez, on the bunk below his, had snored most of the night and Henri had smiled in the darkness when the farts came, evenly spaced between snores.

Henri watched the wood floating by and measured its speed as the logs passed beneath the rope stretched across the bay. The rope ran parallel to the dam, only several yards from it, and about four feet above the water. All along the thick rope and at intervals of four feet or so, short lengths of rope tied to the main rope dropped down into the water. Henri had looked at the rope for a long time and how the current made the shorter ropes stand out at an angle. It reminded him of a hay rake he had seen once being pulled by a team of horses with the driver swaying on the tiny metal seat above the curved tines. "Safety," was what *Monsieur* Lafond said the rope was for. If someone fell into the water, he could grab onto one of the dangling, short lengths of rope to avoid being swept through the gap and over the side of the dam, and into the Gens-de-Terre.

Armand Lafond drove the point of his pike pole into the floor of the boardwalk and leaned the handle against the railing.

"Take a break, Henri," he said.

"They're moving pretty good now, eh?" Henri said.

"Yes, they're moving all right."

The old man began to roll a cigarette. "You have your tobacco?" he said.

Henri nodded, yes, and leaned his pole against the railing. Henri and Armand Lafond stood together with their shoulders almost touching, their backs bent and their elbows resting on the railing, smoking and looking at the logs floating by. Henri stared at the thick yellow rope stretched tightly between the two boardwalks, and the shorter lengths seeming to dance upon the surface as the current held them pointed at a steady angle to the dam.

"*Monsieur* Lafond," he said. "I've been thinking."

"Careful, *mon vieux*," the old man smiled. "You know what that can do. Especially out here in the sun."

Armand held his cigarette cupped inside his hand to protect it from the spray of the gap. Henri watched him taking long drags on the cigarette, and the smoke coming out of his mouth and his nostrils at the same time. The hair below the rim of his hard hat was a yellow-white and his face was tanned. The lines were thin near his ears and growing deeper as they descended below the collar of his shirt. Armand held the cigarette between thumb and index finger. With a flick of his finger, he sent the stub of a cigarette flying. Henri watched it spinning and heaving on the water and, finally, disappearing over the edge of the gap.

"I was thinking about the rope."

"Yes?"

"Well, if I was to fall in, which would be worse, do you think, to go through the gap, or hang onto those ropes and be crushed by a log?"

"Better not to fall in."

"Yes, but what if I did?"

"If you're dead, you're dead. Either way, you don't have a chance?"

"And the ropes?" Henri looked at the man.

"You're young, Henri" Armand replied. "Someday, you'll know about these things. Imagine how it would look in *The Gazette* if you were to fall in. What do you think they would say about you? Not much, I can tell you. But the rope, Henri, they would not forget to mention about the rope, and this railing, even your hard hat. And what if you were not wearing your life jacket? They would say that poor Henri Morin had drowned because he was not wearing his life jacket. But the rope, they would certainly mention about that, and how it would have saved your life if only you had been wearing your life jacket. There would be no talk of the saw logs, twelve and sixteen feet long and weighing who knows how much, and how they come rushing towards the gap."

Armand leaned over the railing and spat into the water. He was a kind old man whose face broke into a smile whenever he spoke. He was not smiling now, leaning against the railing and staring across the length of yellow rope.

"Well," he said, straightening up and slapping the railing with his hand. "I think I'll go and have a tea."

"Yes sir."

It was only nine o'clock. Although the sun was high and much wood had gone through the gap since seven that morning, it was still a half hour before the break.

"A man my age," Armand said, "he deserves more than two breaks a day. What do you think, eh?"

"Ah yes, three or four at least."

"Here, Henri. Stand here near the gap. You want to use my pole? I put a file to it just this morning."

"Sure."

Henri held the smooth handle. It was much lighter and shorter than the one he had been using.

"Six years," the old man said. "Six years I've been using this one. Plenty of logs have been pushed over the gap with this one, I'll tell you."

"Hey, six years," Henri repeated.

"Yes sir. Well, now I'm going."

The old man moved carefully. He walked slowly, moving from one boulder to the next along the shore. He stopped once, at the high-water line, and then began the uphill climb to the cookhouse. Henri watched the yellow hard hat disappear from view as Armand stepped over the crest of the hill.

Standing by the gap and leaning on *Monsieur* Lafond's short pike pole, Henri gazed to the north, trying to see open water. He could not. He could see the small tugboat working in among the logs, Bernatchez's tugboat. And he could see the deckhand, astern, working the boom chain with a pike pole. On the opposite boardwalk, the guys waved to Henri. They were laughing and some were shouting to him but he could not make out the words over the roar of the water. André Guy lifted his hat and made a mock bow. François Gauthier was there too, next to André. Henri wondered how he was feeling. Had they changed at all since coming to Washika? Outwardly, it would seem they had not. They had arrived at Washika as students from the Collège de Ste-Émilie and, as such, would return to Ste-Émilie. Their bodies would be brown from the sun and their bellies flat, perhaps, from working the logs, but they would still be the same *instruits,* those well educated boys as the older men at Washika referred to them. They knew nothing at all when they first set foot upon the shores of the Cabonga and they would leave exactly the same. Or were they? How many fathers would be proud and say, "Three months on the drive, it has been good for my son. He left us only months ago, a mere boy, a pale face and a head full of words. Now look at him. Now, he's a man. Look at how tall he has grown. He knows what it is to live. Now he knows what it is to earn a dollar." Some of the fathers and mothers would be proud and say such things of their sons. Others, perhaps, would say nothing at all.

It was easy to dream. The roar of the water going through the gap had a rhythm, like the old washing machine his mother insisted on using had a rhythm, chug-chug, chug-chug the paddle turned, sloshing the clothes around inside. Henri leaned against the railing, warm in the sun and listening to the song of the water, the melody repeated over, and over, and over again. He thought of returning to Cabonga someday, further down the Gens-de-Terre maybe, within sound of the cascading water. He would set up a camp and fish in the morning. In the afternoons, he would read in the sun and, when he was stiff from sitting on the rocks, he would go for a swim, perhaps, or a stroll in the bush. Someday he would return or perhaps not. He could only hope that time and the acquiring of years would not dull his memory of Washika and the Cabonga; that he would always remember the sound of a breeze whispering through the needles of a pine, and gulls barking, and waves slapping upon a sandy shoreline; that he would always know the smell of sweet fern and spruce gum and balsam; and that he would never tire of seeing the sun sliding downward and making the *chicots* stick up like silver slivers through the flat, shallow water of the bays.

Chapter 60

It was their fourteenth day at Cabonga Dam. As the students filed into the cookhouse for breakfast, they were surprised to see Alphonse sitting there. He sat at the table, opposite Armand. He smiled at each of the boys as they entered. After the last one arrived and sat down at the students' table, Alphonse turned to Armand, and Bernatchez and the deckhand.

"And so, Armand," Alphonse spoke more loudly than was usual for him. "*Mes petits canards* were well behaved?"

"Well, I'll tell you, Alphonse," Armand began. "I was a little worried when I saw them jumping down from the *Madeleine*. And then when I saw them climbing the hill with mattresses on their heads, I wanted to hide. I couldn't believe the Company would do this to me. Not after all these years."

"So, it was pretty bad then?" Alphonse interrupted. He sat with his back to the students and facing Armand. He winked at the old man. "I guess they are a pretty wild gang at that."

Armand laughed. He looked past Alphonse to the students who were pretending not to be listening.

"You know, Alphonse," Armand cleared his throat. "I've been here a long time and I've worked with all kinds of people. This morning I was on the radio with the head office. I was talking with the superintendent, Mister McDougal, and I was telling him about your crew here. He couldn't believe it. I'm telling you, he's never heard of such things."

Alphonse looked behind him to see how his boys were taking it all in. They sat with their backs bent and their heads close to the table, forcing food into their mouths and waiting to hear the bad news.

"Well, I suppose," Alphonse smiled. "It's a new generation, you know. These are children born after a war and who knows what that can bring."

"You're right there, Alphonse. I don't know how I'm going to tell them. You're good at that, Alphonse. Will you tell them for me?"

"Sure Armand, they're used to hearing news from me. Right after we finish eating, I'll tell them."

The students pushed food into their mouths and, once again, molars ground against molars and all washed down with hot tea, but their hearts were not in it. Even Nicole, strutting by the kitchen entrance, failed to arouse their attention. Some of the students glanced back towards the table behind them, looking for signs, for some hint as to what they were in for. Henri looked over at Bernatchez who sat next to Armand. Bernatchez stared right back, a cold, hard stare.

As the students were finishing up, gulping down a last cup of tea, Alphonse stood up from his place at the table and turned to face them.

"Well, my little ducks," he began. "I have a few things to say to you this morning."

The students sat quietly at their places, those closest to Alphonse turning to look at him. The cook and his daughter moved in closer, to hear what was being said.

"Good," Alphonse nodded towards the cook and his daughter. "I am glad that you can also hear what I have to say. I have been speaking with Armand about how things have been going since I left here two weeks ago. All of you know how Armand has worked here at the dam, almost forever. He's seen all kinds of people come and go. This morning, he was talking to me about you guys, my little ducks, the sweep crew from Washika. Never in his life, he said, has he seen a bunch like you. Isn't that right, Armand?"

Alphonse turned to look at Armand. The old man sat with his elbows on the table and his hands clasped over the front of his mouth. The hands concealed the smile on his face but not the look of pride in his tired, old eyes.

"I have known Armand a long time," Alphonse continued. "He's a hard man but he's also a just man. And he can tell good men from bad almost from the first moment he sees them. Well, my little ducks, I think Armand's hit it right once again. He told me about you this morning.

He asked me to speak to you. He says that he's not very good at such things. And so, Armand would like all of you to know that you are the best goddamn bunch of workers that he's ever seen pushing logs into the Gens-de-Terre, and that's what he told the boss in town this morning. And guess what, my little ducks? We're going back to Washika just as soon as you can pack your rags."

The older men were surprised. They expected cheering and applause. There was not a sound. The students turned to look at Armand. As they looked into his eyes they were reminded of another old man and how he had looked at them that day when Lavigne had gone to see Alphonse and the driver of the caboose and returned with a cushion for Fred Garneau's aching bones.

Almost immediately, each boy stood up from his place at the table and went directly to Armand, to offer him a warm handshake and a few kind words. And then, on to Alphonse, and the cook and his daughter who had joined the lineup. From a distance it was touching to see the expression on each of the students' faces as they went from Armand, to Alphonse, to *Monsieur* Laviolette and, finally, to Nicole; for each person, the students wore a different face. As they shook Armand's hand, some looked as if they would soon break into tears while, as they faced Alphonse, they wore their usual, devilish, broad smile. Facing *Monsieur* Laviolette, they displayed their serious, polite smile. For the most part, the looks on all of the faces followed this pattern but, when it came to standing before Nicole, they were not the same. One might say that some of the students wore the faces of shame for all of the bad thoughts they might have had concerning the cook's daughter. Others smiled politely and shook her hand warmly. Even François Gauthier, now recovered from his initial reaction to Nicole's beauty and the seductive way she had looked at him that first day, smiled openly and looked into her eyes with confidence and shook her hand warmly, with his left hand covering their clasped hands. Maurice St-Jean was second from the end of the student line. He offered strong handshakes to all three men, smiling his thin smile and leaving, as usual, the impression of not having any teeth. Henri watched him closely as he stood before Nicole, the young girl he had spoken of so bitterly that first night at Cabonga. As St-Jean held out his hand, the young girl looked straight into his eyes and there were tears trickling down her cheeks. Suddenly, she lunged forward and hugged St-Jean, burying her chin between his neck and shoulder. As she did so, her hair slid slowly over her face and down her back. Henri saw that St-Jean held her close to him and caressed the hair that flowed over her back. Then, without words, Nicole and Maurice left the lineup and went into the kitchen. The cook smiled when he saw them leaving.

"This was supposed to happen almost a year ago," he said to Alphonse standing beside him. "Maurice was younger then."

"Ah yes," Alphonse said. "Who knows how these young ones think sometimes?"

Henri walked up to Armand. He held his hand out and looked into the old man's eyes. Then he prayed. Let me be strong, and not be a fool here. Let me be brave and strong and not be a babbling idiot. Before he knew it, Armand held his hand tightly and, just as quickly, put his arms around Henri and hugged him warmly.

"*Merci*, Henri," he said, softly, "You have made an old man very happy here at the gap. I wish you a very good life, Henri."

The students stared at Henri and Armand Lafond. They had never seen two men hugging. They had mixed feelings, no doubt, but, somewhere, deep down inside, they were also just a bit envious.

As Alphonse stood there, between Armand and *Monsieur* Laviolette, he smiled broadly and was genuinely happy for his crew. Some were hanging around the table talking. Others were trading jokes with Bernatchez and his deckhand. Only St-Jean was missing, off somewhere with the cook's daughter. Things have turned out well, Alphonse thought to himself, now if only they knew what's in store for them at Washika.

Chapter 61

As the *Madeleine* approached the dock at exactly five o'clock, the students could hear the engine slowing and then, suddenly, picking up speed as Alphonse shifted her into reverse to keep from ramming the wharf.

"Okay, you guys!" Alphonse stuck his head out at the cabin door. "Get your mattresses and things back to your bunkhouse. You have time to go to the van. The fire cheques have arrived. But hurry, we don't want to keep Dumas waiting."

The boys threw the mattresses onto the wharf, along with duffle bags and packsacks. And then began the long march, single file, up to the main sleep camp and the bunkhouse-and-office, carrying mattresses on their heads, and packsacks on their backs, with their untied boot laces trailing in the sand.

It was good to be back. The students were cheerful as they tossed mattresses onto bunks and quickly set their things in order before rushing out to the van. The fire cheques had arrived, Alphonse had told them. They were anxious to see the amount written on the second line, just below their name. All of the cheques would be for the same amount. Perhaps Henri's would be more, they teased. After all, he had spent a couple of hours longer than they had on the burn site.

Once at the van, they stood in line facing the clerk. Each in turn was handed a thin brown envelope containing the fire cheque. Before opening the envelope, each student ordered soft drinks, chocolate bars and tobacco, and signed his name in the ledger. As Henri was signing his name, the clerk reached behind him.

"Henri Morin," he said. "Two letters for you."

Immediately, there was a long drawn out "oooooh!" from the guys behind him.

"*Merci monsieur,*" Henri said to the clerk as he stuffed the letters into his back pocket and left with his supplies from the van.

Henri walked quickly. He had noticed a return address on one of the envelopes but he had not read it. As he went by the cookhouse, Richard Gagnier, the cookee, waved to him from a screened window.

Henri placed the soft drinks and chocolate bars on the orange crate bureau by his bed. He dropped the two letters onto the bed and, beside these, the plain brown envelope containing his fire cheque. Like everyone else, he wanted to see how much they had earned. He looked at the other two envelopes. On the one with the return address he read: 70 rue de la Rivière, Ste-Émilie, Québec. He felt, suddenly, just as he had felt when his mother faced him with the results of his High School Leaving Examinations, looking so serious, and not smiling at first. For no reason that he could tell, that was how he felt upon reading the return address. Of course, he knew the address. That was where Sylvie lived. And she had written to him, even before he had. This worried him. Was she writing to tell him that it was all a mistake? Why was there always this negative feeling? Was he being a 'have-not' again? Was this what it was all about?

Henri put Sylvie's letter aside and opened the plain brown envelope. Inside was a form much like the one he had received from *Monsieur* Lafrance at the pay office. There were small squares with titles typed above them: Gross Salary, Provincial Tax, Federal Tax, Unemployment Insurance, Net Amount. The last of these squares attracted his attention, $420.36. They had worked long hours on the fire. The salary per hour was less than on the sweep, but they worked longer hours on the burn sites. At least they were there more hours per day than on the sweep. And, of course, they spent much time sitting, and smoking, and drinking tea on the shore of the river. Henri was satisfied. This amount and what he had saved since they began on the sweep would help pay some of his expenses at university. *Papa* would surely be good for the rest, *maman* would see to that. And there was the pay, still to come, for their work at Cabonga Dam.

Henri picked up the two letters and left the bunkhouse-and-office. He did not want to be disturbed while he read the letter from Sylvie. And besides, what if it was bad news? He did not want the others to see him like that.

Henri walked over the knoll and down to the wharf. He was certain that no one would be there and he could be alone with Sylvie in her letter and with what she had to say to him. The other letter, he would read later.

He opened the envelope and took out the neatly folded pages. He looked at the date. She had written that same day, after their meeting at the fair, and their ride on the Ferris wheel. The letter began, "Dear Henri" and, from there on, Sylvie expressed her great joy at having met Henri at the fair, at how she had felt secure and frightened at the same time: frightened as they swayed on the big wheel but, warm and secure as she held onto him the whole time. Never in her young life had she felt so happy, and she knew that she would sleep very little that night after their meeting. Even her mother had been impressed with Henri, how polite and well raised he had seemed to her. Her father, of course, had made no comment. But even that was a good sign, Sylvie explained. She went on for several pages about when she had first seen Henri and how she had often thought of him. She even mentioned that day when she caught him staring at her breasts, and how he had blushed. Finally, she expressed a desire to be with him, often. She would be at the teacher's college, only a ten-minute walk from the university. They could see each other every day if he wished. And then, she ended the letter with words that almost took his breath away. "Henri," she wrote, "I love you. Sylvie."

Henri sat on the dock with his legs dangling over the edge. He could hear the waves slapping against the *Madeleine*'s hull but, above all, he was sure that he could hear the beating of his heart. He sat there thinking about life, his adolescent life mostly, and how Shannon had left him and how his life had changed. He remembered that time and all of the other boys his age and how easily joy fell upon them while he mourned his great loss. How easily they could slide from deception to joy, from disappointment to happiness without hardly a moment's thought. How they could give themselves completely to merriment and song at absolutely any occasion while he, Henri Morin, seemed left out, different than the rest, unable to release that strangling hold he had placed upon his life. Was it really because of her? Or was there more to it than that?

Despite his young age, had he been correct in assuming that he was, in fact, a 'have-not' and would always remain so? Henri thought about his life as he sat there on the wharf at Washika Bay. He thought about his parents and how fortunate he was to have them, and, now, Sylvie who wanted him to be part of her life. That did not sound much like a 'have-not' to him. He thought about this for a long time before putting Sylvie's letter back into its envelope. He turned to the other envelope. It did not seem important now. He read the address on the envelope to be sure that it was, in fact, for him. He could not imagine who would be writing to him. Even his mother would have included a return address. And besides, it was not the beautiful, flowing letters that he had seen his mother form with her gold-tipped fountain pen. His name had been written with choppy, broken letters, most probably with a ballpoint pen. Henri tore open the envelope and withdrew the lined, single page. At a glance he realized that the letter was from his best friend, David Greer.

The letter began, cheerfully enough, at first. David inquired if his buddy had finally gotten over his misadventure with Francine Villeneuve and, not to worry, there would be other occasions if only he could stay sober long enough. Henri smiled, sheepishly, as he recalled how badly he had behaved at the hotel room in Ste-Émilie. Or was it simply, as he had explained to Sylvie, that he was just too drunk?

Then the letter took a sudden, serious, turn. "By the time you get this letter, Morin," he wrote, "I'll be well on my way to Alberta. I dropped in to say good-bye to mom yesterday and then packed my bags and started hitchhiking west. One of the fellows on the cruise comes from there, from Red Deer, Alberta. He says that there's lots of work out that way. I'll work there a while and save up some and maybe find a vet school somewhere in the province. So that's it, old buddy. I just can't stand the old man anymore. Got to start out on my own. I feel sorry for mom, though. All the best at university, Henri. And try to stay sober with the co-eds. I'll be in touch as soon as I get an address of sorts. He signed the letter, your old buddy, Greer."

Henri sat there for what seemed to be a long time. He sat staring at the water below, how the setting sun's reflection moved with each passing wave. In that time, he saw his long-standing friendship with David Greer go by him: the fishing trips and long treks in his father's wood-canvas canoe, the hikes into the bush on snowshoes and those cold, cold nights camped under a large spruce tree with snow sliding into their sleeping bags, their first taste of alcohol, and the crazy plans they made up for later in their lives. As he held David's letter in his hand, waving wildly as a strong breeze struck up suddenly from the west, Henri could see no further. It was the end of something. He thought of David, standing along a highway with his pack on the ground beside him, holding his thumb out at the sound of a car, or a big semi rolling towards him and, then, feeling a gush of wind moving past him. He could see David standing there, a rejected look on his face, and spitting on the pavement.

Henri's thoughts of David were suddenly interrupted by the dull sounds of the supper bell coming from beyond the knoll. Henri hurried, stuffing the letters into his back pocket and running up the path to the bunkhouse-and-office. He did not want to keep Dumas waiting.

Chapter 62

The older men at Washika had never seen anything like it. Even beyond the fact that the superintendent, Simard-Comtois, was already seated at the table when they arrived. The men entered the cookhouse in a state of shock. On the tables were red and white-checkered table cloths and, at intervals of three feet or so, stood tall lighted candles in glass candlesticks. The men walked slowly between the tables, not believing their eyes. They glanced at each other, all sharing one common thought; Dumas had finally cracked.

Next to enter the cookhouse were the students, preceded by Alphonse Ouimet. Alphonse nodded to Simard-Comtois and went on to join the older men at their table.

"See what I mean, Alphonse," Percy Dumont commented before Alphonse even had time to sit down. "This is the limit."

"Oh, I don't know," Alphonse smiled at the tractor driver. "Looks pretty good to me."

The students looked around them as they entered the cookhouse, wide smiles growing instantly on their faces. They were still feeling the effect of Dumas's words of welcome as each student handed him his meal ticket, how he welcomed each one of them with an open smile and a warm hand on their shoulder. Their hearts were still glowing as they stepped over the doorsill and into the decorated cookhouse. They did not know what to think. Actually, they did not want to think. They were happy to be back. They wished only to savour that moment for as long as it would last.

Dumas entered the cookhouse, closing the screen door behind him. He walked to the centre, to stand between the four tables as he always did. He stood there, beaming, smiling at the students, nodding politely to the opposite table where Simard-Comtois sat.

"Before we start supper," Dumas spoke loudly, holding his hands clasped behind his back. "*Monsieur* Simard-Comtois would like to say a few words to you."

The superintendent nodded, one would say he even smiled towards the cook, a man who had made his life difficult throughout that summer, and many summers before that.

"*Merci* Dumas," the superintendent said as he got up from the bench and stood facing the students. "I have some very good news for you boys this evening."

A sudden groan erupted from the students' table.

"Hang on, you guys," Dumas interrupted. "Listen first. Believe me."

They could not believe their ears: Dumas, defending Simard-Comtois. The students turned to look at Alphonse, for a sign of sorts. Alphonse stared right back at them, with the largest smile they had ever seen on his face.

"I can understand," Simard-Comtois continued. "I know that it hasn't been easy. I have just two things to say to you. First, as you know, you boys have been the first group of student workers that we've ever had here. We were a little worried, I can tell you. We had no idea what it would be like having a large group of young students working here for the summer. Well, all I can say, and it gives me great pleasure to do so, is that we've all been pleasantly surprised. You're a fine group of young men, good workers too according to Alphonse, and we'll certainly miss you when you leave Washika. And that brings me to my second point. This'll be our last supper together. You'll be leaving for Ste-Émilie in the morning as the sweep officially ended today. I wish all of you good luck in your future occupations."

Not many heard Simard-Comtois' good wishes for the future. The cheers that came from the students' table drowned out the superintendent's words. The man smiled proudly and sat down. When, finally, the cheering had ceased, Dumas looked at them, more intently than he ever had in the past. He held his hands clasped in front of him as his face broke into another of his great smiles.

"Okay, Richard," he said, glancing towards the kitchen entrance.

Richard Gagnier entered the dining area carrying a large metal tray with more than a dozen small glasses filled almost to the brim with white wine. Richard made several trips to the kitchen for more of these glasses until everyone in the cookhouse held a glass of iced wine in his hand. Dumas stood at the centre of the room. He held his glass up at head level.

"To the students from the Collège de Ste-Émilie," he said loudly.

When everyone had emptied their glasses, Dumas nodded towards the kitchen doorway. Richard returned with three bottles of the white wine. But he was not alone. Now was to be the greatest surprise of all. Nothing like it had ever occurred in a lumberman's camp, much less in a lumberman's cookhouse. As the cookee returned with more wine, he was followed by a woman. The woman wore a long, floor-length dress, a light green like her eyes, and her long brown hair flowing straight down to the small of her back. She looked straight into the cook's eyes as she entered the room.

Dumas Hébert extended his hand towards the woman. He cleared his throat and looked back to the older men behind him, and then to the students, and the men sitting opposite them.

"Now it is my turn to say a few words," Dumas began. "Some of you here have known me a long time. You know that I never have trouble saying what is on my mind. Is that not right, André?"

The superintendent smiled. Light chuckles could be heard coming from the older men. "I am not always easy," the cook continued. "I know that. I always try to do my best but sometimes, as you know, I can be difficult. I believe, now, that it is all about how you see life and when you see life as I have seen it, you cannot be generous or love people very much. But things can change. I did not believe it, at first. Some events occur that can change how you see life. I believe that now because it has happened to me. I know that some of you are thinking that I have taken to drink. Others, perhaps, are convinced that I have finally gone mad. It is none of these, believe me. I wish, now, to introduce you to the future *Madame* Dumas Hébert, the woman who has saved my life. Lise Archambault, our nurse here at Washika, has accepted to become my wife, my partner in life. We will be married in Ste-Émilie on October twenty-third. And, of course, you are all invited to the wedding."

The applause was accompanied by loud cheering from the students and, spontaneously, all stood up from the plank benches to form a single line, to congratulate the cook and his beautiful fiancée.

It was a most happy gathering of people that evening at Washika Bay, along the shores of the Cabonga. The older workers who had known Dumas those many years were relieved to hear that the man had not, in fact, gone mad or turned to drink. They knew well how empty his life had been since the sudden death of his beloved Bernadette. It had been a difficult birth and both his young bride and their newborn son had perished. All of that had happened more than twenty years ago, twenty years of torment for the cook. But now, that was past.

The students were, of course, surprised to hear that their time at Washika had come to an end. They were overjoyed to hear of the upcoming marriage of Dumas Hébert and Lise Archambault. But, as they sat at the table, eating supper finally, and sipping on the rest of their wine, they looked around them, at the older men, at the scalers sitting at the table across from them, at *Monsieur* Simard-Comtois. There were mixed feelings. Not sadness, really. It was more like the end of something.

Chapter 63

For some, the end of the sweep at Washika also meant an end to long-term friendships. Some would be leaving Ste-Émilie to attend university in the Capital. Others would be staying on in town, attending trade schools, or working at the town mill. There were some who would even be leaving Québec. And so, that evening, after the surprising events at supper, the boys visited each other's rooms, exchanging mailing addresses and sharing plans for their future lives.

In the bunkhouse-and-office, all was quiet. André Guy had left to visit with his new friend, François Gauthier. Seated at a small table next to the oil space heater, Maurice St-Jean struggled with pencil and paper, striving desperately to find the right words. The letter had to be finished by early morning of the next day, as that was when Jean-Luc Desrosiers, the inspector of sweeps, was heading down to Cabonga Dam. Maurice had a great deal to say in so little time. Much had happened in the past year and he wanted Nicole to know about that, and how he felt about her, truly.

Pierre Morrow, Gaston Cyr, and Lavigne had also left the bunkhouse-and-office to spend time with other students in the main sleep camp. That left St-Jean at the table, writing, and Henri Morin stretched out on his bunk.

Henri was thinking of Sylvie. Perhaps, he too should be busy writing. But he would be in town by tomorrow afternoon. There would be no mistake this time. He would call her as soon as he arrived. And he would speak to his parents about her. Maybe on Saturday morning, his father would take him down to the tavern. There they would talk about him and *maman* and how it was back when they first met. Henri was no longer feeling like a 'have-not.' He would speak to his father about that as well.

"Hey Maurice," Henri called from his bed. "You decided to write a book?"

"Don't mention it." St-Jean dropped the pencil. He reached for his tobacco and began to roll a cigarette. "You can't know what it's like. I know what I feel, I think. But I don't want to make mistakes. I don't want to say the wrong things."

"That's for Nicole?" Henri nodded towards the pages on the table.

"Yes. I've been writing the same page since after supper."

"I didn't know that you knew her before. A long time?"

"I suppose. But it did not go well. Her good looks, and me jealous all the time."

"And now?" Henri had never known jealousy. He knew about love lost. He wondered if the two were the same.

"It's okay now. I'm sure of that," St-Jean replied. "It took almost a year for me to learn. Even then, I wasn't sure. Seeing her at Cabonga like that, all the guys wanting her. Something happened then. I can't explain it. Maybe it was Armand and how he treated us, or Alphonse, or even our whole summer here at Washika. All of a sudden I could see how crazy it all was. I was such a fool, you know. All Nicole wanted was to be with me, no one else. I couldn't see it then."

"Maurice," Henri walked over to the table. "You think that you can remember what you just told me, long enough to write it down on your paper there? There's your letter, Maurice. She won't need to hear anything else."

"You think so?" St-Jean reached for his pencil.

"Sure. I ..." Henri was interrupted by a knock at the door. Henri and St-Jean looked at each other. No one ever knocked at the sleep camp door, especially not at the bunkhouse-and-office.

"Yes? Come in," Henri called from the table.

It was the cookee, Richard Gagnier. The whole time they had been at Washika, Richard had never visited the bunkhouse-and-office. It was the hours. Working as a cookee for Dumas Hébert did not allow him the same leisure hours as the rest of the students. A cook's day started at four in the morning.

"*Salut* Richard," Henri greeted him. "Now the sweep's finished you can visit, eh?"

"Well, not really," the cookee began. "*Salut* Henri, *salut* Maurice. I'm still working for Dumas. You see, I'm not going down with you guys tomorrow."

"Oh yeah?" Henri was surprised. He had not known Richard at high school and since they had not worked together during all of their stay at Washika, he really did not know him at all. "But you'll be leaving Ste-Émilie to attend school soon?"

"No. That's finished for me," the cookee stood by the table, his hands in his pockets. "I didn't pass the exams and, besides, I don't really like school. With Dumas this summer I learned so much. And I really like cooking. Dumas refers to me as "*la relève*," that I might be the person to take his place someday. He says that if I work hard and pay attention to what he teaches me, I could become a very good cook. And now that Dumas is getting married, he'll probably be gone more often. They'll need someone to cook while he's away."

"Well Richard," Henri began. "I'm very happy for you. That's really something. You know what you want and, already, you have someone who'll teach you. And you have a job at the same time. Boy, you're really lucky, Richard."

"I guess!" Maurice said, nodding his approval. "I tell you, I wish I knew what I wanted to do."

"Well, I won't keep you," Richard turned to leave. "I may not get to speak to you in the morning so, good luck in your studies. Maybe we can meet in Ste-Émilie someday."

Both St-Jean and Henri extended their hands to the cookee and wished him well. As he reached for the door, Richard stopped abruptly and turned to face Henri.

"I almost forgot, Henri," he said. "Lise Archambault, the nurse, asked me to deliver a message. She asked if you could go to the infirmary. She'd like to speak to you."

As Richard Gagnier closed the door behind him, Maurice St-Jean looked up at Henri, a teasing smile on his face.

"Careful, Morin," he said. "I hear that Dumas keeps a shotgun under his bed."

"Don't worry," he laughed. He was laughing, but he was also a little worried. Why would she want to see him at the infirmary? And what would Dumas think if he saw him going there? After all, they were almost husband and wife. "She probably just wants to take a look at my burn. She's a very good nurse, you know."

Chapter 64

Henri walked on the fine sand, between the bunkhouse-and-office and the cookhouse. The cookhouse was in darkness. Perhaps Dumas was at the infirmary with Lise. He tried not to think about that. Still, he wondered why Lise had sent for him. To say good-bye? Hardly. There were enough good wishes expressed during supper. Perhaps it was his silence that she wanted. But he had promised, and he planned on keeping that promise. If ever he discussed it with anyone, he would never mention her name or where it had taken place.

As he reached the truck scales, Emmett Cronier waved to him from his little hut.

"Quite a surprise, eh?" he looked at Henri through the open doorway. "Who would have thought that Dumas had it in him? Christ almighty, wine and everything."

"Yes, that's for sure."

Henri did not want to linger. He was worried, that was certain, but he was also curious. He had not spoken to the nurse since that morning they had made love together. Not counting, of course, what drunken words he had spoken to her at La Tanière in Ste-Émilie.

Henri kicked at the stones on the road as he went. Finally, he left the gravel road and walked down the short path to the infirmary. The screen door banged against the jamb as he knocked.

"Yes?" the familiar voice sang out. The tone was more cheerful than he remembered.

"Oh Henri," she said, opening the door. "I am so glad to see you. Come in. Come in and sit down."

She had changed since supper. She wore a plain white T-shirt and jeans, and her feet were bare. Henri noticed how tanned her feet were, like her arms and face. She walked ahead of Henri as she led him into the back room. Henri tried to think only of Sylvie, of their ride on the Ferris wheel and her hands squeezing his arm, the touch of her hand in his, her kiss. Lise walked ahead of him and, silhouetted against the bright lights of the room was the roundness of those hips that had swayed above him like waves upon the sand, and those firm bulges that had given him pleasure the likes of which he had never imagined. It was not going to be easy. But, he would be strong. He was a 'have' now, and he would be leaving in the morning.

"You would like a coffee, Henri?"

"*Non, merci.*" Henri felt awkward, for no reason that he could tell.

"Please sit down, Henri," the young woman pulled out a chair and sat down by the table.

Henri sat facing the nurse. He tried not looking into her eyes, but he could not avoid it.

"Lise," he began.

"Wait, Henri," she said. "Before you say anything, I would like to speak. Please. There are things that I must say to you."

She had changed. Especially her eyes were not the same. She looked into his eyes, like she had when he had come to see her with his sunburned chest. But the look was different now.

"Henri," she began. "I think that you are old enough for us to have this conversation. After all that has happened, I think that it is necessary to speak of it. We made love, you and I, and Henri, I want to tell you that it was wonderful. It was wonderful, and warm, and loving. But, most of all, Henri, it lighted a kind of fire in my heart. A long time ago, when I graduated from the nursing school…I was about your age then. I was young, like you, and very much in love. But that love was suddenly taken away from me. There was an accident, a terrible, horrible accident. My love, the man I hoped to marry, was dead, drowned in a lake."

Henri looked at her. Those lovely green eyes had tears in them now. Still, she did not look away, or try to hide her tears.

"I do not know if you will understand this, Henri, but I will try to explain. After that night, when François died, I was not the same. I could never be the same again. I believed that. After a while, my friends stopped calling to invite me out, to join them in their outings. I could not see life any more. It was difficult for me, even to smile. For me life was over. It was just a matter of time before I would also die. That is why I came to Washika: to work and be alone and wait for my time to come, for my time to leave. My position here as camp nurse was exactly what I needed for my solitude. But then, Dumas Hébert came along. I am not blind, Henri. I know that I am attractive to men. And Dumas certainly tried very hard to convince me that he was the man I needed in my life. But I was not convinced. I was certain that my life could never be; that I could never feel desire or a need for it. My body in that sense was already dead. There remained only for my being alive to end. Do you understand, Henri?"

Henri was beginning to understand much more than Lise was trying so desperately to explain. He recalled how he had tortured himself with the idea that he was a 'have-not,' that life had stolen love from him and left him dead, without hope of ever living again. And that had poisoned his life. Somewhere Shannon was still young and alive. But to me, Henri remembered vividly, she was dead. Shannon was dead and so was I. Now, as I listen to Lise, it's all becoming so clear. Neither Lise nor I were 'have-nots.' Both of us had love taken from us, that's true, and for Lise, much more tragically so. But still, in our hearts, we both felt that our lives had been shut down, that everything left had been contaminated and had little interest for us.

"Yes, Lise," he said. "I understand. I understand more than you might think. Please, go on."

The woman placed her hand softly upon Henri's. She left it there as she spoke and Henri could feel the warmness, the intimacy of her touch.

"That day," she continued, "when you came to see me here, you were just another patient, another injury that I had to care for. But, when you returned the next morning, there was something about you, something intense for such a young man, the way you spoke to me, how you looked into my eyes. When you asked to join me in my room, it seemed so natural that I could not refuse. There was a kind of innocence in your being there, in the way you made love to me, how softly you touched me. After, when I helped you, when I made love to you, believe me, Henri, I had never done that before, ever. Not even with François. Something was happening to me. I was becoming alive. I did not think about it then.

But later, when you had gone, I realized that I was alive again. Life suddenly had meaning for me, for the first time in several years."

Henri felt her hand tighten around his. He wanted suddenly to take her into his arms, to hold her tightly against him. But there was another feeling. As he listened to Lise pouring her heart out to him, he realized, suddenly, that he could be doing exactly the same with a certain young lady serving tables at the Café D'Or. Henri's thoughts turned to Sylvie. Sylvie's given me life, in a sense, he mused. She's managed to convince me, in her way, that I'm alive and that I'm not a 'have-not.' I'm a 'have'! Now, have Lise and I been caught in the same trap? Did misfortune in our respective lives convince us that it was over, that there was nothing left? Were we just lying there with one foot in the trap, waiting for the end to come?

A chill came over Henri as he remembered the barred owl he had seen once. The bird's leg had been caught between the jaws of a leg hold trap, a No. 4 steel trap often used for the capture of wolves. The bird had pecked and chewed away at its leg, trying to escape a certain death, trying to stay alive. Without help, without antibiotics, the owl would surely die of infection or starvation even if it did escape from the trap. But the proud bird did not think of that. There was only one thing on its mind and that was to rid itself of this ugly piece of metal wrapped around its leg, to be free, and to stay alive.

"Henri," she said, as tears swelled in her eyes once again. "Henri, you have saved my life. After our time together, I began to understand more, to know what Dumas was trying to say to me, years ago, when I first arrived here. But I was not able to hear then. I could not feel. I love Dumas very much, Henri. This is why I have asked you to come here. I wish to thank you, with all my heart, for making it possible for me to love again, to be able to love Dumas, and to love life again."

That evening, a northwest wind pushed whitecaps up onto the beach at Washika Bay. The sun slowly descended below the grey, dead trees making them appear as silver slivers sticking up out of the water against a stark red background stretching from north to south. In the darkened infirmary, the curtains stood straight out from the opened windows. The whistling of the wind filtering through the window screens was all that cut through the silence. That, and the cries of ecstasy coming from the back room of the infirmary.

Glossary

Definitions in this glossary are limited in scope and are provided as a guide to readers.

French swearwords

During the 1960s when the action in this novel took place, the people of Quebec were gradually withdrawing from the Catholic Church. One result was the adoption of Ecclesiastical words as everyday swearwords. Instead of taking the Lord's name in vain, as was common among the English-speaking population, French Canadians began to use the names of articles used in the celebration of mass to vent their anger. Some of these expletives appear in *Washika*. We have chosen to spell the words phonetically and to put them in italics.

Calis: calice (chalice) is the correct spelling of this French but it is pronounced as though written "*calis.*"

hostie: host, the bread or wafer used for Holy Communion (Eucharist).

sacrament: *sacrement* is the correct spelling in French, but it is most often pronounced *sacrament*.

tabarnacle: *tabernacle* is the correct spelling. However, the expression "*tabarnacle*" is most commonly heard. The tabernacle is a receptacle (often ornamented) used for storing and, often exhibiting, the Eucharist.

Other French Words and Expressions

Acadia: a small tugboat with its engine at the centre of the hull.

ah bien, sacrament: well, sacrament!

allez mes petits canards: to work, my little ducks!

allo: hello.

banane: banana. The canvas fire hose folded into two-foot lengths looks somewhat like a curved banana.

bain de minuit: skinny dipping (swimming naked) at midnight, often men and women together.

brochet: a northern pike.

brûlot: sandfly, a small, bloodsucking, dipterous insect of the Order Diptera, genus Phlebotomus. The insect tends to cause a burning sensation in its victims hence the name "brûlot" most probably based on the verb, *brûler* – to burn. This insect is often found on sandy beaches and, thus, the name, sand fly.

chambre à louer: room for rent.

chicot: tall, dead tree, often found standing in water. Grey in color without, or with very little bark left.

c'est rien: it's nothing. Don't worry about it.

célibataire: a single man or woman.

Chemin de Notre-Dame: Notre Dame Street.

collège: A Catholic college where children were taught at both primary and secondary levels.

commissions: errands.

coup de foudre: love at first sight. (literally: a lightning strike)

crochet: hook. A curved metal hook, wide at one end with a handle of wood or metal. The pointed part of the hook has an L-shaped figure at the extreme end of the point. Men could lift and manipulate the four-foot pulp logs with it.

crosseuses: from the slang word *crosser* meaning, "to masturbate."

Église de Saint-Germain: Saint-Germain church.

étudiants: students

et bien: oh well.

et misère: oh damn, or some such expression to lament one's wretchedness or misery.

gaffe: a blunder.

hein?: eh?

la cabane: the hut; the name of the tavern where Henri's father spent his Saturday mornings.

maman: mom.

merci: thank you.

merci monsieur: thank you sir.

monsieur (name): mister (name); plural, *messieurs*

non merci: no thank you.

papa: dad.

petites américaines: young American girls.

relève: next generation.

sage: wise

salut: hi

van: a store within the camp office where soft drinks, chocolate bars, tobacco and papers, leather boot laces and wool socks, etc. were sold.*vraiment libre*: really free.

English Words and Expressions[1]

beaver dog: usually a small breed of dog used by trappers to locate a beaver hut entrance or trail to the hut entrance. The dog's keen sense of smell allowed it to locate the beaver through snow and/or ice.

Beaver on floats: a de Havilland single-engine bush plane fitted with floats to be able to land on lakes or rivers. The Beaver was the most popular bush plane used during the time period of this novel.

1. Many of these words were used in the forestry industry in Québec during the time period of this novel; the rivers were highways, used earlier by fur traders and later by loggers.

boom timbers: squared timbers (often B.C. Fir), more than twenty feet long with holes bored at both ends to allow for the passage of boom chains. The chains joined the boom timbers together to form a sort of corral around the logs to be towed by tugboats. The tugboats would tow the boom down the lakes or reservoirs to the nearest dam and, from there, the logs floated downstream to the mills. If the tugboat was unable to tow the boom with its engine only, the captain would drop anchor at a great distance from the boom. The tug would then return to where the logs were and hook onto the boom. Then with tug engine working and the winch pulling the tug towards the anchor, the tug would haul the boom downstream.

Cabonga: pronounced, Cabunga. The name comes from the Algonquin *kakibonga* meaning, "completely blocked by sand." This refers to the great expanse of beach sand surrounding the waters of the Cabonga Reservoir.

chore boy: a yard man in the camp, responsible for the smooth running of the camp.

cookee: a bush-camp cook's assistant.

drive (or river drive): collecting logs cut during the winter months and dumped into rivers or large lakes (reservoirs) in the spring. The logs are floated down river or towed down lakes leading to a river in booms. The logs are then directed along rivers to pulp-and-paper mills downstream.

drive boats: long wooden double-bowed boats often used by workers while maneuvering the logs with their pike poles.

fly oil: insect repellent. From the Québécois slang word, *huile à mouche.*

mackinaw: short (usually plaid) coat of thick wool; also called a bush jacket, the red-plaid version is often used by hunters and bush workers.

pàgwàshka: Algonquin word meaning, "a place where a body of water is shallow," very appropriate for Pàgwàshka Bay in this novel.

peavey: stout wooden handle (about four or five feet long) with a sharp metal point at one end and a movable metal hook just below the point. The peavey is used in maneuvering logs, especially rolling larger logs. The pointed end is driven into a log and, as the handle is moved forward, the pointed hook grabs onto the log below where the pointed end is. The worker can then roll the log forward. (NOTE: the "cant hook" is similar to the peavey with one exception: instead of a pointed metal end, there is a double set of short metal teeth at the extremity with a movable metal hook below this point.)

pike pole: a long (about six feet) wooden pole fitted with a double metal point at one end. The metal point consists of a single spear point plus a hook point perpendicular to the latter. The pike pole is used for manipulating logs in water.

The spear point is used to move logs forward and the hook point, to pull them towards the worker.

pulpwood: mostly spruce and balsam logs, four feet long, used in the production of paper. Other logs on the drive consist of twelve and sixteen-foot logs used in saw mills for lumber.

rubby: a drunk, an alcoholic.

Russel: a two-cylinder tugboat, of a smaller size, used most often inside and around pockets of boom timbers. The boat's caged-in propeller allowed it to work in among the logs without problems.

scaler: a forestry company employee whose task is to measure logs (length, diameter, cubic feet, etc.) after they have been cut and before they have been sent down river during the drive. The company can thus determine the amount to pay loggers and what stock is available prior to the drive.

sweep: the final operation of a log drive. After all of the logs (floating) on the lakes or reservoirs have been rounded up and delivered to the nearest river that will take them to a pulp and paper mill or sawmill, workers on the sweep are sent out to search the bays and swamps for stray or entangled logs.

timber cruise: before aerial photos were used to assess the amount of wood available, people on the "timber cruise" would go through a stand of trees and could calculate the number of feet of timber that could be harvested.

washika: pronounced, "Washeeka." The area used to be referred to as Washega Bay. The Algonquin word *washega* means a natural clearing in a forest or shoreline. The change to "Washika" probably took place after the arrival of French-speaking lumberjacks.

Zippo: a very popular cigarette lighter during the period of this novel; extremely wind-proof, inexpensive, and available in the vans at most of the lumber camps.

Acknowledgements

First off, I would like to thank two people without whom this book would never have left the confines of my little cabin near the woods. I am especially indebted to Mary Bialek who has read and reread the novel, I don't know how many times, and probably typed as many pages of notes and suggestions for me. Without her support and the patience and encouragement I have received from Robin Philpot, my publisher, this book would certainly not be what it is today. To both of these people, I humbly say, *Kichi Mìgwech.* I would also like to thank Julia Philpot for her illustration and photos.

I wish to offer many thanks to my friend Mr. Gaston Lavoie of Maniwaki, Québec, for his technical support and salvation each time my antiquated computer decided to manifest an independent life of its own.

Thank you to my longstanding friend Douglas Gagnon for allowing us to use his photographs of tugboats that were once part of the annual log drives on both the Cabonga and the Baskatong Reservoirs.

Finally, I would like to say *Kichi Mìgwech* to my friend Dean Ottawa of Kitigan Zibi Anishinàbeg for the cover painting of this novel.

MORE QUEBEC FICTION FROM BARAKA BOOKS
Also Available in all Ebook Formats

I Hate Hockey
François Barcelo (translated by Peter McCambridge)

Principals and Other Schoolyard Bullies
Short Stories by Nick Fonda

YA Fiction

Break Away 1, Jessie on My Mind
Sylvain Hotte (translated by Casey Roberts)
(Winner of the John Glassco Prize awarded
by the Literary Translators Assocation of Canada)

Break Away 2, Power Forward
Sylvain Hotte (translated by Casey Roberts)

The Adventures of Radisson 1, Hell Never Burns
Martin Fournier (translated by Peter McCambridge)

Nonfiction

A People's History of Quebec
Jacques Lacoursière & Robin Philpot

America's Gift: What the World Owes
to the Americas and Their First Inhabitants
Käthe Roth & Denis Vaugeois

The Orphanage, An Autobiography
Richard Bergeron

Roads to Richmond, Portraits of Quebec's Eastern Townships
Nick Fonda

RECYCLED
Paper made from recycled material
FSC® C103567
www.fsc.org

MARQUIS
Marquis Book Printing Inc.

Québec, Canada
2012

Printed on Silva Enviro 100% post-consumer EcoLogo certified paper, processed chlorine free and manufactured using biogas energy.

100%
PERMANENT
BIO GAS ENERGY